IT HAD
TO BE
YOU

ALSO BY GEORGIA CLARK

The Bucket List

The Regulars

Parched

She's with the Band

IT HAD TO BE YOU

- A NOVEL -

GEORGIA CLARK

EMILY BESTLER BOOKS

ATRIA

NEW YORK   LONDON   TORONTO   SYDNEY   NEW DELHI

EMILY
BESTLER
BOOKS

ATRIA

An Imprint of Simon & Schuster, Inc.
1230 Avenue of the Americas
New York, NY 10020

First Emily Bestler Books/Atria Paperback edition May 2021

EMILY BESTLER BOOKS/ATRIA PAPERBACK and colophon are trademarks of Simon & Schuster, Inc.

For information about special discounts for bulk purchases, please contact Simon & Schuster Special Sales at 1-866-506-1949 or business@simonandschuster.com.

The Simon & Schuster Speakers Bureau can bring authors to your live event. For more information or to book an event, contact the Simon & Schuster Speakers Bureau at 1-866-248-3049 or visit our website at www.simonspeakers.com.

Interior design by Jill Putorti

Manufactured in the United States of America

1 3 5 7 9 10 8 6 4 2

ISBN 978-1-9821-3319-1
ISBN 978-1-9821-3321-4 (ebook)

*For Lindsay, again,
and true romantics, everywhere*

Lovers don't finally meet somewhere.
They're in each other all along.

—RUMI

PROLOGUE

Liv Goldenhorn stared at the cage of bristling birds and tried not to panic.

Like all career wedding planners, she knew tradition and ritual didn't arise from some universal experience of love and commitment. Rituals were reinvented and reinterpreted all the time. The idea that an engagement ring should cost three months' salary originated from the marketing campaign of a Depression-era diamond company. Bridesmaids dressed alike to confuse the evil spirits of ancient Rome. Wedding veils came from arranged marriages, when families didn't want the groom to spot his wife-to-be at the other end of the aisle and think, *No thanks*, then slip out the back door.

Nothing symbolized love so well as a dove, but you never released actual doves at a wedding: you released white homing pigeons. Unlike their delicate cousins, who would get lost and eaten by hawks, pigeons were born with internal Google Maps and were a perfect match for the lovely winged creature so favored by Aphrodite and modern brides alike.

But this was a cage of scrappy gray city pigeons.

"Ugh!" Ralph Gorman, her florist and best friend, grimaced and took a step back. "What are they doing in here?"

The birds clucked and cooed, shedding feathers in a heavy metal cage that sat at the kitchen's service entrance. Liv folded her arms. "Preparing to be a flying metaphor for everlasting love?"

A bird squirted a white stream of poop outside the cage.

Liv snatched a paper towel, thankful the caterers were busy setting up cheese plates in the ballroom. This was Eliot's fault. Her husband coordinated all live-animal deliveries, from ponies to peacocks.

Where was he? The flight from his semi-regular consulting gig in Kentucky had landed over an hour ago, and he'd promised to come straight from the airport. The minutes were falling away like raining confetti; guests would arrive in under an hour.

Gorman—who loathed his given name and only ever went by his surname—inched closer, fingering the patterned silk neckerchief knotted at his throat. "Should they be in the kitchen?"

"Oh, yes." Liv whipped out her phone. "Yes, I'm certain I told the delivery man, please leave a cage of winged rats where food for two hundred is being prepared."

The number for Birds Birds Birds went straight to voice mail—it was Thanksgiving weekend. Liv swore and hung up.

"I can't believe some idiot just left them here! Eliot must've booked the cheapest bird-rental company on Long Island." She toed the metal cage. It didn't budge. "Do you think we could move them?"

"Darling, I do flowers. Not manual labor. And speaking of . . ." Gorman gave her a look. "We have a problem."

From the expression on his face, the non-doves would have to wait.

Liv flung a tablecloth over the cage, then strode with Gorman through an obnoxiously palatial estate, stepping outside to follow the winding path toward the ceremony site: a boathouse overlooking a picturesque frozen lake. Gorman explained that the bushels of lavender the bride had insisted on, desperate to evoke the golden haze of late summer in Provence, were attracting *unwanted guests*.

"Guests?" Liv repeated, her breath fogging in the crisp November air. "What, have some horticulturally inclined ex-boyfriends shown up?"

Gorman flicked something from Liv's choppy black bob. "Bees."

A local hive had moved into the boat shed rafters for the winter. Gorman and his partner, Henry, had recommended flowers with no fragrance and low pollen. The bride refused. The lavender, coupled with the space heaters warming the shed, had clearly made the bees think that spring had sprung early.

"Well, we are out of the city." Liv scanned a run sheet that was rapidly making a genre shift from sober nonfiction to slapstick farce. Where in the world was Eliot? Half the items on the run sheet were *his* responsibility. "We can't ask nature to be less nature-y for the duration of— *Ow!*" Pain needled her arm. "One just stung me!"

Gorman gave her an *I told you so* look. "Henry brought an EpiPen."

"I'm fine." Ignoring the hives already forming on her arm, Liv pushed open the doors to the boathouse. She expected to see the two hundred white chairs draped in French satin and a thousand flickering flameless tea lights. What she did not expect to see under the triangular arbor—reclaimed wood, from the bride's childhood home—was the DJ making out with a bridesmaid. Her hand was down the front of his pants.

Liv gasped. "Zach!"

"Shit!" Startled, Zach Livingstone backed up. His pants dropped to his ankles. He tripped and grabbed the flimsy arbor for support. He and the arbor toppled over, crashing to the floor.

Panic shot through Liv's chest.

The arbor was no longer an arbor. Two pieces of wood lay five feet apart, as if refusing to speak to each other. And Eliot wasn't around to fix it.

"Liv, I'm so sorry." Zach's London accent rendered every word as plummy as Christmas pudding. "I was just showing this young lady the size of the, er, *lake*."

The bridesmaid gave a tipsy giggle.

Henry Chu rushed into the boathouse with two bushels of fresh lavender. "What happened?"

"Arbor," Liv sighed. "Zach."

"Hello, Henry," Zach called, popping to his feet and yanking up his pants.

"Oh, hi Zach." Henry, petter of neighborhood dogs, sender of birthday cards, unflappable designer of all things floral, ducked and wove away from a bee circling his head. He glanced at Gorman. "Have you told her? They're getting worse."

But Gorman's gaze had wandered to the hot, young Brit zipping up his fly.

Liv clicked her fingers in his face. "Gor! Let's try to fix the arbor. Zach, button up your shirt, this isn't Mardi Gras."

Zia Ruiz breezed in, carrying wineglasses. "Oh, Liv," she called, heading for the bar at the back, "looks like there's a couple of pigeons loose in the kitchen."

Liv pinched the bridge of her nose, trying to remember if she'd secured the cage door. Apparently not. "How good are you at catching birds?"

Zia laughed. "Not very." Even in her white blouse and black pants, she retained a whiff of carefree boho backpacker. Maybe it was the ylang-ylang she wore instead of deodorant. If Liv didn't trust her so implicitly, she'd assume Zia would be the kind who'd free a few caged birds.

Weddings were about tradition, but more so, how traditions were changing. Liv's tradition was that the business she ran with her husband was respected, professional, and nimble in a crisis. She'd troubleshot hundreds of events, always able to steer the runaway horses away from the cliff at the last moment. But right now the steeds were bolting and she couldn't find the reins. Liv picked up the two pieces of the arbor, glancing around for something that could be fashioned into a hammer.

Darlene Mitchell, the wedding singer, strode in with a wireless microphone. Her tone was as prim as her appearance: a cream silk dress that showed off her dark skin. "Zach. We need to sound check."

Zach ran a hand through his flop of hair. "Coming, love."

The bridesmaid's lipstick-smeared mouth fell open. "*Love*?! Is she your *girlfriend*?"

He laughed. "Not exactly."

Darlene shuddered. "Not at all."

Satisfied, the bridesmaid continued to ooze over Zach, pressing herself against his side.

And while Liv should have been hurrying the two musicians along, and fixing the arbor, and finding a solution for the escaped pigeons and newly awakened bees, the thought that formed as clear as lake water in her mind was this: it had been months since Eliot had touched her like that. Maybe even years.

"What. The. *Hell*."

Everyone froze.

Liv swung around.

The bride stood in the doorway.

Liv's stomach dropped through the floorboards and into the frigid lake below.

Not the bride. *Anyone* but the bride. Today, the bride was president and prime minister, the CEO, God herself. Things could be a freewheeling disaster behind the scenes. The mother-in-law could slap the priest, or the best man could lose the rings in a bet involving hot dogs (true stories). But the bride must only experience a highlight reel of physical and emotional transcendence. It was her day, and it was perfect. Except now, it wasn't.

"Oh my God, you look *gorgeous*," Liv said.

Ignoring her, the bride addressed the bridesmaid. "You're supposed to be helping me get ready, not screwing the busboy!"

"DJ," Zach corrected, tucking in his shirt and giving her a wink. "And MC, and I'm also a musician. Man of many hats, really."

"Sorry, babe. Got distracted." The bridesmaid hooked an arm around Zach's neck. "It's a wedding."

The bride's gaze found the pieces of wood in Liv's hands. "What happened to my arbor?"

Gorman, Henry, Zach, Darlene, and Zia all looked at Liv, who said, "Everything is completely under control."

A couple of pigeons fluttered past the bride's head. She jabbed a finger in the air. "Someone said those are my *doves*?" She advanced on Liv, a football field of white tulle dragging behind her. "I'm getting *married*. This is supposed to be my *special day*."

Eliot would calm this woman with his own special brand of magic that quieted, charmed, and switched focus to a champagne toast with bridesmaids.

"It is!" Liv said. "And it's going to be *wonderful*. Can everyone please get back to what they are supposed to be doing, and—"

The bride screamed. A protracted just-found-a-dead-body-in-the-bath scream.

Zia dropped a wineglass. Darlene's microphone squealed. Henry, Gorman, and Liv all said "What?" as Zach said, "Bloody hell. Oh, that looks bad."

The bride's bottom lip had swollen to the size of an overripe raspberry. "Thomething bit my thip."

"Bees," whispered Gorman.

"Beeth?" The bride's false eyelashes widened. "*Beeth*? I'm allergic to *beeth*!"

Liv's phone buzzed. *Eliot Goldenhorn (Huz) calling.* Finally: a life raft.

"Eliot! I'm dying here! Where the hell are you?"

But it wasn't Eliot on the other end of the line. It was a girl. Her voice had a light Southern lilt. She was completely hysterical. "I'm sorry, they just found him like this—I got your number from his phone, I know we haven't met—I didn't know who else to call!"

Everything—the boathouse, the bride, the beeth—disappeared. A new kind of horror broke in Liv's chest.

"Who is this?" she demanded. "What's going on?"

The girl took a shuddering breath. "It's Eliot," she wailed. "*He's dead.*"

Eliot was dead.

Impossible. And yet, not.

Myocardial infarction: heart attack. Eliot was forty-nine. The same age as Liv. Eliot was in perfect health. Eliot was in a closed casket. Liv touched the side of it. The wood was smooth and very cold.

It was an icy day at Salem Fields Cemetery in Brooklyn. The sky was the color of dryer lint.

Ben had Velcroed himself to her hip. She could only see the top of her son's small head. He should be wearing a scarf. Liv couldn't remember if he'd worn one. She couldn't remember getting ready.

Liv understood she should mingle with the mourners gathered on the stumpy grass. She told her feet to move toward them. Her feet didn't. She couldn't leave the casket. And so the people started moving toward her. They were speaking to her. She recognized some of them; she was replying to them. But Liv couldn't hear a thing. She was suspended behind a barrier, as transparent and tough as bulletproof glass. From behind the glass, she had a sense of what these people thought they saw. Liv Goldenhorn: someone resilient and impressive, the sort of person you wanted to sit next to at a dinner party. She'd stripped her own floors, gotten her son into the good public school, and once fought off a mugger by bashing him with her *New Yorker* tote bag and screaming she had syphilis (a lie). Even her own cheating husband's funeral was something Liv Goldenhorn had been determined to get through.

But standing by Eliot's casket, she was realizing that Liv Goldenhorn was just an idea of a person. And ideas about people could change.

More words were said. The casket was lowered. Handfuls of soil were tossed on the polished wood. And just like that, it was over. The mourners started drifting toward the street. There was a lightness in their voices and shoulders. Their brush with mortality was over; life was back to normal. Liv's entire world had been obliterated in just one week—her routine, her sense of safety, her livelihood, all snatched away. There was no more normal.

She wrapped both arms around her son, holding him as he finally broke down and cried. Ben was eight but looked younger. His features were fine and expensive-looking, like a porcelain dinner set viewed behind glass.

"I'm here, baby," she whispered over and over again. "I'm here. I'll always be here."

It was the sort of lie done out of kindness.

She held her only child until he quieted, smoothing his dark hair off his fevered face. Her miracle baby. The baby who defied all odds. Conceiving Ben was supposed to have been the great challenge of her life. The absolute hardest thing. And then Eliot died, and four years of IVF seemed like a relaxing holiday.

Liv's mother must've seen something off in her face because she took her grandson's hand and said something about meeting them by the car—*C'mon Benny, let's give Mom a moment*—then they were gone.

Liv stood at the cemetery gates, wondering if she was going to cry but instead feeling an endless absence of everything. A feeling without a horizon.

She didn't know where to put her hands. What time it was. What had just happened.

A week ago, she was married.

A week ago, everything was predictable.

For better, or for worse.

Eight days later, Liv was hauling a bag of mindlessly purchased groceries from the trunk of her car when someone behind her tentatively spoke her name.

Liv's instinct was to ignore them. She did not need yet another pity lasagna. But the safety of her brownstone was half a block away.

A young woman stood on the sidewalk. She appeared both apologetic and, oddly, optimistic.

Liv squinted, momentarily mesmerized by the woman's flawlessly heat-styled doll-blond curls. Liv hadn't washed her own hair in over a week.

The girl was talking to her. First pointing to the brownstone, where Liv intimated she'd been waiting, then saying something about being *sorry for your loss*. She was slathered in so much makeup she looked like a frosted cake. Through layers of lip gloss, she spoke the slippery syllables of her name. With a Southern lilt.

The realization of who this person was cut into Liv's mind so fast she almost dropped the groceries. It was like realizing that the dark shape in the water wasn't a rock. It was a shark.

Liv's heart started beating fast, roaring blood into her ears.

Now she was saying something about emails: ". . . didn't reply to my emails or voice mails. I've already come by twice."

Between them, a thick white envelope. The girl's hand was steady as she offered it. Her fingernails were painted translucent pink.

Liv let the groceries fall to the sidewalk. Her fingers felt as thick as sausages as she ripped open the envelope and unfolded a sheaf of good linen paper.

It was a copy of Eliot's will. They'd both written wills after their son was born; Liv hadn't returned her lawyer's recent calls because she knew Eliot had left everything important to her, and Ben. But this will appeared to have been updated. Three weeks ago. Liv tried to scan the tight black font. She recognized her name. Eliot's name. And, another name with slippery syllables.

She refocused on the girl. There was a pimple near the corner of her mouth, expertly concealed with foundation.

"What," Liv said, "does all this mean?"

Savannah Shipley's glossy lips pulled into a smile. "It means that . . . well, Mrs. Goldenhorn, I guess you're looking at your new business partner."

It was such a ludicrous statement, Liv couldn't get her head around it. The girl's smile turned hopeful. She appeared poreless, like a balloon. Liv imagined popping her. The way she'd whip around midair, deflating, before landing in a soft, spent heap on the concrete.

"That is impossible." Liv handed back the will. "There is no more In Love in New York."

The girl's eyes widened. Of course they were the color of the Mediterranean. *Of course they were.* "But the will says—"

Liv grabbed the groceries and slammed the trunk, obliterating her words. She hurried across the street and up the brownstone's steps, retreating into the safety of her house and its locked front door.

Liv's hands were shaking as she glugged white wine into a glass, hoping to erase the last few minutes from her memory. Praying she'd never see or hear from *that girl* ever again.

PART ONE

IN LOVE IN THE CATSKILLS

1

The first day of Savannah Shipley's new life dawned cloudless, as if there was absolutely nothing standing in her way. The scrubbed-clean March sun that blasted the cold streets of Brooklyn seemed bold and ready to work.

At first, Savannah was stunned that Eliot Goldenhorn had left her half his business. Yes, she'd interned at An Event to Remember, Lexington's most popular event-planning company, for two whole years. She'd met Eliot six months before he died, when she volunteered to give the consultant from *New York City* a tour. Knowing his line of work, she'd gushed about how much she adored weddings—the way they brought people together, the beauty of tradition. Eliot wasn't the most attractive man she'd ever met, but he hummed with magical, big-city energy. Their conversations started in the office, graduated to dinner, and culminated in bed. The sex felt experimental on both their parts. He, "newly separated" (which she now knew to be a lie), and her, newly adult and curious. The way a deliberate moment of eye contact could transmute a relationship was a thrilling, frightening power.

When the shock of his death wore off, it started to feel like kismet. Eliot was a smart guy: he must've had his reasons, even if they weren't clear. And Savannah had an unwavering faith in the universe and the God who created it. This was all obviously meant to be.

She arrived at Liv's brownstone in Prospect Heights a full forty-five minutes early. The New York that Savannah had grown up seeing in movies conjured rows of the classic houses that were all exactly the same, standing to attention like a well-dressed marching band. But actually, the brownstones on Liv's street were all slightly different shades of brown. This one bold mahogany, that one nostalgic sepia, the one next door a chichi caramel. The Goldenhorns' had a weathered, washed-out facade. In the small front garden, a faded LOVE WON poster was stuck at an angle in the last island of dirty snow. Most people in Savannah's small hometown voted against love winning. Savannah didn't consider herself political, but maybe privately disagreeing with the status quo had set her on the path here, to New York, a city that was the same and different from her imagination.

She snapped a selfie in front of Liv's house, swiped for a filter that bettered the color of the brownstone, and added it to her Instagram, @Savannah_Ships. She'd read in a travel magazine that the last American quarry to mine brownstone closed years ago, in Portland. It was actually a mediocre stone—just brown sandstone. Its softness made it vulnerable. An odd choice to clad a city where it appeared resilience was key. But New York also traded in beauty, Savannah thought, smiling at a woman walking two fuzzy Pomeranians. The woman smiled back, and why wouldn't she? Beauty could be powerful, too.

At 10:00 a.m., Savannah picked up the potted orchid she'd purchased as a gift and marched up the wide front steps. She knew this wouldn't be easy. She knew, by some measure, this was completely insane. But she had the moral high ground (she'd really had no idea Eliot was still with Liv), she had the legal grounds (Eliot's will), and most important, she had the unwavering belief that this was the right thing to do. Not just for her, but for Liv. According to her online sleuthing, In Love in New York was currently nonoperational, following a scathing review entitled PIGEONS AND BEES RUINED MY WEDDING! that went mildly viral and now lived on every wedding planner review website. The diatribe was from a wedding last November. The day Eliot died.

Savannah could guess what Liv thought of her: a gold-digging airhead, a midlife crisis, a few mean words inked on a bathroom stall door. And that was just plain wrong. Savannah was determined to prove herself to Eliot's wife and help resurrect a business that did the most noble thing of all: celebrate people's love for each other.

Because Savannah Shipley was always up for a challenge.

She summoned the biggest smile she could muster and rang the doorbell.

Nothing. Her cheeks started to hurt.

She rang the doorbell again. And again.

A voice sounded from inside. "Jesus Christ, *coming!*" The front door cracked. Liv was in an old dressing gown. A cigarette smoldered between her fingers. Her tangled black bob looked like the aftermath of a fire. "What the hell are you doing here?"

Three months had passed since they'd met across the street from the brownstone. Savannah had assumed three months would be enough time to fall apart, mourn, and begin rebuilding. Clearly, Savannah was wrong. But to be fair, she had emailed about all this, many times.

"Good morning, Mrs. Goldenhorn. I'm here for our first meeting. With our new clients."

"What are you doing *in New York?*"

Alarm edged into Savannah's chest. "Like I said in my emails, I moved here. For this job."

"You can't be serious."

"I'm very serious, Mrs. Goldenhorn." Savannah shifted the plant from one arm to the other without breaking eye contact. "I moved here, from Lexington, to run In Love in New York. With you."

Liv let out a hard bark of a laugh. She tightened her dressing gown and narrowed her eyes. "How did you get my husband to change his will?"

Savannah was unaccustomed to being accused. Heat seeped up her neck. "I didn't. Like I said in my emails, I had no idea he'd done it until your lawyer called me. And I did *not* know y'all were still married. He told me you were separated."

Liv tapped her cigarette. Ash floated onto Savannah's shoes. "Do you know what the term *undue influence* means?"

Savannah's smile dropped; she caught it and put it back in place. "Yes. And I know it doesn't apply to me. I had no sway over Eliot at all. Honestly, Mrs. Goldenhorn, I'm here to help you. I sent you a deck. With a business plan, and a social media strategy, and a division of roles, and—"

"Couldn't open it." Liv cut her off with a curt wave of her hand. No ring on that fourth finger anymore. "I don't have Key-whatever."

"Keynote." A program she could download *for free.* "But I got on a plane, I got a sublet, and our first clients are— our first meeting is *today.*"

"Meeting?" The bags under Liv's eyes were the size and color of figs. "In Love in New York has been on hiatus since . . . actually since the last time I saw you." Liv pointed her cigarette at the orchid. "I hope that's not for me. I can't keep anything alive."

Savannah's industrial-strength optimism finally cracked. "But I've messaged you about all this a dozen times: she's an Instagram celebrity, he's a talent manager—Kamile Thomas and Dave Seal—"

"She's a what?" Liv's nose crinkled. "Instagram . . . celebrity?"

"Yes! Her support will help get the business back on its feet. Good reviews are our number one priority right now."

"Our?" The word was slick with contempt.

Tears rushed Savannah's eyes. She'd come all this way. This was her *big break*. "But Dave and Kamile are—"

"Savannah?" An attractive young couple who wouldn't look out of place in a renters' insurance commercial stood behind her on the stoop.

"Early," she finished. Dave and Kamile were here.

Savannah followed Liv inside as if it wasn't the very first time she'd done it. The bones of the brownstone were impressive—high molded ceilings, sturdy hardwood floors. There was framed art on the walls: classy art, the kind that didn't make sense. Somewhere, possibly upstairs, faint classical music was playing. Savannah's shoe clattered against an empty wine bottle, one of many lining the wall. No way Dave and Kamile could miss that. She didn't dare turn around to check.

Liv paused outside the first door to the right. If Savannah's googling served her correctly, this was In Love in New York's office. Liv's hand lingered on the doorknob for a long moment. Savannah said a quick prayer as Liv turned the knob and led them inside.

Savannah could see how the large front room could be a lovely office. A three-cornered bay window looked out onto the quiet, sun-dappled street. A long white desk and two brown leather office chairs were at the opposite end. Four smaller chairs faced them. Above the desk hung the pink-and-black In Love in New York logo, an oval design Savannah felt was dated. A sofa and coffee table were tucked against the far wall, next to a tall bookcase stacked with wedding and photography books. Half a dozen framed magazine and newspaper articles hung on the walls, including the front page of the *New York Times* Style section. MEET BROOKLYN'S IT WEDDING PLANNERS invited the subhead, under a photo of a much younger-looking Liv and Eliot, lounging casually by the bay window. Of all the publicity photographs Savannah had found online of Liv, that one was her favorite. The dark-haired young woman looked cool, confident, and completely in charge. Hashtag boss lady. Savannah tried to replicate that facial expression in approximately one thousand selfies but always came across less like a CEO and more like a snotty heiress who owned too many whippets. The article suggested that a happily married couple working out of their enviable brownstone gave In Love in New York a unique edge. Engaged couples felt buoyed by both the home and the couple's charm and class: *This could be our future, married and living in a gorgeous brownstone in a tree-lined neighborhood*. The article casually noted the celebrity clientele, which included Jesse Tyler Ferguson and Maggie Gyllenhaal, the latter described as "very intelligent, with a strong sense of what she wanted on the big day." Savannah could picture a productive and positive consultation in this room, where everyone hugged at the end instead of shaking hands.

If the room didn't look like a squat.

In the middle of the floor was a bag of golf clubs that had once been set on fire. Strewn next to it were four bulging suitcases, a few boxes of books and records, and about two dozen men's shirts and trousers still on hangers. A framed set of baseball cards under broken glass. Most shocking of all, a dozen vases of long-dead flowers. Most likely, *three-month-old funeral flowers*. They were responsible for the smell. The stench of death.

Savannah forced her mouth into a breezy smile and spun around. "Sorry about the mess: renovations. Come, take a seat." Two patches of sweat circled from her underarms, staining her peach-pink blouse. Her heart, which had been bouncing with excitement all morning, was now thumping like an executioner's drum.

Dave took in the room's disarray with an expression of light confusion. In his expensive-looking chinos and blue-check button-down, he looked a bit like a Kennedy—someone for whom style was an instinct. Kamile wore tight white jeans and a silk shirt printed with tiny flowers. The rock on her fourth finger was the size of a skating rink. Kamile was a sorority sister, president when Savannah was a sophomore. She'd built her extensive online following (@TheRealKamile, on all platforms) by exploiting her natural beauty and her private life. The chance to help plan this successful woman's wedding was Savannah's first real career opportunity. As an intern she'd been indulged but never respected. Never put in the driver's seat. And now she was sinking into the worn leather chair Eliot bequeathed her in his will. Its divot was off-putting; her feet didn't touch the floor.

Rather than join Savannah behind the desk, Liv sat on the white sofa behind the couple. She gave the room a raw stare, took a drag of her cigarette, then ground it into one of the sofa cushions.

Kamile didn't notice, instead angling her phone at herself, trying to find the best light. "Hey guys! Dave and I are here at our very first meeting with our *wedding planner*." Big smile, hair flip. "We have so much to get through, so I'll let you know how it goes. Wish us luck!" Kamile put her phone faceup on the desk and addressed Savannah. "Sorry, so rude. *Hi*. How long's it been?"

"Too long!" Savannah was so flustered she honestly couldn't remember. "It's great to see you again, and meet you, Dave. You look great, and this is just so"—she raised her palms to the ceiling, smiling manically—"great."

"You were the best social chair that Delta Zeta Lambda ever had," Kamile said. "I know you'll be an amazing planner."

Savannah glanced at Liv, so distracted by her lack of involvement that she almost missed her cue to reply. "Thank you, yes, of course."

A pause. Dave and Kamile glanced at each other, then back at her.

"Sorry," Kamile said. "We've never done this before, obviously, so we're not exactly sure . . ."

Savannah looked back at Liv, who slanted her eyebrows slowly, as if to say, *Be my guest.*

A tiny ember in Savannah's chest began to glow hot.

The only thing on the desk in front of her was a pen and an In Love in New York branded notepad. Scribbled on the first page was the word *FUCK*, underlined three times. Savannah tossed it into a wastepaper basket and cleared her throat.

"It is the honor of my life to help you plan your dream wedding. We will merge sophistication and tradition in ways that will surprise and delight you, to create memories that'll warm your hearts for years to come."

Kamile put her hand on her chest, and gave Savannah a moved smile. Dave kissed his fiancée on the cheek.

Savannah beamed. *Exactly* the reaction she wanted. "Well, why don't you start with what you have and, I guess, what you need?"

Kamile nodded, shaking her hair out with her fingers. "Okay. Wow. So we're getting married on May fifteenth, two months away, which is totally crazy, *I know*. I was going to do all the planning myself, but work is *insane*. We've got the venue, thank God, a really cute farm upstate in the Catskills; we just need chairs and tables and stuff. For flowers: I'm thinking lilies, irises, things like that, very elegant and graceful and, um, baroque? No roses, I just don't like roses—I know I'm weird—and obviously no baby's breath or carnations or anything, like, cheap-looking." She was speaking very quickly, gathering speed with every word. "Jazz for cocktail hour, nothing cheesy, sort of breathy and sexy and Norah Jones-y? And then a DJ who can MC—they all do that, right? Not to sound shallow, but I'd prefer someone good-looking—it's probably illegal to say that, but whatever. Cocktails are important, we're sort of cocktail snobs, so we'd love a certified mixologist who's trained somewhere good and uses all fresh stuff; I don't want everyone wasted on Long Island iced teas, that's sort of my worst nightmare, apart from people not using the hashtag, which—given Dave's last name is Seal—is, obviously . . ." She looked at Savannah, as if they should answer together. "Sealed the deal," Kamile finished as Savannah guessed, "Kiss from a rose?"

Kamile looked mildly appalled. "Cute, but no, and literally just said I hate roses." Kamile started ticking off her fingers. "Got my dress; Dave's got his tux. Need hair and makeup, someone who's done a million brown brides before, obviously. I don't want anyone who's, like, 'I don't have foundation dark enough for you!' Like, what a nightmare. Need a photographer who can shoot for social, that's nonnegotiable, I have, like, three hundred thousand followers now; it's nuts. Do you know any good DPs who can livestream? Definitely planning on doing a tasteful amount of sponcon, so it'll be good for you to middleman that. Sorry, should I be saying middle-woman now? You know what I mean. Oh, and the caterer has to be vegetarian/gluten-free/farm-to-table, locally grown, one hundred percent organic but *yummy*." A deep breath. A smile at Dave. "Whew! Did you get all that?"

Savannah looked down at her notepad. *Cat's kills (?) No BB breath. Norah Jones. Baroque MC = hot. Yummy.*

Silence feathered into the still room. Impossibly, Liv was *smiling*. The sight of her smugly amused face spiked a burning flash of rage. The feeling was so unprecedented, so radically unfamiliar, that for a long moment Savannah forgot entirely who she was.

"So . . . you have your . . . dress."

"Yep." Kamile nodded.

"And Dave's got his . . . his tux."

"Yep." Dave nodded.

Savannah pretended to write this down, when in reality she wrote *FUCK* and underlined it three times. "And, you're . . . you're thinking about sponsoring your livestream?"

"No, I'm getting some things sponsored, but I want you to orga-nize the livestream." Kamile cocked her head. Her voice became a little more assertive. "Not to sound rude or anything, but this is our wedding, and I kind of need it to be perfect. You're up for this, right, Savannah?"

Savannah opened her mouth, ready to deflect this silly question-ing of her competence. She was *Savannah Shipley*: head of the year-book committee, champion fundraiser, the best social chair Delta Zeta Lambda ever had!

Not a single word escaped.

Savannah stared at Liv. *Please, please help me. I need you.*

Kamile and Dave twisted around to eye the hungover, half-dressed woman on the couch behind them.

Liv exhaled a short puff of air: *Okay, fine.* "How much? Our fee," Liv clarified, before changing it to "*my* fee: partial planning costs ten percent of the budget or eight thousand dollars, whatever's higher."

Kamile traded a look of unease with Dave before turning to Sa-vannah. "I thought I was pretty clear about that."

"You were." Savannah heard her own voice, tiny as a church mouse. She willed it louder. "You were. Mrs. Goldenhorn, I said we'd do the wedding for free. In exchange for some posts on Kamile's social media."

Liv rose from the couch, dressing gown dangerously close to falling open, and moved to shake hands with Kamile and then Dave. "Nice to meet you. Nice to meet you. This has been extremely . . . ridiculous." She walked out of the room, leaving everyone staring, dumbfounded, after her.

2

Ralph Gorman tightened the blindfold around Henry's head and asked if he could see anything.

"Not a thing. Totally in the dark." As always, Henry told the truth.

"Okay, birthday boy. Ready?" Gorman's baritone vibrated with excitement. Henry had always found it sexy—the voice of a late-night radio host playing love songs by request—but tonight it gave him an extra jolt of nerves. *This was it. It was happening.*

"I am ready." Henry Chu was ready to get married. And on the evening of his thirty-seventh birthday, he was certain this new chapter was about to begin, with a proposal and a shiny gold ring.

They'd been together for only a few months when Gorman told Henry he had no intention of ever marrying: *I'm from a different generation. It's just not for me.* Henry had just turned thirty. Apart from falling in love with this stylish, erudite older man, he didn't know what he wanted. He was fine being domestic partners while he and Gorman co-opened Flower Power, Honey! in Carroll Gardens. While purchasing the apartment above the shop together and feeling like an adult for the very first time. While holidaying for Gorman's fiftieth in Mallorca; while visiting Henry's family in Flushing for homemade Chinese dumplings and congee; while buying sheets or coffee or bickering about whose turn it was to wash the sheets or make the coffee. They were a committed couple. What was the difference?

But over the past year, Henry's ambivalence started to tilt into urgency. All the couples he knew were placing orders for wedding bouquets, then baby shower flowers. Gorman might be part of the previous generation, but Henry was from the current one. He'd started dropping hints, first microscopic, then visible to the naked eye. Henry Chu wanted to close his open relationship and get hitched.

Ralph Gorman, the old lush, was a consummate deflector. But he could not deflect Henry's thirty-seventh, a date Henry implied strongly he wanted to be engaged by. In turn, Henry had sensed a softening. He knew Gorman didn't want to lose him. They lived together, ran a business together, they argued and made love and texted things like *can you get half + half 🥛 love u! ❤*. What was the difference?

"Okay, take my hand." Gorman led Henry from their bedroom and down the hallway toward their living room. He assumed Gorman's decorative strategy would be flowers. Which was nice: that was their thing. They loved flowers and the theater and dead French queens, and Henry didn't care if that made them clichés. He didn't care if wanting to be married made him a cliché, either.

Blindfolded, the familiar hallway became entirely new territory. The disorientation was exciting. Maybe they'd find another use for the blindfold later. . . .

As they entered the living room, Henry clutched Gorman's hand extra hard, passing him love and confidence. *You got this, babe!*

Gorman loosened the blindfold. "One . . . two . . . three!"

Henry blinked as his eyes adjusted, glancing around for a room filled with red or cream or multicolored hybrid tea roses . . . but there were none. Or candles. Or champagne, or chocolates. Instead, Gorman was gesturing at a large box on their coffee table. "It's . . . a stand mixer," said Henry.

"Yes!" Gorman patted it proudly, as if it were a clever pet. "Just like you've been saying you wanted."

Had he? Maybe once or twice in passing.

Henry thought he'd been obvious about wanting a ring. But maybe he'd mistaken Gorman's equivocation for consent. Or, more distressingly, he *had* made his needs clear—and Gorman had ignored them.

"Gor—" Henry started, only to be cut off by a flat female voice on the other side of the room.

"Don't look so pissed, Henry. You can always take it back for cash."

"Liv!" Now Henry really *was* surprised. "You're here."

She crossed the room to peck his cheek with a dry kiss, handing him a glass of wine. "Happy birthday, Henry. Although I really should say *commiserations*. It's all downhill from here. Trust me." She refilled her own, much larger glass.

Henry recognized the label. "I thought we were saving the Penfolds."

"If the past few months have taught me anything," Liv said, "it's drink the damn wine." She emptied the bottle into her glass and headed into the kitchen. "Why wait? Could step in front of a Fresh Direct truck tomorrow."

Henry gave Gorman a look.

"She just showed up!" Gorman whispered. "Ben's at his grand-mother's—she said she didn't want to be alone."

"But it's my birthday." Henry's fourth finger felt naked. He couldn't even look at the damned stand mixer.

Gorman fiddled with his silk kerchief, as if unsure whether to tighten or loosen his signature piece. "If you want me to ask her to leave, I'll ask her to leave."

Liv's voice rang out from the kitchen. "You won't believe who showed up on my doorstep today. The slut." They heard the fridge door open. "Got any olives, Gor? I feel like a martini. Or seven."

In the warm lamplight of the living room, Gorman's wave of white hair glowed. He gave Henry a small, apologetic smile. "I'm sorry, Choo-Choo. But she's my best friend."

Henry knew what the word *friend* meant to Gorman. Friendship was not a Hallmark card. Friendship was Shakespearian. A Greek myth, a Russian novel. Friendship was a bone-deep, decades-old un-derstanding of another human's deepest flaws, and loving them *be-cause* of those flaws, not in spite of them. Gorman might be a lush, but he was loyal. And his friendships were more loyal than most marriages.

Henry tossed the blindfold aside. "I'll put on some pasta."

3

"Obviously, it's complete lunacy, the entire situation." Liv speared her third olive. "Showing up like that. As if she could just waltz on into my life!" Anger sparked in every cell in her body. It was a welcome respite from the cold, airless muteness that pressed on her heart and lungs most days. People expressed sympathy for "her pain," websites talked about "the pain" of loss, everyone seemed to think she felt "pain." All Liv usually felt was absence. Nothingness. Savannah's irritating, sun-bright confidence revved her up, like gasoline on a fire. The anger felt good: clean and enlivening.

Liv broke the olive's flesh with her teeth. "That business is my life's work. I'm not going to share it with some twenty-three-year-old *ditz*."

"You might have to." Gorman removed his glasses and handed Liv a piece of paper with a figure circled several times. Having balanced the books for Flower Power, Honey! since they opened, Gorman knew his way around a profit-and-loss statement. Over marinara and martinis, Liv had allowed him to extract the Goldenhorns' full financial picture. And it was no masterpiece.

Liv blinked at the circled number. "That'll get us through this year, at least. It's actually more than I thought."

"That's your *debt*, darling," Gorman said.

"What?" Liv snapped to attention. "What about the life insurance?"

"It'll float you for a minute. But it's not a permanent solution. Eliot left behind some pretty impressive credit card debt, and you're still paying off the last of the mortgage. Plus you haven't contributed to Ben's college fund in years. You're going to have to . . ."

"What?" Liv asked.

Gorman took a perfunctory sip of his martini. "Get a job."

Liv blanched. "They don't hire forty-nine-year-old women, Gor. They use us to scare millennials into wearing sunscreen."

Henry emptied the leftovers into Tupperware. "Would it really be so bad to bring on a business partner? I thought the deck she made was very impressive."

"Yes, you really need to get better with the computer, darling," Gorman said. "Being flustered by attachments makes you seem positively Jurassic."

"Don't you mean geriassic?" Liv quipped, and Gorman laughed.

Henry put the leftovers in the fridge and shut the door a little harder than necessary. "All I'm saying is Savannah seems very keen. Organized. Passionate."

"So was Hannibal Lecter!" Liv exclaimed. "Besides, I barely have any vendors on the books anymore. No caterers want to work with me, after the whole shitshow with the pigeons." The Long Island Bridezilla made a point to mention the escaped non-doves in her one-star review, as well as the bee sting, the broken arbor, and the fact Liv left an hour before the ceremony.

"You still have us." Henry patted her shoulder. "At our usual generous rate."

"Thank you," Liv mumbled, unable to meet his eye. Humility was not Liv's strong suit.

Gorman pushed aside the bank and credit card statements. "Do you still think she had something to do with it? Getting E to change his will, I mean."

It was a theory Liv palmed back and forth over the last few months. But now it was clear Savannah Shipley was less a conniving mistress and more a shiny red convertible. "No. Unless she's a sociopath, and I don't think she's that interesting."

Gorman and Henry exchanged a glance that indicated Savannah's innocence was something they'd already come to believe. "How are you?" Gorman's voice was gentle. "Really?"

Liv lifted her hands in tired bewilderment. "What do you want me to say, Gor? Shocked. Sad. Angry, hurt, humiliated, just really . . . *blargh!*" She slumped over the table. "Is this really still something I want to do? Be a *wedding planner*? I am a feminist, you know, and somehow, I've ended up in this archaic industry that forces women to do even more unpaid emotional labor while worrying about being too fat. The whole system is designed to equate spending with happiness, and it honestly makes me sick! Maybe I should become a communist and move to the mountains! Get some goats. Goats are easy to keep, aren't they?"

Henry and Gorman traded another look. Liv-the-commie-goat-farmer had made her appearance in a few other conversations since the funeral.

Henry went first. "Sure, the wedding industrial complex is a hysterical money pit designed to emotionally manipulate couples—we all know that. But the way you plan weddings helps people realize what they actually want. To put a sensible budget first and everything else second. You've always kept your prices market rate, and you never upsell couples on things they don't need."

It was true. If clients wanted to custom color match the table linens to the bouquet, or ride in on a bucking white bronco, Liv would make it happen. But she also made it clear to couples who had concerns about throwing the now-standard three-day wedding extravaganza that a wedding was to a marriage what a birthday party was to the year ahead: you could skip the party and still have a fabulous year. More than once, she'd talked couples *out* of hiring her, knowing the resentment and panic of the final bill would not be worth it. Liv also understood that many couples in love in New York (especially Brooklyn) didn't want a normative, traditional wedding, they wanted a fun, classy party where two people happened to be legally wed. As such, In Love in New York had garnered a healthy reputation for being the city's best alternative-wedding planner.

"You always plan events that are authentic to the couple," Gorman said. "Plus, for better or worse, people are always going to get married and hire wedding planners. Why not you?"

Liv harrumphed. But she was listening.

"Besides, don't you want to go back to work?" Gorman speared an olive from the jar. "You love work. They'd barely cut Benny's umbilical cord and you were running out for a site visit."

"For Chrissake, she's my husband's girlfriend!" Liv slapped the table, sloshing half a glass of gin.

"Not to sound crude, but he's not technically your husband anymore," Henry delicately pointed out. "You can't be married to someone who's been deceased for three months."

"And barely his girlfriend," said Gorman. "She was a fling! You were his *wife*. And from what you'd been saying to me for the past few years, he was your husband in name only. Things weren't exactly thriving, were they?"

Liv made a petulant face—*no, not exactly.*

"So be the bigger woman," Gorman continued. "Transcend all that female competitive bullshit."

"Besides, maybe E really did know something you don't," Henry mused. "He must have had a reason, as weird as it all is."

Liv slurped the rest of her martini, the liquor bitter in her mouth. The truth was, she wanted to *want* to work. As ludicrous as the meeting with Dave and Kamile had been, it'd given her a taste of her old life. She missed ambition. That invisible, powerful impulse that guided and goaded and gave a day meaning. Liv Goldenhorn had no idea how to get her lust for life back.

But that's because she hadn't yet met Sam.

4

Jammed into a subway car so crowded she couldn't even check her phone, Savannah Shipley was beginning to think she'd made the biggest mistake of her life.

Giving up everything in Kentucky had been the hardest thing she'd ever done. Not to mention the fact she'd basically—okay, she'd *definitely*—lied about the origins of her new "dream job" to her loving, trusting parents, Terry and Sherry. Her parents' devotion to their only child was as unwavering as their Sunday church attendance. If they knew their daughter had once purchased a vibrator, let alone carried on an affair with a married New Yorker, Terry and Sherry would have twin heart attacks.

Savannah's extended circle of friends had been excited for her move to Brooklyn, but her best friend, Cricket, took the news as a betrayal. Savannah tried to make it sound like an exciting, short-term opportunity for both of them—*Come visit me! I won't be there forever!*—but she wasn't surprised to see something crumble behind Cricket's eyes. It was essentially a nonsexual breakup.

Her internship, her best friend and the apartment they shared, her proximity to clean air and wide streets and place in the order of things: all gone.

At first, that all seemed worth it. As represented by her New York vision board, Savannah's future in the greatest city in the world was one of bright lights and laughter, yellow cabs and pink cocktails. The words she'd placed at jaunty angles—*Love! Success! Adventure! Romance!*—felt like certainties. As did the image in the center of her vision board, the one that held the most mystery, the most promise: a gorgeous man in a tux. A twinkle in his piercing blue eyes.

Who are you?

Where do I find you?

Savannah Shipley hadn't just moved to work for In Love in New York. She had moved to find this person, and in the meantime, fall in love with New York itself.

But so far, it was no romance.

The city was cold, dark, and confusing. Home was now a matchbox-size room in a grotty loft with three strangers in a neighborhood where no one said hello to one another and everything was three times more expensive than it should be. When Savannah finally pushed her way off the sardined subway and onto the chilly, wet streets of her new neighborhood of Bushwick, raw, painful thoughts formed in her mind: Was she in the right place?

Living the right life?

How did you find love in a city that, so far, didn't seem to believe in it?

Shivering, she turned a corner and stumbled across 'Shwick Chick. A down-home fried chicken joint. The restaurant's cheery neon sign shone through the cool, misty rain enveloping the city. Even though she was living on her savings and on a budget, Savannah pushed open the door. The warm, salty-sweet smell almost brought her to tears.

Home.

It was late on a rainy Monday, but customers filled the dozen tables, which were decorated with red-checkered tablecloths and vases of daffodils. She didn't mind waiting. The energy—of the patrons, the hip-hop playing, and four staff members doing the work of ten—lightened her dark mood. Finally, a seat opened up at the bar. Savannah's mouth pooled in anticipation of a plate of her favorite food in the world. As Cricket always said, "Fried chicken is like sex. Even when it's bad, it's good." Savannah had laughed in agreement with this, but now, as she studied the small, handwritten menu, she realized it wasn't true . . . when it came to sex. In her experience, sex was often just bad: awkward and unromantic, less magical, more mechanical. Even Eliot was a better conversationalist than he was a lover.

A bartender in a cute Rosie the Riveter bandanna and plaid shirt rolled at the sleeves slid in front of her. She had two delicate gold earrings in each ear and wore her curly dark brown hair in a pixie cut. Ruddy freckles sprayed across skin that was pockmarked with acne scars. Like all the staff, she appeared overworked but cheerful. "Whatcha havin', darlin'?" Her Southern twang sounded as cozy as hot toddies in front of a fire.

"How's the fried chicken?" Savannah asked. "And I hope you say it's damn good."

"It's damn good, Kentucky." Then, off Savannah's look of surprise that this woman had picked her accent so precisely, she added, "And so am I, apparently."

Fifteen minutes later, Savannah was presented with a meal that *was* better than sex. The juicy, golden-brown chicken was crispy and crunchy on the outside, moist and tender on the inside. Each deep-fried piece was soaked with a spicy-sweet honey sauce that was so good, Savannah asked for an extra side of it. She resisted the urge to moan as she ate, every bite sating a desperate, bone-deep craving. Around her, the staff whirred like a well-oiled machine. The girl with the pixie cut was the most efficient of all, equally friendly and adept. Savannah had been done for less than ten seconds before she swept by to clear her plate, flashing a brief, gap-toothed grin.

"That was just about the best fried chicken I've ever had," Savannah hurried to offer. "Usually the leg is my favorite, but that breast was perfect."

"Breast is best, right? Actually the honey-fried chicken's my recipe. Named after myself." The woman thumbed her necklace. *Honey*, in cursive, on a gold chain.

"Are you the owner?"

Honey tipped her head back and laughed. "I wish! One day." Her arms were inked with fine tattoos: a dachshund, a triangle, the words *Girl Almighty* in tiny block letters. The only makeup she wore was a bright slash of red across her lips. "What about you, Kentucky? What do you do?"

"I'm a wedding planner." At best it sounded like a fantasy. At worst, a lie. It'd been almost a week since the meeting with Kamile and Dave. Liv wasn't returning her calls. "But not a very good one. I can't even find a caterer."

"You live here or just visitin'?"

"I live here."

"Then I expect to see you back here," Honey said, sliding the picked-clean bones into the trash.

"I'll be a regular at anywhere serving Pappy Van Winkle." Savannah pointed at her favorite bourbon whiskey. "Best bourbon in the world."

Honey arched an eyebrow, seeming impressed. "I agree. And we're the only restaurant in Bushwick who serves it." She grabbed the bottle. "This one's on me."

Honey poured her a glass, winked, then turned her attention to the guys at the other end of the bar. Savannah watched their eyes slide over Honey's body, lingering at the swell of her breasts. Half the men who came in here probably fell in love with her.

Savannah had never been short of male attention, but she'd never truly connected with any of the guys in the South. They always felt too familiar or too shallow. Sexless, like a big brother or a best friend. New York had already presented one worldly lover. It was sure to present another. Someone confident and hardworking, with a cheeky glint in their eye. Maybe that was the reason why she uprooted her life and moved to a new city where she knew no one and was unequivocally the tiniest fish in the world's biggest pond. Because if love wasn't in New York City—where was it?

Savannah lingered over her drink, not wanting the evening to end. But when the servers started putting chairs onto tables, she knew it was time to face reality. As she slipped off her stool, Honey came out from behind the bar and handed her a folded napkin.

"Here."

For a disorientating moment, Savannah thought Honey was handing over her own number. But the name *Sam Woods* and a cell number were printed on the napkin.

"Catering recommendation," Honey said. "We used to work together. Tell him Honey Calhoun sent you."

A wave of warm tingles prickled Savannah's skin. The restaurant, the recommendation, even Honey herself felt like the first glimpse of that New York magic she'd heard so much about. "*Thank you.*"

She couldn't stop herself from reaching out to squeeze Honey's arm. To her delight, Honey pulled her in for a hug. A real hug: warm and sincere.

"All right, Kentucky." Honey let her go. "Even though you're not a *real* Southerner, I like you. So come back soon, okay?"

Savannah nodded. "And I'm Savannah." Not Kentucky. Not anymore.

Honey tilted her head, impressed or maybe just amused. She flipped the OPEN sign to CLOSED. "Good night, Savannah."

Savannah stepped out onto the chilly street, zipped up her jacket, and dared to feel hopeful.

5

Sam Woods didn't typically cook test meals in potential clients' homes. But Savannah Shipley had been both insistent and charming, and so, here he was on a Wednesday afternoon, outside a lovely old brownstone. A family home. Sam felt an unfamiliar pang of envy as he pressed the doorbell.

The door was answered by a woman in sweatpants and a threadbare T-shirt. Unsmiling, but not unattractive. Liv Goldenhorn, presumably. She was about the same age he was, maybe a pinch younger, which was a relief: clients in their twenties and thirties tended to be too demanding or too indecisive. Her gaze flicked to the bags of groceries at his feet.

"Kitchen's straight through, do you mind?"

He went to explain he wasn't a delivery man, he was the chef she'd been expecting, but Liv had already disappeared up the stairs. So Sam picked up his grocery bags and did as he was told. He walked down a hallway lined with art, past a wooden staircase curling up, and into an open-plan kitchen and dining room. Certainly, the brownstone was a cozy home, exuding a familial, artsy charm; a fridge papered with school artwork, a dining room table scattered with books and unopened bills, a fruit basket piled with overripe apples and bananas. But it was also a mess. The sink was heaped with dishes. The recycling bin was overflowing. Marie Kondo would have a fit.

"H-hello? Liv?" Silence but for the faint patter of a shower. Savannah Shipley promised she'd be there. He set down the bags and moved toward the patio doors to send her a text. The overgrown backyard was dominated by a fifty-foot weeping willow. It was, sadly, dying. Several of its beefy limbs were already deadwood. The whole thing needed to be chopped down.

The text to Savannah didn't deliver.

Unsure what else to do, Sam started unpacking the groceries. There was barely enough room on the countertops, so he tossed the oil-slick take-out containers in the trash, wiped down the bench, emptied the dishwasher, and filled it up again. After locating an apron (brand-new and floral), he began chopping onions.

Ah, the noble onion. As reliable and ubiquitous as the faithful hound. Cooking onions actually diminished their bold taste but increased the flavor of the food around them, which Sam felt was generous. With deft, methodical fingers, he peeled his first onion, sliced it lengthwise, and placed it in the center of the chopping board. Then, angling the knife, which he noted was a little blunt, he made five even slices horizontally, cutting back toward the end, then sliced vertically. The result was a small white mound of perfectly diced onion. Cooking relaxed Sam, sending his body and brain into a meditative state. When things got bad, and they had gotten bad, the kitchen was where he felt safe.

He diced the rest of the onions and had all but forgotten about the earlier misunderstanding when Liv hurried back in, tightening a dressing gown. Her hair was wrapped in a towel. Her post-shower skin was pink and moist. She had a lovely complexion, alabaster and luminous.

Liv saw him. Stopped dead. Choked in a panicked, guttural gasp.

Shit. "Oh," he rushed, "I'm not actually—"

Her gaze flashed to his hand.

He was holding the knife he was using for the onions. "No, I'm not—"

Liv rocketed to the dining room table, scrambling for a weapon, which turned out to be . . . a banana. "Stay back or I'll scream."

He flung the knife in the sink. "No, I'm Sam, I'm Sam—"

"I don't care who you are! I'll put you in jail, motherfucker!"

"Liv, Liv, Liv, I'm Sam, Sam Woods—"

"How do you know my name?" Liv brandished the banana again, but the gesture had become a distracted inquiry, as if trying to pinpoint why he was wearing a flowery apron.

Sam spoke slowly and clearly. "Savannah Shipley, who I believe runs a wedding-planning business with you, organized for me to come do a test meal. I'm Sam. I'm a caterer."

The banana thumped onto the table. "*You're* Sam."

"Yes! Yes, I'm Sam." He gestured at the front door. "I think you thought I was from the grocery store, but then you went upstairs and—"

"Right, right. That explains the apron. God almighty, I almost lost my mind."

"Me too," said Sam.

Their fright went out of them in a huff of laughter.

Liv twisted the towel off her damp hair and dropped it over the back of a dining room chair. "Look, I appreciate you coming over and Jamie Oliver–ing my kitchen. But I don't think this will work out."

It felt like cutting open a perfectly ripe avocado to find it brown and smelly inside. "That's a shame."

The front door opened. "Mom?"

Liv's entire face lit up. "In here!"

Oh, Sam realized. *She's really pretty.*

Footsteps sounded down the hallway. A young boy ran in and threw himself on Liv in a hug.

She hugged him back in the way only a mom did. "Hey, baby. How was school?"

"Good," replied the boy. He looked to be about seven or eight.

Liv asked him something about how a carpool went: he must've been dropped off by one of the other parents. It didn't feel like there was a father in the picture. The house, the boy, the woman, were all absent of a spouse, somehow. Divorce? Divorcing? Or maybe something worse. That would explain the kitchen.

The kid went on. "We did an experiment with eggshells to see how soda stains teeth and wears down enamel."

"Whoa!" Liv poked him in the side. "Did it make you want to drink less soda?"

"Nope," he said, before noticing Sam, and becoming shy.

"Ben, honey, this is Sam. A . . . friend."

"Hey Ben." Sam bent down to Ben's level. "I like your backpack. Is that Spider-Man?"

Ben nodded, his eyes on the ground.

"I have a question," Sam said. "Who would win in a battle between Superman and Spider-Man?"

"Superman."

"Really?" Sam was intrigued. "Then why isn't he on your backpack?"

"Well, Superman is stronger but Spider-Man's funnier and more, um, relatable." Now Ben was looking at Sam. "He was just a regular kid."

"Sounds like you know what you're talking about," Sam said.

"I'm intellectually curious," replied Ben.

Sam grinned. Liv was smiling too, proud and pretending not to be.

Ben wandered into the kitchen, taking in the groceries. "What are you doing?"

Sam rose to his feet. "Well, you know how your mom plans weddings?"

Ben nodded.

"I'm a cook. I make food for weddings. And I'm here to audition for your mom. You know what an audition is?"

Ben shook his head. A small smile edged his mouth.

One of those kids who loved learning. Like Dottie. Dottie loved learning new things, too. "It's like a test. A trial. If your mom likes what I cook, she might hire me." Sam and Liv traded smiles, easy as an underarm lob.

Ben rocked back and forth on his toes. "What are you going to make?"

Sam looked to Liv. She shrugged, then nodded. Permission granted.

"Zucchini lasagna, fresh pea risotto, and a few appetizers," Sam said. "Vegetarian, gluten-free, one hundred percent organic, and *yummy*. Wanna help me?"

"Can I, Mom?"

A micro expression of surprise flashed over her face before Liv replaced it with something more neutral. "As long as you don't chop your fingers off."

"Don't worry, I am an expert in not chopping off fingers." It'd been a while since Sam had met someone he found interesting. Liv was interesting. Her gaze brought a little flush to the back of his neck. Maybe she was in the same sort of situation he was in. "All right Big Ben, I am going to show you how to shuck peas."

6

An hour or so later, Liv was tasting the best pea risotto of her life. One bite and she saw delicate young shoots and careening swallows and the gorgeous vermilion roses that burst forth along the back fence every May, unbidden and relentlessly alive. God, this winter had been long. Soon it'd be warm enough to eat dinner in the backyard under the old willow tree. If she could bring herself to pull out the one thousand weeds.

"Do you like it, Mom?" Ben was bouncing with excitement. "I shucked *hundreds* of peas."

Ben's interest in food prep was a surprise. His grief counselor said this would be a marathon, not a sprint. In some ways, Ben would never get over losing his father. The disruption to the family unit would play out his entire life: his attachment style, his choice of partners, maybe even the way he parented himself. The last three months had been fraught; Ben couldn't sleep alone or with the lights off. He was prone to anxiety and tantrums. *Pay attention to difference*, said the counselor. *To change*.

Cooking wasn't a Goldenhorn tradition. But it wasn't exactly an unpleasant sight, the handsome caterer helping Ben stir a pot of simmering risotto.

"It's delicious," Liv told her son, accidentally looking at Sam instead of Ben as she added, "Well done, sweetie."

"You're welcome, sweetie," Sam replied, deadpan.

Liv laughed out loud. She honestly could not remember the last time she'd done that. She'd find out later that Savannah was currently stuck on a stalled L train with no reception, panicking. At that moment, Liv didn't care where she was.

Sam put the last of the bowls in the dishwasher. There were some strands of silver in an otherwise full head of dark hair. He was over six feet tall, but his posture was as relaxed as the old T-shirt he was wearing. If height was power, Sam didn't feel the need to dominate. Eliot, at five seven, had always carried himself with the straightest spine possible and wore shoes with risers.

"Right, the lasagna needs another thirty minutes in the oven. Apps are here" Sam gestured to a platter of brightly colored dips and finger foods—"and you've got enough risotto for a week."

"Can't we shuck more peas?" Ben whined, trailing him to the front door.

"Can't, champ," Sam said, "got to get home to my own family."

Hot, hard disappointment punched Liv in the belly. The reaction was deeply embarrassing. She was too old to have a crush, or be the subject of one, and besides: he was married. Of course he was. Sam was gentle and funny, and his warm brown eyes crinkled nicely when he smiled.

"Your partner's lucky," Liv said, as they reached the door. "My, um, ex was a pretty bad cook. I'm not much better." It felt odd calling Eliot her "ex": she wanted Sam to know she was single but not the reason why.

"Oh, my ex-wife is a great cook. It was monogamy she sucked at."

She surprised herself with a girlish giggle. *Get a grip, lady. You're a middle-aged widow with saggy tits and a mild drinking problem.*

"Yeah, it's just me and Dottie." Sam slipped a tan leather jacket over broad shoulders. "My daughter. Little younger than Ben. Not as into Spider-Man."

"Ha!" Liv's heart was pattering. She hoped she wasn't blushing. "Well, thanks for the food, and the cooking lesson, and for not being a home invader."

"No worries."

She rubbed at her forehead, pulling the wrinkles with her fingertips. "Look, I should mention . . . Things fell apart a bit workwise last year."

"Yeah, I know. Think I read something about pigeons and bees?" *Screw the internet, seriously.*

"Don't worry about it." He smiled at her. Sam's eyes were the color of butterscotch pudding, of brandy, of warm, delicious things. "Guess I'm willing to take the risk."

"Thank you. I'll be in touch."

"Sounds great." The only caterer in New York willing to work with her ambled down her front steps. "Night, Liv."

The early evening was unseasonably balmy. The air almost felt silky on her bare arms. A handful of stars twinkled in the lavender sky, delicate as fine jewelry.

"Night, Sam."

Liv closed the door after him, letting the lock click into place with deliberate slowness. Her house was redolent of butter and onions. It smelled like a home. Enjoying the way the smooth wooden floorboards creaked under her footfalls, Liv wandered back into the kitchen. It was, impossibly, completely clean.

7

The next morning, Savannah was shaken awake by Arj, one of her new roommates. The skinny bartender did not look pleased. "There's a crazy bitch downstairs who says she knows you. Also, I work nights. I was in the middle of my REM."

Confused, Savannah pulled up her blind and peered down at the street. Liv was standing on the pavement, leaning on the horn of a beat-up Subaru. Savannah heaved the window up, bracing against the rush of cold morning air. "Mrs. Goldenhorn?"

Liv was wearing oversize sunglasses and a hot-pink pussyhat, the one made famous by the first Women's March. "Hurry up, Shipley. We've got things to do." She got back in the car, calling through the window. "And for God's sake, call me Liv!"

An unseen neighbor yelled, "Shut the hell up, Liv!"

Liv almost smiled.

It took a long moment to land. Then Savannah bolted out of bed, threw on some clothes, and flew down the stairs. She'd never been less put together when she climbed in next to Mrs. Golden—*Liv*. But her business partner didn't seem to notice.

After missing Sam Woods's test meal thanks to a subway drama, Savannah figured she'd blown it and was planning on spending the morning booking a flight home. But now, she was in Liv's inner sanctum. Faded stickers on the glove box. A blue evil eye charm hung from the rearview mirror.

"Here's how it's going to go down." Liv clicked in her seat belt. "Rule one: I'm in charge. Rule two: I'm in charge. Rule three?"

"You're in charge."

"Exactly." Liv was wearing lipstick. It made her look pretty, softening her edges. She started the car, and Alanis Morissette's snarl blasted: "*A slap in the face, how quickly I was replaced, and are you thinking of me when you fu—*" Liv hit the eject button, mumbling something about breakup music. She reached into the back seat and groped for another CD from the dozen sliding around. Savannah had never once purchased a CD.

Savannah got her license at sixteen, eager to have the freedom and responsibility of a car. She'd only ever driven in Kentucky, never in New York. And at this moment, as Liv careened between lanes, riding the brakes and the horn, all while fiddling with the CD player and gulping coffee from a thermos, Savannah didn't think she'd ever have the chance. It'd be a miracle if they got wherever they were going alive.

"The thing about wedding planning," Liv shouted over the nervy jangle of vintage-sounding rock, "is it's less about what they *say* they want and more about what they can—*out of my lane, prick!*—afford. Everyone comes in with big dreams—the cake, the dress, the destination wedding, but—*what the hell are you doing?*—all that adds up. So do they want to double their budget, or do they want some creative solutions? Because even though people hire a wedding planner because they'd rather spend their money than their time, you have to—*learn to drive, ya dildo!*"

On the three-hour drive north to the Catskills, Savannah tried to scratch the surface of twenty-odd years of wedding-planning wisdom while Liv blasted bands Savannah had never heard of. Despite the terrible first meeting the week before, Kamile was still open to working with In Love in New York. No other wedding planners were interested in exchanging two months of unpaid work for social posts, and Kamile was not prepared to fork out ten grand for a planner, or do it all herself.

In the Catskills, the rustic red barn was huge and completely empty, surrounded by apple trees. Twenty feet away, a pond glinted. The first thing Savannah said to the owner was "Adorable! What a perfect place for a romantic spring wedding!"

The first thing Liv said was, "I need to know about parking, power, liability insurance, sound restrictions, your preferred vendors, and the wet-weather plan."

*   *   *

And they were off. The pace never slowed. The list of tasks was
endless: design the wedding website, negotiate vendor contracts,
connect with the officiant, coordinate the cake tasting. It was less
"sophistication and tradition merging in surprising and delightful
ways" and more . . . matter-of-fact. Budgets, dates, deadlines. De-
cisions were made quickly and often. Savannah assumed wedding
planning would be about love and logistics. But it was so much more
about anxiety and assurance. Kamile's anxiety. Liv's assurance. Was
it okay to not do a receiving line, even though her parents expected
her to? Of course it was: receiving lines were out of style in the era of
a newer, more casual approach. Was this dress too short to wear to
the rehearsal dinner? Of course not: great legs should be shown off!
Anxiety, due to the fact that the first thing an engaged couple was
expected to do was plan an enormous, expensive event that was part
family reunion, part group holiday, for everyone who'd ever meant
anything to them, that would also express their identity as a couple,
without going broke or mad. Assurance that it could be done. Tradition and ritual were being reimagined, or revoked, every single day.

A few weeks in, the two women sat working in the front office,
still surrounded by dust and debris. Savannah was testing the new
submission form on their website, wondering how many referrals
they'd get from Kamile's posts. Five? Ten? Fifty? Liv looked up from
her ancient laptop. "Have you got a contract?"

"For what?"

"For Kamile. And all this"—Liv waved her 1:00 p.m. glass of white
wine around—"exposure you think she's going to get us. Me. Get me."

Savannah gave the older woman an indulgent smile. "Kamile is
my friend."

Liv put her wine down with deliberate accuracy. "So, we're working for free, for months, and if Kamile decides not to post about us,
then legally we can do absolutely nothing. Correct?"

"Liv! Kamile is a *sorority sister*. If she says she'll do it, she'll do it."

"If you're not comfortable with sending her one, I'll do it."

"A contract will make it seem like I don't trust her! Like I'm expecting her to screw me over! It's like a prenup. Why would you get
one unless you were expecting a marriage to fail?"

"Because so many do," Liv said. "Even if you don't expect it."

Alarm spiked in Savannah's chest, making her angrier. "I don't need a contract. Kamile will post for us, on the Sunday morning after her wedding, just like she promised."

"But what if she doesn't? What if she forgets? What if she gets so used to having free wedding fairies at her disposal that she mistakes our hard work for her due in life and heads off on her honeymoon, totally oblivious?"

"I can *guarantee* that *won't* happen."

"No, you can't," said Liv, and Savannah wanted to scream. Liv didn't get it *at all*. And she wasn't much of a teacher, either.

As Savannah put it to Honey, later that night, over a plate of crunchy fried chicken, "It's like she's keeping me at arm's length, and I only learn things if I squint real hard and happen to catch her doing it."

Honey splashed more Pappy Van Winkle into Savannah's glass. She'd heard the backstory of Liv and Eliot from Savannah's regular appearances on a 'Shwick Chick barstool. "Be patient, darlin'," said Honey. "You didn't expect to be weaving friendship bracelets together from day one, did you?"

"No. We're very different people." Savannah chewed her drumstick thoughtfully. "I think she's still trying to work out if she trusts me."

"That takes time." Honey folded her arms and cocked her head at Savannah.

"What?" Savannah asked, worried. "Don't you think I'm trustworthy?"

Honey smiled, shaking her head like *That's not it*, as she took a drinks order from another customer. With her tattoos and short hair, it was hard to picture her from small-town Alabama. Her lack of makeup had inspired Savannah to experiment with wearing less. Now, instead of primer, foundation, concealer, bronzer, blush, eyelid primer, eyeshadow, eyeliner, mascara, brow pencil, lip liner, lipstick, lip gloss, and a setting spray, she was *only* doing primer, foundation, blush, mascara, brow pencil, and lip gloss. It felt nice not to have on a full face. Liberating.

"When did it start feeling like home for you?" Savannah asked when Honey returned. "New York, I mean."

Honey pulled beers for the couple next to Savannah, thinking. "That's a good question. I'll have to get back to you."

Savannah sipped her bourbon. Still the taste of tailgating and bluegrass and long summer evenings on someone's porch, listening to the screech owls. "Do you miss the South?"

"Nope." Honey cleared Savannah's empty plate and tossed the scraps in the trash. "I really don't." She didn't meet Savannah's eye when she said it.

8

Spring started as a timid, whiplashed affair. On the first day the mercury spiked over sixty, New Yorkers packed away their oppressive winter coats and flocked outside, only to unpack the coats the following week, scowling as the weather dipped back into the forties. Nevertheless, spring persisted. Day by day, buds emerged on the bare branches of the willow tree in the backyard. The farmers markets' root vegetables and pickles were replaced with leafy greens and the daring hint of a tomato. Finally, the definitive sign that the seasons had changed: the city's restaurants removed their cold-weather vestibules and set up outdoor seating. Spring had sprung.

And while time passing was meant to be a good thing, sometimes Liv wanted it to slow down, or stop altogether.

There was still a wedge of Eliot's brie in the fridge. It stunk up the kitchen as it decomposed, day by day, but she couldn't make herself toss it. To recycle the sports section stuffed next to the toilet. To empty the drawer of his mismatched socks. He called them misfit socks. That used to make her laugh.

Mornings were the hardest. Waking alone; no tuneless singing in the shower, no smell of burning toast. Just Liv, silently lying in bed, tears leaking down her temples, thinking about everything she'd lost.

But as Liv let herself be drawn into Dave and Kamile's wedding planning, she discovered it was good to have a focus. It pulled her out of the muck of her own mind. She had to learn new parts of the process, the things Eliot usually did. The human side of negotiation, figuring out the rental toilets, exactly how much power a site needed. Sometimes an entire hour would pass and Liv was so involved in a task that Eliot didn't enter her mind at all.

But Savannah was always there. Asking questions. Making sugges-
tions. *Cleaning* things. She replaced the cigarette-singed couch with a
pale pink sofa (sourced on Craigslist; Liv couldn't afford a new one)
and put Eliot's things in the fourth-floor attic. She brightened the
front room with a fresh coat of paint and inspirational posters (Liv
vetoed CREATE YOUR OWN SUNSHINE and ALL WOMEN ARE QUEENS!,
begrudgingly accepting DON'T DREAM ABOUT SUCCESS: WORK FOR
IT). "But it's not as if she's actually helpful with anything to do with
planning," Liv complained to Henry and Gorman, in the back room
of Flower Power, Honey!

"Because, you're not actually letting her do any." Henry added
a few delicate white anemones to an airy table display. "Do you
think Kamile would go for something like this? Very wabi-sabi,
very chic."

"She'll approve anything I tell her is 'extremely Instagrammable,'"
Liv replied. "Which is rather a neat trick."

Gorman looked up from his copy of *Who's Afraid of Virginia
Woolf?*, which he was reading for his Monday-night playwriting
class. "And who taught you that trick, darling?"

Liv huffed. The smartphone obsession was highly irritating, all
these kids carrying phones around like miniature oxygen tanks. But
it was true Savannah understood that inane world. "She's very good
at appearances," Liv said. "How things look. How she looks."

"But what's going on on the inside?" Henry added another anemone to the display. "That's what's interesting."

"Not much," said Liv.

"Then what'd E see in her?" Gorman closed his book. "He was
always a flirt, but I didn't think he was the type to cheat."

"And it wasn't like we *never* had sex," Liv said. "Every now and
then I'd get drunk and relent."

"Hot," said Gorman.

"The current thinking on affairs is that it's less about the relationship they're leaving or even the new relationship they're having,"
Henry said. "It's about the new relationship with the *self*. Eliot liked
who he was when he was with Savannah."

Someone unencumbered by his identity as a husband and father.
Someone vibrant and intelligent, all inspiration, no obligation. Liv
could fathom this, even if she couldn't understand his willingness to

let his second life shatter hers. "But by that logic, Savannah could've been almost anyone. So why leave a business to her?"

"That," Henry said, "is what I'm still trying to figure out."

As far as Liv was concerned, Savannah was one of those women who chose cultivating a conformist personality as survival. Admittedly she wasn't unimpressive, and she didn't lack confidence: she'd arrived in New York City with the zeal of a conquering hero and she was, Liv had to admit, a fast learner. But Liv was sure Savannah would fall victim to the thing that took down most mainstream girls in America: the belief that being pretty enough and smart enough and kind enough was, in short, enough. Savannah Shipley would succeed as that version of a woman. She didn't have true potential to be interesting.

On the night before Dave and Kamile's wedding, Liv and Savannah pored over every last detail for the third time. Liv peered at the final run sheet through black-rimmed glasses. "The band is sound-checking—"

"At two p.m. while they're doing family photos," Savannah recited. "When we'll also test the mics and AV."

"Hair and makeup—"

"Arriving at the bridesmaids' rental house at seven a.m. sharp."

Kamile had hoped to trade all her vendors' services for social media posts. Only a few took the deal: makeup was one of them.

"Are you sure you don't want me to start an Instagram?" Savannah asked. "After Kamile posts about us, it'd be so good if she could tag us."

Post about *us*. Tag *us*. Savannah insisted on making out as if they were some kind of team. Liv removed her glasses. "Remind me of rules one, two, and three?"

Savannah let out a scoff of annoyance.

Liv raised an eyebrow.

Savannah realized what she'd done and blushed. "I'm so sorry. I just . . ."

"Had an emotion other than peppy? Don't apologize for that." Liv zipped up the emergency kit, a bag filled with everything from bobby pins to bandages, plus a backup copy of the couples' vows and list of must-play songs. They had plans, and contingency plans, and contingency plans of the contingency plans. In Love in New York was ready. Or, as ready as they'd ever be. Liv felt an unfamiliar wobble of nerves. It had been so long since she'd had a wedding go off without a hitch. A self-destructive part of her almost wanted tomorrow to implode. It might be preferable than doing all this again with Savannah Shipley. "It's late. Go home and get some rest."

Savannah rose obediently. "Liv—"

"Let's not," Liv cut her off. "You're so grateful for this opportunity, and you can't wait to celebrate the wondrous thing that is true love and blah blah blah."

"I was going to say we should bring antiperspirant deodorant. Dave sweats a lot."

"Oh," said Liv. "Yes, of course. Well, see you tomorrow."

She watched the girl stride up the darkening street toward the subway. Prospect Heights to Bushwick: that was a long commute. Complicated, too. The 3 to the L? The B to the M? But Little Miss Hush Puppy had never said a word about it or (apart from the test meal with Sam) been late to a meeting, not once in the two months they'd been working together. A pinprick of respect glowed quietly in the soft plum twilight.

Ugh! Liv slapped it away like a mosquito and yanked the front door shut.

9

kamile nia thomas
&
david anthony seal

Invite you to share in the celebration of their love

Saturday, May 15	Robertson Farm
Four o'clock in the	North Branch
afternoon	Catskills, New York

Reception to follow
#sealedthedeal (please use the hashtag)

"So there I am, in the middle of the jungle in Southeast Asia: no cell phone, no map, totally lost . . . and it's starting to get dark." The next morning, in Queens, Zia Ruiz was relishing the adorable sight of her spellbound niece and nephew, mouths open in wonder.

"What did you do, Auntie Zia?" lisped Lucy.

"Were there monsters?" shouted her older brother, Mateo, limping in a circle around her. His right leg was in a cast from a playground fall.

"Cambodia is known for being home to lots of different animals." Zia made her voice spooky. "Like snakes. And spiders. And big, man-eating tigers!"

The kids screamed as she leaped forward and tickled them, an explosion of shrieking giggles.

"Hey, hey, hey: inside voices, please," Layla called from the cramped kitchen. "Or I'll set those tigers on you."

Zia and Layla shared a family resemblance, inheriting their father's olive skin and their mother's loose curls. But Layla looked much older than her thirty-five years, closer to forty. She was a single mom of two, and it showed in the indigo circles under her eyes. Zia looked a pinch younger than twenty-seven, with a full, carefree smile and startling green eyes that inspired painters and bad pickup lines.

"What happened?" Lucy asked her aunt.

"I stayed up all night and found my way out the next morning," Zia replied, kissing Lucy's forehead. "Got eaten alive by mosquitoes. But the jungle at dawn . . . man, it was unforgettable. A symphony of life."

"Just another day in the globe-trotting life of Zia Ruiz." Layla dried her hands with a dish towel. Her smile was wry.

Zia wrapped her arms around her big sister, feeling the same way she always did when talking about her work overseas: unbearably guilty. "One of these days, you have to come with me. You'd love it."

"Okay." Layla shrugged, addressing her kids. "You guys are old enough to stay home by yourself for a few months, right?"

The kids chorused, "*Yes, totally!*"

The sisters exchanged a smile.

"Yeah, I bet. Okay, if we're out the door for day care in five, you can watch *Paw Patrol* tonight," Layla bribed. "Again."

That sent Lucy scampering and Mateo after her, his cast banging against the floor.

Layla slipped on her CVS vest. She'd been working for the pharmacy ever since she kicked the kids' deadbeat dad out of their one-bedroom years ago. "I missed you so much, sis. You were *gone forever.*"

"Four months," Zia corrected. Four amazing months helping build a school in rural Cambodia. Zia worked as a paid volunteer coordinator for Global Care, an international NGO devoted to humanitarian and environmental causes. She'd joined a team in its local field office and would stay as long as they needed her. Sometimes a disaster would mean an influx of interest that needed managing; sometimes she was just covering someone's maternity leave or overseeing a construction project. Between jobs she wanted to take, Zia picked up cater-waiter work in New York and spent time with her sister.

Working for Global Care didn't feel like work. It was a promise she'd made to herself, the ability to pack up and leave on a day's notice. It was a freedom she was still getting used to having again. For reasons she didn't like to think about.

Layla pulled her hair into a ponytail. "Just promise you're not ditching out on us again anytime soon."

Zia's throat tightened. She was already looking for another overseas assignment. "I didn't ditch you. I'm just, y'know, living my life."

"I know." Layla sighed. "I'm just jealous. I wish we could trade places for, like, forever." She massaged the joints in her hands, wincing. Zia's older sister had rheumatoid arthritis, and even with medication, it still gave her pain. "Are you sure you can't babysit? Day care's so expensive."

"Sorry. I'm working a wedding upstate for Liv Goldenhorn."

"Didn't her husband bite it?"

"Layla! He didn't 'bite it.' He died." Zia had worked on and off for Liv since she was seventeen. Eliot's death made her more determined to live life on her own terms. "I gotta go. Darlene's driving, and she hates when I'm late."

"Before you run off again . . ." Layla handed her a medium-size box.

Zia read the front. "It's an air mattress."

"Yup. Unless you wanna keep sleeping in the bed with me." Layla tossed her a grin. "Just like when you were a kid."

Zia put down the box, a sense of claustrophobia closing in. "Thanks, but I might crash at Darlene's tonight."

Layla paused. "It's a really good mattress."

"Babe, I've been here every day since I got back," Zia said lightly. "And Darlene has a sofa bed."

"The doc wants a million follow-ups for Mateo's leg." Layla piled dishes into the already full sink. "No idea where I'm getting the money for that. And I really need a dishwasher. Swear to God, I spend my nonexistent free time up to my neck in dirty dishwater. It'd be great if I had an unburdened little sister who could finish up here before she disappears. Again."

"I can't. I'll be late." Zia stuffed her sleep shirt and toothbrush into her backpack, trying to mute the impulse to flee.

"Okay." Layla blasted water over the dishes. "Have fun."

"It's not fun, it's work."

Layla opened her mouth. Reconsidered. Shut it. She pulled her sister in for a hug. "Love you." It sounded like a reminder.

"Love you too." Zia backed toward the front door. "And you can have all my tips from tonight. But I really gotta go." Then to the kids, "Bye, monkeys! Have fun at day care!"

On the street outside, she inhaled a breath of fresh air, letting the tension of the morning melt away. It was a beautiful day in Astoria. Things with her sister would work out. Even if she was envious, Layla wanted the best for her. She'd never really stand in her way.

Zia breathed in once, twice, and set off on her bike, coasting down the wide, sunny street. *You're free*, she told herself, still trying to believe it.

10

It was a gorgeous, sunny morning in SoHo—the kind that makes the city look like a backdrop for a movie where everyone gets what they want in the end. Sunshine splashed over the yellow cabs and glinting skyscrapers. Why would you live anywhere else?

The bagel shop guy rang up Darlene Mitchell's breakfast order. "Eighteen dollars."

Ouch: that was why. Darlene was frugal, but being frugal in New York was like trying to be sober at a wedding. Still, it was satisfying the order came out even. Darlene's car volume, thermostat, and her alarm were always set to even numbers. Just a little bit of symmetry in an uneven world.

She was humming as she reached for the twenty-dollar bill tucked in her wallet. The twenty-dollar bill that was decidedly not there. No: it had to be. She definitely had a twenty. A twenty . . . that she spent on a cab last night. She'd waited three hours for a five-minute slot at a crappy open mic in Sunset Park. By the time her name was called, it was 2:00 a.m. and the audience had reduced to drunk white guys who stared at her boobs. A cab seemed like an act of self-care. Now, the familiar low-grade panic about being a doomed, broke musician made it look like a foolish indulgence. Darlene handed over a credit card, trying not to think about her elephantine student loans and astronomical rent. She left a good tip—relying on tips herself, it was impossible not to—and stepped outside.

A few minutes past their agreed-on time, Zia glided to a stop, dismounting her bike with the ease of someone who enjoyed outdoor activities. "Hey babe. Sorry I'm late: took the scenic route. Such a beautiful day!"

"Hey lady." Darlene hugged her tightly. "So good to see you!"

She and Zia had met while carpooling to an In Love in New York wedding years ago. They talked so much Darlene had to remind herself not to overdo it before singing all night.

"How was Cambodia?"

Zia locked up her bike. "Incredible: the food, the kids—I wanna go back."

"Take me with you," Darlene groaned. "The most adventurous thing I've done since I saw you last was go to Sunset Park."

Zia laughed. "Where's Zach?"

It was 10:35 a.m. "Officially five minutes late. But if he appeared right now, he'd actually be fifteen minutes early, according to Zach time."

They got into the rental car parked outside Zach's chrome-and-steel apartment complex. Zach rented his condo from his parents, probably for less than Darlene paid for her postage-stamp-size spot in East Williamsburg. The two women began on breakfast: cream cheese bagel for Zia, who had the metabolism of an Olympian, and a large green juice for Darlene.

"Oh my *God*," Zia groaned. "*So good*. I want to marry this bagel."

"A lot of men are going to be sad they lost out to a piece of boiled bread."

Zia snorted. "Yeah, right." She'd always regarded her attractiveness with neutral detachment, even mild embarrassment, which Darlene both admired and felt a little jealous of.

"What about you?" Zia asked. "Still dating that political commentator guy—Charles?"

"Broke up a few months ago." Darlene flipped the driver-side mirror down and adjusted the wig she usually wore to wedding gigs. Bouncy waves of shiny black tickled her skin. "My love life is officially on hold until I record an EP."

"Awesome." Zia licked cream cheese off her pinkie. "How's all things music?"

It was a polite inquiry, and a genuine one. Everyone was interested in the path of the artist, excited for success, sympathetic about setbacks. Firm in their belief that for good people, tenacity and talent paid off. But what Darlene didn't realize about choosing to forgo a reliable nine-to-five in favor of the nebulous dream of being a full-time musician was how often she'd have to play the role of optimistic striver. No one wanted to hear that dream chasing could be tiring, demoralizing, and financially crippling. Not that she wanted to share that uncomfortable truth. While Darlene Mitchell could sing songs that were full of emotions, she was not particularly good at expressing them. There was something about that sort of vulnerability that made her feel exposed. Or worse still, pitied. So when people asked about how her music "career" was going, she'd usually slap a smile on her face and say, *Great! I'm performing pretty much every weekend!* (Unpaid open mics or jazz gigs covering other people's songs, but still: the truth.) But Darlene didn't need to pretend around Zia. She huffed an exasperated breath. "I'm twenty-nine. I need to get off the wedding-party circuit and into an actual studio. Record my own songs."

"With Zach?"

Darlene let out a soft snort. "No."

"Why not? You always say he's so talented."

"He is. But Zach has other . . . priorities."

As if on cue, a uniformed doorman opened the building's front door for Zach and a buttery blonde in a miniskirt. This was Lauren (Laura?), a pharmaceutical rep. They'd met at a wedding; she'd been a bridesmaid. She and Zach had been dating for about six weeks. Zach dated someone for about six weeks a lot.

Lauren (Laura?) put her arms around Zach's neck. He leaned down for a kiss, which quickly lengthened into a full-on make-out.

A scalding rush of anger that only Zach could inspire exploded in Darlene's stomach. Could he go one month without charming the pants off some Bachelorette wannabe? And did they all have to constantly hook up in front of her? She leaned on the horn, hard. The sound broke the lovers apart with a satisfying jump. Zach shot her an apologetic grin, the kind of warm, winning smile that forgave just about anything. After one more stomach-churning kiss, he loped toward the car . . . before stopping to let a jogger pass. Then a dog walker. Then he was chasing the dog walker halfway down the block to return the guy's dropped glove. Jesus, they were already late! Finally, he popped the trunk to store his guitar, the case plastered with UK flags and a BRITS DO IT BETTER sticker.

"Morning, Mitchell." He slid into the back seat. "Hello, Zia, love: long time. Ooh, is that bagels I smell?"

The trio hadn't worked a wedding together since November, nearly six months ago. The one on Long Island, where a flock of pigeons got loose in the kitchen and Liv found out poor Eliot had died. The last time Darlene had seen Liv was at the funeral. She'd been surprised to get another booking. In Love in New York was still alive.

"Hey, Zee-Bot." Zia twisted around in her seat. "Blondie was cute. Predictable, but cute."

"Don't get attached." Zach arched his back like a satisfied cat. "I think our time together is coming to an end."

You could set your watch to it. Darlene pulled into traffic.

Zach eyed the bagel in Zia's hand and tickled Darlene's neck. "Tell me you got ol' Zachie some breakfast, Darlene, my darling?"

She swiped him away. "You didn't reply to my email about the new arrangement for 'At Last.'"

He met her eyes in the rearview mirror, eyebrows up. "The one you sent at midnight last night?"

"'At Last' is the first dance," she pointed out. "It's special."

"I know, I know. Well, we can go through it now. We do have a three-hour drive ahead of us." Zach ran a hand through his hair and yawned. "As long as I can work in a quick nap. Barely got a wink last night."

"You're so unprofessional," Darlene muttered, changing lanes.

"They'll put it on my gravestone. *Here lies Zach. He lived unprofessionally.*"

He did. Lavishly and without regret. With his flop of light brown hair, decent body, and that outrageously effective smile, Zach was cute. Less hot, more attainable. Very, very attainable. And so Zach Livingstone lived unprofessionally. Sometimes twice a night. He fixed Darlene with disconcertingly blue eyes through the rearview. "Bagel?"

Darlene sighed and plucked the bag between her legs. "Sesame. With scallion cream cheese."

"My favorite!" Grabbing it, he smooched Darlene's cheek. Scratchy stubble and warm, soft lips. The spot where he kissed her pulsed, sending a false alarm down her entire body. Flustered, she almost swerved into the next lane.

"Watch it," she snapped, as the car next to them blared its horn. "Or that gravestone'll become a reality."

"Easy, Mitchell. I come bearing treats." Zach leaned forward between the girls, presenting both fists. Zia tapped the closest. He opened it to reveal a fat joint. In the other, a lighter.

Zia laughed and high-fived him.

"You're not smoking that in here," Darlene said.

"Duh. We'll get high at a rest stop and buy loads of terrible junk food. My treat." Zach grabbed the car's auxiliary cable and plugged in his phone. The swaggering, slippery groove of Salt-N-Pepa filled the car: "*Shoop shoop ba-doop shoop ba-doop, shoop ba-doop ba-doop.*"

Zach turned it up, seat-dancing in time with Zia, twisting left, then right, left, then right. "'*Here I go, here I go, here I go again . . .*'"

As if Darlene could expect anything less from Zach "I Bring the Party" Livingstone. And it was always fun to hear him sing in an American accent. Giving up, she joined in—"'*Girls, what's my weakness? Men!*'"—pulling onto the West Side Highway.

Just over three hours later, the trio pulled into the service parking lot of Dave and Kamile's wedding venue. It was a glorious May day in the Catskills. A warm breeze ruffled the apple tree blossoms, sending white petals floating through the clean, country air. Darlene was still climbing out of the front seat when a very enthusiastic blonde appeared out of nowhere, introducing herself as "Savannah Shipley, from the emails." A small-town beauty queen not quite pretty enough to take State. She handed Darlene a form. "It's an *NDA*." Evidently, Savannah-from-the-emails was excited by this. "Non-disclosure agreement. We have a *celebrity guest* attending today's wedding."

Darlene skimmed the form and scrawled her signature. She'd performed at plenty of weddings with high-profile guests. They didn't really affect her but for the fact the other guests were usually paying more attention to them than her, the person onstage.

Savannah thrust a form at Zia, beaming. "You're a server, right? You'll be circulating around our *celebrity guest.*" She bounced on her toes. "It's Clay Russo!"

The name was vaguely familiar, but Zia couldn't conjure a face. "Football player?"

Savannah's jaw dropped. "*Movie star.*"

Zia didn't really keep abreast of popular culture. The idea of sitting in a dark room for hours on end, staring at a screen, felt a bit oppressive. She'd rather be outside, in her body, in the air. She signed the NDA and handed it back. "I'll keep an eye out."

"It's better you *don't* keep an eye out," Savannah corrected. "He's actually very private, and I think he's going through a breakup, according to the tabloids, so we should all—Oh. Hello."

Zach emerged from the back seat, yawning. "Gosh, I just had the most amazing dream." He locked eyes with Savannah. "Or maybe it hasn't yet ended?"

Darlene shuddered. Zach did land most of their gigs by flirting with female wedding planners or bro-ing out with male venue bookers. But seeing white male privilege in action was still gross.

"This is Liv's new business partner," she said pointedly.

"Welcome to the family." Zach smiled. "Although surely you being here is a little unfair."

The girl's eyes pulsed in . . . was it alarm? "What do you mean?"

Zach's smile was conspiratorial. "How does it look for the wedding planner to be more beautiful than the bride?"

Darlene mimed gagging to Zia and popped the trunk. "We have to set up."

Savannah addressed Zach. "You're the DJ, right? Do you need a green room?"

Darlene exchanged a look of incredulity with Zach. Not the first time he was treated like an artist, while she was treated like staff.

"I don't need a green room." Zach winked at Savannah. "But next time, feel free to offer that to Darlene too. She's the actual talent here."

The two musicians lugged their equipment to a small wooden stage overlooking the grassy field where they'd be playing cocktail hour. It was a pretty venue, typical for the area, but Darlene wasn't taking in the lush trees and nearby pond. The thought of Zach seducing Savannah made her feel a bit ill. Reading her mind, Zach chuckled.

"Don't worry. She's not my type."

"She's the human equivalent of a vanilla cupcake." Darlene plugged in the amp. "She's exactly your type."

Zach laughed and placed the mic stand center stage. "What, are you jealous?"

"Besides losing my voice or waking up with crab claws for hands, dating you is actually my worst nightmare."

"A fair point, well made." Zach plugged the mic into the mixer and started adjusting the levels. "How's everything going with your EP?"

Darlene glanced over in surprise. She'd only mentioned her dream of recording an EP—a shorter version of a full-length album—to Zach once.

"I remembered." He almost sounded offended. "I'm excited for you. You're a genius, Mitchell, and soon, everyone will know it."

That was the thing about Zach. Just when you decided to be annoyed with him, he'd turn around and be disgustingly earnest. "I haven't got any finished songs yet. But I found a producer I like. He's not cheap, but he's good, and he gets me. Now I just need the cash." She positioned the tip jar at the front of the small stage.

"Why can't you just ask your dad for money? Didn't he write a million books?"

"He's written four." Darlene's father was a professor of African American studies at Oberlin. But the Mitchell family motto was basically *Do it on your own*. "I haven't asked my dad for a thing since I moved out."

"There's such a thing as being too self-sufficient. Let people help you." Zach plugged the pedals into his guitar, testing them one by one. "You know what they say. Behind every strong woman is an almost-as-strong man."

"Not behind me. I don't want my success handed to me. I want to earn it."

"Honorable. You know you're my hero, Mitchell." Zach pushed his hair out of his eyes, watching her reach up to swivel the PA. "I might actually be in love with you."

Darlene rewarded this with a withering smile. "Save it for the bridesmaids, Livingstone. All I need to hear is you learning the first dance in less than thirty minutes, please."

"Yes, ma'am." Zach pulled a guitar pick from his pocket and faultlessly started the new arrangement of "At Last."

II

One of the things a newly engaged couple didn't realize about their decision to have a wedding was that their task was not to plan a ceremony. Or a party. It was a show. A high-stakes, high-drama, once-in-a-lifetime show. That was one of the things that hooked Liv in—the sight of everyone dashing around as they drew closer to the curtain call, perfecting the set for the arrival of the cast (the wedding party) and the audience (their guests). It recalled the thrill of acting in New York in her early twenties, except these shows were real life, and she was actually being paid.

But today, Liv was an actor who couldn't remember her lines. She kept feeling there was something missing. Over and over again, she'd check the run sheet, sensing a major oversight. And every time, she remembered what it was. Or rather, who it was. Eliot and weddings were as interconnected as an infinity ring. They'd met at the very first one Liv had planned.

She was twenty-five. Her hair was long, and her dresses were short. The dream of becoming the next Winona Ryder was starting to crumble under the weight of ego-crushing auditions. Appalled at what a snobby Manhattan planner was charging an old friend from acting class, she offered to help. It turned out beautifully, a relaxed late-summer affair in Prospect Park with a jazz quartet and lawn games. The couple said their *I dos* with wet cheeks and full hearts, and just for a moment, the world was perfect. Love was real, and people were good, and there was hope for the entire human race. Liv didn't know it at the time, but that sort of feeling would sustain her for years to come. It renewed her passion, buoying her through the less fun (aka utterly shitful) aspects of full-time wedding planning. Maybe she'd catch it in the father-daughter dance, or the best man toast, or the way a newly married couple would gaze at each other, so full of wonder. The world was run by madmen and bastards. But we could also love one another. We could also be tender.

As the dinner finished up, and everyone was feeling nicely tipsy, Liv had tucked her long locks behind her ears and tapped her glass, commanding the attention of the guests. She'd told a few jokes and a suitably embarrassing story about the bride mistaking an audition call for Sun-Maid raisins as being for *A Raisin in the Sun* and presenting a theatrical monologue for a dried-fruit commercial, to waves of satisfying laughter. "I want to end with one of my favorite poems. 'Pathways,' by Rainer Maria Rilke. To me, this poem speaks to how much everyone needs love. Even the loners. The seekers. The wanderers." She cleared her throat, and began. " 'Understand, I'll slip quietly, away from the noisy crowd, when I see the pale stars rising, blooming, over the oaks. I'll pursue solitary pathways, through the pale twilit meadows, with only this one dream: *You come too*.' "

The crowd murmured their appreciation.

Liv raised her glass, addressing the newlyweds. "May you always walk side by side, seeking the stars and new horizons. To love."

"To love," echoed the crowd.

Liv sat back down, giddy with a post-performance rush. She was only able to refocus as one of the groom's college friends took the microphone. He wore a tux with a bow tie undone. Dark hair, confident nose; Jewish, like her. Handsome, with a glint in his eye. Liv sat up straighter.

The speaker pointed at the groom. "This guy has always been a prick."

The crowd laughed.

The man continued, now indicating Liv. "I mean, who makes his best man follow that? A beautiful woman speaking heartfelt words?"

The crowd laughed harder. Liv's cheeks warmed, suddenly feeling the effects of the seventeen thousand glasses of wine she'd knocked back.

Eliot continued, the microphone loose in his hand. "Everything you're going to see from me is going to resemble a chimpanzee throwing his own feces. Which reminds me of the time we all got drunk at the zoo."

The college friends howled, thrilled. A tawdry tale was being exposed, but Liv didn't hear a word of it. This guy, whoever he was, was cute.

Later, Eliot had found Liv at the edge of the tent, taking a break from the dance floor. An unlit cigarette hung from his lips. "Got a light?"

"Don't tell me you smoke."

"I don't." He tossed it. "Anymore."

She almost smiled, but Liv was a pretty cool cat in those days. She informed Eliot that smoking was disgusting and bad for his health.

Eliot lapped it up, leaning against the tent pole. "Then why do I keep doing it? What's wrong with me?"

"Are you self-destructive? Hedonistic, even if it risks your health?"

Eliot clamped his hand over his heart. "It's like you've known me all my life."

That did get a laugh out of her.

Charmed, Eliot dropped the schtick. "You're Olive, right? You helped plan this bacchanalia?" In front of them, everyone danced to "Brown Eyed Girl" played by a DJ wearing hammer pants.

"I am and I did," Liv replied.

"Impressive. Your speech was terrific."

Liv side-eyed him. "Yours too."

"I like this." Eliot handed her a glass of prosecco she didn't even see him procure. "Let's always believe in the best in each other. That's how we'll make it work."

Liv looked him properly in the face for the first time. Beneath the mischief, his eyes were warm. She decided to go to bed with him. "I'm in."

"Liv!"

Darlene stood in front of her, arms crossed.

"Sorry, what?" Liv struggled to get her bearings. She was beside a barn, not a tent, and the person in front of her was Darlene, looking at her with wary concern.

"The Wi-Fi isn't working." The singer sounded like she was repeating this. "We need it for the playlist—there's no cell reception."

"Right, yes." Liv opened her binder. It was upside down. "Wasn't the password on your—"

"It's not working," Darlene repeated, almost testily.

"The Wi-Fi?" Savannah popped up at her elbow, like a gopher in wedge sandals. "I just restarted the router. It'll be back on in a minute."

Darlene nodded and strode back toward the stage.

"Also, here are the NDAs." Savannah handed them to Liv. "*So* exciting."

Liv frowned at the stack, wondering how she'd got them signed so quickly. "Don't lose your head over Clay Russo."

"I won't," Savannah replied, as if the possibility was nonexistent. "Going to check on flowers."

Liv watched her point something out to Henry, who was twisting a hundred white peonies into the arbor that'd been set up under the apple trees.

Was Savannah being professional, or was Clay Russo really not her type? Was Eliot her type? Did Eliot really lie to her, and if so, how did she feel about his betrayal? And why on earth did Eliot force his wife to meet—no, *work with*—the woman with whom he'd had an affair?

Her walkie-talkie crackled. The chef wanted to see her.

Amid the frantic ballet of the kitchen, Sam was sniffing the contents of a saucepan with the intensity of one solving a crime. Liv's instinct was to appear cool and casual, as if she'd just bumped into him while engaging in a leisurely spot of gardening. "Oh, hello," she said, stopping herself from adding, *Aren't the marigolds looking divine?*

"Liv. Just the person I need." He spooned something into a teaspoon and handed it to her.

It was the tomato-basil cream sauce, made with cashews instead of dairy. Velvety, salty-sweet ripeness, which promised so much. Spring. It was finally spring.

"Heaven. But don't add any more salt, it's just on the edge."

His brown eyes crinkled when he grinned. "Knew I could trust you."

"I feel like I can trust you too," said Liv, before hearing the unchecked sincerity and blushing. God, how desperate did she sound? Gorman radioed her to come approve the bouquets. She made herself brusque. "I trust you'll be right on time for five p.m. cocktail hour."

"You got it, boss." Sam dropped the teaspoon in the sink. "Hey, Liv," he called after her. He tossed an apple in the air and caught it. "This is fun, isn't it?"

He was smiling at her, as if he was genuinely having a good time. She used to enjoy herself at weddings. She used to enjoy herself.

Liv made herself smile back at Sam, but she knew it was wonky and cheap, a knockoff. "Better get back to work."

12

Clay Russo was not enjoying himself. Slumped on the end of the plush hotel bed, he couldn't take his eyes off the magazine. The latest *People*, the one with him and Michelle on the front cover, both looking angry, above the bright yellow coverline that was giving him nightmares: CLAY DUMPS MICHELLE! And under it, in neon pink: WHAT TORE THEM APART AND WHAT'S NEXT FOR MICHELLE.

"Knock, knock." Dave came in, balancing two shot glasses of whiskey, shutting the door behind him. He spotted the magazine in Clay's hands. "Dude. C'mon."

"I know." Clay sighed, tossing it away. "I'm ignoring it. I am."

"We knew it was coming."

"Doesn't make it any easier. And now you're here to tell me more bad news."

Dave handed him a shot. "It can wait."

"No." Clay got to his feet. "Lay it on me. I want to hear it before any of the two hundred people at your wedding."

Dave faced him. "Michelle's writing a book. A friend at Simon and Schuster slipped me an early draft. There's a few chapters on you that suggest you like being"—Dave drew a breath, keeping his eye contact steady—"bossed around in bed."

"What?" Clay slammed the shot glass onto the hotel desk. Hearing his kink voiced by his manager and best friend had his voice vibrating with angry embarrassment. "That's private!"

"You could own it," Dave suggested. "It'd be a surprise, but everyone's into authenticity these days."

"No way. That's the whole problem."

His ex-girlfriend had always dissolved the boundaries between public and private life. She claimed it was for "authenticity," but Clay suspected it was to sate a hungry ego with the addictive feedback loop of social media. And now she was threatening to expose his private life in a way that was even more intimate and revealing.

"I can't believe it." Clay found Michelle's eyes on the magazine cover and felt a hot thrust of pain under his ribs. "I trusted her."

"I know. It's bullshit. But that book will never come out. We've got an army of ruthless lawyers on it. It'll be a bloodbath, with billable hours." Dave blew out a sigh. "Look, thanks again for coming. I know you'd rather be . . . anywhere but here."

Clay looked over in surprise. "Hey, this is the only place I want to be. You're getting married, dude. You're one of my best friends. I love you, man."

Dave smiled, stretching the tiny scar on his upper lip from a layup Clay missed, back when they had nothing better to do than play basketball and sink cheap beers. "You're one of the good ones, Clay Russo. To friendship."

"To friendship. And to love." The whiskey surged through Clay's bloodstream, unlocking some of the tension in his shoulders. This would be fine. He'd stay for dinner, then slip out after the DJ started. Hopefully none of the guests would ask for a selfie.

Dave checked his hair in the large oval mirror by the door. He'd put Clay in the second-nicest room, after his own. "Fair warning: I think Kamile's put you at the singles' table."

"That'll be a disappointment for the singles. I'm officially a monk."

"Begin Operation Monk. Understood." Dave clapped him on the shoulder. "All right. Let's get me married."

"Behind you."

Clay picked up the magazine, tempted to throw it in the toilet and flush. But then the toilet would clog and some poor maid would have to come up and fix it. So into the trash it went. He met his own eyes in the mirror. The breakup had taken a toll physically, but it was likely only he could see it: the deepening lines in his forehead, the shadows under his eyes. He knew he was handsome: good genes and a good haircut, really. But no one at this wedding would be seeing the real Clay.

He arranged his face into that of his public persona, his heart hidden behind a stone wall constructed from neutral, pleasant-looking bricks, and followed Dave out of the room.

13

Cocktail hour was crowded, and Zia knew negotiating it was an exercise in anticipation: of unexpected hugs and dashing children and wild gesticulation. She had just started her fourth circuit, rounding a clump of increasingly tipsy bridesmaids, when she saw him.

Even though she had no idea what he looked like, she knew, without a doubt, that this was the *celebrity guest*. Because this man was radiant. Like the other groomsmen, he was wearing a tuxedo. It made him look like an ad for cologne or very expensive watches. Broad shoulders filled out a crisp white shirt. And his face . . . Plenty of guys were good-looking. But Clay Russo was beautiful. Dark stubble shaded a jaw so square, it'd make mathematicians weep. He was tanned, or more accurately golden, a hint of the Mediterranean in the thick eyebrows that gave his face such a sturdy, masculine authority. He was an exquisite human being.

Zia let out a quick breath, regaining control. He was just a guy, no more special than anyone else. He was probably a womanizer. Or worse, boring.

Clay was standing in a small group. No one had any food, and they were exactly in her circuit. She straightened her shoulders and approached.

"Loved you in *Adam Atlantis*. That chase scene around Rome? So epic." One of the guests, a finance bro type, held up his phone. "Can I get a selfie?"

"Sriracha tempeh slider?" Zia offered the tray.

The group shook their heads, but Clay said, "Yes, please," and suddenly everyone wanted sriracha tempeh sliders.

"Like I was saying," the guest continued to Clay, holding a mini burger he clearly did not intend to eat, "a selfie—"

"What are these?" Clay looked at Zia. His eyes were light hazel, almost gold. To her surprise, her skin prickled.

"Sriracha tempeh sliders," Zia replied with a smile.

The corners of Clay's mouth curved upward. His lips were dark pink and soft-looking. "Sriracha . . ."

"Tempeh sliders," she finished, a laugh in her voice. It sounded funny when you kept saying it. Clay smiled back broadly. There was nothing snobby or sleazy in his eyes. In fact, she just saw warmth.

The finance bro clicked his fingers. "Just want to get that selfie, dude—"

Zia gave the bro a big shit-eating grin. "I can take a picture for you."

A whisper of irritation crossed Clay's face. Zia caught his eye. A look of understanding was exchanged.

She put her empty tray down and took the phone, tapping the icon to flip the screen. "Oh yeah, this is nice." As she made a show of snapping the group together, the only thing she was actually photographing was her nostrils. Zia turned the phone off before handing it back. "There you go. And, Mr. Russo, the wedding planner asked me to pass on that you have an urgent call."

He looked surprised for only a second before catching on. "Right. Yes, I'm expecting a call from . . ."

"Your dry cleaner," Zia improvised.

Clay's face turned serious. "I'm very close with my dry cleaner. We speak daily. Excuse me."

He followed Zia, who was heading for the kitchen to restock her tray, skirting the mingling guests. Zia was laughing. "I love the idea you check in every day with your dry cleaner."

"Absolutely I do." He fell in step with her. "I must have updates: solvents, what's new in eco-friendly practices."

"Folding," Zia offered.

"Folding is our favorite topic!" Clay exclaimed. "Don't get us started on the correct way to fold a fitted sheet." He chuckled theatrically. "We can talk for hours."

Zia giggled. She didn't think of herself as funny, but she loved funny people. Maybe Clay was a bit of a goofball.

Clay's smile oscillated between pleased and embarrassed. "Sorry. I make a lot of dumb jokes."

They paused on a slight rise overlooking the party. "Lucky for you, I love dumb jokes."

His smile settled into pleased. "Good."

She tucked the tray under her arm and scooped up a champagne flute from the grass. When she turned around, Clay was gazing out at the two hundred guests, all chatting and laughing and downing the specialty cocktail. The late-afternoon sun poured over the trees and shrubs and turned the nearby pond into a sheet of gold. On the small stage, Darlene was singing "London Boy" while Zach accompanied her on guitar. " '*You know I love a London boy, I enjoy walking Camden Market in the afternoon.*' " It was lovely. Romantic and happy. If only life could always be like this.

Clay nudged Zia's shoulder with his. "Hey, thanks for saving me back there. I'm Clay."

"You're welcome, Clay." His face was so perfect, it was almost uninteresting. What made Clay attractive was the way his thoughts and feelings surfaced and then submerged, quickly, like moving water. It made him seem intelligent. Zia wondered what he was really thinking. "I'm Zia."

"Zia. That's a really beautiful name."

Zia smiled, not so much at the compliment but the sincerity with which it was delivered. "It means 'light' in Arabic."

"It suits you." Clay blinked, as if consciously pulling himself out of a too-intimate moment. He moved back half a step and turned to the party. His voice became deeper and more formal. "So who should I talk to? I don't really know anyone that well except the groom."

Zia scanned the crowd. "Avoid the bridesmaids. They're all wasted and would eat you alive."

"Ha. No, definitely not up for that."

It seemed this guy was no Zach Livingstone. At least, not today. "Best to avoid the sad aunts and uncles," she continued. "They're all talking about their knee surgeries and what's wrong with the younger generation."

"Buzzkill," he agreed.

"The high school friends are all taking a lot of photos, which you don't seem that into."

Clay's gaze dropped to his shoes. "I'm, ah, pretty private." He said it like it was a minor flaw. "By the way, did you flip the screen back there?"

"You know it." They high-fived.

"This is good." Clay indicated the party. "You're good, keep going."

"Oh, I've got it. Stylish older ladies, eleven o'clock." She indicated a group of brightly dressed women in their sixties, all laughing and toasting with white wine. "They're all in the art scene somehow. Smart and fun, and they're not going to throw themselves on you. Probably."

"Perfect." Clay crooked his neck to smile at her.

The openness she saw earlier was back.

"Although I'm a little sad I can't stay here talking to you," he added.

Was it possible Clay was flirting with her? "What would we talk about?"

He shrugged and angled his body toward her. But he didn't try to brush her arm or lower back. He respected her physical boundaries. "You."

"What about me?"

"I know your name and that you're clever and that you're the purveyor of delicious sriracha tempeh sliders. What else?"

The memory that came to mind was one she hadn't thought about in years. "When I was about seven, I started a club that rocked PS Eighty-Four. POCTA."

"POCTA?"

"Prevention of Cruelty to Animals."

Clay repressed a laugh.

Zia did not. "I know, not the most catchy acronym. We raised thirty-five dollars in a bake sale and donated it to the local animal shelter. But then one of the guys in our class started calling us Perverted Old Cows Together Again, and the whole thing fell apart."

"Still, you made an impact."

"Yeah, I'm kind of into that. Being a good person. Or, trying to," she added.

"I'm kind of into that too," Clay said. "But I've got nothing on POCTA."

"Zia!" Liv strode toward her, a determined look on her face. As her eyes moved to Clay, her expression changed, lightening from disapproval into wonder.

"I'm so sorry," Zia said to Liv. "I was just about to—"

Liv waved it off. "Welcome back, honey. It's good to see you."

Zia found herself being hugged. She certainly considered Liv a friend, she'd worked for her on and off for ten years, but Zia had been closer to the more playful Eliot. Liv's warmth was because of Clay, somehow.

He introduced himself, and he and her boss exchanged a few pleasantries. Then Liv tactfully informed her there was another tray of sriracha tempeh sliders with her name on it, and headed off.

"Duty calls." Zia squeezed Clay's upper arm. The sensation of her touch flickered lightly over his face. "Have fun on the dance floor—the DJ's great."

"Oh, I'm leaving right after dinner." Clay offered his hand. "But very nice to meet you, Zia."

"You too, Clay," she said, shaking it. He let it linger. Just for a microsecond. But enough for the feeling to race up her spine, sparking across her back. She could feel him watching her when she left, happy to be wrong about the very charming celebrity guest. Or if he'd been acting, at least she'd never know. She'd likely never talk to Clay Russo again.

14

Cocktail hour became dinner. Speeches were made. Glasses were topped up for one, two, five toasts. Kamile danced with her father in her Chantilly lace dress, weeping in his arms. After the song ended, Dave and Kamile embraced, and everyone spilled onto the dance floor around them. From outside the tent, Savannah's eyes welled. "They're so beautiful. Love is just so beautiful."

Liv stubbed her cigarette out on a tent pole and put the butt in her fanny pack. "I give it ten years."

Savannah fixed her with a disapproving look. "How can you say that? Look at them. They're besotted."

"Of course they are," Liv said. "They're young and gorgeous and in perfect health. They found a best friend and a lover and a confidant and a co-parent and an adventure buddy and a muse. They found their soul mate, and they're *so lucky* because not everyone does. But after the literal and metaphorical honeymoon is over, they'll find that being an amazing lover *and* best friend *and* parent *and* every other little thing on their list is a pretty tall order. And after a while, or maybe all of a sudden, the way she's so outspoken doesn't make her strong, it makes her a bitch. And the fact he opens bottles of expensive wine every night doesn't make him classy, it makes him an alcoholic." Liv didn't sound angry. She sounded resigned. "She'll get crow's-feet, he'll get a potbelly, and they'll start investing a lot of time and money in not aging. Bickering becomes woven into the fabric of their relationship until it carpets the entire house. There's nothing new to talk about, nothing left to discover. Even sex is a drag, and it's no longer spontaneous and passionate, it's planned and it's boring. And one day, they'll wake up and realize they haven't just gotten sick of each other: they *can't stand* the person they married. That the person lying next to them in bed is just doing a comically bad impression of the man they used to love."

Behind the decks, Zach was playing "Brown Eyed Girl" and everyone was up and dancing, singing along: "*'Sha la la la la la la la la, la te da, la te da.'*"

Savannah picked her words with care. "That doesn't happen to everyone, Liv."

"No. Not everyone." Liv's eyes didn't leave the couple, laughing as their friends and family danced around them, sloshing glasses of organic wine. "But half the weddings I've planned in the last twenty years ended in divorce. And they all looked exactly like this."

When Savannah met Liv's eyes, she expected to see bitter smugness or cold satisfaction: game, set, *match*. But what she actually saw surprised her. In Liv's usually hawklike eyes, the eyes that didn't miss a trick, was soft and billowing sadness.

"Come on," Liv said, turning away. "Let's start on the pack-up list."

15

The formerly busy kitchen was quiet. Zia emptied the leftovers of what had to be her hundredth plate into the garbage. She didn't mind being on cleanup, but it was depressing that almost a billion people lived on less than two dollars a day, and here she was throwing away landfills of locally grown salad and green-pea risotto. She filled three takeout containers for her sister, closing the lids with a satisfied snap.

"Hello?"

It was Clay Russo. The actor had a slightly embarrassed look on his face and a giant red-wine stain on his shirt. His mouth lifted in a pleased smile. "Hello again."

"Hey." Zia smiled back. "Interesting after-party look."

"Dance-floor mishap. One of those drunk bridesmaids you were warning me about."

"Dangerous. Let me see if I can find some club soda." Her heart picked up, pattering. "I thought you were leaving after dinner."

"You were right: the DJ's great. Haven't danced that much in ages." Clay looked flushed and a little tipsy—not drunk, just less careful than earlier. His eyes were bright, fixed on her in a way that was comforting, and strangely thrilling. "I didn't see you during the dinner service."

"I wasn't working the floor. Just cleanup. How was it?"

"Excellent. The risotto was fantastic. Basically licked my plate clean."

At least she wasn't throwing away Clay's leftovers. She held up a can of club soda. "This'll get that stain out." She looked at him expectedly.

Clay's eyebrows flickered down. "Should I just . . ."

Zia gestured around the kitchen. "Everyone's on cake duty. There's no one else here."

He unbuttoned the top button. "As long as I'm not sexually harassing you by stripping down."

She laughed. "I'm basically ordering you to."

"Not mad about it." In one fluid motion, Clay slipped off his shirt, revealing his bare torso.

Zia almost did a double take. Clay's body was the brutal, beautiful wedge of a Greek warrior. Smooth, bronzed skin. A quilt of stomach muscles. His arms were the right sort of big, both biceps bulging and thick. She was vaguely aware Clay was in action movies, and yes, this was the body of a man destined to save the day, and look damn good doing it.

"Wow. You have a beautiful body." She took the shirt off him, matter-of-fact. "You must get that all the time."

He chuckled, and was he actually blushing? "Not to my face."

Zia tipped the soda water over the stain. "Life's too short not to say what's on your mind."

He stood next to her at the sink, looking a little uneasy at being semi-naked in her presence, which was, Zia thought, pretty cute. "Unfortunately I don't get to do a lot of that."

"Well, what are you thinking right now?"

"Right now?"

She tingled. She was flirting but pretended she wasn't. "Yeah."

"I'd say . . . that . . . you have a beautiful body too, Zia."

Blood rushed her cheeks. She focused on the shirt. "I'm pretty active. Biking, rock climbing, surfing."

"Surfing, nice. Never tried it."

She wrung out the material, squeezing hard. Her skin felt tender. "It's amazing. Total feeling of freedom. Nothing like it in the world."

"Nothing?"

His eyes were the color of a jungle cat. His lips were parted, which made Zia conscious of her own mouth. This man was attracted to her. She was always the last person to figure it out, but right now, she was certain. The idea of kissing him flashed in her mind. A sticky wave of heat pulsed through her body. She swayed an inch closer to him. He did the same.

Holy libido: get a grip. Zia backed up a step and exhaled. "Let's get this dry."

Clay snapped back to reality. He looked as confused as she was. "Yeah, I need to get going."

In the white-tiled bathroom, the dull roar of the hand dryer made conversation impossible.

She snuck a glance at him and caught him watching her. His gaze bounced away. She could not kiss Clay. He was basically a stranger, and she was working. Plus she'd signed some sort of contract about this guy, and not mauling him with her mouth was probably in the fine print.

As soon as the shirt was wearable, she all but thrust at it him and busied herself with washing her hands while he buttoned it up. But when she turned around, a light laugh escaped her lips. His shirt was askew. "You missed a button."

He followed her gaze and let out a soft, amused breath.

Without thinking, she moved toward him to rebutton it. Being so near to him was like seeing a statue come to life: startling, beautiful. She was so close he could take her in his arms. So close she could tilt her head up and feel his mouth touch hers. His presence pounded through her like a storm. Zia had always assumed the ability to be wildly, uncontrollably attracted to someone was just a rare human quirk, like having two different-colored eyes. But it was happening to her, and she didn't know what to do. She could barely ease the black button through the stiff buttonhole. She was undressing him. As if for bed. As if for sex. His body on top of hers, moving together in a hot, hungry rhythm.

Her fingers found his bare chest, touching the smooth, hard muscles. Clay inhaled. His chest rose beneath her fingertips. His musky, masculine smell made her mouth water. Her body was one hot surging mess of driving need. Desperate for contact. Desperate for this man.

She dared to look up at him. His eyes were glazed and hooded. Drilling into her. His voice was low and almost strained. "Zia . . ."

She yanked his shirt toward her.

"The thing about straight weddings—"

Before their lips had a chance to meet, Henry's voice crashed over her like a bucket of cold water. They sprang apart like guilty teenagers as Henry and Gorman entered the bathroom.

"—is no one knows how to dance . . ." Henry trailed off as both he and Gorman stared at Clay. Then at Zia. Then back at Clay, a tennis match of surprise. Zia's face was burning. Clay's shirt was half unbuttoned.

Gorman cleared his throat, his fingers resting lightly on his chest. "That's because straight people feel so guilty about sex. Don't you agree, Zia?"

Usually Zia enjoyed the florist's dry humor, but at that moment, she couldn't even look at him. Or Henry. Or the man she'd just been about to kiss. Her heart was striking a steady beat of *What? The? Hell?*

"I'll, um . . ." Clay's attempt at speech was a failure. He gave Zia a parting look of mute bewilderment, and left the bathroom.

Henry looked rattled. "Did we just walk in on a Me Too moment, Zia?"

"No!" Zia shook her head. "No, that was . . . I don't know what that was. But I liked it."

"I'll bet you did," murmured Gorman.

Zia's gaze fell to the floor. Something square, made of dark brown leather, was at her feet. A wallet. Even before she flipped it open, she knew who it belonged to.

"Good," said Henry. "And, bonus: now you know who Clay Russo is."

16

Henry packed the table arrangements back into boxes, extracting the dainty flowers from a battleground of soiled napkins, spilled booze, and discarded menus. Dave and Kamile didn't want to keep the arrangements, so whatever the other guests hadn't taken, they'd donate to a local assisted-living facility. It was an excuse to stay till the end, really: he and Gor wanted to keep an eye on Liv, especially given the free-flowing alcohol. But the wedding had turned out pretty much perfectly. Possibly the part where the bride mentioned the hashtag in her vows was a little odd. But otherwise, gorgeous.

Henry finished one box and started another.

Clay and Zia. Huh. If they got married, maybe Henry would get to make a speech. *Zia and Clay are a passionate couple. I walked in on them about to share their first kiss . . . in a public bathroom!* Henry had made a dozen speeches at weddings over the years. People said he was good at them. He just always imagined the sort of speech he'd want to hear at his own wedding.

In the weeks following his birthday and the infamous stand mixer, Henry had begun to feel increasingly insecure. Maybe he'd been too subtle about wanting to get married, maybe not. Either way, it was obvious Gorman didn't want to marry him. But instead of addressing the issue as he typically would, his lack of confidence made him fold back on himself. Maybe he should just let the idea go. Gay marriage as fiction, as performed normativity—could he make it his truth, if he had to?

It seemed impossible. Painful. Dangerous. Why?

Because if he followed the impulse all the way to its logical root, he wanted a baby.

Henry's hand stilled in midair. He'd never let the desire form so perfectly, so unapologetically. Instead, Henry buried his paternal urges under layers of practicality and, somewhat shamefully, fear. Even in progressive Brooklyn, he and Gorman were far from a typical family: an interracial gay couple, a generation apart in age. But how much longer could Henry deny the precious and delicate truth that he wanted to be a father? He'd never just wanted a proposal—he wanted shelter for a family. An indication Gorman wanted one too. Marriage was a need for a love that was strong and reciprocal enough to create the future he was terrified to imagine.

"Can I have a flower?" Behind him stood a little girl, her small face pink and puffy with sleep.

Henry's heart just about fainted. "Of course you can, sweetheart."

He selected a white frizzle tulip. The child accepted it gravely, just as her mom came up behind her. They looked so alike: same close-set eyes, same narrow chin.

"What do you say to the nice man?" Mom prompted, and the girl responded with the requisite "Thank you," cut short by a big yawn.

They left. Henry felt his smile fade.

For straight couples, the news they might not be able to conceive a child was devastating, a turn of events they'd spend thousands of dollars and years of effort to overcome. Because what greater achievement could there be in making a person with the person you love? The literal expression of your union, there in a child that has Mom's pretty eyes and Dad's sense of humor. Straight people expected shared DNA would form their family and anything less was subpar. But subpar was where gay couples started and no one ever said anything about it. The tragedy that Henry could not make a baby with Gorman, or even bring up the notion of children in the first place, was a sadness he alone had to carry.

He hefted the crate of arrangements and headed for the car.

17

Liv had just finished stacking the last of the take-home items in her Subaru's trunk when someone appeared in her peripheral vision. Sam.

"Oh, hi." Her stomach flipped. She ignored it. "What are you still doing here?"

"Tying up some loose ends. My first time on the job, wanted to make sure I got it all perfect." He smiled at her, and his eyes did the crinkly thing she liked.

"You did a great job. Everyone was raving about the food, and perfect execution, timewise. That's usually the hardest part."

"Thanks."

Liv shut the trunk. "Can I ask you a question?"

"Sure."

"Why'd you take this job? Given the horror stories you read about me online?"

He chuckled. "You don't seem like a—what'd that review say?—*demogorgon bitchface*."

Liv winced. "Oy vey."

"Also, getting divorced is expensive. And it made me realize everyone deserves a second chance."

He smiled at her again, and this time, she smiled back, not at all worried that she probably smelled like leftovers and cleaning spray. Something very small and tender emerged between them. A few Januarys ago, she and Eliot had rented a house in Maine for a week. One evening, they came across a deer in a clearing. For a couple of lifelong city dwellers, it felt akin to glimpsing a winged fairy. She couldn't move, even breathe, for fear of frightening it away. Then Eliot's phone rang, blasting his latest novelty ringtone: "Love Shack." The deer leaped off through the forest.

Savannah appeared around the corner, arms laden with Dave and Kamile's boxed gifts.

Sam's eyes flickered from hers. "Better hit the road. Night, Liv."

"Night, Sam."

He fumbled the keys slightly as he unlocked his car.

What had just transpired? And did she want it to happen again?

She and Savannah settled back in the Subaru.

"Not too bad." Liv shuffled through the loose CDs, selecting one by the Pixies, a band that formed over a decade before Savannah was an embryo. "Considering we only had two months. How are you feeling?"

"Starving." Savannah sighed. "What I wouldn't give for some honey-fried chicken."

"There's some food for you in the back seat."

"For me?"

"Sure. I always ask the caterers to make up a plate for the people who don't get to eat: the couple and us."

"Wow. Thank you, Liv." Savannah peeled back the aluminum foil. "Still warm!"

The car filled with the delicious smell of green-pea risotto. The other night, Ben asked if Sam could come over and cook it for them again. Liv said no, explaining Sam had already gotten the job.

By the time Savannah finished eating, they were on the highway home. The Pixies ended. For a few moments, they drove in silence.

Savannah turned to Liv. "Why are you a wedding planner?"

"Too old to intern, too young for social security."

"No, really. If you're so cynical about love, and such a feminist"—Savannah pointed at the pink pussyhat on the back seat—"how'd you end up a planner?"

Liv shrugged. "Everyone else does it so badly."

Savannah didn't say anything. She just waited.

"I guess I just never quit. Which is how a lot of people end up in their careers. And I might have cynical moments, but I'm not a cynic. Most of my weddings, even if they don't last, are . . . beautiful. Life-affirming. And being a feminist wedding planner isn't an oxymoron. Our whole thing was about bringing men into it, so it wasn't just 'women's business.' When Eliot was . . ."

Alive.

Out of the corner of her eye, Savannah nodded.

They drove in silence. The wedding's success made Liv feel capable, but it also muted her emotions, leaving her cool and clear-eyed. If she didn't do this now, it might never happen. "How did you meet?"

Savannah blinked, half asleep. "Who? Honey?"

"Is that what you called him?"

"Him?" As it landed, she straightened and looked at Liv, as if to say, *Are we doing this?*

They were.

"At work," Savannah replied, nervous. "I gave Eliot a tour of our office."

"The events company. Where you were an intern."

Savannah nodded.

Liv swallowed. "What was he like? When you first met."

Savannah directed her answer at her hands. "He seemed very . . . sophisticated, I guess. Being old . . . er. Older. From New York. And smart. He knew a lot of weird facts about Kentucky."

"He always was a font of useless information." Liv recalled the two of them in bed together, her with a novel by Margaret Atwood or Velma Wolff, him with a copy of *The Best Bar Trivia.* "And I guess he asked you out?"

Savannah nodded again.

This hurt. But in the way getting a shard of glass out of your foot did: pain, in order to heal. "Drinks?"

"Dinner."

"And what was that like?"

Savannah sounded anxious. "Impressive. I mean, when I went out for dinner it was barbecue on paper plates and margaritas in plastic cups. He took me somewhere with white tablecloths and a valet."

Eliot's ability to disassociate was better than Liv imagined. Because how else could he enjoy dinner with a young woman while his wife and child were at home, oblivious?

"What was he like?" Liv asked. "Personality-wise."

"He was . . . big."

"Charming."

"Yes."

"Maybe a little manic. Scattered."

"Yes."

"And he made you feel like the most interesting person he'd ever laid eyes on."

Savannah let out a soft breath. "Yes."

Liv took it like a blow. "And so, dinner and then . . ."

"Liv." Her name was a tiny sound, uttered toward the passenger window. Not even enough to fog the glass.

"Dinner and then . . ."

"I didn't sleep with him after our first date, if that's what you're implying."

"So after the second? Third?"

Savannah exhaled angrily. "Fifth, actually."

Fifth. Well. "I slept with Eliot the first night we met."

Savannah looked over. A small smile passed her lips. "Oh."

"How many . . . I mean, how long did . . ." Liv braced herself. "How many times did you do it?"

"Five. And a half."

Ugh. Eliot went to Kentucky ten times during his stint as a consultant for Savannah's events company. Which probably meant they'd started dating the first or second trip. Liv tried to recall the sound of his voice when he'd call to speak with Ben—peppy? Relaxed? She couldn't remember. She was too busy enjoying having the house to herself. Liv changed lanes. "So did he ever . . . mention me? Or Ben?"

"He said he had an ex-wife: that y'all were separated and getting a divorce."

That prick. The pain of Eliot's betrayal had lessened as time passed. But it still seemed so cruel. That he'd erase them so cavalierly from the picture of his life. In death, this was not possible. Liv had flown to Kentucky the day Eliot died. Middle seat, no movies, four tiny bottles of wine, a lot of dumbstruck staring. At the dinky, understaffed hospital, an orderly gave her E's wallet, the money in his pocket, the wristwatch she'd given him for his fortieth birthday. She was the one who signed all the forms and called Eliot's parents in Boston and flew his body back to New York. "It should've been me."

"I'm sorry?"

"He should've . . . Even if he was"—in lieu of saying *sleeping*, Liv flicked her wrist—"with you. He should've died with— It should've been *me*."

"Yes," Savannah said softly. "It should have."

Liv's hands tightened on the steering wheel. "So why were you seeing him? Were you in love with him?"

There was a brief, noisy silence. Liv could hear Savannah breathing.

"No. I wasn't in love with Eliot. I mean, maybe, if it had continued, and I did care about him. But no. Not when . . . when it ended."

"When he died," Liv said. "In the hotel room you screwed in."

"Oh gosh, Liv! What do you want me to say? I didn't love him! I was sleeping with your husband, and I didn't even love him, that's the truth. I'm twenty-three, I'm still figuring myself out!"

Savannah's intensity stoked Liv's own. "So what was it about? If you didn't love him, what was it about?"

"I'm just trying!"

"To do what?"

"To fall in love!" Savannah cried. "But it wasn't Eliot, and it was never going to be Eliot, but now I'm here and I'm with you, and maybe that's how it was meant to end up." She twisted to face Liv. "I'm sorry. I'm sorry Eliot lied to you, and I'm sorry Eliot lied to me. But I'm not sorry Eliot brought us together. That was the one good thing he did. The one thing."

Liv kept her eyes on the road, breathing hard through her nostrils. After a minute or so, the hurricane inside her began to subside, and she was able to speak. "I believe you. I believe you didn't know we weren't separated."

Savannah started to cry. Liv took a hand off the wheel and found herself awkwardly patting the girl's arm. Her own eyes were watering, too.

For months, she'd wanted to hate the person next to her. But she was just a girl, flattered by a charismatic older man's attention. When he was his best self, Eliot could be as bright as the sun. Where Liv saw a society run by corrupt politicians and greedy corporations, Eliot saw a world full of wonder, full of shining examples of human achievement. He loved people, and coincidences, and acts of bravery or kindness. His optimism lightened her pessimism. Without it, the last six months had been a brutal, lonely place as she sat at home alone and darkly processed the entire world.

And yet, there were his mood swings. The depression. High highs. Low lows. Eliot hated doctors, and the medical system in general, which is why Liv kept her theories about his mental health to herself. ADD, ADHD, even bipolar: she always suspected he was right on the edge of a diagnosis. But because he was responsible enough to co-own a business, and take Ben to baseball games, and make her laugh harder than anyone else, she let it slide, and focused on the good side. Her untamed wanderer. Her unpredictable dreamer.

He'd come alive like that for Savannah. On top of feeling sad and angry, Liv felt *jealous* that it was Savannah, not her, who'd gotten to enjoy that Eliot in his final days.

"So why did he do it?" Liv bashed away a tear with a fisted hand. "Why did he change his will and leave half the business to you?"

Savannah took a long moment to answer. "I've thought about that so many times. And I always get to the exact same answer."

"Which is?"

Over the horizon, New York appeared, glittering against the night sky. From here, it was silent and monolithic, belying nothing of the grit, the heat, the weight of each city street. Each corner its own kingdom. With its own closely held secrets. "I have absolutely no idea."

18

"What do you mean you almost kissed the waitress?" Dave's incredulous voice reverberated through Clay's earbuds. The shopper next to him at the busy Whole Foods threw Clay a suspicious look.

Clay returned it with a sheepish grin and moved to the next aisle. "I mean just that."

"What happened to Operation Monk?"

The answer was simple. Zia happened. Clay met plenty of good-looking women. These days, it was part of the job. But no one had gotten under his skin as fast and hard as Zia Last-Name-Unknown. It wasn't just that she was beautiful and smelled good and was possibly the world's best shirt buttoner. She treated him like an equal, and Clay Russo didn't get a lot of that these days. Her breezy attitude made him feel a decade younger, back when he had to work for women's attention . . . and he liked the time travel. Zia was authentic and honest in a way that wasn't just attractive but also felt *necessary*. Whatever it was, it'd snapped him like a cheap chopstick. Clay ambled into the supplements aisle, tossing things into his basket at random.

"I don't know, man. The operation was temporarily disabled."

Dave sighed. "Help me help you, you know? At least she signed an NDA. And none of my sources are reporting any stories."

Clay trusted Zia. But he'd also trusted Michelle, and look where that had gotten him. "And my wallet?"

"She has it. Phoned it in via the wedding planner. Do you really need it back? All the cards and stuff are canceled."

"It was a gift from my mom."

"Jesus, Clay. Okay, we'll get the waitress to courier it to the shoot this afternoon."

"Zia. Her name is Zia." It really was a beautiful name. And she really was a beautiful person. Clay paused, the sounds of the busy supermarket fading around him. "Unless . . ."

They met up in person. Checked out a museum, grabbed a drink. Or, maybe dinner. There was a great Italian spot in his neighborhood. The thought of seeing that smile again—big and radiant and genuine—filled his lungs with fresh air. The women he usually dated were industry people. Astute, ambitious women who knew just what a picture of him on their arm did for their careers. In his world, people traded each other like stocks, and his valuation was high. But he wouldn't be surprised if Zia hadn't even heard of him.

"Unless . . . You know . . ."

"Clay. Brother. I'm going to cut to the chase because, one, you're my best friend, and two, I really have to get back to my brand-new wife." Dave's voice became direct and unflinching: the *Listen to me, you idiot* tone. "If you don't want to appear in the tabloids, don't give them anything to talk about. A date with a waitress you met at a wedding is a story."

It was irritating that this was true. "People should be worried about clean water and climate change, not who I'm dating. I need the freedom to take a woman on a date."

"Sorry, but you don't have that anymore. You gave it up when you booked *Adam Atlantis*. I did warn you about this."

Clay bristled. "Having a public career doesn't mean my life belongs to the public. I deserve privacy, just like everyone else."

"Look man, I can't get into the whole should-celebrities-expect-privacy thing with you now. Suffice to say, if the gatekeepers think your name will sell Michelle's book, it makes it a lot harder for us to kill it. And that book'll really get people talking, for the reason we've discussed. If you want to fly under the radar, like you keep telling me you do, be thankful the waitress didn't sell the story, and leave it at that."

"But—"

"Let's stay focused on your career. We're in a good place, but transitioning you from action to drama is delicate. The next move is crucial: we need a script with Oscar potential. Something weighty and topical. Maybe even edgy. Flings with waitresses, flings with anyone, is not the game plan. We need full control over how you're being perceived."

Irritation surged into anger. Clay was raised for loyalty, one of six in a close-knit family, which meant his current search for autonomy as an actor was akin to a rebellion. And now his manager was telling him who he could and couldn't date. "It's not like I'm Oprah Winfrey! I'm not that well-known."

"Well, I just got a Google alert that you're buying a colon cleanse at Whole Foods."

Clay stared at the supplements in his basket in horror. He swung around. Curious gazes bounced away, like small animals scattering. His skin bloomed hot. It wasn't just embarrassing. It was an invasion. "I'll call you later."

"I'm actually on my honeymoon, so—"

"I hate the internet."

Clay abandoned his basket and pulled a baseball cap low. As he exited the store, three shoppers unashamedly filmed him. Like he wasn't even a person. Like he was a thing.

Someone like Zia wouldn't want any part of his messed-up life. A life where everything from his groceries to his kinks were reported as breaking news. He felt hunted, and it was exhausting. Clay loved his work, but he also wanted to spend an afternoon wandering around the Met with a cute girl, flirting in front of the artwork without worrying that it'd end up in *People*. But today just proved that he didn't have nor could he expect any privacy. And privacy was what you needed to let a relationship grow.

Around him, New York City pulsed relentlessly. The streets swallowed him up until, thankfully, he was just another face in the crowd.

19

Greenpoint had traditionally been a Polish neighborhood, but in recent years, the busy end had been claimed by hipsters, and the industrial end by film and television productions. Nondescript warehouses were filled with secret, fleeting worlds—a bloody crime scene, a sunny high school cafeteria, a 1950s street corner. And it was one such warehouse that Zia approached a few hours later.

She'd been sent an address to courier Clay's wallet, and instructions on how to recoup the charge. But when she called to book it, they'd quoted her a hundred dollars for a same-day delivery. One hundred dollars, and it was only a short bike ride away!

She wasn't going to see Clay. A very cool project had just come up through Global Care. A six-month volunteer coordinator position at a women's resource center in Quelimane, Mozambique. The pay was modest but livable. Per the job description, the center helped empower local women to do everything from start their own business to leave abusive relationships. Which resonated. If she got the job—and could work up the courage to tell Layla she was leaving New York again—she'd be off on another mission. With a few clicks, she'd emailed her résumé and expression of interest to the team leader. Done. And right now, she'd drop off the wallet, then ride home along the waterfront.

Easy.

In a scrappy front-office-type area, people milled about, some on their phones, some lounging. It appeared casual, but there was a buzz in the air. Something that mattered to these people was happening. The charge got under her skin, and Zia stood a little taller. She got out the warm, worn leather wallet, and looked around for an assistant.

And that's when she locked eyes with Clay.

Well, not actually Clay, but his headshot, taped to a wall with *C Russo Team* and an arrow scrawled underneath it.

His eyes. That mouth. She wondered what he saw when he looked in the mirror.

A young woman in a headset burst into the space, looking around with open desperation. To Zia's alarm, she beelined right for her. "Are you hair and makeup?"

"No, I'm Zia Ruiz. I'm just dropping off—"

"We're running so late." The young woman scanned the foyer. "The only person getting in to see Clay is hair and makeup."

And then Zia did something that caught her, and the assistant, entirely by surprise. "Oh, *hair* and makeup? For the Clay Russo shoot?" Zia attempted to look professional. "That's me."

In a daze, Zia followed the harried assistant down a series of twisting hallways. Why had she done that? Zia was not a liar. A risk-taker, yes. Impulsive, for sure. But a liar, no. Something just . . . came over her. What if it freaked Clay out? Would he call security? She didn't even have a makeup kit; she barely wore makeup herself. Maybe Clay would be with another girl. This was a mistake. A monumental mistake. They'd asked her to courier the wallet, not stalk the owner.

"Excuse me," Zia squeaked to the assistant. "Actually I, um—"

The assistant opened a door and disappeared inside.

Zia looked left, then right. She had no idea how to get back out of the enormous building. "One more for the memoir," she muttered, following the assistant.

A mirror dominated one wall, lined by soft yellow globes. A few people sat on a long couch, working on laptops while a couple of others were huddled into a corner in conversation. Sitting at the far end of the room, with a sheaf of paper in one hand and his phone in the other, was Clay.

"Mr. Russo, hair and makeup's here," the assistant announced.

Clay looked up. His eyes pulsed in surprise.

Zia inhaled, her heart hammering.

A slow smile spread across Clay's features, like sunshine warming the corners of a dark room. All of Zia's concerns evaporated. She smiled back and stepped forward. "Hi, Mr. Russo," she said, channeling the easy warmth she'd seen the hair and makeup artists offer at weddings. "So nice to meet you."

Clay was on his feet. "Hi." The papers he was reading slid to the floor. "Hello. Hi."

The assistant narrowed her eyes, sensing disturbance. She eyed the purse slung over Zia's shoulder. "Wait, where's your kit?"

Zia looked at Clay. "Clay, um . . ."

"I decided on a very minimal look for this shoot," Clay said.

Zia scrabbled through her purse. She didn't have a makeup bag, but she did have a small emergency bag, containing things like a tampon, whistle, copy of her passport. She held it up. By makeup-artist standards, it was microscopic. "I have a very down-to-earth approach."

The assistant still looked skeptical. But after checking the time, she informed Zia she had twenty minutes, and left. No one else in the room was paying any attention to them.

"I hope this isn't weird," she whispered. "I just wanted to see you."

"I'm so glad you did." He was alert. Entirely focused on her. "Really. I wanted to see you again too."

"What if the real makeup artist shows up?"

"She just texted. Family emergency."

"But I don't know how to . . ."

Clay waved it off. "Honestly, it's not rocket science. And if I don't say anything, no one else will."

"Okay." Surreptitiously, Zia slid Clay's wallet back to him. When he took it, their fingertips touched. Not by accident.

Clay pocketed the wallet. "I guess you know all my secrets."

"I didn't look through it. I promise."

"I believe you."

It wasn't just that he was beautiful, with those gold eyes and thick brows and six-pack hidden beneath his shirt. He was staring at her, rapt. And she could feel it, everywhere. The simmering heat between them threatened a rolling boil. Which it couldn't, and shouldn't: they were in public, and Clay had to work. They both blinked, swaying back, as if waking up to their reality at the same time.

"All right, Mr. Russo. Let's get you ready." She stood up behind him, determined to keep it together. The long mirror reflected a striking, perfectly passable couple. *Not bad.* She rested her hands on his shoulders. The hard heat of his muscles radiated through a thin cotton T-shirt. "Shall we start with hair?"

Clay's eyes were dancing. "Absolutely, let's start with hair."

Zia ran her hands through his hair, relishing the chance to dig her fingers into the dark strands. Clay's eyelids fluttered. "Oh, that feels . . . so good." He groaned. A low, sexy grunt. The idea of giving Clay pleasure made her insides squeeze deliciously.

One of the randos sitting on the couch glanced up at them, perturbed. Giving the talent a head massage was probably not how Hollywood makeup artists rolled. Using the only hair product she had in her bag, a travel-sized bottle of Moroccan hair oil, she began styling. Zia had never done a man's hair before, but she treated herself to a decent haircut three or four times a year, so she tried her best to make it just-got-out-of-bed sexy.

"You have lovely hair," she said, working the ends. "So thick. Strong."

Clay grinned. She hadn't meant it to sound flirtatious. "I get it from my mom, she's Italian. What about you?"

"Puerto Rican on my dad's side, but he's not in the picture, and my mom's Moroccan."

"Where did you grow up?"

"I was born in PR, but Mom moved my older sister and me to Astoria when I was three. Mom moved back to Morocco to look after her mom a few years ago. After my *abuelita* passed, she stayed."

He nodded. "*¿Hablas español?*"

"*Sí. ¿Y tú?*"

"*Sí. Yo estudié en Barcelona en la universidad.*"

"What did you study?"

"Theater major. You?"

"Double major in business and human services at Queensborough Community College." Finished, Zia examined her handiwork. It sort of looked the same as when she started. "What do you think?"

His gaze stayed on her. "*Hermosa,*" he murmured. "My hair, I mean. My hair is very, very beautiful. I often comment on it."

She laughed and came to sit in front of him for the makeup part of her new job. He was clean-shaven: no stubble. She reached up and smoothed his thick, unruly eyebrows. An itch she'd been waiting to scratch. A smile flitted across his lips. He liked this. He liked being touched by her. For a moment, she couldn't do anything but admire his beauty. His eyes didn't leave hers. There was something raw in them, hidden deep. A well she wanted to swim to the bottom of.

Clay's gaze dropped to her mouth.

"Five-minute call!" The assistant slammed the door behind her. The moment shattered into a thousand shining pieces.

"Makeup," Zia repeated, biting back a smile.

The photo shoot took place in a warehouse. Under blinding-white lights, against a white backdrop, Clay posed in a series of casual menswear outfits—leather jacket and distressed jeans, unbuttoned white shirt and white pants, some very flattering swim trunks. Zia was quite proud of her amateur makeup effort from the three products she'd found in the bottom of her purse. Tiny bit of Burt's Bees lip gloss, little concealer under his eyes, and mascara to make his dark eyebrows extra smooth and impressive. She could never have faked it with a female celebrity, but so much less was expected of men. And Clay was already so handsome.

The shoot was fun. Zia chatted and joked with the other assistants, fitting right in. It was easy and enlivening to drop into different worlds like this. Being a chameleon was Zia's superpower. There was nothing she liked more than ending up in the most unlikely place. She was glowing. Every time Clay caught her eye, the glow got brighter.

At the end of the shoot, Clay found her by craft services, putting some leftover salmon and tuna salad into containers she'd charmed from the caterer. Omega-3s were good for her sister's arthritis, and Layla couldn't afford prime cuts of fish. "Thought I'd drop some food over to my family."

"Awesome idea." He helped her stack them into a tote bag. "A lot of food doesn't get eaten at these things."

"Twenty percent of landfills is wasted food," Zia said. "And half of that is from businesses."

"That much? I should know that." Clay addressed a passing assistant. "Hey, can we do something about all this leftover food? Donate it to a shelter, and order less next time? We shouldn't be throwing anything out at the end of a shoot."

The assistant nodded, making a note. Zia was impressed and maybe a little jealous that for someone like Clay, it was easy to make change.

He lingered. "Thanks for that. And for today. I really like the down-to-earth approach."

"I had a feeling you did."

"Well, bye." He opened his arms. She moved into them for a hug. Their bodies pressed together, hip to hip, her soft breasts against his hard chest. Warm, solid muscle enveloped her. A feeling of complete safety filled her entire being. Her eyes drifted shut, relishing the closeness. The intimacy in Zia's life was all platonic. It'd been way too long since she'd held another person like this.

Someone called Clay's name. Zia pulled away.

He pressed a folded scrap of paper into her hands. "*Gracias, Zia. Por todo.*"

Clay was hurried off, the center of a traveling circus onto the next town. Zia headed for the exit, feeling like a tightrope walker who'd just made it safely back to solid ground.

20

Zinc Bar was a well-regarded jazz club in New York's West Village, the backroom of which generally hosted a respectful audience of locals and tourists. Except for Monday nights. Monday nights were different.

They were reckless. Wild. Completely unhinged. And that was because Zach Livingstone was in the house, whipping the crowd into a Dionysian frenzy. Look at him now, standing in front of the Steinway, shirt soaked, hair a mess, fingers dancing up the keys.

"C'mon, New York, let's hear you!"

Darlene revved into their crowd-pleasing closer, "Rehab" by Amy Winehouse. "*They tried to make me go to rehab—*"

"*I said*, No, no, no,'" scream-sung the crowd.

The set started lukewarm, the audience chatty and distracted and not planning on getting wasted on a Monday. But song by song, Zach worked the crowd, getting them hot. Now, people were dancing on tables, doing shots, and making out with strangers. Darlene was on the floor, in the crowd, belting it out in that smoky, sexy voice of hers, "*Yes, I've been black, but when I come back—*"

"*You'll know, know, know!*" shouted the crowd.

Despite the chaos, Zach never missed a note. This feeling of being in sync with another musician, and the audience, and himself, was better than anything. Even sex. And there was no one he was more connected with than Darlene. Maybe it was the way their differences fit together: she was technical, he was instinctive. She was polished, he didn't own an iron. American, Brit; Black, white; girl, boy. Or maybe it was just that indefinable thing called chemistry. Offstage, it was muted. But onstage, it was neon bright, and everyone in the club could see it and hear it and feel it in waves.

They finished with a flourish, crowd and musicians singing as one: "*He's tried to make me go to rehab, I won't go, go, GO!*"

The crowd went nuts, cheering and screaming and stamping their feet. Darlene caught Zach's eye and laughed, the stage lights bouncing off her hair and body. She looked absolutely bloody beautiful.

This gig was always, without fail, the highlight of Zach Livingstone's week.

Offstage, Zach high-fived the bartender and returned with two shots of tequila. He and Darlene did them together, and it filled him like fire, like starlight, like love. He shouted over the still-noisy crowd, "You killed it!"

She waved it off. "I was pitchy in that last chorus—"

"Mitchell! You crushed it!" And somehow they were hugging, which they never did, his arms around her soft, perfect body, holding each other hot and close, spontaneous and free.

Life was very, very good.

After a few too-short seconds, she let go. He could see her organized brain putting a wall back between them, moving them onto load-out and logistics. A young man with surfer-blond hair and an obnoxious tan swaggered in front of them. Annoyingly, Zach was forced to back up.

"Hey." The surf rat smiled at Darlene. "Ripper of a set. You guys were on fire."

Australian. How soon till this idiot mentioned kangaroos?

Darlene smiled back modestly. "Thank you so much."

"Yeah, you had me bouncing around like a bloody kangaroo." Australia ran a hand through his hair just to show off his bicep. "Buy you a drink, gorgeous?"

As if Darlene was going to go for this peroxide prole. She only dated men with brains the size of planets. Her last boyfriend, Awful Charles, was a smug git who was constantly publishing articles about what an intellectual wanker he was. With his scrub of ginger curls, and Father Christmas paunch, Charles was no pinup, but he was a celebrated mind, and he and Darlene dated for what felt like *forever*. So Zach was more than surprised when Darlene accepted the offer. "Vodka tonic. But we need to load out first."

Australia grinned. Zach readied himself to step in, but before he could, someone slung an arm around his neck. "Hey, lady-killer." The female version of Zach—summer-blue eyes, thick brown bangs— smirked at him. It was his older sister, Imogene. Behind her were their parents, Mark and Catherine.

"Guys!" Zach hugged them one by one. His family had seen him and Darlene play only once or twice over the past two years. "What are you all doing here? You didn't tell me you'd be in town!"

"I had meetings in the city." His dad's voice boomed over the noisy club.

"And Mum's helping me with the never-ending search for a wedding dress. Honestly, kill me." Imogene was getting married to Mina Choi, her girlfriend of five years and fellow overachiever, at the family's Hamptons estate in September. In Love in New York had been hired a year and a half ago to plan the wedding. The key vendors had all been locked in before Eliot passed, but Zach hadn't quite gotten around to sharing the current state of the business, purely out of loyalty to Liv. Fortunately Imogene had been more focused on finding a dress that wasn't a giant marshmallow.

"We wanted to surprise you, Zach." His mum's vaguely pretentious habit of elongating random vowels produced his name with an extra syllable: *Za-ach*. Catherine looked formidably refined in a snow-white sheath dress. Her pale blond hair was expertly twisted into a cross between a seashell and a croissant. His mother's bloodline boasted some distant dukes, but in his parents' circle, that ancestry was as common as pennies and postmen.

"We're *starving*," Imogene announced, hooking her arm into his. "C'mon, Zook: let's go stuff our faces with pasta."

Relishing the chance to interrupt her conversation with the Aussie tosser, Zach asked Darlene if she'd mind handling load-out so he could have dinner with his family. "I swear I'll make it up to you," he said, bribing her to stop by for a cocktail or two before she went home, with the promise his father would pay. "Best negronis in the city."

Darlene rolled her eyes but agreed, so Zach guided his family to Babbo, an elegant Italian restaurant a few streets over, slipping the maître d' a fifty to secure them a prime table.

Zach's father, Mark, had met his wife, Catherine, at Oxford while studying business. Zach and his sister had grown up in a London neighborhood chosen for its proximity to good restaurants and gilded theaters. He'd spent his childhood in box seats at the Royal Opera House and all-ages gigs at the Roundhouse. Zach was permitted to study his first love of music, as long as it was at the prestigious Royal Academy of Music. There he was a middling student academically, but very popular socially (*If Zach applied half the attention he gave to the female students to developing his own considerable talent . . . et cetera*). When Imogene got into Harvard Law School, Zach followed his big sister to America, settling in New York. His parents soon followed, buying a house in the Hamptons and a pied-à-terre in Chelsea, after Mark received an offer as managing director for a New York–based venture capital fund. His mum sat on several charity boards, but her idea of philanthropy was largely attending black-tie balls. Zach was on a visa and still felt close to his English roots. The accent, after all, was a bloody effective aphrodisiac.

"So, Zachary," Mark began, after the wine was poured and they'd all ordered mains. "How are things?"

"Same old, same old." Zach leaned back in his chair, still feeling high from the show. "Sex, drugs, rock 'n' roll."

His father's mouth hardened. His mother looked openly appalled.

"Guys, I'm kidding!" Zach said. "I play jazz, not rock 'n' roll."

Imogene laughed.

His parents traded a coded look. "What about grad school?" Catherine's question was as delicate as the pearl drop earrings hanging from each lobe.

"Grad school?" Vague memories of tossing this out at a previous family dinner emerged. "Yeah, that's on the back burner for now."

His father had both hands flat on the table. "That's what you said last year."

"I didn't realize we were keeping score!" Zach tore off a hunk of bread and drenched it in olive oil. "Grad school isn't in the cards for me right now."

"So grad school isn't in the cards." Mark ticked off his fingers. "And neither is a full-time job, or an internship, or any kind of postgraduate education."

"Way to make a guy feel bad," said Zach, even though he didn't. His phone buzzed. Not Darlene: just a random girl.

Catherine fingered her neckline of her sheath. "What about . . . relationships?"

Zach almost choked on his bread. "I'm sorry: it sounds like you're inquiring about my *sex life*."

"Zach!" his mother hissed, glancing around. "Please. We're just worried about you. Might we remind you that by the time Genie was your age—"

"Please don't drag me into this, Mum," Imogene said.

"Yes, we're all aware how brilliant Imogene is," Zach muttered.

"She was clerking for a Supreme Court justice!"

"C'mon, guys," Imogene said. "Zach's just having the fun I never had because I was so busy being boring and studying all the time."

"Zach is twenty-six," Catherine said. "A young man clearly in need of the grounding a solid relationship would bring."

"I have solid relationships!" Zach exclaimed. "God, you're making me out to be some sort of depraved Don Juan—"

"Zach?"

The table looked up.

Zach felt a hard jolt of alarm. "Lauren!" The woman he was intending on breaking up with was at his table. Under usual circumstances Zach would find her skintight miniskirt quite delightful, but right now it seemed a little . . . revealing. "H-Hi."

"You always said Babbo was fantastic, so I'm here with my roommate." She tucked a lock of blond behind one ear coyly. "So funny running into you."

"Yes, absolutely, um, hysterical." He didn't want to hurt Lauren, he just couldn't imagine a successful relationship with her. Or, anyone. He'd get bored, or (more likely) they'd get bored. So it was safer to enjoy an extended fling, then sensitively end it. But, not in front of his parents.

Lauren addressed the table. "You must be Zach's family. So nice to meet you. How long are you in town?"

His mother's smile was tight. "We'll stay the night and drive back tomorrow."

Lauren let out a laugh. "To London?"

Zach winced.

Catherine cut her eyes to Zach. "To Southampton."

It was a stupid lie, but one he regularly told. It just made things easier if his girlfriends never expected to meet his family. Lauren glanced back at Zach, who smiled weakly. Christ, he was a knob sometimes. He could see her deciding to give him the benefit of the doubt. "Okay, I guess I'll see you tomorrow night."

"Tomorrow night I have rehearsal with Darlene." Zach glanced at his parents—*See? I'm responsible!* "But I'll, um, definitely give you a call. Sometime."

He may as well have dumped her then and there. A ripple of emotion distorted Lauren's face before she pressed her lips together, gave Zach a perfunctory smile, and began to walk off. She'd taken only a few steps before swinging around. "Are you sure you're not too busy calling the girl who texted you the other night? The one wanting to *suck your big D*?"

Catherine dropped her salad fork.

Panic shot through Zach's chest.

Lauren continued, her voice rising. "Meant to ask you about your last STD check, but obviously I should just get tested ASAP."

Zach's entire face was on fire. He could barely get the words out. "I'm always, um, careful . . ." But Lauren was gone.

Zach was adept at handling his family's outsize expectations. But this was different. This was a screwup. Of *Titanic* proportions. He cleared his throat. "Funny story, actually—"

"Oh, save it, Zach." His mother was uncharacteristically sharp. "Your father and I are withholding your trust until you get your act together."

He understood each word separately but not in that exact order. "I'm sorry, what?"

"Your trust fund," his father said. "You're not getting it."

Still, utterly incomprehensible. "But—but—but that money's mine. That's *my* money."

"No, Zachary, it's our money," Catherine corrected. "That you're clearly not mature enough to handle."

"But Imogene—"

"Spent hers on a portfolio of well-researched investments and charitable donations." Catherine cocked her head. "What would your plans be?"

Zach gripped the side of the table. His entire life had been leading up to his twenty-seventh birthday—the age his parents felt a young person's brain finally finished developing—whereby an embarrassing amount of money would be discreetly bequeathed to him to do with whatever he damn well pleased. Which was play music with Darlene, have sex with random bridesmaids, and enjoy life to the best of his ability. That's why he didn't need a job or further education or even a plan. It was crude to admit, but the fact was, his family was rich. He was rich.

Except now, he wasn't. He racked his brain for an angle, a convincing argument, a counterpoint. None emerged. *No!* This could *not* be happening.

"The thing is," he began, licking his lips.

"Yes?" His mother sipped her wine.

"The thing is," he repeated. "The thing . . . *is—*"

"Hello, Livingstones." Darlene stood at the table, smiling politely. Under her cropped denim jacket, she was wearing what she usually wore to jazz gigs: a floor-length, high-necked ivory silk dress, plus a glossy black bob wig. Sexy, yes, but also modest. Classy.

Zach was on his feet. "The thing is, I have something to tell you. *We* have something to tell you."

"We do?" Darlene asked.

"Yes, we do. We weren't ready to do this because it's so new—very, *very* new—but given the, uh, circumstance." Zach put his arm around Darlene's shoulder and gave it a squeeze. "Darlene and I . . . Well, we're . . . in love."

Darlene stared at Zach in total disbelief. "We're in what?"

21

At first, Gorman found the concept of adult education vaguely embarrassing. Wasn't there something sad about a roomful of adults well past the flush of youth sitting around a poky little classroom? Like wearing overalls or doing shots, it did not seem suitable for those over fifty. But Eliot's death, and Savannah Shipley's arrival in New York, had reminded Gorman that life was short. The week after E died, Gorman signed up for a playwriting class at a local community college. He'd spent his actual collegiate years wrestling with his sexuality by having closeted sex with wrestlers. But now, Gorman was an adult-education convert. His Monday-night playwriting class was one of the best parts of his week. He enjoyed meeting with "the over-forties Breakfast Club" for high-minded discussions about how form serves content or the sonic effect of alliteration. Each student spent the year working on a full-length play of their own, and the whole venture felt like a salon or a secret society. He was comfortable with this routine—Gorman always sought comfort wherever he was—but as he entered the classroom on Monday night, his cozy tradition had unexpectedly transformed.

"We have a new student," announced Jon, a rotund, bearded young man who'd had two productions staged at downtown theaters. "Gilbert."

Gorman twisted in his seat. He expected to see a former bus driver seeking the sublime or a supermarket employee who fancied himself a philosopher (they already had one each of those). Gilbert was neither.

"Hello." Gilbert gave a little wave.

"Hello." Everyone chorused. Everyone except Gorman.

Gilbert was adorable. Sandy-blond hair, round glasses, and a cute, friendly smile that revealed bleached white teeth. Easily a decade younger than the next youngest person in the room. Gilbert couldn't yet be thirty.

"I sent Gilbert all of your works in progress to catch up on." Jon smiled at the new student. "Hope we didn't overwhelm you."

"Not at all," said Gilbert. "I'm loving them. Especially *Tears of a Recalcitrant Snail*. I can't put it down, my roommates are like, 'Enough with the snail!'"

Gorman's cheeks burned. He felt slightly dazed.

"Well done, Gorman," Jon said. "Always nice to get some positive reinforcement. Okay, gang, let's pick up where we left off. Act Two of *Who's Afraid of Virginia Woolf?*, and we're keeping an eye out for the social and historical context."

The class thumbed through their books. Gorman swiveled around again. Gilbert smiled back eagerly, pointing to a dog-eared printout of Gorman's play and mouthing, *Love it!*

Gorman dipped his head in thanks and returned to his copy of *Who's Afraid of Virginia Woolf?*, having completely forgotten where he should be directing his attention.

Afterward, most of the class decamped to a nearby Irish bar known for its generous pours. Gilbert didn't join them, which was both disappointing and oddly relieving. Gorman had just gotten comfortable with a glass of fruity merlot and was preparing to discuss the second act of *Woolf* with the sublime-seeking bus driver when a cheerful voice sounded behind him. "Is this seat free?"

The class made room for Gilbert to sit next to Gorman. Gorman's heart picked up, like someone realizing they were, in fact, standing next to a celebrity.

"Sorry I'm late." Gilbert unzipped his jacket, revealing a T-shirt that read *No Bad Days!* "There's a credit card minimum; had to find an ATM machine that does ten-dollar bills."

Good grief, that really did take him back to college. "It's just ATM, you know," Gorman said. "ATM machine is redundant. Automatic teller machine machine."

Gilbert widened his eyes, like a baby owl. "You're right. That's hilarious. You're obviously brilliant. Really glad I signed up for this class."

"Why did you sign up for this class?" Gorman asked, and Gilbert began a monologue about dropping out of college to become an actor in LA but finding it too sunny and thinking maybe he'd move to the mountains to write a novel but then his sister telling him that was a dumb idea because he'd never written anything longer than an email . . . It was not uninteresting, but it certainly wasn't interesting. Confidence, Gorman realized. That was a defining quality of youth. Confidence that what you had to say was worth listening to. And people did listen to you, when you were as pleasing to look at as Gilbert.

They fell into an easy if not especially stimulating conversation about the class and living in New York and the downtown theater scene. Gilbert's worldview was so much more expansive and permissive than Gorman's had been in his midtwenties. Back then, a same-sex kiss on TV would set everyone's hair on fire and send advertisers fleeing. Gay marriage was a wildly radical fantasy. How much had changed for the younger generation. Their confidence made them expect equality.

While Gilbert was certainly fond of his own voice, he was also fond of Gorman, who he'd apparently decided was someone worth listening to. *I hope he doesn't ask me to be a mentor*, Gorman thought, as he bought the pair their third round of drinks. He didn't really see himself as the mentor type.

But that wasn't what Gilbert had in mind. "Have you heard of HERE Arts Center, Gorman?"

Gorman nodded, handing Gilbert his rum and Coke. "Off-off theater in SoHo?" By the corner of Spring and Sixth, near a now-closed piano bar he used to frequent in the nineties.

Gilbert nodded. "My aunt owns it. And I think this"—he brandished Gorman's play—"would be perfect for it. I love the absurd humor, feels contemporary and totally classic at the same time. And I love that Egor actually turns into a snail at the end—*very* Ionesco."

Heat seeped under Gorman's collar. Gilbert was more fluent in theater than he expected. "That's exactly what I was going for." When he was young, life was full of magic and opportunity. These days, surprises were few. This, he felt, was a true plot twist.

"I'd love to show it to my aunt and talk about a run," Gilbert continued, "if I got to play Egor."

Egor Snail was the lead. A clever, slightly vain aesthete who was struggling to accept his sexuality and largely defined by his relationship to his mother, an emotional terrorist. As suggested by the rest of the class, a thinly veiled version of Gorman as a younger man. At Gilbert's age.

Was it a fit? Gilbert certainly wasn't a physical match—in his youth, Gorman had the kind of face one couldn't decide was fantastically handsome or frightfully ugly. Gilbert held no such paradox. And Gorman had no idea if he could act or not. But perhaps that didn't matter. Possibility edged over the horizon, changing the black night sky to a subtler but distinctly lighter gray.

Gorman pushed his wineglass aside and leaned forward on his elbows. "You'd be absolutely *perfect*."

22

Darlene gaped at her bandmate. Why the hell had he just told his family they were in love?

"It's true, isn't it, darling?" Zach gave her shoulder another tight squeeze. "Beautiful, really. All this time playing together and what I was really looking for was right in front of me."

This was absurd. No: humiliating. Half the restaurant was staring, unsure if this was a grand romantic gesture or a joke. Their gazes closed around her like a trap. Darlene tried to wriggle away. "But—"

"I know we said we'd keep it a secret while we figured out our feelings, but I'm sorry, I want the world to know." Zach's voice rose in declaration. "I'm in love with Darlene Mitchell!"

For the second time that evening, they were the center of everyone's attention. Mark and Catherine looked speechless. Their blindingly white alarm at her presence beside their son exploded inside Darlene as fury and, embarrassingly, shame.

"Zach." She kept her voice firm. "I have no idea why—"

"We work as a couple, yes, I know, it surprised me too. I'm me and you're"—Zach glanced at her; Darlene glared back—"well, you're you, aren't you, darling? So sensible. Responsible. And it's really rubbing off on me." He addressed a passing man in a suit. "Put this dinner on my tab, will you?"

Catherine's gaze lingered on Darlene, even as she addressed Zach. "That wasn't a waiter, and you don't have a tab here."

"How long has this been going on?" asked Zach's father. Mark had always been polite enough to Darlene, but now he was frowning, his entire body tense.

"Yes, tell us your love story." Imogene made her voice swoony— she obviously believed this as much as Darlene did. "You're just like Harry and Meghan."

"You're right," said Catherine. "Especially how Meghan is so . . ."

Darlene braced herself, preparing for the worst.

"American."

Zach slapped his hand to his forehead.

Darlene pushed herself from Zach's grip. "I actually have to get going."

Zach spluttered, "No, darling. Sit down, stay for a drink."

"I have an early start," Darlene replied, her voice edged. "Good night, everyone. Goodbye, Zach." She moved swiftly back through the dining room, being sure to keep her head high.

Zach was on her heels. "Darlene, baby, wait!"

He followed her out of Babbo, onto Waverly Place, chasing her to the other side of the street.

"What the hell, Zach?" She spun on him, confusion solidifying into anger. "Did you lose a bet or something?"

"Darlene, I'm sorry. My parents threatened to withhold my trust unless I 'got my act together' and was in a 'solid relationship.' If they think you and I are together . . ."

Oh. Of course. "You get paid."

"Exactly. On my twenty-seventh birthday, which is only a teeny-tiny five months away."

"Five months?" She moved past him, raising her hand to hail a yellow taxi. "No way."

"Please?"

The taxi pulled up. "You're insane."

"I'll pay you!" He was back in front of her. "Ten thousand dollars."

Ten thousand dollars? That would pay for half the recording costs of an EP. "Twenty-five."

"Ha!" Zach saw she was serious. "Twenty."

The cab honked at her.

Darlene barely heard it. "Twenty-five."

"Okay, fine. Twenty-five thousand dollars for five months of dating. Done."

The number billowed in front of her. It took her a few moments to catch up to it, and what had just happened. Twenty-five thousand.

Dollars. It'd be the most amount of money she'd ever make in one go. Her tongue ran over her bottom lip, a nervous habit. "You better not be playing."

Zach's gaze was on her mouth. He caught himself staring and refocused. "I'm not."

The taxi drove off. Darlene backed up. "No. No. I'm not some *thing* to be paraded around in front of your— Sorry, Zach, but it's obvious what your family thinks about people like me."

"They think you're amazing. As do I."

Zach was always the first person to tell bookers, clients, his friends how brilliant she was. A few weeks ago, someone had mistaken him for the singer and her for backup, and he'd gotten so outraged on her behalf the tops of his ears went red.

Still, she gave him a look. "And why would I want to help you?"

"Because I'm Zach! Your musical better half. And the trust will help me play music, with you, without getting a real job."

Annoyingly, there was some truth to that. Other musicians had to plan around day jobs. Zach was always available. "Music is my real job."

"Of course it is! And this will help me help you do that job. Please?" he begged. "I know it's not the best plan."

"It's not a 'plan' at all! Who would believe you and I are a couple?"

"C'mon, Mitchell. We've got a thing going. Onstage," he clarified. "That's why we work so well together." He took a step toward her, his eyebrows raised. "You know what I mean."

Blood heated her cheeks. "Chemistry," she allowed. "But that's just a performance."

"So is this! Think of it as the easiest, best-paid gig ever."

That could very well be true. Her next question was one she'd wondered about. "Have you ever even dated a Black woman?"

"As a matter of fact I have. Safiyah." His eyes went a little starry. "She was a premed student from Nigeria. We dated for six months after uni."

"Oh." Darlene didn't expect this. Six months was a significant amount of time. Zach would've walked down the street with Safiyah. Heard any comments people made. He would've watched her get ready for bed.

"Safi was awesome." Zach smiled at a mental picture in his head.

"Smart and talented and sexy." His gaze landed back on Darlene. "Like you."

Weirdly, Darlene almost felt jealous of this smart, cool med student who put such a smile on Zach's face.

Twenty-five thousand dollars would pay for an entire EP without bootstrapping it: quality recording, great production, marketing budget, a DIY tour, everything. And a well-produced album was the first step to becoming an artist. Her own songs. Her way.

She made her voice cool. "What would I have to do?"

"Nothing you're not comfortable with. I'm not Harvey Weinstein, Mitchell: I'm not one of those guys. This'll only work if *you're* happy faking it. Strictly first base."

"First base?" Hand holding. Kissing. Maybe some touching. That seemed feasible.

"Yes." Zach placed his hands lightly on her shoulders and took a step closer. Closer than they'd ever stood before. Closer than friends. "Like this." His blue eyes were soft and serious. No mischievous spark in them. "Do we have a deal?"

She could smell him: a hint of red wine on his breath, and something that was uniquely, undeniably Zach. It all smelled . . . yummy. She spoke before she could second-guess herself. "Okay. But so we're clear, I'm doing this for me, so I can cut an album. And if you screw me over, I will destroy you."

"Understood." The warm pad of his thumbs brushed her collarbones, moving in a slow circle. "Don't look now, but my family are currently spying on us from the front of the restaurant. I said don't look!" he said, as Darlene went to swivel around. "We've been having an argument about me deciding to come clean about our relationship. And about the fact that I only just broke up with Lauren. Who didn't mean anything to me," he added quickly as she pulled back an inch. "I promise." Tentatively, he skimmed his fingers down her arm. Like a boyfriend would. Affectionate. Loving. "Now, you've forgiven me, and I think we should kiss."

"Now? Here?"

"Well, we are in love, right? Just a little makeup kiss. Are you okay with that?"

Zach's proximity was having the oddest effect. She was trying to stay alert and rational, but her bones felt like butter left in the sun. *Focus! This is just acting. This is not real.* "Fine."

"Bang on." His smile was surprised and just a little bit wicked. There was still a foot of air between them. "Come closer."

She moved a half step forward.

"Closer."

She couldn't make her feet move. This was Zach: the bane of her existence, the most annoying person in the world. But he was, objectively, attractive. And she was pretty sure he felt the same way about her. She inched toward him, until they were almost touching.

"Put your arms around me."

She put her hands on his hips, middle-school-dance style.

He tried not to laugh. "C'mon, Mitchell. Pretend I'm someone you actually like."

After a long moment of hesitation, Darlene circled her arms around his neck. Their bodies pressed against each other. Zach's hands dropped to her lower back, sliding against the slinky material of her dress. A bright wave of heat shimmied up and down her entire body. None of this was permitted. None of this should be happening. And that excited her.

"Ready?" His voice was husky.

Darlene tilted her face up to him. Her heart was beating so ferociously there was a good chance it'd burst out of her chest. "Yes."

Slowly, inch by inch, Zach lowered his mouth onto hers. At first, Darlene kept her lips shut, unable to relax and stop thinking: *Zach is kissing me, Zach, Zach Livingstone, right now, in the middle of the street!* But Zach persisted. His mouth moved over hers, kissing her top lip, her bottom lip, her top lip again, his lips warm and confident against hers.

She couldn't fight it anymore.

A barrier inside her broke. She opened her mouth and started kissing Zach back. Really kissing him back.

And that's when things got kind of nuts.

Her fingers dug into his hair, his stupid flop of perfect hair. It was just as soft and thick as she always thought it'd be, which made her feel angry and turned on in equal measure. She fisted the strands and tugged, wanting him to feel it. He let out a groan of pleasure, pulling back to flash her a look of surprise. Not kissing was way worse than kissing. Annoyed, she dropped her hands to his shirt collar and yanked him to her, kissing him hard. He kissed her back deeply. His hands were on her back, pulling her body onto his. The feeling of the power in his hands, those hands that could pick up any instrument and make it sing, made her blood run white-hot. She pressed her teeth onto his bottom lip, sucking and biting down. Zach mumbled something like, "Jesus," and she said something like, "Shut up," opening her mouth wider. Zach groaned low in his throat, squeezing her ass. The feeling of his hands on her butt and the moan in his voice unlocked something even wilder in her. She backed them up against a brick wall. Their kiss turned desperate. His hands cupped her jaw, her hips, the back of her head, hot muscle pushing against her rhythmically. She couldn't get enough, would never get enough. She needed more, more of his mouth, his body, his hair, his hands, which were everywhere, sending waves of pleasure *everywhere*, all crashing cymbals and crazed piano held together by the *throb throb throb* of a low, insistent bass, that was getting louder, and faster, reaching a peak—

A car alarm sounded, close, noisy. It jerked Darlene out of her body. Back into her head.

She froze.

He froze.

She was back, in the West Village, on Waverly Place, her arms around Zach. *Zach*. She inhaled hard and pushed him off her.

He almost fell over. "Um, wow. That was . . ." He looked absolutely stupefied. "Who are you, and what have you done with Darlene Mitchell?"

She couldn't answer. Could not speak, think, process at all. She was a blank sheet of music. An empty stage.

What the *hell* had she just done. . . . with *Zach*?

Zach adjusted something in his pants—she would not think about that, no she would *not*—and looked over his shoulder. "And I guess we had a bit of an audience."

Only now did Darlene remember that the Livingstone family had witnessed the entire make-out. Crowded at the restaurant entrance, Mark's eyes were slit with suspicion while his mother looked somewhere between stunned and scandalized. Imogene looked genuinely amazed.

Darlene stared back, feeling caught out. She spent so much of her life listening to her father lecture her about how she presented herself. Darlene knew respectability politics were bullshit, but she did like to be in control. Unless she was kissing Zach, apparently. Which was only for money: a *lot* of money. It didn't matter what his family thought: she was the one getting the upper hand in this situation. She'd negotiated the terms, she'd only do what she wanted to. She was playing him. Darlene ignored the wild thrum under her skin and took another step back, away. "I'm getting a cab. Go finish loading the rest of the gear."

First base *only*. She would never kiss him like that *ever* again.

23

Zia flopped onto Darlene's couch, limbs aching. She'd intended to simply drop off the leftovers from Clay's photo shoot to Layla but had somehow gotten roped into cleaning the bathroom, then cooking dinner. Boundaries. She had to get better at boundaries. She loved her sister and wanted to help, but she'd always been susceptible to guilt and Layla knew how to work it. It felt manipulative, and it irritated her. Back at Darlene's apartment, where she'd been crashing most nights, Zia tried to shake it off. She popped open a Montauk Summer Ale and contemplated the piece of paper Clay had given her.

His cell number.

Of course Zia wanted to see Clay again. But a new horizon was beckoning.

She reread the enthusiastic email she'd received from the team leader in Mozambique. Yes, they'd *love* to hire her as a volunteer coordinator at the women's resource center. Six months in Africa. Wanderlust stirred, stretching like a cat waking up from a nap.

Zia was intrigued by Clay, but she was also wary of what falling for someone could do to her. Had done to her before. The loss of freedom. The loss of self.

She'd been intrigued by Logan, too.

Her ex-boyfriend's name still made it feel like there were spiders under her skin. He'd been her first serious relationship, back when she was only twenty. He was almost thirty, devoted to owning good suits and making good money. The kind of man who thought everything they wanted already belonged to them.

Logan had made everything that happened feel like a consequence of her behavior. Now she knew abusive relationships were never the fault of the survivor.

Air drained from her lungs, replaced by a suffocating blackness closing in.

The feeling of being trapped. Completely powerless.

Don't think about Logan. Don't go back there.

The front door opened.

"Darlene!" Zia swiveled around, grateful for the distraction. "How was the gig? Zinc Bar, right?"

"Fine." Darlene looked pensive and distracted, but also light. Like a girl with a secret.

"Dee. What's going on?"

"If I tell you something, you have to promise not to judge me. Or ask any follow-up questions."

"Okay."

Darlene sank down next to her on the sofa. "I kind of . . . just . . . made out with Zach."

A bolt of surprised excitement made Zia grab Darlene's arm. "What? When? Finally!"

Darlene was blushing. "Finally?"

"C'mon, you guys have mad chemistry. I knew this would happen." Zia edged closer, grinning. "What was it like?"

"I said no follow-ups!" Darlene couldn't stop a smile unfolding over her face. "But it was pretty hot."

Zia laughed. "So, what—do you want to date him?"

Darlene exhaled, looking conflicted. "Can you keep a secret?"

Zia could. She'd kept Clay a secret. And it felt like freedom to release herself into Darlene's world. Zia grabbed a beer from the fridge and handed it to Darlene. "Tell me *everything*."

24

"You said Kamile would post about us on Sunday." Liv wedged her phone under one ear, stirring a pot of green-pea risotto in her kitchen. "It's *Friday*."

Savannah blathered something about being "on it, totally on it." The girl was an atrocious liar. She didn't wear her heart on her sleeve; she was parading around in a giant heart costume.

Kamile had agreed to share her "fantastic, flawless" experience of working with In Love in New York in the first public photograph from her wedding day, which would be the most valuable to her fans. There was indeed a picture posted last Sunday morning, which Liv was able to see online, even without an Instagram account. A *Vogue*-worthy shot of the beatific bride gazing at her devoted groom, both awash in golden-hour light. The caption? *Married my best friend yesterday #sealedthedeal.* Over twenty-four thousand likes. Two thousand comments. Hundreds of reposts. No one tagged except for Dave. Even Liv knew what that meant. And it wasn't just her business: Kamile had promised a few other vendors the same kind of trade, vendors Liv felt responsible for. She muted Savannah, and asked Ben to set the table. As soon as he was out of earshot, Liv unmuted the call and cut Savannah off.

"Listen, Shipley. I worked for eight weeks on that wedding. You promised she'd post and that we'd get so many referrals we'd be instantly back in business. But there's no post, and no referrals."

There was a tense pause. Savannah sounded strained. "I have another friend, who's getting married this summer . . ."

Liv almost dropped the phone in the saucepan. Panic flared in her chest. "*Another*— No. I can't wait that long." Liv squeezed her eyes shut, humiliated. "I'm broke."

"So am I," Savannah said passionately.

Being broke in your twenties was a rite of passage. Being broke in middle age was frightening. Liv was cooking to save money. Between the mortgage, bills, and all their weekly costs, the Goldenhorns were hemorrhaging cash. She'd enjoyed working on Dave and Kamile's wedding. She'd actually let herself see a spark of faith in Savannah.

"You're a naive idiot," Liv hissed. "I never should've trusted you."

"But, Liv—"

Liv hung up and let the phone clatter to the messy kitchen counter.

Was this why Eliot changed his will—to punish her for falling out of love with him by pairing her with a ditzy business partner doomed to fail?

"Ready, Mom!" Ben sung out.

Liv inhaled a breath. When she was Savannah's age, she said whatever was on her mind and indulged every passing emotion. Who knew acting would be so handy as a parent? Ignoring the stress tears in the corners of her eyes, she swung around and made herself smile. "Great job, honey!"

The risotto looked runnier than the one Sam made. Perhaps they added too much stock? She'd only eyeballed the measurements.

Ben pursed his lips at his bowl. "We can still order a pizza."

"No pizza." Liv took a seat opposite her son. "We made it from scratch."

Ben's expression indicated this was the problem.

Ben forked risotto into his mouth. Disgust flickered over his face. Liv made herself swallow a bite. The worst pea risotto in history slimed down her throat.

"Let's order a pizza," she said. "Quickly."

She couldn't really afford it. But they had to eat.

Liv scooped up both bowls. It was a pretty good excuse to call Sam, ask for advice. But surely the frisson between them was just in her head. Like Eliot, Sam's next partner would probably be someone Savannah's age. It was risky and silly to think about love and sex (*Wait, why am I thinking about sex? Stop thinking about sex!*). There was no way anything would, should, or could ever happen between her and Sam Woods.

Liv tipped every last grain of risotto into the trash. "I don't know what happened. We followed the recipe." More or less.

"Sometimes, things just don't work out how you think they're going to," Ben said. He got quiet.

Liv scooted a chair next to him and ran her fingers through his hair in the way that always soothed him. "You thinking about Daddy, honey?"

He nodded, eyes on the floor.

"You miss him?"

He nodded again.

Her heart felt like a wet dishrag being squeezed until it was bone-dry. "I miss him too." She kept stroking his hair. "Hey, remember all the crazy costumes Daddy would make for Halloween?"

A smile almost lifted her son's mouth. "Yeah."

"How many can you remember?" She ticked off her fingers. "There was the year he was Willy Wonka and you were an Oompa Loompa, and then, what else?"

"I was Harry Potter and he was Dumbledore."

She'd made a wizard robe out of an old blanket. Ben looked adorable in his stripy scarf and round glasses. "That's right. Oh, what about the year Dad was a Ghostbuster and you were the Stay Puft Marshmallow Man?"

"I don't remember that." Ben sounded worried.

"Yeah, you were still pretty little, but we have about one thousand photos. So we won't ever forget."

Her son looked up at her. "Do you think I'll ever forget Dad?"

"No!" A pit opened up in Liv's stomach, its depth surprising her. She felt horrified. "No, sweetie, I don't, I really don't. You won't, I promise."

"But how? I don't remember being the Stay Puft Marshmallow Man."

Liv hadn't contemplated the fact she'd be the primary bearer of Eliot's memory. And that would mean swallowing her betrayal forever, only giving Ben the highlights. That was her maternal duty. But it also felt a bit like lying. "Because we're going to talk about him. And look at pictures and tell stories and keep him alive in here." She pressed her hand against her son's chest. "In our hearts."

"Mom," he said, "that's really cheesy."

She laughed. "Maybe. Maybe it's okay to be cheesy. Every now and then."

"Mom?"

"Yes, baby?"

"Can I order the pizza now?"

Liv unlocked her phone, checking there was no *Amazing news!!* text from Savannah. There wasn't. "You got it, mister."

Financial ruin, here we come.

"No, I want to call."

She raised her eyebrows. "Do you know how?"

He nodded.

"Okay." She handed him her phone.

Ben tapped and scrolled until he found the number and dialed. "Hello? I'd like to order a large cheese pizza. Yes, that's the address. We'll pay in cash. Thank you."

"Look at you, ordering a pizza like a pro." Liv knew she was biased, but it was quite possible her child was the smartest kid in Prospect Heights, and maybe even the entire world. She wanted to give him everything. "So clever, Benny."

"Well, I've seen you do it a million times." He sounded more upbeat than a few minutes ago. "You and Dad didn't really cook a lot."

"That's true. What were we doing all the time?"

Ben pushed his glasses up his nose. "Working."

He was right. They did work all the time. But in different ways.

When Ben was still a mysterious lump in Liv's belly, she'd had many conversations with Eliot about equal parenting. She intended to raise a feminist, and that meant seeing his dad cleaning and his mom sitting at the head at the table. "He should know masculine and feminine is all on a spectrum," Liv would say, rubbing her swollen belly while munching dill pickles. "My unborn child will respect women or I'll have failed as a parent."

"He will, sweetheart," Eliot promised, helping himself to the last pickle. "And if we're especially lucky, he'll also be a genderfluid poet who wants to save the whales."

"One can only hope." Liv chuckled.

But somewhere along the way, Liv's gender-neutral parenting dreams had been diluted. On top of running In Love in New York, she was the one doing the majority of the physical and emotional labor of raising her son: the one who packed the lunches and did his laundry and consoled him after a fall. Even progressive Brooklyn was behind the times: the parenting group she joined was called Prospect Heights Moms, the attendees of which complimented her as a *career woman* and, more upsettingly, a *girl boss*. "There's no career men," Liv would point out. "Or boy bosses." The moms would all ooh, fascinated, and switch the topic to keto diets.

Things changed between her and Eliot after Ben was finally born, following their punishing four-year IVF journey. Benny was a fussy baby, mother-hungry, and cranky with Eliot. Their couple identity didn't flow easily from "couple trying to conceive" to "couple being parents." Eliot wasn't a bad father, but he wasn't an exceptionally good one. Liv suspected he liked being the baby of the relationship, vaguely resentful that Liv was no longer on tap to indulge his need for reassurance—that he was lovable, or a genius, or impressively virile. Liv had a new love. A tiny, unreliable god in the shape of a frog-faced baby she adored with swoony fierceness.

Liv's desire to have a second child, a baby girl, pushed them further apart. Every time she brought it up, Eliot would look at her like she was absolutely mad. "You're too old," he'd say, or "I think we have our hands full with one." Unequivocally *no*. And so her secret fantasies of teaching a girl how to be a woman, sharing all the important things her own mother did, or didn't do, went unmet. Instead, she focused on Ben's needs, and the needs of the business, a demanding and fulfilling entity that she also deeply loved.

Liv's line of work involved negotiating tradition (what was expected) with change (what was truly desired). She met the life she was given with the ideals she thought she had and tried to make it work. So did Eliot. But it was only after they became parents did the ravine between their two approaches become clear. At the time, it seemed like the only way. But now, just like a bride who was deciding not to wear white down the aisle, Liv was beginning to understand there were *so many more possibilities* than what she thought she saw at the time.

As Liv put the risotto bowls in the dishwasher, the question presented itself to her with frightening clarity: Was being a wife something she still prioritized after Ben was born? Or had it somehow been lagging in third place, behind mother and business owner? She was probably a better friend than she had been a wife, given all the time she spent drinking with Gorman. For years, she'd been certain that seeing Eliot every day, in the home they shared and the business they owned, had been the highest form of intimacy. But now, Liv had to wonder: Had she still been married to her husband?

Or to everything else around her?

25

The next day, Savannah let the city distract her from the fiasco that was In Love in New York.

She took the subway to the Upper East Side to visit the Metropolitan Museum of Art, ending up in a room full of modern masters: Georgia O'Keeffe, Salvador Dalí, Pablo Picasso. One of Modigliani's famed reclining nudes gazed back at her, eyes heavy-lidded, flesh glowing and creamy. Transcendent. New York was like this—unexpected pockets of beauty and history, offered as casually as one tosses bread crumbs at pigeons. She'd turn a corner, and suddenly, there was Carnegie Hall or a naked cowboy with a guitar or a supermodel in sweats. Once, she saw Lady Gaga, in a full, glittery ball gown, getting into a black Suburban on Park Avenue. For one brief second, they locked eyes. Savannah swore that Lady Gaga *smiled* at her.

At first, it felt like a waste to have these experiences alone. She and Honey would occasionally text each other perfect little New York moments a subway saxophonist playing "New York State of Mind," a particularly excellent lox bagel—but still, physically, alone. Savannah was used to defining herself in relation to others—a daughter, an intern, a best friend. Alone, she was just herself, discovering who she was when no one else was around. Her own mother never had this opportunity: Terry and Sherry were high school sweethearts. They'd never spent more than two nights apart. But having been in New York alone for the past few months, Savannah could feel herself changing. Like the best work of art or a glass of good whiskey, her layers were beginning to reveal themselves.

And yet, even the magic of New York couldn't fix her current predicament. It was almost closing time on Saturday night when Savannah hauled herself onto a barstool at 'Shwick Chick and let out a heavy sigh. "I need a drink."

Honey reached for the Pappy Van Winkle.

Over the past week, Kamile hadn't replied to any of Savannah's increasingly desperate texts and voice mails. The newlywed was lying on a beach in the Bahamas, ironically unplugged. That *wasn't* how the world was supposed to work. You give, you get.

Honey left to clear a table, returning a minute later to ask, "But haven't you got a contract or something?"

Savannah closed her eyes in defeat. "No." Why had she pushed back so vehemently on sending Kamile a contract? Liv had been right. One hundred percent, absolutely, fundamentally *right*. The reputation of the business Savannah co-owned was still in the toilet, and the past few months of full-time work had amounted to absolutely zilch. "I'm such an *idiot*."

"No, you're an optimist." Honey squeezed her hand. "Savannah, what you're doing isn't easy. You threw yourself into a new job in a new city with a woman who has every right to hate you. You brought in the first client and pulled off an awesome wedding against a lot of odds. We're always our own harshest critic, but as your biggest fan on the sidelines, I'm telling you, you're killing it."

Savannah closed her eyes, trying to let the kind words into her heart. Why was it so easy to see the best in others, but not in yourself?

Her phone pinged. A text. From her father. *Hey Pookie! I know it's late, but are you free for a chat? Nothing urgent, we love you!*

She flipped her phone over, feeling an unfamiliar snap of annoyance. She was fairly certain she was the only Gen Z transplant in Bushwick who talked to their parents multiple times a week.

Honey flipped the OPEN sign to CLOSED, and invited Savannah to hang out while the staff cleaned up and balanced the books. Savannah felt like she'd just been invited backstage. A new level of intimacy, unlocked. She watched her friend expertly wipe down the bar. "What's your plan, Honey? Think you'll stay here for a while?"

"This is the best restaurant job I've ever had. But I'm just crazy enough to open my own spot, one day. I hear it's real easy."

Savannah perked up. "Really? That's so cool."

"*Honey's Fried Chicken.* It's got a ring to it, doesn't it?" She leaned across the bar, her brown eyes sparking. "I've worked every front-of-house job, so I know how to staff up. I'm only an amateur cook, so I'd hire someone to run the kitchen. Maybe somewhere in Greenpoint, or Bed-Stuy."

Savannah nodded eagerly. "You could start with a dinner series. Like, a pop-up. Fifty bucks for all-you-can-eat fried chicken and beer. Build a mailing list, get a logo designed, maybe start a YouTube channel. The Brooklyn food scene is so popular right now, and having a niche is smart."

"You're smart," Honey said. "They're all really good ideas." As Honey cleaned, they riffed on the concept. The honey-fried chicken was one of the most popular items on 'Shwick Chick's menu, and the only dish that wasn't created by the head chef. It made Honey feel confident she knew enough about food to hire the right cook. Honey was only twenty-five but the food scene was a good place for the young and ambitious; the owners of 'Shwick Chick were two guys in their early thirties. And Honey's ex was a designer. "You know—for the logo and stuff."

Honey had never mentioned anything about her private life. Savannah didn't know if this was a mistake or an invitation. "That's handy." And then, because she really was curious about how relationships in New York started: "How did you meet?"

"Online. It's one of those on-again-off-again-I'm-losing-my-mind-again things."

It wasn't a mistake. They were definitely in the waters of a deeper friendship. "Maybe I should give that another go. Online dating, I mean, not getting back with my ex." *He died.* Savannah saw his dead body, something she tried not to think about but would come back to her in disturbing flashes. Poor Eliot's death was obviously why the idea of dating guys in New York still left her so cold. "Think you'll get back with your guy?"

Honey inhaled a breath and wrinkled her brow. "It's a long story. For another time. Sit tight and I'll get some leftover pie to wash down that whiskey. Then if you're up for it, come get a drink with us." She indicated the rest of the staff. "There's a dive around the corner we usually hit up."

Savannah was surprised she'd been deemed cool enough to be invited along. "I'd love that." She leaned across the bar to give Honey a kiss on the cheek. "Thanks for being such a good friend, Hon. It's really good to have someone to confide in."

"You're welcome. And don't worry about Kamile. You'll figure it out." Honey topped up her drink. "Go the extra mile. Roll up your sleeves and just get it done."

Go the extra mile. Just get it done.

Yes.

Savannah swirled the whiskey, mind whirring. A plan started to form.

26

Zia picked up extra shifts, working parties and events, in an effort to save for Mozambique. Global Care would pay for her flight and accommodation, but the weekly stipend was tiny, and she'd spent all her savings on helping her sister. It didn't make sense to text Clay. But while her brain made a perfectly rational case, her subconscious had other plans. Clay Russo filled her dreams. Every night. The feeling of his mouth on hers, bold and sensual. Frankly, she was stunned at the way she was responding to this man. The crush was interesting, but learning something about her own body was fascinating. Come Saturday night, her resolve broke.

> **Zia, 8:35 p.m.:** Hey, it's Zia/your favorite makeup artist. I'm going out dancing tonight. Bembe in BK. Wanna come?
>
> **Clay, 8:41 p.m.:** Hello! Nice to hear from you. Dancing sounds fun, but crowds can be tricky. A drink at my place? No funny business, would just like to talk.
>
> **Zia, 9:06 p.m.:** I hope your funny business rule doesn't extend to Bill Murray, I love him 😀. I need to move tonight, so Bembe's my jam. 💃
>
> **Clay, 9:18 p.m.:** Totally get it. Can we make a plan for next week? Dinner + a Bill Murray movie? 🎬
>
> **Clay, 10:15 p.m.:** Are you still going tonight?

By day, Bembe didn't exist. It was just a faded black door, messy with graffiti, notable only for its location tucked under the giant steel beams of the Williamsburg Bridge. But by night, long lines braved muggy heat or bitter cold to get into the city's best global music dance club. Bembe was a place people came to dance. Feel-the-music-in-every-cell-and-let-it-move-your-hips dance. Salsa and dancehall and Afrobeats, all with live percussion. Zia squeezed her way onto the crowded dance floor and let the beat start to dictate her movements. Feeling lithe and supple, all thoughts of Clay left her head.

An hour or so later, a man in aviator sunglasses and a baseball cap grooved up next to her. When she turned away, he was back in front of her. *Take a hint, bro!* The man took off his glasses, and winked.

Clay. He showed up. Despite the worry about crowds.

He must really like her.

Giddy, she lost the beat, bumping into the people around her.

"Two left feet?" he teased, showing off his own skills with a fluid hip swivel. The man knew how to move.

Zia refocused. She may not have experience flirting with mysterious movie stars who showed up at tiny Brooklyn clubs. But she could dance. She leaned in close to his ear, one hand on his bicep. Still as warm and hard as she left it. "*¡Vamos, chacho!*"

Once again, Zia was back inside the music, snaking her hips and shaking her shoulders. But this time, she wasn't alone.

It was well into the witching hour when they decided to call it a night. "Can I give you a ride home?" Clay asked.

Zia wiped off her forehead, sweaty and spent. Almost postcoital. "I'm staying with a friend ten minutes away. You can walk with me, if you want."

Clay nodded, pursing his lips. "Let me talk to my security."

He conferred with a serious, swarthy man, both of them huddled in the shadows. A glimpse of Clay's larger world, the one that required him to have a bodyguard, edged into Zia's consciousness. It was like glimpsing the ocean for the first time: something vast and thrilling with an undercurrent of danger.

Clay reappeared, smiling as he shrugged on a leather jacket. But when she moved toward the front entrance, Clay turned her around. "Cameras just arrived." Then, off her look of confusion: "Paparazzi."

Clay's security guard, Angus, led the pair into a back office. Clay handed Angus his hat and sunglasses. Angus was the same height and build as Clay, and was wearing the same outfit. He would be the decoy, and the paparazzi would follow him back to Clay's apartment in SoHo, allowing them to leave via the service entrance at the back of the club.

They snuck into the empty, quiet alleyway, walking quickly up to the street, turning onto Wythe Avenue. Clay was alert, but there was no one around except tipsy locals. Above them, a subway train rattled over the Williamsburg Bridge. It felt like they'd just robbed a bank. She couldn't parse out her feelings about it. Or him. Who was this person walking her home? She'd been in sync with Clay on the dance floor, but it was clear they were from completely different worlds. The sight of his perfectly proportioned face, a face that belonged on magazine covers and fifty-foot billboards, both relaxed her and made her more tense.

"Are you all right?" he asked.

She almost laughed. "I'm just . . . I mean, this is a little bit . . ."

"Look, ask me anything, Zia. Seriously, I'm an open book."

Zia wrapped her arms around herself. "Okay. What's it like being Clay Russo?"

He mulled it over for a moment. "Mostly, it's good, and sometimes it's complicated. What's it like being Zia . . . ?"

"Ruiz," she supplied, and he repeated it, like he was rolling a sweet around in his mouth. She considered his question. "I guess, ditto."

"See," he said. "We're not so different."

They talked all the way back to Darlene's apartment, an easy back-and-forth that moved fluidly between banter and scattered bits of biography. She told him about the time she'd spent abroad—Haiti, Cambodia, Bangladesh. He shared his work as cofounder of Radical Water, a clean-water initiative that'd taken him to Uganda three times in the past two years. When he wasn't on location for a film, he divided his time between New York and LA. Zia had met wealthy people in her travels—many of the donors who funded Global Care projects were part of the 1 percent. But celebrity wealth was different, tied to the value of one specific person. Her sister always said, "The only people who say money doesn't matter are people who have a lot of it." Zia put this out of her mind. Money didn't define a person; it was usually the least interesting thing about them. Their heart was what mattered.

She stopped outside Darlene's building. "Well. This is me."

"Okay. This is you." Clay smiled at her, almost shyly, his hands in his pockets.

He hadn't touched her since they left the club. He didn't assume she was his.

She said, "There's a roof deck . . . ?"

Zia handed Clay a Sierra Nevada Pale Ale as they took in the sprawling mess of Brooklyn, the restless East River, and behind it, the most unmistakable skyline in the world. Manhattan. There was something about being up here, part of the cityscape and far from the ordinary reality of the street below, that seemed permissive. Intimate.

"So, when you say your life is complicated," she said, "what does that mean?"

He eyed her. "You promise you're not, like, a journalist or anything? I spill my guts, it ends up on the internet?"

"No! God, no! No, I was just . . . totally prying, and you definitely do not have to answer." She held his gaze. "But you can trust me. I promise."

He tapped his foot against the concrete balcony that separated them from the drop to the street below. "Well, first, let's be clear: I'm lucky. I'm not the best actor in the world; every single critic will tell you that. But through a series of coincidences and persistence and dumb luck, I ended up in this pretty incredible job that gives me the kind of life I honestly never even dreamed of." Clay shook his head. "People talk a lot about privilege these days, and man, I got privilege coming out the wazoo. I got my health. I can help good people do good things. I got a lot, Zia, more than I deserve, for sure."

"But?" Zia asked.

He took a sip of beer. Stalling. "But everything comes with strings attached."

"Like?"

Clay let out an uneasy laugh. "I don't want you to think I'm ungrateful, because I'm not."

"Clay," Zia protested. "I asked."

Clay sighed. "In a nutshell . . . everyone feels like I owe them more than I'm giving. More than I'm able to give."

Zia didn't say anything, giving Clay room to continue.

"I got a big family and I'm from a small town. And so when I was starting out in LA, nobody really gave a crap about me when I went home for Christmas. And that was fine; we all just ate turkey and watched the game and tried to stop Uncle Enzo drinking too much grappa."

Zia chuckled.

Clay smiled too. "Anyway, so after I did my first big movie, people who I hadn't heard from in years started coming out of the woodwork, inviting me over, asking me to invest in their business, wanting me to be their kid's godfather." He rubbed his eyes. "I am so many people's godfather, it's crazy. And when I started to say no, because I said yes way too many times, people got pissed. Like, really pissed. And it's not just family shit." He ticked off his fingers. "Directors want more time. Press want more interviews. Fans want more of me. Even my friends want more. Next week I have to fly to Tokyo to do some kind of energy drink sponsorship, which I'm only doing because . . . I don't even know why. I hate energy drinks!" He ran his hand through his hair, looking slightly bewildered. "Sometimes, I don't even feel like a person. I feel like a gateway to something else: money, influence, power. I owe a million emails and phone calls and tweets and favors and introductions. I constantly feel like I'm letting everyone down because there's not enough of me to go around. I'm just one guy. One guy whose ex-girlfriend wrote a book full of way too much personal information, who has no privacy, no downtime, but can never complain about it because . . ."

"You're so lucky," Zia finished.

"And, I am," he said with a shrug. "So, that's my life. It's good. But complicated."

Zia let all this sink in. The few celebrities she'd encountered on projects abroad treated their experience like a fun, rustic adventure or a fix for a PR problem. She'd assumed people like Clay existed in a world of excess and gratification. She'd never really thought about a balance: that for every benefit received, something was expected in return.

"Say something." Clay sounded nervous. "You think I'm a jerk?"

"Of course I don't think you're a jerk. I'm just taking it all in. It makes me feel . . . sad. I feel for you." She peeled the edge of her beer bottle label, thinking. "What do you have that's just yours?"

"Tonight. I bailed on a dinner, said I was sick. No one knows I'm up here with you. So maybe . . . you." His gold eyes drilled into her. "You're just for me."

Zia shivered with something darker. She had to look away, at the distant city skyline.

"What? Did I say something wrong?"

"I know you're saying that to be romantic. And it is. But if we're being honest . . ."

"Please."

"I have mixed feelings about being someone's everything."

Clay tilted his head. Open to whatever she was going to say next.

Zia had never told the story to someone she'd only just met. And she wasn't about to lay it on Clay now. But interestingly, she felt that if she did, he would listen. "I have family commitments. Expectations of my time, my focus. So I can relate to feeling bad about freedom." She could tell Clay knew it wasn't the full story. But the serious stuff was making her feel closed and she wanted to feel open. She finished her beer and held it up. "Another? I'm still so thirsty."

"Hey, what a coincidence. Me too."

They found some plastic folding chairs and spent another two hours on the roof, talking, joking, flirting. Clay was different from what she'd imagined, in some ways more confident, in some ways less. Sensitive and a little shy, but also funny, also charming. He was a person, not a billboard. "You're easy to talk to," she said, after they'd finished their third beer.

"You too," he said, nudging her foot with his.

She held his gaze, letting the moment fill with something more loaded than friendly banter.

He gazed back, drinking her in. He was attracted to her. The reality of this ran its fingers all over her entire body, heating her skin.

Zia put down her beer. "Look, I should tell you: I'm leaving New York soon. For a job in Mozambique."

"Africa? For how long?"

"It's a six-month position."

She watched the way it landed, invoking surprise, disappointment, and finally, a question.

Now what?

She got to her feet, tugging him up. Suddenly, they were standing only inches apart.

"Hi," she said.

"Hello," he said.

Zia stuck her hands in her back pockets. His remained hooked in his jeans. An adult game of chicken: Who'd break first? She could see each little hair shading his jaw. Smell the musky mix of clean and dirty: soap and dance-floor sweat. The air between them thickened. "I think," she said, "I have a crush on you."

"Oh, I definitely have a crush on you."

She laughed. Edged closer. His breath ghosted over her lips. "You're kinda cute," she said.

A smile flitted across his face. His eyes were on her mouth. "Zia," he said, "you're insanely hot."

Zia grabbed the front of Clay's T-shirt, and then his mouth was on hers and they were kissing. His stubble was rough against her skin, his mouth hot and eager. She let out a moan, her desire overwhelming her. Clay pulled her closer, one hand in her hair, the other sliding down her back. Time, space, place, who he was, who she was, it all disappeared. It was just them, and this kiss, this glorious, intense, insanely hot kiss.

After ten minutes or ten years, he pulled back to gaze at her, twisting his fingers into a stray tendril. "I have a crazy idea."

She ran her fingers through his hair, relishing the chance to touch him. "I like crazy ideas."

"Come to Tokyo with me next week."

"Sure," she joked. "That sounds fun."

"No, I'm serious. Come to Tokyo. I have to go for this energy drink thing. It's only four nights, and if you hate it, I'll fly you home." He squeezed her hands, saying something about a private jet, five-star hotel, sightseeing in his downtime. Spending time with his best friend and manager, Dave, the guy whose wedding they met at. "It'll be so much better if you're there. Please?"

"Clay!" She laughed, amazed he actually seemed serious. "I can't go with you to Tokyo. I don't even know you."

"It's a fourteen-hour flight. Plenty of time to get to know each other." Clay took her hands, his voice becoming soft. "We don't have to rush anything, I promise. Separate beds, all that. I just . . . really like you, Zia. I want to see where this could go."

She'd never been to Japan. She'd always wanted to go. Clay seemed trustworthy. If he wasn't, she could handle herself. It wouldn't eat into her savings too much, and she could trade out the freelance shifts she had lined up. One more for the memoir, right?

"Okay." She shrugged. "But only if you take me out for sushi."

"Really?" He cupped her face. "You're amazing." He kissed her. "Thank you." He kissed her again, deeper. "One favor: I just need for you not to put any of it on Instagram or anything."

Zia knew he didn't just mean the trip. The need for discretion made sense, but the rule unsettled her. Her ex-boyfriend had a lot of rules, too. *But Clay's not Logan*, Zia reminded herself. And she'd promised herself not to let her past—a past that unfolded over seven years ago—dictate her future. "I'm not even on social."

"Perfect. That's just . . . *perfect*." He kissed her a third time, and she giggled, giddy with the thrill of a new adventure. And a new man.

Clay rubbed his thumbs gently over her cheekbones. "Where did you come from, Zia Ruiz?"

"Special delivery," she replied. "From your dry cleaner."

Their joke from the wedding. Clay only paused for a second before tipping his head back and starting to laugh.

Zia ignored a wiggle of fear in her stomach and laughed along with him.

27

When Gorman suggested dinner at Frankies, "their spot," Henry tried not to get ahead of himself. Five years at a flower shop had taught him that human beings were capable of deep care and affection. But it seemed unlikely Gorman would've so quickly boomeranged from "Here's a stand mixer" to "Here's a gold ring." His partner was stubborn and did not like being told what to do. "Darling, I already have a mother," he'd remark when challenged. "I don't particularly want another." Yet, as Henry dressed for dinner, he couldn't help but fantasize. A ring at the bottom of a glass of champagne, glinting like a treasure on the ocean floor. The prospect felt like a door opening, and the relief was palatable. Henry didn't dare expect. But he hoped. He hoped, so much.

Which is why Gorman's announcement came as a particularly unpleasant shock.

"Let me make sure I'm hearing this correctly." Henry put down his wineglass, careful not to raise his voice. Even outside in the garden, they were seated quite close to the couple next to them. "You want to put on your snail play with some young guy from your class, and you want to spend ten thousand dollars of our savings doing it."

"We'll get the money back, Choo-Choo." Gorman's face was alive with excitement. "In ticket sales. It's an opportunity. For me. For *us*."

This seemed like both an afterthought and a stretch. "Who is this boy? Graham?"

"Gilbert. Oh, just a cute young thing with a particularly good connection. Connections, really—he said his aunt could help us find a top director. This could be the first step. My play. Onstage." Gorman hadn't been this enlivened since being cut off in traffic by Bette Midler. "They review off-Broadway plays, you know."

"They?"

"The *New Yorker.* The *New York Times.*"

Ah, the lifelong scramble for approval. First parents, then friends, then East Coast media. "When?"

"HERE programs years in advance—"

"Years?"

"—but, they had a slot open in September. If we can come up with the money, we'd start casting, well, tomorrow."

September. Months away. A server hovered, offering to refill their fifteen-dollar glasses of wine. Henry dispatched him with a grim smile. "Ten thousand dollars is a lot of money, Gor. Especially if we're not certain we'll get it back."

"It's an investment!"

"Yes, and all investments are ultimately gambles, aren't they?" Henry pushed his plate aside so he could thread their fingers together. "Sweetie, I just . . . I just thought we'd be using that money for something different."

"What, exactly?"

In the long run? Maybe adoption-agency fees. Diapers, childcare, cheesy matching pajamas for snowy Christmas mornings. "For a wedding."

Gorman actually looked confused. "Whose wedding?"

Henry felt like he'd just been slapped.

"Oh, *oh.*" Gorman got it. "Well—I mean . . . One day . . ."

Henry kept his voice calm. "When?"

"One day. In the future."

Henry's entire body constricted. He instructed himself not to cry. "Do you not want to get married?"

Gorman sat back in his seat. "Darling. I know I have a youthful zest, but I'm from a different generation. We didn't grow up expecting to get married: that was all bourgeois nonsense. It's still a bit of a new idea for me."

This "new idea" had been New York State law for a decade. It was so frustrating being in this position: wanting something his partner didn't want to give, that society technically allowed him, but didn't always celebrate. Something that straight couples expected and usually got, in a way that was not just easy, and feted, but also ascribed as normal. Henry felt needy and pissed off and sad. "Well, it's not a new idea for me. And it's what I want."

"Why?"

"Why, what?"

"Why do you want to get married?"

Anger streaked in Henry's chest even as he knew he wasn't angry with Gorman. He was angry with himself. Why, after everything, after coming out dozens of times over the years and living as honestly as he knew how, couldn't he tell the truth?

Because he wanted children. "Because I love you."

"And I love you. I don't need a ring or a piece of paper to tell me that. That's the truth."

Henry couldn't tell Gorman what he wanted because Gorman wouldn't agree, and then he'd have to live a compromised life *or* go through the harrowing process of untangling himself from someone he lived and worked with, who he still loved. *That* was the truth.

"Henry." Gorman caught his gaze and held it gently. "I'm not saying never. I just need more time. And, in the interim, I really want to put on my play. I'm not sure how many more chances an old guy like me is going to get. It's my baby."

And it was this that almost broke Henry. But they were in the nice garden of a nice restaurant, surrounded by dozens of other couples who were all keeping their shit together, despite the cruelty of modern life. Henry took a deep breath and let it out slowly. "You're not old. And, sure, you have my blessing. Let's just keep talking, okay?"

"And continue our great conversation," Gorman said, with warmth. "For as long as we both shall live."

28

Liv's peaceful Sunday morning was shattered by someone pounding on the brownstone's front door for a full ten seconds. "Jesus Christ, *coming*!" She pulled open the door, careful not to spill any coffee from her *My Favorite Season Is the Fall of Patriarchy* mug.

Savannah was holding out her phone like she was presenting Liv with an Oscar.

"If you think I can read that without my glasses, you're in for a rude shock when you're my age," Liv told her.

Inside and bespectacled, Liv peered at the screen. "What am I looking at?"

"Our Instagram!" Savannah was practically vibrating. "I know you said you didn't want to start one, but I did—"

"Savannah!"

"And look—we have three *thousand* followers! Kamile posted about us—"

Liv looked over her glasses. "You're kidding. Why? How?" Then, peering into Savannah's tote bag: "What's all this?"

Savannah shoved the glittery WELCOME HOME DAVE + KAMILE! sign back in the bag. "I might've *lightly* ambushed her at the airport. Turns out she'd just forgotten to post with all the post-wedding craziness. But I offered to drive her home, and she ended up writing the *nicest* thing." Savannah read aloud. "'Absolute dream to work with @Savannah_Ships'—that's me—'and #LivGoldenhorn. Cannot recommend these two talented wedding planners from @InLoveInNewYork highly enough.' She only posted an hour ago, and we already have *six* email inquiries."

Liv scrolled through @InLoveInNewYork's Instagram account.

"There's a picture of me on here." In a meeting with Kamile in the front office. Liv was pointing to the seating chart and Kamile was smiling. It was a pretty good shot, candid and natural. Savannah had obviously used some kind of filter—was that still the lingo?—because her skin looked, well, young.

"There are a lot of pictures of you," Savannah said. "And me. We're the brand."

God, there were dozens of photos on the account. How surreal to see the last few months of her life reflected back in such a colorful and charming way. "Wait, did you say six inquiries?"

Savannah nodded, beaming.

"For partial or full service?"

"Both!"

This seemed to mean—it sounded like it meant—business. Customers. *Money*.

The elephant sitting on Liv's chest hauled to its feet and ambled away. She let out a long, grateful breath. *Finally*.

Her phone rang. "Yes, this is Liv Goldenhorn . . . On . . . Instagram? I mean, yes, on Instagram . . . Oh, thank you so much."

Savannah whispered to her, "I put both our cells on the new website—" Her own phone rang. Another inquiry.

Liv Goldenhorn still didn't know why Eliot had played matchmaker in bringing her and Savannah Shipley into each other's lives. But right now, with the early-summer sun streaming through the front window and an eager-sounding customer on the other end of the line, she didn't care.

The truth would present itself in due course.

PART TWO

IN LOVE IN MANHATTAN

29

As the weather heated up, so did wedding season.

The wedding-planning business was a long game. Full-service planners would generally start working with a couple at least ten months out, overseeing every detail from save-the-date cards to after-party nosh. But while In Love in New York was starting to plan for clients who were getting married the following year, they didn't have many marrying over the coming summer: those folks had taken one look at the infamous pigeons-and-bees review from last November and flown the coop. It was Savannah's idea to promote a special for day-of coordination: a modest fee to show up on the big day and run a wedding they didn't actually plan. This was where Savannah got her first peek into the wide spectrum of weddings in New York. There was the one with the WASPy couple who incorporated the hora, not because they were Jewish, but because the boisterous chair dance just seemed like fun. The one where someone's uncle who, in lieu of giving a toast, read his recently published essay on the future of driverless cars. The rich-kid weddings where everyone was on coke. The sober weddings were everyone drank Coke. The first dance to that song from *Dirty Dancing*, complete with a passable lift at the end. They even ran a solo wedding, a new trend originating in Japan, where single women married themselves.

But despite the fact Savannah owned half the business, Liv still treated Savannah like hired help. Clients assumed Savannah was Liv's assistant. Liv complained that Savannah made the coffee too weak, that she used too many exclamation points in her emails, that she was too intimate with clients. "They're not your *friends*," Liv warned. "Don't overpromise. Or get too close."

Savannah ignored this advice. She'd been raised with an open-door/no-ask-is-too-big policy. Which is how she found herself spending an entire weekend hand-addressing three hundred save-the-dates for a tearful bride who'd run out of time. "She's paying us," Savannah protested weakly, starting envelope number 126. Her wrist was already burning.

"Not to do this," Liv said, almost smugly.

Liv was good with boundaries and expectations, even if, to Savannah's taste, it made her come across a little cool. But it did suit the client base. In the South, you waved at every car and smiled at every stranger. In New York, pedestrians and drivers were in a constant battle for the road, and smiling at someone resulted in an odd look or pickup line. Brides in the Big Apple didn't have time for endless hours of cozy chitchat.

Liv explained her sales system: inquiry (usually via email), intake interview (ideally coffee, in the front office), mutual approval, custom quote, negotiation, close the deal. Her contracts and quotes were good, but Liv recorded intake interviews on yellow sticky notes, then typed them into Word documents saved to her desktop. Mind-blowingly archaic.

"We could set up a CMS—a content management system—to keep track of everything," Savannah suggested. "And some plug-ins in our in-box to help keep everything in a pipeline."

Liv scoffed. The doorbell rang. "My system *works*. Remember," she added, "don't overpromise."

Vanessa Fitzpatrick and Lenny Maple met the old-fashioned way. Online. For their first date, they planned to see *Jurassic Park* in Central Park, both being fans of outdoor entertainment and Jeff Goldblum. A boisterous summer storm had other ideas. As fat drops splattered and scattered the moviegoers, Vanessa and Lenny ran hand in hand to the park's boathouse restaurant overlooking the Lake, to wait out the deluge with a glass of pinot. Four hours later, they were still there. They hadn't stopped talking since.

Their wedding was to be held at the Harvard Club in Manhattan, a dark wood, old-world social club for the alumni of the Ivy League. The venue was to appease Vanessa's father. General Tucker Fitzpatrick was a West Point grad with a master's from Harvard, retired military, and a fan of tradition. "In general," as Vanessa put it. Lenny squeezed her thigh supportively. He was skinny and kind-eyed, with shoulder-length hair tucked behind large ears. The couple exchanged a glance stuffed with a thousand unspoken words. While perfectly poised, Vanessa's painted fingernails twisting the ends of her long blond hair gave away her concern.

"All I want," she said, articulating each word carefully, "is for my father to walk me down the aisle on my wedding day. I know it's old-fashioned: the idea of a man giving away his daughter. But it's what I've always wanted. And maybe, it'll bring us back together." She exchanged a glance with her fiancé. "My dad and I haven't really talked in a few years."

In her intake interview, Vanessa shared with Liv and Savannah that she'd been dreaming about her wedding day since she was six. The vision of herself in a dramatic ball gown of tiered white tulle had been the very first indicator that the male body she'd been born into had been a "clerical error." Vanessa had come out as trans in college and transitioned to female five years ago. Savannah had been extremely nervous to meet the couple. She'd never met a transgender person before and was terrified she'd make a slipup or break some unspoken rule. But then Vanessa and Lenny started sharing their heartfelt plans for a wedding that honored their community as well as their love for each other. They were excited and loving and clueless about how to pull it all off. Just like every other couple. All Savannah's worries flew out the window. She admired Vanessa's determination. The idea of standing up to her own father over anything felt foreign, even frightening.

"I think that's lovely," Savannah said. "I'd want my dad to walk me down the aisle, too."

Liv asked the bride-to-be, "Have you told your father that?"

Vanessa shook her head.

Liv gave her an encouraging smile. "We can certainly help facilitate that conversation when he arrives."

They moved onto music selection for the cocktail hour—jazz classics that invited ("Let's Fall in Love"), flirted ("I've Got a Crush on You"), and declared ("Yes Sir, That's My Baby"). But the pending arrival of General Fitzpatrick underscored everything with panicked violins. When the doorbell rang, Savannah felt it like the crash of a cymbal.

General Tucker Fitzpatrick was the kind of man who sucked all the air out of the room and all other buildings in a one-mile radius. And it had nothing to do with size. He was only five foot six, with the compact build of a bulldog and dark hair combed neat. His handshake was crushing. As he sat on the pale pink sofa, Liv attempted light banter. They parried awkwardly for a few minutes about traffic and parking before Liv steered the conversation to logistics.

"Vanessa and Lenny would love to include you in the ceremony."

"Well, I'll be there." General Fitzpatrick spoke to Liv. "Just like I said I'd show up here."

Liv looked at Vanessa.

Vanessa nodded. Sweat beaded her upper lip. "Dad."

He tipped his head, indicating he was listening, without actually meeting her gaze.

"Dad, I know you've already expressed you don't want to do the father-daughter dance with me—"

"No one wants to see me dance," the general said to Liv. "A brick wall has more rhythm."

"I know, Dad, and I told you that's okay," Vanessa said in a way that indicated it really was not. "But it would mean a lot to me, and to Lenny, if you at least walked me down the aisle."

The general rubbed the space between his eyebrows. "I don't think you want an ugly old badger like me up there."

"Actually, I do," Vanessa said.

He let out a tense breath. "My knee's been playing up."

"It's twenty feet!"

The general snapped, "Look, I'm not going along with this dog and pony show, okay?"

Vanessa froze.

Lenny swore under his breath.

Savannah couldn't stop herself gasping. She hadn't imagined he'd actually say no. It was Vanessa's *wedding day*. That happens *once*.

Liv took a deep breath and calmly dove in. "Well, let's think this through. It is, of course, *tradition* for the father of the bride to walk his daughter down the aisle. And the terrific thing about traditions is they're human, like us. They change as we change."

The man's face remained eerily unmoved.

"General Fitzpatrick." Savannah took the reins. "It really is such an honor to be able to give your daughter away. Especially to a wonderful groom like Lenny. And as father of the bride, you—"

The general interrupted. "Can we all stop saying that?"

"Saying what?" asked Savannah. From the corner of her eye, she saw Liv flinch.

"*Father of the bride.* I'm sorry, but whatever it is you've become, Adam: it's not a *bride.*"

It landed like a bomb. Hard heat shot into Savannah's body, rippling every muscle.

In a low voice, Vanessa said, "Please do not use that name, Dad."

"It's your name. The name I gave you. The name I gave my son." The general's voice was close to breaking. "First I lose your mother. Then you go and do . . . *this.*"

Lenny raked both hands hard through his hair. "I'm so sick of this."

Liv raised a hand. "Lenny, let's try and stay—"

"Do you realize how strong this woman is? How much she's been through?" Lenny was on his feet. "And now all she wants is for you to walk her down the aisle. One day. One goddamn day."

The general's face was blotchy with anger. He rose from the pale pink sofa and moved toward the door. "I'm not listening to this crap."

"Dad, please." Vanessa got to her feet. "I'm only doing this once. I never ask you for anything. I know things between us are tough, but weddings bring people together. I think we'll both regret it if you're not an important part of my day."

"I don't know who you are anymore." The general met Vanessa's eyes for the first time. "I don't know what any of this is. How can I walk someone I don't even know down the aisle?" He pressed one shaking hand to his face. For a moment, it seemed he might cry. Then the general drew in a thick breath and squared his shoulders. "I am sorry, Adam. But I just can't." He nodded curtly at Liv and left the room.

"I'm sorry." Lenny was red-faced and wiping his eyes. "Babe, I'm so sorry."

"It's okay," Vanessa whispered.

But Savannah didn't think it was.

After the couple left, Liv leaned back in her chair, gulping some coffee. "I try to keep an open mind about everyone, but wow—he's going to make it hard. Oh, well: if Vanessa wants him to walk her down the aisle, that's what we want."

Savannah nodded. She felt the same way. Her instinct had been to hug Vanessa tearfully and promise they would *absolutely* have her father walking her down the aisle. But she was glad she hadn't: she couldn't guarantee that. Maybe Liv was rubbing off on her.

Liv handed Savannah the mess of sticky notes she'd been scribbling on in the meeting.

Savannah accepted them gingerly. "What should I do with these?"

Liv flapped a hand about, reddening. "Put them all into that CMS plug-in thing you've been yammering on about. And then, I don't know, show me how to use it."

A huge swell of warmth made Savannah smile. She'd always respected Liv. But now, she was actually starting to like her.

"Good coffee," Liv added, turning back to her computer. "Why don't you make another pot?"

30

The sun rose blood-orange over the beautiful, smoggy sprawl of Tokyo. Clay slipped on his leather jacket and checked the time on the clock next to the hotel bed. "I should be back by seven. There's a gym downstairs. And the concierge can probably recommend somewhere to get lunch."

Zia finished lacing up her boots. "I'm going to get the train to Shibuya, find somewhere for a traditional breakfast, and explore for a few hours. Then I'll head to Harajuku for lunch—gyozas, definitely. Do the Meiji Shrine, walk along Omotesando Avenue, people-watch for a bit, then end up on the observation deck of the Mori Tower for sunset and a sake. But I'd love to meet you for dinner."

Clay looked, frankly, amazed.

Tokyo exceeded Zia's expectations. The person she became when far from home was her template for living: open and good-humored, confident and curious. She loved who she was when the only agenda was learning, experiencing, and stepping outside the day-to-day. Her senses felt sharper, treated to the smell of salty miso, the taste of chewy ramen, the sight of so much color and life.

Spending time with Clay was effortless, a new language she some-how spoke fluidly. When he slipped his fingers into hers as they explored the crowded Shinjuku Chuo Park market, browsing vintage kimonos and 1950s toys, it didn't even register it was the first time they were holding hands. It just felt normal. She loved watching him interact with the locals, gracious and genuinely interested. Over late-night dinners in quiet, elegant restaurants, she grilled him on Radical Water, the clean-water initiative he'd started. He was so engaged and enthusiastic about the cause: how far Ugandan girls and women

walked to get water that just made them sick, how much of a difference one well could make to an entire village. How clean water was
linked to climate change. Being a performer had become a means to
an end for Clay. "I don't want to belong to a world where someone
like me gets all this privilege with no obligation to the millions of
people who live on less than two dollars a day."

Polite servers whisked their empty plates away. Clay wasn't famous
tonight. He was just an American, on a date with a woman he couldn't
take his eyes off. Under the table, she rubbed his calf with her foot. "I
love how passionate you are. You really care about people."

"Don't you?"

"Of course. But my impression is people in your position can just
donate a bit of money and leave it at that."

"But the planet is dying. It's an emergency."

Zia's heart swelled, her crush finding more justification with every
passing minute. "I totally agree."

Clay kept his word about separate beds, booking Zia her own
room. On the second night, she joined him in his bed, and they made
love. It was as exhilarating as discovering the new country she was
in. Their mutual desire, impassioned and primal, felt like delicious
delirium. She came first. And then, again. Afterward, as they lay together in a newly vulnerable space, Clay shared that he liked to be
dominated.

"Dominated?" Zia repeated, stunned. "Like, S and M?"

He shrugged, tracing his fingers up and down her arms. "I call it
power play, but you could call it that."

Zia had been dominated in bed, but not in a "power play" way. In
a sex-with-an-asshole way. "I've never really done anything like that."

Clay explained that kink was about communication and boundaries. If she wasn't into it, no problem. If it didn't feel good, they'd
stop. They'd have a safe word. He was direct and unembarrassed, but
he wasn't trying to talk her into it. If she was curious, they could try
it. Baby steps. "Maybe, when we're back in New York," he offered.

Zia pictured handcuffing Clay to the bed. Telling him what he
could and couldn't do. The idea felt like a piece of heavy furniture
being moved out of her way. "Maybe."

The more Zia thought about calling the shots in the bedroom,
dictating when he came, when she came, the more she liked it. In-

triguing, tantalizing, but also safe. On their last night in Tokyo, she sashayed into his room, wearing just the hotel dressing robe. He grinned and went to tug it open.

"Uh-uh," she admonished, her heart beating fast. "No touching."

He quirked an eyebrow. "Okay."

"Lie back on the bed. Hands above your head. And *don't move*."

Clay obeyed.

For hours.

As they climbed back aboard the private jet to return stateside, Clay was light and relaxed, joking with their pilot and flight attendant. His manager, Dave, pulled Zia aside. "Whatever you're doing, keep doing it. I've never seen that bastard so happy."

As summer spread itself sunscreen-thick over New York, Zia Ruiz and Clay Russo started seeing each other. In secret. As Clay explained, as soon as the press knew they were dating, they'd be hounded and Zia's personal life would no longer be personal. Trolls would come out of the woodwork. Her online footprint would be mined for information. "They'd be obsessed with getting a photo of us," he said, unable to hide his annoyance. Privacy gave the relationship space to breathe, and grow, he said. And they'd have lots of time together, since the job in Mozambique unexpectedly fell through. The project lost funding. Zia expected to feel disappointed. Instead, she felt relieved. Excited. There'd be other jobs, and her feelings for Clay were growing.

If they were out late and Clay's security gave the all clear, occasionally Clay would stay over at Darlene's. Darlene had sworn to take-it-to-the-grave secrecy, as had Zach, who'd popped by one night and ended up bonding with the actor over a shared love of nineties British rock bands. ("That guy seriously has the world's best body," Zach told the two women. "I can say that because I'm comfortable in my manhood.") But usually, it was safer, and more convenient, to stay at Clay's penthouse apartment. Zia had complicated feelings about the wraparound terrace and California king bed. Her ex had soured the taste of unearned luxuries. The only luxury she needed was time with Clay. Truthfully, Zia was happy to be discreet about her relationship. Minimizing it would help if things didn't work out, and more important, it avoided having to tell her sister. It was easier to enjoy getting to know an interesting new person, and push the past away.

"What's with you?" Layla demanded. "Are you getting laid?"

Around them, Lucy and Mateo pinwheeled, cabin-fevered and crazed. A summer storm had canceled Sunday afternoon at the park, so they were stuck inside. It felt like a hundred children were bolting around the one-bedroom apartment. Seated on the sofa, Zia lifted her legs to let a squealing Lucy scamper underneath. "I'm happy."

"*I'm happy?* What does that mean?" In another life, her sister could've been a detective. She pointed at Zia's neck. "Is that legit?"

Zia fingered her new necklace. 光: the Japanese symbol for light, on a delicate chain. Clay had surprised her with it on their last night in Tokyo. She was pretty sure it was real gold. "I got it in Chinatown for five bucks."

Her sister's eyes stayed on her, waiting.

Zia slipped the necklace under her T-shirt. "Fine, I'm seeing someone."

"Another finance guy?" Layla's question was sharp. It really meant, *Another asshole like Logan?*

Zia shook her head. "No. He's a . . . gardener. His name is Tom."

"Tom," Layla repeated the name, testing for the truth.

"He's a good guy. Nothing like . . . Tom's sweet."

"Good." Layla swigged wine from a Winnie the Pooh juice cup.

Zia frowned. It wasn't even 4:00 p.m.

"Self-medicating," Layla muttered, massaging her knees. Pain flickered over her face.

"Are you taking your arthritis medication? Can I help?"

Layla scowled and rolled her eyes. She welcomed help around the house and with the kids, but her health always seemed off-limits. "So, what, is Tom really ripped?"

"He's good-looking. But it's not just that. He's really kind. And smart. And funny." Zia smiled, thinking about their silly inside jokes and running gags. "But he's also really sensitive . . ."

"Okay, okay." Layla snorted a laugh. "I get it: you're gonna marry Tom."

"No, I'm not!" Zia couldn't imagine telling anyone about Clay, let alone *marrying* him. As much as she focused on Clay as a person, who he was to everyone else was undeniable. Clay Russo had millions of followers on Instagram. They could order takeout from any restaurant in the city and never worry about what it cost. Last night he was texting with Steven Spielberg. Marrying him was as likely as moving to the moon. "I'm really not."

"Yes, you are. It'll be dope. You'll live in Brooklyn and make babies and become a mom with me. Hashtag mom life. Get ready to drink a lot." Layla refilled the juice cup and raised it in a toast. "You got pictures?" Zia's phone was in Layla's hand.

"No!" Zia snatched her phone back.

"Whoa, chill out. Delete your nudes and show me your future hubby."

The funny thing was, even if she told her sister the truth about her relationship, Zia had absolutely no evidence. Clay never took random selfies of them, so Zia didn't, either. The only proof was the necklace, which could've come from anywhere, and their texts, which could be from anyone. The truest proof was her memory. Love was abstract: it was a concept, a shared agreement. Maybe that was what made love so magical, so delicate. In this three-dimensional world, we crave the ethereal. The certainty of something that barely exists.

"Layla, I'm not going to marry Tom."

"Why not?"

"He lives in LA."

"LA? So what, you're gonna start spending all your time there now?" Layla looked testy. "Also, he's a *gardener* and he lives in LA? Why is he out here?"

Zia tried not to flounder. "He's more like a landscaper. He, um, designs gardens for famous people."

Layla's face lit like a match. "Famous people like who?"

"No one."

"Famous people like who?"

"No one."

"*Like who?*"

"No one! I don't know!"

Layla laughed. "Calm down! I don't actually care." She sipped her wine, amused. "Look at you. Getting all riled up."

Zia took their lunch plates to the kitchen.

Layla trailed her, wiping the nose of a whiny Mateo, whose leg cast was covered in wonky Sharpie scrawls. "Omigod, what if he knows, like, Beyoncé. We can pretend to be his assistants."

"What? Why?"

"We can swipe a coaster or something. You know how much people will pay for celebrity shit online?"

"Layla!" Zia popped the trash can lid. "You can't joke like that."

"I ain't joking." Her sister's eyes glinted. "I think this is dope. You want my advice? Keep Tom happy. The closer you are to insane wealth, the better chance we have to catch some crumbs." She leaned against the doorframe that separated the living room from the kitchen. "You still have the looks."

But Zia was only half hearing the words. On top of the trash was a scrunched-up bill: Layla's credit card. Fifteen thousand four hundred and twenty-two dollars. Zia stood frozen with her foot on the pedal of the trash can, staring at the ungodly amount.

She was used to her sister having problems. But this was a different kind of problem.

"Zia?"

Zia jumped. Panicked, she slid the scraps into the trash. "What?"

"When are we gonna meet Tom?"

Layla had insurance. The bill was probably for the emergency room visit for Mateo's broken leg, and she just hadn't been paid back yet. Because her sister didn't have a spare fifteen dollars, let alone fifteen thousand. "It's way too soon."

For the first time, Zia didn't just feel apprehensive about her sister finding out about Clay. As she started on the dishes, the kids clambering over her like a jungle gym, Layla making more bad jokes about stealing Tom's clients' stuff, Zia actually felt afraid.

31

Sam wanted to call Liv and ask her out to dinner, so he procrastinated by cooking. Mole sauce, from scratch.

Each step a small, fragrant piece of the puzzle. Dry roasting the chilis and tortillas. Blackening tomatoes and tomatillos. Blending both with chicken broth. Onion, garlic, peanuts, raisins, thyme, cinnamon, cloves, and spices sautéed, then blended. Mixing everything together with hunks of dark chocolate, more salt, more broth. He'd learned the recipe from his host family when he was living in Oaxaca in his twenties. The trick, his *abuela* insisted, was timing. You couldn't rush a single step. *Todo tiene su tiempo.* Everything has its time.

Finally, the rich, red-brown sauce was finished and simmering, making his newly rented garden-floor apartment smell rich and deeply delicious.

Pick up your damn phone and call!

He paced the kitchen as her cell rang. It'd been so long since a woman had made him feel this way: anxious, elated, slightly obsessive, slightly scared. He was almost hoping it'd go to voice mail when she picked up. "Hello?"

"Sam!" he said, a little too loudly. "Is me, and I'm calling you, Liv." He leaned against the counter, eyes squeezed shut, wincing. "Hi."

"Hi," she replied, sounding a bit surprised. "How are you?"

"Grunderful." *Oh, for Pete's sake.* "Great. Wonderful. You?"

"Busy. Which is also grunderful." Then: "Savannah, don't mix up those name cards, they're for two different weddings." Back to him. "Sorry. What's up?"

"I was wondering if"—*you'd like to have dinner with me. You'd like to grab a drink. You like Mexican?*—"you got the menu I sent you. For the Fitzpatrick-Maple wedding." *Coward!*

"Yes, I sent my notes back. Didn't you get them? Savannah set up a new email, and she probably didn't—"

"Oh, no, sorry—here it is. Went into my spam for some reason." It hadn't. "Good call on the lobster. Perfect time of year. And green-pea risotto for the vegetarians, nice."

"Well, you're so good at it. You're a very talented chef, Sam Woods."

In pleased surprise, he brought his free hand down hard, hitting the wooden spoon sitting in the mole, flipping it out. Dark red sauce sprayed all over the ceiling, like a savory Jackson Pollock. "Oh, fu— antastic. That's fantastic you think that."

"That one." She was talking to Savannah again. "That's really cool, actually. But maybe change the font color to that red you had before?" Then back to Sam. "We're designing a new logo. It's a mad- house in here. Training someone new, et cetera."

"I'm jealous," Sam said, wiping up a puddle of mole. "I wish I had a partner. In work," he hurried to clarify. "It gets lonely on my own. In the kitchen," he rushed to add. "I'm not a sad, lonely guy or anything."

Liv let out a laugh. "Well, I'm a sad, lonely woman, so if you want to join my club, you're absolutely welcome."

Was that an invitation? Before he could figure out what to do with it, he heard a doorbell at Liv's end.

"I have to run," she said, "Client meeting. Guess I'll see you at the Fitzpatrick-Maple wedding. Looking forward!"

"Me too! Bye, Liv."

"Bye, Sam."

He hung up.

Well. That was an epic failure. But she did say he was a good cook. *Very talented* were her exact words. And dating post-divorce would be baby steps. And stepladders, Sam thought, turning his attention to cleaning a ceiling decorated in red mole.

32

Darlene Mitchell liked being in control. Of her brain. And her body. And of her heart. She did not like feeling as if her heart was bounding around outside her body. She wasn't even going to think of the reason's name. She needed to think about *herself*. Her career. Her future. One she was not going to threaten with a preposterous "fake relationship" that'd drag on for months. "Dating" a privileged white guy as some kind of tokenized prize would destroy her integrity. She'd make that twenty-five grand on her own, even if it took another ten years of working bougie weddings and crappy open-mic nights.

She'd played with he-who-should-not-be-thought-about at a half dozen gigs since the night at Babbo, but had skillfully managed to avoid one-on-one conversation, as well as his many texts. Instead, she focused on translating the effect of he-who-should-not-be-thought-about's kiss into something productive. Lyrics. A hook. A feeling, a tone. It was so much easier for Darlene to write about feelings than to feel them. Writing about feelings gave some distance, and some practical use, to the messy, complex, vaguely embarrassing experience of having them.

He's my dark secret; she thinks he's a keeper.

It wasn't about Zach. It was probably about Zia and Clay.

He's my dark secret; she thinks he's a keeper. She let the lyrics slip and slide over a thousand different iterations of the rhythm, trying to find the one that fit. Writing songs and making music was one of the few times Darlene disconnected from conscious thought, losing track of time, of logistics, of the sense of her own body, even identity. If she was in the zone, as she was now, she felt cut off from the world, connecting with something mystic. *He's my dark secret; she thinks he's a keeper. She likes to run, but he makes her stand still. . . .*

The doorbell wrenched her back into the present.

Zach stood in her doorway looking like a rumpled rock star who just woke up. He was wearing an unironed white button-down pushed up at the sleeves and light-wash summer jeans that were probably expensive. His eyes traveled past her cropped tee, landing with glee on her hot pants. "Now *that's* why I didn't call. I knew you were a secret minx." He prowled in, ogling every inch of her skin. "Good lord, Mitchell."

Darlene snatched a kimono from the back of the bathroom door and smothered herself in it. "What are you doing here?"

Zach had visited Darlene's one-and-a-half bedroom apartment exactly zero times. It was only a walk-up—no doorman or elevator like Zach's place—but it was cute and charming, and Darlene kept it nicely decorated. Zach's eyes roved over framed photos of her friends and family. A signed poster of Janelle Monáe. A bookshelf of Zadie Smith, Proust, and mortifyingly, a sticky-note-filled self-help book that promised badassery and wealth.

"You're such a Virgo." He yanked open the fridge. "Um, why is everything labeled? Don't you live alone?"

"Zia's crashing here."

Zach made a show of searching the fridge. "And her food is . . ."

"If she gets groceries, she won't get confused." Darlene shut the fridge door and positioned herself in front of it. "What are you doing here?"

"Can't a fake boyfriend pop in to see his fake girlfriend unannounced?" Putting both hands on her hips, he easily moved her aside.

The sensation zip-lined through her body, landing in her lower stomach. "Look, I thought it all through and my answer's no. I'm sorry, but I can't be your fake anything."

"What? Why?"

"Because it's risky! And unprofessional. And—" The kiss outside Babbo played back, slowed down with an orchestral score. She doused it in kerosene and lit it on fire. "Distracting."

Zach's confidence faded. "I got the impression you were . . . into it."

"I was pretending."

She expected him to look offended or laugh the idea off. Instead, he deflated, and sat down on her couch. "Oh."

Oddly, she wanted to console him. She sat next to him. "C'mon, Zach. It'll never work."

He looked pained. Which was sort of . . . sweet. "Please, Mitchell? Pretty please? I get that kissing me repulses you and that I'm definitely *not* your type. But you're literally the only person I can think to ask who my parents would actually approve of."

Mark and Catherine's twin looks of surprise flashed in her mind. "Yeah, I don't think your parents approve of me."

"Of course they do!" Zach exclaimed. "You're smart and sophisticated and career-driven and a bunch of other things that I most definitely am not."

Darlene's throat tightened. "That's not what I meant."

It landed. Zach waved the idea off, reddening. "My sister is marrying a *Korean woman*. And honestly, they couldn't be happier."

Darlene took a deep breath. This could partly be explained by the fact Zach wasn't American. "It's different," she said. "Korean . . . African American: it's different."

Zach's gaze rested on her. Listening.

"You know—not all racism looks the same. Look at the pay gap. Asian women make way more on the dollar than Black women. And white guys make the most of all."

"I know. It's gross." His voice was quiet. "I really like it when you tell me stuff like this."

"Oh, I didn't realize I was your private African American studies tutor. I'm going to need my own office. And benefits."

"That's not what I mean," he said, bashful. "I'm just saying, I like when you do. I want to be a good ally. I want to be, like, woke."

In spite of herself, she felt oddly touched by his earnestness. "Start with not saying *woke*. I can say that: you can't."

"Okay." Zach nodded. "Noted. Look, I know my parents are terrible, and yes, dealing with them would be part of this. I want freedom from them too. But I promise they're not totally insane, and they do actually like the idea of us being together. It really won't be much work, and you'll get an album out of it. Which I'll play on for free if you want. I'll literally do whatever you want for the next seven hundred years."

He was begging her to let him pay her to kiss her. And Zach was a good kisser. Too good. "Well, I guess I'd need a contract."

"A contract?"

"Yes, this Virgo needs a contract!"

"Okay, okay. I'll get one drawn up. So you're in?"

No. I'm not going to debase myself for money by letting you put that hot, eager tongue into my— "Fine, *fine*."

"Thanks, Dee." He took her hand, his blue eyes sincere. "You're a real friend."

Friend? She'd only ever thought of Zach as a necessary evil. Darlene pulled her hand away. "I better get back to work."

"Not so fast." Zach brightened, swinging back into his usual mode: entertainer. "It has come to my mother's attention that despite my assurance you and I are deeply in love and engaging in regular bouts of horizontal folk dancing—"

"Ew."

"—you are entirely absent from my digital footprint."

"Meaning?"

"Meaning we need to be just as obnoxious as all the other coupled fools and document our happiness." He held up his phone and fluttered his eyelids. "For social media."

"Your mom follows you on social?"

"*Stalks* is a more accurate description. Nothing gets past her. She makes MI5 look like a bunch of bumbling idiots, and I don't know how much longer I can tell her you're just very private about online PDA. I figured we shoot a few here, then go for a jaunt around the neighborhood. I can pepper them all in over the next five months."

"On which account?" Darlene had a public account for their duo and a private account for herself.

"Yours, obviously. I think Mum's already requested to follow you."

Unless she texted every single person who followed her, that'd make her friends think they were together. Zach was, objectively, good-looking—there'd be some cachet in casting him as her boyfriend. But he was also Zach. She imagined her book club texting behind her back.

Doesn't she know he's f*cked half of NY? ◗◗◗

Srsly thought she was smarter than this 😩

Darlene drew the kimono tighter. "I don't know."

"Fine." He flipped off the couch and headed for the door. "I'm not going to beg. Anymore. I'll find someone else who wants to fund their first EP for appearing in a handful of selfies."

Anxiety gripped her. It'd take years to save twenty-five grand. She needed progress. Forward momentum. "I'll get changed."

"No need." Zach was back on the couch. "Lose the kimono and get over here, minx."

She rolled her eyes. "At least let me do something with my hair."

"Like what?" His gaze brushed her fuzzy natural curls.

"I don't know. Maybe a wig."

"Would you wear a wig to Netflix-and-chill?"

She shrugged. "Probably not."

"Then just leave it as it is. I think the 'fro is so much cuter anyway," he said, sounding genuine.

Darlene felt surprised. Then, flattered.

Zach whipped his phone up. "Oh yes, that's so cute. Look at you being all shy and adorable."

"Zach!" She laughed, batting at him.

"Oh, that's good! Cuteness overload. Blowing every cuteness meter we have! Can't even handle the cuteness!"

"You are such a dork," she told him, giggling.

He gave her a crooked grin back. His button-down was undone enough to glimpse a small scruff of chest hair. His hair was sticking up in the heat. Tousled. Sexy. If he really was her boyfriend, she'd lean over and kiss him.

"All right, got some winners there. Now, scooch a little closer."

She shifted next to him, until their legs were pressed. He smelled like sandalwood soap, mixed with something distinctly masculine. Distinctly Zach. She had the urge to wrap her arms around him and crawl into his lap.

"Lean in." He held the camera up. In the small screen, their two faces smiled back at her. Like a real couple. Zach pressed his lips to her forehead. She closed her eyes, savoring the feeling. "Aw, so pretty." His voice was close and soft. She opened her eyes. "The photograph," he clarified. "I'm a regular Diane Arbus."

Darlene bit back a smile. "Diane Arbus photographed freaks."

"Did she? See, Dee, I *am* just a pretty face."

Again with the Dee.

They shot more pictures: noses pressed together, both pulling funny faces, pretending to be surprised, then mad. Sweet but tame.

Zach licked his lips. "Okay. I think all we have left is, um . . ."

She knew what was coming. What she wanted, with surprising urgency, to happen. The idea corkscrewed through her chest, landing between her legs. "I guess we have to. As gross as kissing you is."

"Oh, so gross," he quickly agreed. "Really unpleasant."

"Maybe I should, um, take off the kimono? Just so it looks like a different day." She stood and let the colorful material slip off her shoulders. He watched with the panicked excitement of a young man getting his first lap dance. Which she was basically giving him. Now in just her cropped tee and hot pants, she gestured clumsily at Zach's lap. "Where should I . . ."

"Where do you want . . ."

"Should I just . . ."

"Works for me."

Sitting in Zach's lap was the most physically awkward thing she'd ever attempted.

Unless she was onstage, Darlene resided in her head. Being in her body, obeying its wishes and demands, felt reckless. Even dangerous. *Stop thinking*, she told herself. *Just feel*. She nestled into him, and relaxed. When Zach held the camera out, she almost forgot why. "Are you ready? For . . ."

She could feel his heart. Which was beating alarmingly fast. "Disgusting PDA."

"Right. Right, disgusting."

Their lips were inches from each other. She ran her fingertips down his cheek, feeling the light rough of a day's stubble. This permission to touch him felt stolen. Criminally exciting. Slowly, she moved toward him. Perhaps their first kiss was an anomaly: so passionate and intense because it'd been a minute since she kissed anyone, and Zach just happened to be the one to break her dry spell. But as soon as their lips touched, it was clear that first kiss was no one-hit wonder.

This time, there was no tentativeness. She sank into Zach, for a slow, lush kiss. His hand rubbed up and down her back. Up and down, each stroke sending her deeper and deeper into woozy pleasure. Zach was so good at this, this back and forth of lips and tongue and shared breath. Always, a consummate improviser.

She was barely conscious of straddling him. All of a sudden her legs were hooked around his waist, and the inside of her thighs were pressing against his hips. White-hot bliss. Everything about them fit. Everything felt right, an effortless bridge sailing into a chorus you want to sing along to at the top of your lungs.

The pace quickened. The kiss turned messy, graceless. His hands were on her ass, pulling her into him, at the point where they both felt the most heat. She groaned and pulled him onto her, needing to feel his full weight. Now they were sprawled out on her sofa, Zach on top of her. Their bodies found a rhythm, grinding in sync. His mouth was on her neck, licking and sucking, kissing her skin until she was moaning, pulling at his shirt. One of his hands was inside her tee, inching up over her stomach toward her breast, and she wanted—she needed—him to touch her nipple—

Zach's phone dinged. It was on the floor. Definitely not documenting all this.

Darlene paused, breathless.

Zach pressed his lips to her neck. "Ignore it."

His phone dinged again.

And Darlene just *knew* it was a girl. Maybe one of many. Who Zach was currently sleeping with. Exactly the kind of thing that'd make her the subject of her book club's casual, pitying gossip. She pushed him off her.

"Dee, wait—"

They were close, they were this close to—she couldn't even think about it. Darlene hauled herself upright, facing away from him, trying to drown out the wall of noise her body was making. "I'm not doing this for your entertainment. Don't give me a reason not to trust you."

She could hear him sitting up. When he spoke, his voice was uncertain. "So—that's it?"

Darlene tossed him an annoyed look. Through his pale jeans, she saw the hard outline of an as-yet-unwitnessed part of Zach's anatomy. Something he'd referred to more than once as his "Jolly Roger." The sight of it sent a fresh wave of blood gushing to her face. What would he do if she reached out and touched him? Held his gaze, deliberately, as she did?

"You should go."

There was another painfully long pause. "Okay. I'll just use the loo."

He disappeared down the hall. Checking the bathroom door was closed, Darlene dipped a finger between her legs. Her underwear was soaked. Her entire body felt heavy and sweet, like an overripe summer fruit that needed to be plucked. Intellectually, she knew Zach wasn't a friend, let alone a lover. But her body had no idea. It had just learned its new favorite song.

By the time Zach came back out, Darlene was standing by the open window on the other side of the room. She'd wrapped the kimono around herself as tightly as a sushi roll. He offered her his phone. "Photos turned out great."

The sight of them making out would send her over the edge. "Please, no. I don't want to lose my appetite permanently."

"Well, you'll see them when I tag you." He rocked back on his heels, attempting "peppy." "So how about a neighborhood wander? We could get a soft serve at Milk Bar and I could do the whole licking-it-off-the-top-of-your-nose thing."

The idea made her tingle violently. She clenched hard to make it dissipate.

"My sister's down to meet up," Zach added deliberately. "That's who was texting me."

She wanted to believe this. She didn't know if she did. "That was Imogene?"

"*Yes*. Darlene, I'm not— Look, I only want to hang out with you."

He sounded tense and sincere. But even if he was telling the truth, it was too late now. She'd already pulled the plug. "I have to work on some lyrics."

He let out a rough, exasperated breath. "Fine." He strode for the front door. "So how do we sort out this contract, Mitchell?"

The boundary should feel good. For some reason, it didn't. "I thought you were going to sort it out."

"Oof, I don't really have the brain for all that legalese." Disdain colored his words. "My sister is the brilliant one. I'm just comic relief. The heir and the spare! I'll pay, just run the lawyer's name past me first so I can try to find out if they know Imogene, or Mina. Christ, that would be an embarrassing way to get caught."

Darlene followed him to the front door. "Of course you have the brain for legalese; you're really smart."

"Ha!" He was already out in the hallway, heading down the stairs. "Zach, wait!"

But the spare was already gone, the front door to her apartment block banging loudly as he left.

33

Summer was growing season: the warm weather coaxing even the most stubborn varietals into full, lush bloom. And just as the delphiniums and gardenias and dahlias began to open up and show their true colors, Henry watched Gorman come to life. Casting had begun for *Tears of a Recalcitrant Snail*.

"It's so thrilling to hear my words read by actual actors." Gorman buzzed around the kitchen, opening one drawer, then another. "The director is incredible. A New School grad—we were lucky to get her."

"And everything's going well with Gilbert?"

Gorman opened another drawer. "Yes."

Was it Henry's imagination or was Gorman blushing? "What are you looking for?"

"Wine opener."

"There." Henry pointed to the cutlery drawer. "Where it always is."

"Rehearsals start soon." Gorman began pulling the cork out. "I'll need to be there every day."

"But you're just the playwright."

"The playwright sits in on rehearsals for rewrites." Gorman spoke in the authoritative-and-offended voice he used when he just learned something five seconds ago. "That's industry standard."

Henry served two generous bowls of chicken chow mein, garnished with green onions and sesame seeds. Gorman poured them both a glass. They sat across from each other at the dining table, draping linen napkins over their laps. Gorman switched on *Dancing with the Stars*, put it on mute, and asked Alexa to play Chopin.

"So I'll be there from five every night. Oh, this is delicious, Choo-Choo. How'd you get the chicken so—"

"Wait a sec. From five p.m.? Every night?"

"Every weeknight."

Henry stared at Gorman. "What about the shop?"

Gorman fussed with his napkin, not meeting Henry's eye. "Yes, well, I was thinking we get that part-timer back in for a few weeks. She was good; you liked her."

Henry's chopsticks paused midway to his mouth. The shop was open till 9:00 p.m. over the summer. Twenty hours a week at twenty dollars an hour. "So not only are we spending ten grand on getting this thing up, now we have to spend four hundred dollars a week on a part-timer to cover you? Starting when?"

Gorman's gaze darted from his bowl to his wineglass. "Rehearsals start, er, tomorrow."

This was typical.

Their therapist, Jennifer, a gray-haired septuagenarian who wore cat-eye glasses and Bakelite necklaces, once said they could choose to lean into their similarities—shared interests, strengths, and values—or focus on their differences. Differences that included Gorman's tendency to obfuscate conflict. Or how Henry handled holiday cards and birthday presents while Gorman just showed up. Or how Henry was close to his family, while Gorman tolerated his. Or how— Henry stopped the spiral. They were different. But they loved each other. And love was a choice.

"Fine," Henry said. "I'll look into it after dinner."

Gorman looked surprised. Then relieved. Then suspicious. Then sheepish. "I can look into it. It's my problem to solve."

"That would be great," said Henry. "Turn on the volume. I want to see this cha-cha."

"Choo-Choo loves the cha-cha," intoned Gorman and Henry giggled. It was true. He did.

Later, after Gorman had cleaned up and they'd made love (they usually had sex after *Dancing with the Stars*), Henry watched Gorman sleep. The soft rise and fall of his lover's chest always soothed him.

When Henry was younger, he thought that loving someone was supposed to feel good, always. If it didn't feel good, that wasn't good love. But over the years, he'd learned that loving someone meant doing things he didn't want to do. Go to a party he didn't want to go to. Indulge a hobby he found tedious, a friend he found boring, a behavioral pattern he found annoying or strange. Pay for a part-timer to allow his significant other to pursue an expensive, time-consuming pipe dream that was quite possibly motivated by a crush on someone barely out of college.

Henry was up for it. Gorman was his best friend and he'd made many compromises to give Henry the life he wanted: the flower shop was primarily Henry's dream. Gorman was good with numbers but he didn't enjoy balancing the books like he enjoyed writing. Henry trusted that eventually, his partner would provide what he needed. But that hadn't stopped Henry from shoving the stand mixer deep into the back of the pantry, unopened. The sight of it still made him upset.

34

When Savannah lived in Kentucky, she'd cook dinner for her room-mate-slash-best-friend, Cricket, every other night. Chicken tacos or mac and cheese eaten in front of the TV while they caught up on the always-depressing news or a ridiculous reality dating show. It was one of the best parts of her day; homey, but also more fun than being home with her family. So it came as a shock to realize at the beginning of her fifth month in New York City she'd not once prepared a home-cooked meal for her Brooklyn roommates. Savannah and Cricket lived parallel lives, privy to each other's every waking thought. But Arj, the grumpy bartender; Cool Leonie, who she only ever saw leaving for or returning from an online date; and Yuli, the hippie with anxiety, ranked only a notch above strangers. Her three roommates' daily activities, relationships, and yes, meals, were a complete mystery. Living with them was like watching a scene from an unfamiliar TV show: things were happening, but it was unclear what it all meant.

It was a hot, sunny Sunday. A full day before she'd have to throw herself back into the challenge of Vanessa and her misguided father and the business of weddings. She'd cleaned her room, a precisely organized shoebox decorated with the cheerful, aspirational women she admired so much: Michelle Obama, Reese Witherspoon, Ellen DeGeneres. She'd caught up on a few text chains, gone for a run, and gone to church, a hipster Christian event in Williamsburg. It was more like a concert than a service. There was a VIP section, and the pastor wore edgy streetwear that wouldn't be out of place at New York Fashion Week. But connecting with God in the company of other Christians still felt comforting. God was real. He had a plan for her. With life changing all around her, this could still be her one constant.

She called her loving, absentminded father, Terry, which descended, as always, into an IT tutorial. "Dad, you have to flip the screen so I can see you."

"I'm making quesadillas!"

All she could see was a sliver of ceiling. "Dad, *flip the screen*."

Her father's bespectacled face filled the small screen. "We miss you, Pookie Bear. Look, I made salsa!" He tasted a mouthful and gagged. "Must've used sugar instead of salt. Okay, that's no good."

"Miss you too, Dad." She loved talking to her parents, even if it was disorienting. The life she'd left was still happening without her. Her dad's bad cooking, her mom's endless knitting, Pickles, the ancient cockapoo, perennially underfoot.

"This is great!" Terry wandered into the living room, away from the meat sizzling on the stove. "What's this called?"

"FaceTime, Daddy."

"FaceTime! How much is it?"

A dog yelped.

"Well, I didn't see you, Pickles, I'm talking to Savannah. C'mon, outside."

"Free, Dad. It comes with the phone."

"Free? How about that! So, what else, honey? You booked your flight back yet?"

"Back where?"

"Home! You said you'd be home by Christmas!"

Technically, her parents had said she'd be moving home by Christmas, and at the time, she hadn't disagreed. But the first half of the year had flown by and she was still finding her feet. What would her life even look like back home? An easy job somewhere on Main Street, drinks with Cricket and the girls at the same three bars, seeing her parents every weekend for countless hours doing who-knows-what. New York was challenging, but it wasn't predictable.

"Here's Mom, knitting a—what is that, honey? A hat?"

"I'm making you a scarf for fall, Pookie!" Sherry sang out. "Do you like the color?"

"I can't see you, I can only see Dad."

His giant forehead filled the screen. "How do I flip it? Ah, here we—" He hung up on her.

Savannah decided to make pan-fried chicken for her roommates. Her grandmother's recipe. Nothing brought people together like fried chicken. Maybe she'd bring Honey a piece. She twirled her keys as she skipped out the door.

The L train, her straight shot from Bushwick into Manhattan, wasn't running: weekend repairs. The subway, while noisy and crowded, was fast and efficient: thoroughbreds at the top of their game. Which made the rumbling city buses dispatched to cover for the train seem like slow-footed Clydesdales one misstep from the glue factory. The trip to the Trader Joe's by Union Square should've taken twenty minutes but instead took a staggering hour and a half. Oh well: onward. Savannah marched to the sliding doors, only to be stopped by an acne-sprayed employee. "There's a line," he said, pointing to it.

Mildly confused why the line for the register started outside the building, Savannah explained she didn't have anything yet.

"It's a line to get in," he clarified. Savannah almost laughed out loud. A line to get in? What, was Billy Joel playing a free concert in the frozen food section? Billy Joel was not. Instead, it seemed every New Yorker on the island of Manhattan had decided to get their groceries at the exact same time. Savannah almost had the last bunch of collard greens snatched out of her hands by a salty grandmother in a T-shirt reading *Not Your Bitch!* Savannah waded through the crowds, finally procuring everything on her list . . . only to join *another* impossibly long line that snaked up and down all the aisles she'd just combed through. The heavily tattooed girl in front of her was simply shopping as she waited, tossing groceries into her basket as the line shuffled forward. *That would've saved me half an hour.*

"All in one bag?" asked the unnaturally jolly employee.

Savannah nodded. She did not need wasted paper on her conscience. But as soon as she had stepped off the shuttle and taken the first of approximately one thousand steps home—centrally located, her apartment was not—the bag handle ripped clean off. Like the contents of a popped piñata, groceries bounced over the sidewalk and onto the street, where all three pink plucked chickens were un-

ceremoniously crushed by the departing Clydesdale. A genderqueer
hipster stopped to take a Polaroid of the massacred birds. They did
not offer to help.

Savannah carried everything that hadn't touched the sidewalk in
the remnants of the busted bag. Her arms ached. Her feet throbbed
(why had she worn heeled sandals? Stupid!). Two blocks from the loft,
a wild summer storm her weather app hadn't predicted unleashed.
By the time she limped back into the apartment, she was soaked
and sore and on the brink of tears. The only thing that stopped her
was seeing, miraculously, that all three roommates were home at the
same time. A sign! Yuli, Arj, and Leonie were slumped on the two
beat-up sofas in the common space, scrolling through their phones
in companionable silence. She didn't even wait for them to inquire as
to her groceries, before announcing her intention. Fried chicken for
all. "Which I'll have to buy again, somehow," she added, trying not
to sound pissed. "But I will, and it's happening. Dinner. Eight sharp."

Arj didn't look up from his phone. "I'm working."

Cool Leonie examined a new Pikachu tattoo. "I have a date."

"I'm a vegan," Yuli informed her, eyes darting around the groceries. "You're not planning on using my Pyrex, are you?" He dribbled a
nervous laugh. "Not, like, cool."

It was too much.

New York was exhausting and demanding and expensive, and for
what? A poky little room in a noisy loft populated by people who
didn't give two shits about her. Savannah wanted so badly to walk
into her family home, scoop up the dog, and eat ice cream on the
couch. But she couldn't. She was stuck in Bushwick. With Leonie and
Arj and Yuli, who was *still* listing the kitchen utensils she couldn't use
to make dinner for everyone.

Savannah slipped off her sandals and walked into her bedroom.
She picked up her pillow, buried her face in it, and screamed.

35

The Gowanus Whole Foods was so sparsely populated it was positively relaxing: Liv knew it was a good idea to go as late as possible to skip the dinner-rush crowd. She picked up a pineapple and studied it thoughtfully. She loved pineapple, as did Benny, but preparing it was such a chore. So much peeling and slicing and removal of spiky bits. Was the hard work worth the reward? The skin was yellowish but also greenish. Was it even ripe? She took a sniff. Smelled like . . . pineapple.

"Hi." Sam Woods stood a few feet away. A snappy little zing, like a wave of unexpected citrus, zipped around her chest.

"Oh, hi." She repressed the instinct to hug him, instead offering a small wave. She wasn't expecting to see him in person until the Fitzpatrick-Maple wedding next month. A mental scan of her outfit confirmed a slouchy jersey jumpsuit and old yellow sneakers. Possibly hairy armpits. Definitely no makeup. Could be better but had been worse. The days of leaving the house in her bathrobe were thankfully in the rearview mirror.

Sam was in a 'Shwick Chick T-shirt and broken-in blue jeans. A shopping basket swung from his forearm. His biceps bulged modestly. The chef nodded at the pineapple. "Looks like you're making a momentous decision."

"I can't tell if it's ripe."

He tugged at one of the spiky leaves. It didn't budge. "Nope." He selected another one. This time, the leaf came off easily. "That's how you can tell."

"So wise." Liv put the pineapple she assumed she was now purchasing into her basket. "What other tricks have you got up your sleeve?"

Sam selected a cantaloupe. "This should feel heavier than it looks." He weighed it in his palm. "And it should smell sweet." Raising it to his nose, he sniffed. "I'd say this one is pretty much perfect."

She took it. Not because she was planning on making a fruit salad, although that was clearly how this shopping expedition was going to turn out. Because of those kind, crinkly eyes that seemed, for some strange reason, to like what they saw. "How about some cherries? I love cherries."

"Hm, they're not quite at their peak yet. But I'll keep an eye out." He selected a few organic apples for his basket. "How's Big Ben?"

"Good. At my mother's tonight, getting spoiled rotten in between anecdotes about the Holocaust. How's Dottie?" Liv asked, more surprised than pleased that she'd remembered Sam's daughter's name.

"Great. Very into *Peppa Pig*. With her mom this weekend."

"That must be tough." Liv had ruminated on what would've happened if Eliot had recovered. She had no idea if they'd have gotten a divorce or tried to figure it out.

"At least we're still friendly." Sam grabbed a knob of garlic. Bits of papery white skin floated to the floor. "I've known couples where it got really ugly. Then it's really hard on the kids. Claudia—that's my ex—we still do Christmas and birthdays and school stuff together."

"How mature." A word that probably would not have been applied to a separation from Eliot. Her gorgeous, gregarious husband had been funny and frank and always the first on the dance floor. But he was also irresponsible, unreliable, and self-centered. A hypochondriac who regularly diagnosed indigestion as stomach cancer. An extrovert who needed constant stimulation. Around Eliot, Liv was always *on*. So now, without his enormous, unwieldy needs, she had time for her own. Needs like the time to sit. To let long thoughts unspool. So the question was:

"What do you need?"

Liv blinked twice. She hadn't been saying all that out loud, had she? "Me?"

"Do you have a list, or is it all up here?" Sam tapped his temple. "In that brilliant brain of yours?"

Liv used to make shopping lists, itemized and neatly printed. She'd get back in that habit. She liked having a list. "I think I want to make a pie."

"Ooh, nice. What kind?"

"When I was a kid, my mom would put a tin of condensed milk in boiling water until it turned into caramel. She'd pour it into a pie shell and serve it with vanilla ice cream. It was outrageously good." Liv looked up at the man next to her. How strange to have a desire for something and state it out loud. Conjuring the abstract into matter. "I think I want to make that."

"Well then," said Sam, looking around. "Let's find the baking aisle."

They finished their shopping together, conversation skating around topics like cooking and kitchen staples. Safe topics: Sam was a vendor, and she was a business owner trying to repair her company's reputation. But he was so easy to talk to, she kept forgetting they weren't old friends. Being with Eliot had been like wearing couture. Being with Sam was like slipping into comfy sweats.

Outside, they were going opposite directions. "Nice to run into you." She hitched her tote bags of ripe fruit and pie crusts over her shoulder. "See you at the Fitzpatrick-Maple wedding."

He dawdled. "Yes, see you then."

She gave him a nod, and took a few steps in the direction of her car.

"Do you want to get dinner with me?"

The question came so unexpectedly, it pulled her up short. "What, like . . . like, a date?"

"No! I mean, yes. Yes, like a date. You and me. Eating. Me paying for eating. Unless you want to split, which would also be"—Sam drew in a breath, face starting to flame—"highly acceptable. Not right this second. Just . . . soon."

The concept of a date was akin to alien technology. Everything about it felt beyond the realm of comprehension. "When?"

"Whenever. Wednesday?"

"Oh, Wednesday I have a thing." Liv was surprised to find herself lying, each word layered on top of the last like a messy brick wall. "A cooking class. I mean, a yoga class. A hot yoga class where you cook a hot meal after."

"Liv, it's fine." Sam retreated a step, his smile wounded but intact. "My apologies. I misread . . . I won't mention it again. Good night."

He walked evenly to the end of the street, rounding the corner to disappear.

Liv caught herself staring after him, returning with a thud to the reality of her four bags of heavy groceries. She couldn't stop a sinking sensation that it was all going to go to waste.

36

"We don't have any butter?" Savannah's voice cracked. "What kind of monsters don't have *butter*?" She slammed the fridge door shut and pressed one hand shakily to her forehead. A woman on the verge of a dairy-related breakdown.

The buzzer sounded.

Thank. *God.*

A minute later, Honey placed two uncooked birds on the kitchen table, furrowing her brow at the pile of crushed groceries. "What's going on?"

Through gritted teeth, Savannah explained the failed dinner attempt and now-absent roommates, topped off by the indignity of a lack of butter, a key ingredient in everything worth eating.

Honey rubbed her shoulders. "Hey, it's okay. I'll go to the bodega and grab whatever you need. Then you and I can cook dinner. Even if it's just the two of us, we'll have a time."

The familiar, selfless hospitality prompted Savannah to take Honey's hand. "Oh, Honey, that's so sweet of you. But I can't make you cook on your day off. Making fried chicken in this dinky little kitchen is probably the last thing you feel like doing."

"The only thing I feel like doing is hanging out with you. And trying out your grandmother's recipe. Gotta get to know the competition."

Savannah met Honey's eyes. The color of Hershey's Kisses. She was so lucky to have found someone who felt like home in a city so far from it. They melted into a hug, the afternoon's tension draining away. Honey could always reset her mood.

"That would be wonderful."

And just like that, everything was okay.

As the rain got heavier, the kitchen got cozier. Together, they made Nanna's fried chicken, the recipe for which called for a fresh buttermilk brine and a handful of crumbled Cheetos in the coating. Savannah pan-fried the different parts, filling the apartment with the warm, salty smell of a backyard barbecue. Honey put a pan of cornbread in the oven and made a bowl of creamy grits. They traded playful insults and made each other laugh. It was both easy and enlivening to be in Honey's presence. Two Southern girls in New York City, chasing their dreams, figuring it out. Honey got excited around food, talking and moving faster than usual. She was at ease in the poky, understocked kitchen, a deft improviser. Her confidence in all things made Savannah feel confident, like what she wanted in life was actually attainable. But more so, as a single girl, it was just so nice to have someone to rely on, for a laugh or a chat or comfort when things went wrong. Just like she used to rely on her best friend from home, Cricket. Except where Cricket was small-town, Honey was big-city, the one who introduced her to the restaurant reviews in the *New Yorker* and hidden speakeasies dotted all over Brooklyn. As the collard greens simmered on the stovetop, Savannah opened a bottle of cheap white wine. They toasted to friendship.

"Speaking of," Savannah added, "I have something for you."

She handed Honey a T-shirt. When Honey unfolded it, she saw it was emblazoned with a Honey's Fried Chicken logo. Honey's eyes went wide. "What? How . . . ?"

"It's just a first draft," Savannah was quick to point out. "I'm not much of a designer. I just thought you could wear something like it when you do all this"—she indicated the food—"yourself."

Honey couldn't stop staring at the shirt, a gap-toothed grin plastered on her face. "This makes the whole idea a thousand times more real. *Thank you.* And now, I don't have to ask my ex about it."

Savannah sipped her wine, curious. "What's going on there?"

Honey sighed, folding up the T-shirt carefully. "Me and Rowan, that's . . . complicated."

"How so?"

"We got together when I first moved to New York. Rowan means a lot to me. Always will. I just can't figure out if we're meant to be."

"If you're not meant to be with him, what sort of guy are you meant to be with?"

Honey met Savannah's gaze. As if she knew the answer to that already. Savannah scanned the available men in Honey's life. Guys who worked at the restaurant, friends who'd drop by for happy hour, a few colleagues from past jobs whose meals Honey always comped. None was a match for Honey: she was so much better than all of them combined. Being unable to guess the riddle felt like losing equilibrium.

"Who?" Savannah pressed. "Do I know him?"

A strange smile played at Honey's lips. "Savannah. It's not—"

The front door unlocked. Leonie was soaked. "My date was a total psycho!" She dumped her bag and busted umbrella. "Oh my God, it smells amazing in here!"

Savannah cleared the kitchen table and set it with cloth napkins and the nicest plates she could find. As Honey began serving pieces of chicken, Yuli arrived home.

"The cornbread's vegan!" Savannah pointed eagerly. "And so are the collard greens!"

Yuli took a seat.

The four feasted. Leonie regaled the table with online dating horror stories and Savannah laughed so hard she got a stitch. She had no idea Leonie was so funny. Yuli ate three pieces of cornbread and canvassed for advice about a job he was going for at a charter school. He taught eighth-grade English and wrote young-adult romance novels under the pen name Summer Winters. Again, a revelation. Just as the wine ran out, Arj returned home from his shift. "I was going to drink this in my room, then try and get some REM," he said, extracting a bottle of burgundy. "But if there's fried chicken going . . ."

"Best fried chicken I've ever had." Leonie reached for a drumstick. "Yuli, you're missing out."

"Screw you," said Yuli companionably. "I have my cornbread. No!" He batted Arj's hand as he tried to take the last piece. "Mine!"

"That reminds me," Leonie said, chewing on a drumstick, "of the time I went on a date with this guy who wouldn't stop eating off my plate."

The table groaned, laughing, as Leonie launched into another anecdote.

Honey met Savannah's eyes across the table and grinned, as if to say, *You did it!*

We did it, Savannah wanted to say. *We're a team.* She hadn't thought about a girlfriend like that since Cricket. She and Cricket were a team: a two-for-one deal. In fact, Cricket kind of looked like Honey. Both were small, spunky brunettes with big smiles and expressive eyes. *Maybe I have a type*, she joked to herself. *A girlfriend type.*

She paused, a forkful of cornbread frozen midair. Honey met her gaze. Blinked. Turned to Leonie, laughing a bit too hard at whatever she'd just said.

Which is when it all started falling into place.

Her roommates were yawning and stacking the dishwasher by the time Honey was at the front door, a bag of leftovers in hand.

"Honey?" Savannah kept her voice low so that her roommates wouldn't hear.

"Yes?"

"About Rowan . . ."

Honey looked up at her quizzically. No. Expectedly.

Everything was shifting, the horizon at a slant. "Rowan's . . . not a guy. Right?"

Savannah couldn't read what was in Honey's eyes. Apprehension? Relief? An eternity passed before her friend slowly shook her head.

"No. She's not." Honey leaned up on her tiptoes and brushed Savannah's cheek with a kiss. "Good night, Savannah." She headed quickly down the stairs and into the rainy, summer night.

The following morning, Savannah and Liv sat side by side in the sunny front office of In Love in New York. Before them were two open laptops and two oat milk cappuccinos. Dolly Parton, a shared favorite, played softly on the Sonos. To an outside observer, a perfect tableau of women at work. And yet neither woman had moved in the last fifteen minutes.

Why hadn't Honey told Savannah that she was gay? The first and most horrifying thought was that Honey, whom Savannah believed to be her closest friend in New York, thought she wouldn't be accepting. Judgmental. Which she *wasn't*.

Okay—maybe it had been a shock.

It had definitely been a shock.

The queer people Savannah knew were obviously gay, definitely gay, no-surprise-to-anyone gay. Lavinia, a witchy lesbian in her study group. Ryan, her middle school "boyfriend" who currently did musical theater. Scout, a beautiful nonbinary model who floated around campus, making weird art-house films that no one understood but everyone went to see because Scout made them. Lavinia and Ryan and Scout were different, and that was great: live and let live. But while they were different to her, Honey was the same. Honey was like her. And so if Honey was gay, then all bets were off and literally anyone else could be too. The rules of who and what you were felt paper-thin and flammable. And that made Savannah uneasy.

But not as uneasy as the fact Honey hadn't returned any of her last three texts. Logically, Savannah knew they'd speak again, and soon: they were adults (basically); they'd clear this up. But to make herself feel bad, she imagined that the previous night was the last time she'd ever see Honey. That one kiss, her lips warm and light on Savannah's cheek, and then, poof. Gone. The idea carved out her chest and left her hollow.

Savannah exhaled noisily, strong-arming herself back to the present. The Fitzpatrick-Maple wedding. The recalcitrant father. "If my father couldn't walk me down the aisle, he'd be crying more than me."

"Mmm," said Liv.

"There must be some way of appealing to the general's better self."

"Mmm." Liv's eyes were glazed, somewhere between dreamy and worried.

"Liv!" Savannah peered at her. "Have you been listening to a word I've been saying?"

"No," Liv sighed. "I haven't."

Savannah caught a whiff of intrigue. "Why not?"

"No reason. Let's get back to . . . whatever it was you were talking about."

Savannah folded her arms. "What's going on?"

Liv sighed and recounted the World's Most Awkward Date Rejection, explaining there was absolutely no way she could go out with Sam. No way she was ready or that it'd even be appropriate. He worked for her. And it hadn't even been a year since Eliot had died. "I mean, I couldn't very well say yes, could I?"

Savannah's eyes were the size of beachballs. "Of course you should go on a date with Sam! Everyone should go on a date with whoever they want!"

Liv swayed back from Savannah's gale-force enthusiasm. "I don't think so. I mean, look at me."

"I am looking at you. And I see a smart, successful woman who he is obviously attracted to. And why wouldn't he be?"

Liv frowned. "What about Ben? Isn't it too soon?"

"Of course it is—for Ben. But you don't need to tell him you're going on a date. It's just one little date!"

Liv looked down at her baggy overalls. "What would I wear?"

"I'll help you get ready!" Savannah was out of her chair, kneeling besides Liv. "It'll be so fun, and I'm actually dying to give you a makeover."

"You think I need a makeover?"

Savannah nodded, fervently. "Nothing drastic. We could just shape your brows and do a bright lip, and I bet I can do something cool with your hair—"

"Okay, point taken. I suppose I could ask Henry and Gor to babysit."

"And if they can't do it, I will!" Savannah clapped her hands. "You deserve this, Liv. And Sam is wonderful. You'd make the best couple."

"'Couple'? What happened to 'one little date'?" Liv was up and pacing. "So, what, should I just call him back and accept? Isn't that a bit weird?"

"I don't think he'll mind." Savannah bounced back to her feet. "This is so exciting! And honestly, I need the distraction."

"From what?"

From soft lips and summer tans. A woman's curves; a topographic map she felt called to explore . . . "Nothing," Savannah replied. "Go on, call him!"

Was there something perverse about convincing her dead ex's widow to go on a date with another man? Yes. Yes, there was. Yet somehow, that's what was happening.

Liv scrolled through her phone, locating the chef's number. She winced, rubbing her stomach. "Gosh, I feel so weird."

"Weird how?"

"Like I'm hungry. Or getting sick. Or like I'm . . ." Liv's eyes pulsed in recognition. She met Savannah's gaze, looking a bit sheepish. "I think I'm excited."

Savannah smiled. Liv deserved this.

Everyone deserved to love, and be loved. However they damn well pleased.

Liv tapped Sam's number. "Here goes nothing."

37

Zach's thumbs moved cautiously over his phone. *Hey! I'm here!* No, too eager. *Yo, downstairs*. Too American. *Miss Mitchell, your chariot awaits*. Oh God, could he be more pretentious?

"Bloody hell." Zach tossed the phone onto the passenger seat and raked his hair with both hands. What had gotten into him?

That was obvious. Darlene had gotten into him.

He'd always had a low-key crush on his bandmate, but it was filed in the Never Going to Happen folder, with a backup copy in Not Her Type and Off-Limits (re: Work). But one impulsive lie followed by two mind-blowing kisses had set those folders ablaze. The kiss outside Babbo started replaying, a tape so worn it was a wonder it hadn't snapped. The feeling of her mouth against his: eager, passionate. All burning heat and crazed, pent-up desire. God, it was hot. So much more than a kiss. It was a floodgate smashing. A hundred wild horses stampeding. It'd taken him a full week to recover. The idea of texting Lauren or the handful of girls he was chatting with promptly seemed ridiculous. After you fly private, you can't go back to coach.

And then there was the photo shoot. If the kiss had been hot, the shoot had been a nuclear explosion. The way she pulled him on top of her, *definitely* into it, both of them writhing and groping and grinding against each other—

"Oh, Christ," Zach moaned. He'd always been horny. But Darlene Mitchell was turning him into thirteen-year-old boy. It was mortifying. The only way he could control himself was by remembering that Darlene was unquestionably out of his league. There was a photograph of her meeting President Obama while she was at Princeton hanging in her hallway! Darlene was beautiful and brilliant. And he was a ridiculously randy idiot.

"Go away!" he hissed at his lap. "Seriously, Jolly Roger, get the hell out of—"

Someone rapped on the passenger window.

"Darlene!" He hurriedly adjusted his pants, abandoning the plan to open the door for her. She slipped in next to him, filling the car with the sweet smell of coconut and jasmine. Somehow she managed to look both adorable and ravishing. Zach did not let his gaze linger on her luscious mouth. Or her perfect breasts. Or her gorgeous ass.

"Were you yelling at your penis?" Darlene asked, placing her purse on the back seat.

"No, don't be absurd." Zach started the engine. The Mercedes purred to life. "You look glorious," he added, risking another glance over as he pulled into traffic. "I like the wig. I mean, I prefer the 'fro, but I like the wig."

Darlene smoothed her neat, glossy bob. "Not a lot of Black people in the Hamptons. Didn't want to freak your folks out with the 'fro."

"Ha. They could handle it."

Darlene flipped the passenger mirror down, checking her makeup, which was, as always, immaculate. "I want to make a good impression."

"You always make a good impression."

Darlene's smile was complicated. "That's because I'm always trying."

Darlene did always look incredible when they were out in public or onstage.

"But, you're not *always* trying around me. I seem to recall some pretty ripe T-shirts and very baggy sweats at rehearsal."

She laughed, relaxing into the passenger seat. "Okay—maybe I'm not *always* trying around you."

"I like that," he said. "I like I can see all sides of you."

"Most sides," she corrected.

"With a view to working my way to all," he replied, unable to resist wiggling his eyebrows at her until she laughed and punched his arm.

They chatted easily as they drove. Not having to look into her sizzling dark eyes helped. They always had plenty to talk about, but their banter was slightly different than usual. Usually, Darlene was annoyed with him about something he no doubt deserved—she was in the right, and he was in the wrong. But tonight, she was gentler with him. Laughing at his jokes and even paying him a few offhand compliments. He had to admit, it was pretty damn lovely. By the time they pulled up to his parents' driveway, he was sad the two-and-a-half-hour car ride was over. And more than a little anxious that the reality of his family's wealth, a reality he chose not to underline, was now on full, gaudy display. Darlene took in the size of the estate, bemused.

"Okay. You didn't mention your parents lived in a palace."

"Damn, I should've warned you." They parked in the circular drive and ascended the sweeping front steps. "I'm such an—"

But his next word—*idiot*—was cut short by Darlene's lips pressing firmly on his. When she pulled back, he blinked, stunned.

"—incredibly fortunate person. What was that for?"

Darlene blushed and ran her tongue over her bottom lip.

"Come on in, lovebirds," Imogene called from the front door. Behind her, his mother was peering at them, intrigued.

"For the ruse," Darlene said, taking his hand.

Of course: Darlene's kisses were for the money. Dinner with his family was in their newly signed contract, after all. And even though the whole lunatic scheme was his idea, Zach was surprised by how much that hurt.

38

Darlene accepted a warm hug from Imogene and a *Don't wrinkle my outfit* air-hug from his mother, Catherine. She shook hands with Zach's father, Mark, and was introduced to their house manager, Debra, a brisk, friendly woman in her forties, who looked Indian or Caribbean. They exchanged a smile and small nod of recognition. Darlene was relieved not to be the only nonwhite person in a fifty-mile radius, even though Debra, despite working on a laptop and not serving drinks, was still technically staff. It was hard not to think of *Get Out.* When Debra disappeared into a study to work from one of the comfortable leather chairs, Darlene stopped herself cracking a joke about the Sunken Place.

"I thought we'd start with a little tipple on the patio," Catherine said, resplendent in a red silk wrap dress and fresh round of Botox. "Just something casual."

It was neither little nor casual. The patio was the size of a ship, looking out over a spangled Olympic-size pool and acres of immaculately landscaped green. Catherine handed Darlene a rum-based cocktail she needed two hands to wrangle.

Zach requested a seltzer. His mother looked shocked. "Zach, you're not drinking?" She said this in the same way one might exclaim, *Zach, you can fly?!*

Zach explained he was driving, laying a hand on Darlene's knee. The sensation zipped up her spine with such hot, unexpected electricity, she twitched. Reading this as reproach, Zach removed his hand.

"Why didn't you get a driver?" Mark asked. Casually, Zach's dad was in a three-piece suit, and shoes a crocodile had casually sacrificed its life for. "Don't you usually get a driver?"

"Don't you get it?" Imogene sipped her cocktail, her blue eyes flashing. "They wanted to be *alone*."

"Oh," Zach's parents said. They exchanged a slightly mystified look. Unclear whether it was because of Zach's sobriety, or that Darlene would want to be alone with their son.

The conversation moved on to Imogene and Mina's upcoming wedding, an event Darlene was expected to attend with the family. On one hand, she felt guilty. The Livingstones were investing in her emotionally, and she was lying to them. But another, less noble part of herself was looking forward to it. Not just because she'd be attending a wedding with Zach that they wouldn't have to work at. Because she'd be attending a wedding with Zach.

It was odd witnessing Zach at home with his family. Darlene was used to him being the life of the party, which was sometimes fun and sometimes annoying, but here Zach was muted. Perhaps he saw entertaining people as work. He wasn't working now. He and Imogene seemed like partners in surviving two dramatic narcissists, in a place where expectations were so impossibly high he wasn't even bothering to please them with a performance. And the irony was Zach's parents still treated him like a clown.

Zach-as-annoying-idiot was a role he'd written for himself and played with aplomb ever since Darlene met him. But it had become less circumstantial, based on fact, and more institutional, based on assumption. Zach put himself down a lot, and often set up everyone around him to do the same. *The heir and the spare.* He wasn't the spare. He wasn't inferior. He was thoughtful and sensitive and flustered by her in a way that really was very cute. Darlene had realized that if she gave Zach the benefit of the doubt, she liked him more than she expected.

She scooted her chair closer and took his hand. An almost shy smile quirked his lips in a way she found absolutely adorable. Their hands settled between the two chairs, connected.

Imogene watched with a curious tilt of her head.

After they were all well on their way to getting drunk, it was time to head into dinner. Darlene excused herself to use the restroom. Gold-plated taps and instead of a hand towel, a pyramid of tiny rolled towels the size of handkerchiefs. On her way out, an abstract expressionist painting caught her eye. Bold slashes of color, as alive as it was unapologetic. She knew this painting.

"Fantastic, isn't it?"

Darlene started at the sound of Imogene's voice. "Absolutely."

Zach's sister came to stand next to her, admiring the colorful artwork. "So spontaneous. Unrestrained."

Darlene nodded. "Joan Mitchell was ahead of her time."

An approving noise sounded from the back of Imogene's throat. "You know your stuff."

"I did a minor in postwar American art," Darlene said.

"At . . ."

"Princeton."

Darlene watched the typical expression of impressed approval flit over Imogene's face. She didn't add that Princeton was much like the rest of society—a place where she had to work twice as hard for the same reward.

Imogene looked back at the painting. "You're not really Zach's girlfriend. This is all so he gets that stupid trust." Imogene side-eyed her. Not accusatory. Just certain. "It was so obvious he was lying the night he told us. So you're not really together. Right?"

If Zach hadn't told Imogene the truth, Darlene wasn't going to. Her allegiance was with Zach. "What makes you think we're not together?"

Imogene gave Darlene an easy-breezy smile. "Darlene, you have your shit together in a thousand ways that he doesn't. I love my little brother, but we both know women like you don't go for train wrecks like Zach."

Darlene's skin burned. She wasn't sure if this was something Imogene actually believed, or if it was some sort of test. Darlene cocked her head at the painting. "It's funny: I never saw Joan Mitchell as a particularly spontaneous artist. To me, this is very controlled. Deliberate." Darlene gave Imogene an easier, breezier smile. "Guess it just depends on your perspective."

Dinner was served in a room the size of a small country. The cutlery was heavy, solid silver, sliding through the juicy steak as if it were butter. Catherine offered Darlene a smile. "So, Darlene. Imogene mentioned you're a Princeton grad. Scholarship? Sports team?"

"*Mum!*" Zach choked on his steak. "Darlene's a straight-A student!"

"Well, I didn't know," Catherine said, so unflustered it was almost funny. "I hear Princeton's quite expensive. Do you miss college, Darlene?"

"Sometimes," Darlene said. "But I'm enjoying working as a musician. I'm actually getting ready to record an album of my own songs."

Catherine's frozen forehead mimed delight. "Congratulations. One day we'll say we knew you when."

"Are you doing it with Zach?" Imogene asked.

An image of her and Zach in flagrante barged into Darlene's mind. The two of them on her couch but with distinctly less clothes. "Excuse me?"

"Are you and Zach collaborating?" Imogene clarified.

Her mind had moved so quickly to the gutter it had basically time-traveled. "Oh. Well, no."

"Why not?" asked Imogene.

Zach affected confusion. "Yes, babe: why not?" He forked some peas into his mouth and slipped her a grin. "Don't you think I'm talented?"

"Of course you're talented. I just have a sneaking suspicion you'd show up late to every recording session, drunk as a skunk," she teased.

"Hey," Zach replied, affecting outrage. "That's . . . accurate. I'm a terribly stinky creature who can't tell time. Pepé Le Pew, without a watch."

Darlene giggled.

Mark wiped his mouth with his napkin. "It's because Zachary doesn't have the brain for business."

It was like witnessing someone slap a child: a quick, domestic horror. Darlene chilled.

"Making a living out of music isn't just about boozing and parties," Mark continued. "It takes discipline. Commitment. Intelligence. Not really Zachary's strengths."

Zach kept his head down, focused on his meal. The suggestion of pink colored his cheeks.

Darlene took a large gulp of wine, hoping it would mute the angry throb of her heart. "I just want to make a solo record."

"And you probably will," Mark said. "But even for someone as clearheaded as you, it's not really a financially stable career, is it? And that's what you need, son," he added, addressing Zach.

"C'mon, Dad," Imogene said. "Plenty of people work as full-time musicians."

Mark's expression said, *Not people like Zachary.*

"I think making your own record is marvelous, Darlene." Catherine cut a tiny bite of steak. "You're so ambitious. Focused. You could really learn a thing or two from her, Zach."

Darlene let out a sharp puff of surprise. Her voice was a few decibels louder than she intended. "Zach is not an idiot."

The four Livingstones glanced at Darlene. Equally surprised.

"We know," said Catherine. "But he does have plenty of room for growth."

The roles of Darlene-the-fake-girlfriend and Darlene-the-real-person mixed and merged. She was playing a part, and speaking entirely from the heart. Which felt equally terrifying and thrilling. She kept the smile on her face but now, it had a glint of steel. "We all have room for growth," Darlene said. "But surely we can acknowledge that Zach is a very talented and charismatic musician. Perfect ear, fast learner, fun to work with. All our clients adore him."

Mark raised an eyebrow in sarcastic acknowledgment. "Being liked is not the same as being successful."

Darlene's smile dropped. She sat up straighter and addressed Mark and Catherine directly. "I'm sorry, but the way you talk about Zach is really limiting. You've raised a kind, warm, open-minded young man. He deserves your support and your respect."

Silence blared.

No one said a thing.

Zach's expression started on bewilderment, whipped to awe, before settling on openmouthed disbelief.

Darlene's mouth went dry. *Oh God. I just chastised my fake future in-laws.* Who were looking equally embarrassed and irate. Darlene coughed and got to her feet. "I'm just going to excuse myself for a minute." She took a few steps, pivoted back to grab her wine, and then beat a hasty retreat.

39

Per Savannah's suggestion, Liv ordered the Uber to be five minutes late. "There's nothing wrong with making Sam wait," Savannah assured her. "To build up a bit of tension."

Liv watched the black town car round the corner, the service her mother was convinced was a convoluted kidnapping racket. Perhaps Savannah used the five-minutes-late strategy with Eliot. The prospect didn't make Liv as furious as she expected. She still loved Eliot, but she was no longer *in* love with him—ridiculous semantics she'd always pooh-poohed but now rang true.

Savannah mimed smiling, tapping both cheeks with her forefingers. "Bye!" She waved both arms above her head, as if Liv was leaving for life on a new continent. "Have fun!"

Liv stared back, feeling out of her depth. Savannah had approached the date like she approached everything: with fervor. Like she wanted to live vicariously. Had she met someone, too? Hopefully not. The business could only handle one love-distracted person, and right now that person was Liv. Savannah Shipley would do well to focus her drive and smarts on hitting another wedding out of the park. She was turning out to be quite a valuable asset.

Ten minutes later, Liv walked into a farm-to-table restaurant Sam had suggested. It was lively without being unbearably noisy, which was good: like neck tattoos and nail art, shouting to be heard in restaurants was something best left to Generation Z. A hefty wooden bar ran against one wall, while a few dozen tables were scattered over creaking floorboards. This place was new: Liv hadn't even heard about it. The persistent evolution of the city regardless of her personal tragedy recalled the old Robert Frost quote: "In three words I can sum up everything I've learned about life: it goes on."

"I'm meeting a friend," she told the maître d', just as she spotted Sam sitting at the bar, chatting to the bartender. He was dressed in dark jeans and a denim shirt rolled at the sleeves. Even dressed up for a date, he looked like the kind of man who could chop down a tree and build a table with it. Her pulse, at a steady trot while she got ready, began cantering freely, showing off with jumps and little kicks. She hadn't felt this nervous in years. It recalled her early days of auditioning, hoping desperately to be picked from a sea of faces and invited to be someone else. But tonight she was auditioning as herself.

Liv placed her purse on the bar next to him.

Sensing movement, Sam flicked his gaze at her. And then turned back to his beer.

Was this what the kids meant by ghosting? "We did say Wednesday, didn't we?"

Sam glanced back up. "Liv! Holy . . ." Disbelieving eyes raced from collarbone to calf. "I didn't recognize you."

And suddenly, the two-and-a-half hours of preparing and plucking and painting of color onto skin and nails were entirely worth it. Liv had been worried that putting herself into the hands of Savannah Shipley would result in a look more suited to a tequila-soaked bachelorette. But the dress Savannah pulled from the back of the closet was her Elan Behzadi: black silk with capped sleeves, V-neck, falling just below the knee.

"Oh, this dress." Liv's eyes had lit up. It'd been her go-to for art openings and the theater, things she and Eliot did every other week before Ben was born. Back when she was always *on*. "It can't still fit me." But it did.

Savannah had swept Liv's hair back off her face, a bold look she'd never tried. But when paired with darkened eyebrows, a pinky-red lip, and just a hint of cream blush, she looked quite . . . chic. The only thing left was shoes. Liv was angling for black flats, even as she knew they weren't entirely right. Savannah held up a tote bag. "I brought a pair of mine to try: we're the same size. Just keep an open mind, okay?"

"All right." Liv wanted to giggle, so she did.

With the panache of a game show host, Savannah presented a pair of patent leather, sunshine-yellow stilettos.

Liv had gasped. "They're so pretty."

"I know! Aren't they fun?"

"Oh, I can't wear these." She slipped them on. Savannah was right: they were the exact same size.

"Whoa." She wobbled toward the mirror. "Don't know if I can walk in heels anymore."

"You already are."

Liv examined her reflection. It was like looking at an actress chosen to play the movie version of Olive Goldenhorn: someone thinner, younger, and a lot better-looking. She was certainly in need of a workout or twenty, but she definitely did not look shlubby. The black dress and sleek hairstyle was classy, but the heels made the whole look . . . fun. Even sexy. Not bad for almost fifty. "Are yellow heels age appropriate?"

"Liv," Savannah had said seriously, "there's no such thing as age appropriate. Wear whatever you want."

Liv flicked her a suspicious look. "When did you get so wise?"

Savannah shrugged, brushing a bit of fluff off the dress. "Maybe when I started working for you."

"With me," Liv had corrected, adding a bangle. "We work together." She busied herself with selecting a purse. But Liv did not miss the slow, thrilled smile that crept onto Savannah's face. It wasn't a smile she saw often, and it made Liv think, again, of Savannah's courtship with her husband. The idea didn't hurt her. Curiously, she felt aligned with Savannah, and the sense of mystery that came along with an exciting first.

Eliot was a question mark again: something to be turned over and reconsidered.

Now, Sam's eyes lingered on Liv's feet as they sat at a table by the window. "And I really like the shoes," he murmured, almost to himself.

Liv permitted herself a grin. "Foot fetish?"

Sam spread the napkin over his lap. "Never too old to cultivate a new interest," he said, and Liv laughed.

Two glasses of pale champagne appeared on the table, set by a woman with a buzz cut, who bowed elaborately. "On the house."

Sam introduced her as Nico, one of the owners. Nico had two sleeves of tattoos and black-rimmed glasses: the look of those new Brooklyn chefs photographed laughing on cool cookbook covers. Generous, with a slightly wicked streak.

"I sous-chef here," Sam explained, looking a little embarrassed. "But I told them not to make a fuss."

"No fuss will be made," Nico said, evidently enjoying making Sam squirm. "Just wanted to say hello." She grinned and addressed Liv. "And tell you that this is a rare breed of man."

Sam put his head into his hands.

"We all love Sam." Nico indicated the bar where the maître d' and bartender were pretending not to be watching them; caught, they both waggled their fingers in greeting. "He's one of the good ones."

Sam groaned. "This might've been a mistake."

But Liv didn't think it was. She thought it was cute. They ordered a selection of small plates, and when the champagne was drained, two glasses of a New Zealand sauvignon blanc. Even though it had been a good few decades since she'd been on a date, she still recalled alcohol as a primary component.

Their conversation was fluid, intimate; interesting. Formative years: Liv's on the Upper East Side, Sam's in coastal Maine. College: NYU, Berkeley. Childhood dreams: actress, firefighter.

"Firefighter?" Liv forked a salted peewee potato in her mouth. "I always had a thing for firefighters."

Sam cocked an eyebrow. "Maybe I'll have to ditch the cooking."

It wasn't until they were onto an ooey-gooey chocolatey dessert and glasses of exquisitely sweet port, the room emptying of patrons and Ella Fitzgerald crooning over the speakers, when the heavier stuff came up.

"We were married for fifteen years." Sam's eyes were soft and serious. Liv could tell this was a painful memory but not one he was going to burst into tears over. Eliot was a regular crier. Sam seemed like the once-a-year type.

Sam told her how they met at a friend's potluck housewarming party when he was thirty-four and Claudia was twenty-five. He brought homemade pulled-pork sliders. She brought a bottle of prosecco and a bag of Flamin' Hot Cheetos. Claudia—spin class junkie, people person, lover of salty snacks—was already a rising star in the marketing department of a youthful makeup brand. Which is where, years later, she met Anton—fellow department head, bowling league teammate, diehard Lakers fan . . . and the man she had an affair with for three years.

"*Three years*." Liv didn't intend to underline it. "Sorry. That's just so . . ."

"Long," Sam finished. "I know."

"I was going to say cruel. My husband was cheating on me for six months, and I thought that was an eternity. And then of course, there was the will."

"Will?"

Liv found herself opening up to Sam, divulging the nature of the Savannah, Eliot, Liv triangle.

He put his dessert fork down, looking shocked. "I'm amazed."

"Affairs are amazing. In the less positive sense of the word."

"No," he amended. "I'm amazed you had the strength to put it behind you and work with Savannah, day-to-day. That must be taking incredible inner strength."

Liv flushed with the compliment. "But three years. That must've destroyed you."

"Maimed. Tortured. Possibly lost a limb. But I'm still standing. And it's nothing like"—Sam paused—"I was going to say 'losing her,' but what I really mean is her dying."

There was no handbook for talking about death. But at least Sam could say the words. Eliot was dead. That was a fact.

"I've been wondering," Liv said. "What would've been less worse: Eliot dying or us having to deal with the affair. Of course, I'd do anything to bring him back, even if we weren't together. For Ben, mostly. But sometimes—and I can't believe I'm admitting this—I feel . . . relief that it happened. Because that choice was taken out of my hands."

If Eliot hadn't died and they'd had to deal with the affair, Liv would only have had her preconceived notion of being a scorned woman, a cuckolded wife, to deal with his betrayal. A role as calcified as their marriage had become. But because things happened in the weird way that they did, she'd come to see the incompatible side of her husband with fresher eyes. She met Sam's gaze. The color of butterscotch pudding, focused entirely on her.

"So, here I am."

"Dating."

Liv screwed up her face. "Don't say it."

Sam chuckled. "Yeah, it's a bit of a blood sport. Most women don't want to date a guy with a kid."

Liv finished the last bite of dessert. "I think most women just don't want to get treated like an idiot." She thought for a second. "Or raped."

Sam choked. "Did you just say *rape* on our first date?"

Liv pushed the empty plate aside. "Okay. Here's what you should know about me. I don't suffer fools. I work all the time. I love my kid, and I will murder anyone who touches so much as a hair on his head. I don't like women who speak in baby voices or men who think their dicks are some sort of passport to power or respect. And because women have been treated like second-class citizens since the dawn of time, yes, I will acknowledge the existence of rape." She sat back in her chair. "So. Are we done?"

Sam chuckled, unfazed. "On the contrary." He flagged their server down and ordered another round of port. "We're just getting started."

40

Zach found Darlene on the far corner of the patio, facing the pool. The light from under the water patterned her pretty face in shifting silver. He wanted to take her in his arms and kiss her and never stop. "Oh my God! You were amazing back there."

She let out a laugh. "I'm pretty sure your parents hate me right now."

"What? No! That was the nicest thing anyone has ever done for me." He let himself gaze into those clever dark eyes that could see right through him. At that lovely mouth that just said all those lovely things. He'd always tried to be open-minded and kind, but no one had ever reflected it back to him. It felt like there was no one in his life who challenged him, admired him, or believed in him as much as Darlene. "Thank you, Darlene."

She smiled at him. "You're welcome, Zach."

The need to touch her built to a fever pitch. Zach jammed his hands in his pockets to stop him mauling her like a hungry beast. "So was that all just part of the act? Or do you actually think that about me?"

Darlene ran her tongue lightly across her bottom lip. "I think both are true."

Stunned, happy disbelief billowed in his chest, puffing him up like a prize-winning peacock. Who cared if it was also for the money? Darlene Mitchell, world's most perfect human, did not think he was a total and complete knob. She actually, maybe, liked him. As a person. Zach could not stop a smile spreading over his face. He inched a step closer.

She inched a step closer.

"My parents might be watching us," Zach said. "So maybe we should kiss."

Darlene laughed, her eyes bright and alive. "That is the creepiest thing anyone has ever said to me."

And because she wasn't flinching or backing away, he did what he'd been wanting to do all night. Lift a hand to skim her soft cheek. Find the small of her back and slowly move her closer, until they were pressed right up against each other. Thigh to thigh. Belly to belly. Skin to skin. A clenched, anxious part of him finally settled. She was in his arms. Where she was always meant to be. He could feel her heartbeat, loud and fast, echoing his own.

"God, Dee," he managed, his words rough and unchecked. "You drive me crazy."

She pulled his mouth toward hers until their lips were hovering, almost touching, and he saw stars and planets and distant galaxies. "You too," she whispered, and then they were kissing.

Zach had kissed his fair share of women. Correction: Zach had kissed his unfair share of women. Like music, it was something he had both natural and practiced talent for. But kissing Darlene was unlike anything he'd ever experienced. There was so much passion in her body. Passion that wasn't at all obvious when they weren't kissing. But as soon as their lips connected, sensible, sweet Darlene turned into a sexy, insatiable vixen. If Zach was capable of conscious thought, he'd realize this transformation was not unfamiliar to him. Because who was the electric performer who could hold an audience's attention, moving and grooving and owning the stage? The same girl in his arms, sucking his lower lip until he groaned against her mouth.

There was no one but Darlene. They must be together, like this, always, every day, every minute, every second. His hands found the curve of her ass, squeezing both cheeks. He was losing control, the embrace turning fiery. He wanted her, all of her, right here on the bloody pool deck. Why were there still so many of these damn clothes between them?

Darlene broke it off, panting a little. "Okay, that's enough. I'm not a peep show."

"Roger that." No devouring Darlene in public, got it. He fought the urge to reach out for one more kiss.

A voice sung out from the back door. "Guys!" It was Imogene. "Dad wants to play canasta. Darlene, you're on my team."

The pair exchanged an amused look. They'd been summoned. Darlene did up her top button that had somehow become undone and straightened her dress. "How do I look?"

Zach pushed a hand through his hair, raking his eyes up and down her body as if he were a man about to lose his sight and it was the last time he'd ever get to see her. "Absolutely bloody gorgeous."

41

Darlene played two hours of canasta with Zach and his family. No one said anything about her earlier outburst, but when Zach played the winning hand, his father offered a seemingly sincere *well played* to his son. Darlene intuited the Livingstones were still processing her statement and the fact she'd dared make it in the first place. Maybe that was why the game was especially, noticeably, boisterous. Now, on the road back to New York, Darlene turned to Zach and laughed. "That was all a bit . . ."

"Bonkers," he said, both hands on the wheel. "I know. My family's a lot."

She relaxed into the passenger seat, feeling warm and a bit woozy from the wine. "Are they always so critical?"

"They've always treated me like a court jester, but the pressure to get a good job and date someone respectable"—he tossed her a grin—"is a new thing. Dad has high expectations. I mean, look at Imogene: killing it at work, marrying someone just as successful and brilliant as she is. They're both Scorpios: talk about a power couple. Mum and Dad just want that for me too."

She looked over at him, charmed. "When did you get into astrology?"

"I've always been into astrology. You just never noticed. Typical Virgo." He shook his head, and she chuckled. The highway was lined with trees. Only the ones closest to the road were visible, the rest hidden in darkness. "What about your family?" Zach went on. "What's your wound?"

And even though Darlene never talked about this, she didn't hesitate in telling Zach the truth. "Expressing love."

"Really?"

She gazed ahead at the darkened road. It felt safe, not facing each other, in the new, open space they'd created over the course of the night. "Dad's just not good at it. We can talk about work and politics and culture and stuff." She smiled, recalling their many debates at the dinner table. "And I know he's proud of me. The one time I saw him cry was when I got into Princeton. But we've never been, like, touchy-feely."

Zach checked the speedometer. They were under the speed limit. "Your mom passed away, right?"

Darlene nodded. "Car accident. When I was twelve. The other driver ran a red light."

"How horrendous. I'm so sorry."

She remembered that night in shards—two cops at the door, her father thinking that at first they'd come for him, then breaking down. Having to make her own dinner for the very first time. The night she stopped being a child. "Thanks. She was pretty great. Mom *was* touchy-feely."

"How so?"

"My mom was the heart of my family. She was the kind of person who had an open-door policy, so there were always people dropping by for dinner, always something in the oven. She could sing, too. Not professionally, just around the house, but I get that from her. And she gave great hugs. All the time. Big on hugs." Darlene wrapped her arms around herself, remembering the earthy-sweet-acidic smell of her mom's Luster's Pink hair oil. The way it felt to be small and safe in her arms. "After she was gone, my dad didn't know what to do. How to replace all that. So, he didn't. He worked, all the time. He was a good provider—I wasn't missing anything, like, superficially—but we were never *close* close." She paused, thinking. "I actually can't even remember the last time he said *I love you*."

Zach looked moved. "Oh, Dee."

Darlene had never shared this with a guy. Somehow, Zach made it easy. "Maybe that's why it's hard for me to talk about my feelings." She sighed. "Music's where I express my emotions, I guess."

"I don't know how anyone couldn't express emotion around you." He gave her a heartfelt smile. "You're very expressible."

She rolled her eyes, secretly pleased. It was quiet in the car. Darlene felt surprisingly happy, even unburdened, as they drove in comfortable silence.

Zach turned up the car's heat a little. "Speaking of music, have you written anything new for your album?"

"Maybe."

"Let's hear it." Then, as she hesitated, "C'mon. I promise not to bite. Unless you want me to."

"There's something about it that's not quite right." She sang the chorus for him. "*He's my dark secret; she thinks he's a keeper. She likes to run, but he makes her stand still.*"

"I like it." He hummed the bars, casually harmonizing. "What's not working for you?"

"I don't know. It's not . . ." She inhaled, thinking. Sometimes talking about music was like dancing about money: square peg, round hole. "Raw enough, or something."

Zach sang the lines a few more times, playing with the rhythm and pitch. "What's it about?"

You and me. "Zia and Clay."

Zach had met Clay; he knew of the secret romance. "Right, of course." He changed lanes to overtake a lumbering truck. He was a better driver than Darlene remembered. "What if you switch the pronoun to *I*?" He sang to demonstrate. "*He's my dark secret; I think he's a keeper. I like to run, but he makes me stand still.*"

The lyrics fell around her like Tetris pieces falling into place. Because it was about her and Zach: he was her secret; he was a keeper. She kept her voice as neutral as possible. "Yes. That actually works."

"You're actually welcome." Zach grinned at her. "What other lyrics have you got?"

"Nothing yet."

"Let's write it together."

The prospect was equally scary and intriguing. "We've never written a song together."

"So let's give it a go. We have got another two hours to kill."

Darlene wiped her palms in her dress, suddenly nervous. "Okay."

"So, it's about Zia and Clay, right? What's your hot take on their relationship?"

"They're lucky," Darlene thought aloud. "To have found someone special. But it's hard for them. Who he is, and everything. He's greater than the sum of his parts."

"Oooh, I like that." Zach tapped out a beat on the steering wheel, singing. "*He's greater than the sum of his parts, which doesn't make it easy on my heart.*"

"*He's not a player, he's a stayer, but he keeps himself farther from me than . . .*"

"*Australia,*" Zach finished, and they both laughed.

Goofing around was fun. But they probably could write a decent song together. Zach was as relaxed and open as she was careful and cerebral. The thrill of creation flowed into her like adrenaline. They had only two hours! She twisted to face him. "Let's do it for real."

The street was empty when Zach pulled up outside Darlene's building. They'd pretty much finished "Dark Secret": most of the lyrics and harmony and nailed down the hook. It sounded *good*. She couldn't wait to start cutting a demo.

Zach turned off the engine. "Thanks again for coming. You were brilliant tonight."

"You're welcome. It was very . . . illuminating."

"For me too." He gave her a smile that was sweet . . . but also sad. "You know you're way too good for me, right?"

"Don't say that." Darlene touched his hand. She wanted to raise it to her mouth and kiss each fingertip. "You deserve the best, Zach. I mean that."

He waited till she'd unlocked the building's front door to call through the driver's side window. "Hey, Dee? I . . . *fake* . . . kind of . . . really like you."

Darlene knew he was flirting—that the words were more true than false—and it was so radically impossible that this was the same Zach she'd known for two years. But the smell of the city soured the perfection of the car ride just a little, reminding her that she had to be sensible. Careful. No one changed overnight. The only thing certain about this entire situation was the $25,000 she was making. "Good night, Zach."

42

While she'd typically come by 'Shwick Chick when it was busy, Savannah waited until Honey was just about to lock up. It was after midnight when they sat at what Savannah had come to think of as her table, a bottle of bourbon between them like a lifeline.

"I feel like an idiot for assuming you were straight," she said, as plainly as she could. "I'm sorry."

"To be honest, I didn't know how you'd react," Honey said. "I'm still a little cautious about letting new people in."

"You can let me in," Savannah said. "Honestly, I'm really interested."

Honey said she knew she was gay as soon as she knew what being gay was. "I didn't want to be. I spent years shoving it down, hoping it'd go away. I was so ashamed. So alone. I didn't know anyone who was gay, apart from, like, celebrities who lived in a completely different world to me. Completely."

"What do you mean?"

Honey etched her fingernail into the dark wood paneling of the restaurant walls. "My family is super religious. I grew up in a part of Alabama where you wear a purity ring and sex before marriage is worse than drowning puppies. You wouldn't even recognize me back then. Long hair, makeup. Dresses, always."

"No tattoos?" Savannah guessed.

"Ha. No. I never planned on telling my parents about who I really was."

But they found out.

"I'd been talking to a girl I met online," Honey continued. "She lived in the UK; we'd message each other now and then. She was queer too, in a similar situation." Honey drew a long breath. "I forgot to log out."

"What happened?"

"My mom was hysterical. Told me I'd broken her heart. My dad told me I was disgusting, I was going to hell, all that stuff. They took me to church." Honey shook her head at the memory. "Had me exorcized."

"Are you joking?"

"I wish. Our pastor, who I'd literally known since I was a baby, told me I'd never find happiness, never find love. It broke me. I packed up my car, and left. My parent's last words were *don't come back*."

"Oh my gosh, Honey." How could anyone be so cruel to someone so warm and wonderful? Her own parents were so loving and accepting. Savannah couldn't imagine them turning anyone away.

But she'd never thought about what would happen if she brought another woman home. She couldn't imagine Terry and Sherry being relaxed and easy in that circumstance. It was just so outside what her parents expected of her. What she'd led them to believe about herself.

Honey sipped her whiskey. "That was three years ago. I moved to New York, found other queer people, worked a bunch of different restaurant jobs until I ended up here. Dated Ro, but I think we've outgrown each other. I really want that, though," she added, without quite looking at Savannah. "A girlfriend. A real relationship."

Savannah could tell she meant it. "What about your family—have you spoken since?"

"A few months ago, I got a voice mail from my dad, asking me to call."

"Did you?"

"No."

"Are you going to?"

"I don't know. Three years is a long time to feel totally rejected by your own parents—" Her words caught in her throat, almost a sob.

Savannah squeezed her hand as hard as she could, wanting to say so many things at once: *I care about you. I will never reject you. I'm here for you.*

Honey drew in a breath, regaining control. "I don't know if I trust my parents. I have to protect myself." She met Savannah's eyes, sad but resolute. "Maybe that's why I lied to you."

"What do you mean?"

Honey drew in a long, slow breath. "I don't want to get my heart broken by a straight girl."

It took a moment to land. "Me?" Savannah asked. "I'm the straight girl?" It almost sounded as if she was asking if she was, indeed, heterosexual, so she rephrased it, as a statement. "I am a straight girl."

"Right." Honey let out a mild, amused laugh. "It's just . . . we spend a lot of time together."

And when they weren't together, Honey was never far from Savannah's thoughts. She'd become the lens through which Savannah viewed the city. "Because you're my friend," Savannah shot back. "We're *friends*."

"And that means a lot to me," Honey said. "I'm just trying to point out that what we have isn't that different from . . ."

A relationship. Savannah's heart was beating so fast she was almost panting. She wanted to play dumb or laugh it off. But that would be childish.

"It's different," she said, "because I don't date girls. I never have. I'm not into that—I wouldn't even know—that's just not *me*—"

"Okay, okay." Honey held up a placating hand. "I don't want to freak you out." Her eyes shifted out the window. The street was empty, the moon kidnapped by clouds. Nothing lighting the way. "Let me put it this way. When I lived in Alabama, I was a huge football fan. I mean, we all are. Roll Tide, all that. I went to all the games, knew every player's name. But after I finished high school, something changed. I couldn't get into it. Then one day, we beat Tennessee in this epic game, nineteen to fourteen. My whole town was going nuts, and I felt . . . nothing. I suddenly realized I didn't actually care about football. I only liked it because everyone else did. Liking football was what I did to fit in." She leaned forward across the table, her brown eyes bright. "I liked it because I hadn't been given the option not to."

A faint ringing, like a distant alarm bell, went off in Savannah's chest.

Honey's words were soft in the quiet, empty restaurant. "I think life is just about figuring out what you like and what works for you, regardless of what everyone else is doing."

Savannah's breath had turned shallow. She felt like she was stark naked. She wanted so badly to push the chair out from underneath her, mutter an excuse, and scurry home, refusing to think about what Honey was implying. But instead, she picked up the whiskey bottle and poured herself another drink, determined not to run away.

43

Zia untied Clay's wrists from the slats on his headboard, still slick with sweat and breathing hard. "Is it just me," she panted, "or does that get better every time?"

"It's not just you." Clay rubbed his reddened wrists, then wrapped her in his arms, nipping at her neck. She giggled, squealing. They rolled over, kissing, laughing, completely lost in each other. Their experiments with power play were a revelation for Zia. As a man, Clay was respectful but inherently powerful. As a lover, Zia was in charge. She settled in the crook of his arm, warm, solid muscle secure around her. She'd never felt so safe. So comfortable. Clay had been in LA the past few weeks, and she'd missed him. Her fingers found the gold necklace resting in the dip of her throat. The Japanese symbol for light. She never took it off.

Outside, the sun was setting, and the city looked like a giant glowing picnic basket. So many different things would be happening that evening. A thousand different adventures, just waiting to be had.

"Let's go out," Zia said.

"Bed. Must stay in bed."

"We've been in bed all day. It's a miracle our muscles haven't atrophied."

Her lover groaned, stretching. Every muscle in his body was toned and taut, like a jungle cat. "You're right. Need sustenance. I'll cook for you!"

"You don't have any groceries. We could go pick some up?"

"Not a good idea, unfortunately." Clay pulled on the briefs that'd been torn off when the sun was still high in the sky. "I'll order some. How do you feel about . . . Italian?"

He made it sound like a spontaneous suggestion, but Italian was the only food Clay liked to eat, order, or cook. And he wasn't a particularly gifted chef. At first, keeping the relationship discreet suited Zia. But she was starting to feel claustrophobic. She wasn't entirely certain why Clay wanted to keep a giant wall between her and the rest of the world.

"Let's go out. There's a free jazz show in Central Park." Darlene and Zach were going, allegedly to maintain a trust fund–related ruse, but actually to film themselves making out while denying the fact they were into each other.

"Sounds like it might be crowded."

Zia slipped on one of Clay's T-shirts and followed him to the kitchen. A wall of windows offered a 180-degree view over lower Manhattan and the glinting Hudson River. "Baseball cap and sunglasses. It worked at Bembe."

"Bembe is a tiny underground club in Brooklyn. Central Park is . . . central. It's right there in the name."

"Okay, how about this Ethiopian place in Bushwick? It's so good: you eat with your hands, all vegetarian." Plus, there were always tons of leftovers that she could drop off to Layla the next day. She'd probably never tried Ethiopian. And it'd ease the guilt Zia felt over still dating "Tom the hot gardener."

"We could hit a few bars—"

"Babe," he interrupted her gently. "How many times do I have to say it—we can't go out in public. I want space for us to grow."

"There's no paparazzi in Bushwick."

"This"—he held up his cell phone—"is a portable film studio. That almost everyone owns."

"Then let's go somewhere romantic." Zia hopped up on one of the stools at the kitchen island. She spun in a circle, eyes closed, one finger outstretched. As the stool settled, she set her eyes on: "The Freedom Tower! I've never been on the observation deck. Maybe you could pull some strings. Go up after they close."

Clay was focused on his phone, tapping silently. She knew he was ordering groceries.

A strange, unsettled emotion unspooled in her belly. They hadn't finished discussing their plans, and he was already making them. She wanted to show him New York, her New York. He didn't seem even tempted by the idea.

Logan's face flashed in her mind. Square jaw. Cold eyes.

"Baby?" She hopped off the stool to circle her arms around Clay's neck. "Doesn't that sound fun? Apparently you can see all the way to Philadelphia."

Clay's attention was on his phone. "I'm actually not great with heights."

"What?" She laughed in surprise, unsure if this was an admission, or an excuse. "Seriously?"

"I mean, I'm not *afraid* of heights," he amended quickly. "I just would prefer not to be able to see Philadelphia from anywhere other than Philadelphia."

"But you live all the way up here in the sky!"

"Where no one can see in."

And where Zia was all alone. A prisoner in a gilded cage.

Clay tapped his phone triumphantly and held it up. "Done! Groceries will be here in an hour." He put on a very bad Italian accent, pulling her into his arms. "I'll make-a you a *delizioso* lasagna." He planted a kiss on her mouth, and then another. And another. A look of wonder warmed his gold-green eyes. "You make me so happy, Zia Ruiz."

She knew he cared about her. Clay wasn't Logan. Logan was hard and cruel and troubled. Clay was a giant marshmallow in the body of a Greek god. Last week he cried at the end of *Thelma & Louise* and wasn't even embarrassed. If she told him she was going out with Darlene and Zach, he'd tell her to go and have fun, and mean every word. But she didn't want to leave him. She didn't want to be apart. Her worry was erased, gradually but certainly, by the sweetness in his gaze.

"I just want to be out in the world with you. For you to see my real life. I love your place, but we spend a lot of time here."

Clay relented, tucking an untamed curl behind her ear. "How about dinner next Friday? I'm shooting all day but no plans at night. I'll find somewhere . . . discreet."

"Next Friday, I'm working." Zia padded toward the shower. "Wedding at the Harvard Club."

"Get someone to fill in for you."

"I need the money!" she called back, closing the door to the bathroom. The white marble glowed in the soft lighting.

Zia knew Clay respected that she worked. He let her pay for things whenever she wanted: splitting the bill for takeout or picking up their cappuccinos from the café downstairs. But the difference of their incomes was like the difference between the earth and the sun. It wasn't easy to understand or look at directly.

And adding to her stress was the fact Zia hadn't found a way to bring up the overdue bill she'd seen in Layla's trash with her sister. She'd done some research about the cost of a broken leg: even in New York, fifteen grand was high. Layla was cagey about money, and proud: she'd never admit outright that she needed help. The gentle prodding Zia tried—*How's everything going with the insurance claim? Any complications with his recovery?*—had been shut down. But it was obvious there was a problem. Her sister had stopped buying name-brand food. Broken things went unfixed. Layla never spent a dime. Zia wanted, even needed, to tell her sister about dating Clay. Ever since they were small, new to the city with only one parent, the sisters had been charged with taking care of each other. Not telling the truth felt like failing some sort of test. But Zia felt strongly that confiding in Layla would unequivocally be a disaster. Just as she knew the longer the relationship was kept secret, the worse it'd be if Layla ever found out.

44

Gorman raised his wineglass and gave Liv a meaningful smile. "To second chances."

"Don't be ridiculous," Liv replied. "It was one date." But her eyes were sparkly, and there was a funny little smile at the corner of her mouth. Gorman knew not to push it.

They relaxed into folding chairs to soak up the last of the sun, taking advantage of the fact that it was just the two of them. Henry wasn't a huge fan of the brownstone's backyard, which the Goldenhorns had let go to shit over the past few years. But as long as the wine was flowing and the chair was comfortable, Gorman didn't mind. Outdoor spaces were rare in New York. They must be enjoyed.

Liv popped a potato chip in her mouth. "How's life as the next Arthur Miller?"

"Fabulous," Gorman purred, regaling her with tales of rehearsals and rewrites. "And you'll love the lead actor. He's absolutely adorable."

"Gilbert," Liv recalled.

"Yes, that's right. Have I mentioned him?"

Liv hooked an eyebrow. "Once or twice."

Gilbert was turning out to be not a bad actor. Not a great one, per se, but not bad. The sandy-haired boy in the cute round glasses and Fire Island tan had thrown himself into rehearsals with the committed, hungry enthusiasm of youth. Gilbert wanted to *understand* the role of Egor Snail, which meant he wanted to *understand* Gorman. This had entailed several long boozy evenings at various drinking establishments where Gilbert listened, rapt, to Gorman wax lyrical about growing up in a time that predated Grindr and PrEP and Neil Patrick Harris. Occasionally Gilbert would offer a comment that was a little tactless ("I honestly can't imagine what's harder: growing up without marriage rights or TikTok") but overall, it was flattering. Fun. And yes, a little flirty. Which was all quite yummy. Henry was mortgage payments and meal planning. Gilbert was *tell me more about Stonewall in the nineties*, then heading off there to dance all night.

When was the last time Henry danced all night?

"So," Liv asked. "Are you boffing?"

Gorman choked on a potato chip. "Boffing! Good grief, Goldenhorn."

"Are you?"

"No."

"Do you want to?"

Gorman brushed a few chip bits from his shirtfront. "Does the pope shit in the woods?"

Liv chuckled. Her gaze wandered over the weeds that'd taken the flower beds hostage. "I never really got how all that worked. An open relationship."

Gorman shrugged. "It's sex. That you're open about."

"But don't you get jealous? Of Henry sleeping with other people?"

Gorman twirled his wrist airily. "That's straight-people stuff. We don't really think that way. Besides," he added, "Henry hasn't slept with someone else in"—he frowned, doing some calculations—"gosh, it must be at least three years. Maybe four?"

"And you?"

"Less."

"So really, *you're* in an open relationship."

"Oh, darling," Gorman sighed. "Don't bore me with your bourgeois values."

Liv took a sip of wine. She was wearing blush, Gorman noted, and were those new earrings? Second chances, indeed.

"Do you think you'll ever get married?" Liv asked.

"Christ, you sound like Henry."

"Henry's brought it up?"

Gorman's lower back pinched. He shifted in his chair. "Henry wants to get married."

"What? When?"

"Yesterday would've been preferable."

Liv bolted forward. "Gor! That's wonderful! Congratul—"

"Deactivate, darling. I don't know if all that's for me. I don't know if I'm marriage material."

"Why not?"

"It just feels so . . . final. Committing to one thing. One person. One life."

"You'd still be able to sleep with other people, according to your rules."

"Henry wants a closed marriage. But it's not just about the sex, believe it or not." Gorman squinted, mopping his forehead with his kerchief. He'd never worn sunscreen when he was younger, and now, he regretted it. Far too many wrinkles. "There's a certain freedom in being unmarried, isn't there? Married is . . . married. When we couldn't get married, I felt like, *Fine, who cares?* All these institutions we were excluded from: the military, marriage, government, boardrooms: I saw them all as capitalist hetero nonsense. They didn't want me, I didn't want them. Now the world's changed, but I don't know if I have. I just want that . . . freedom. To live life on my terms."

Liv pffted.

"What?" Gorman was offended. "That's what I think."

"Apart from the fact you're pissing on the institution I gave up a lot for—and that my business, and a lot of yours, is built on believing in—it sounds like what you actually want to do is run away with Gilbert after he falls in love with you. Which is more juvenile than the boy in question."

"Witch." Gorman snatched the wine and refilled his glass. All right, yes: perhaps Gilbert was playing a part in his thinking. Perhaps he had indulged in a few fantasies of dating a much younger man: spontaneous weekends in Paris and Rome. Lounging by a pool as blue as a Hockney. He didn't want to lose himself. Cut ties with the young man who'd screwed in club bathrooms and the piers along the Hudson River. The young man who'd once taken the stage of the Pyramid Club in drag as Miss Demeanor, and had everyone singing along to "I Will Survive."

He recalled a moment in last week's rehearsals. The scene where Egor comes out to his mother.

Egor: I'm not going to end up like you, Mother! Bitter and angry and dead on the inside.

Mother: And how exactly do you think you'll avoid that, Egor? We all become our mothers, eventually.

Egor: I'm going to suck the marrow out of life, Mother. I'm going to suck it!

Gorman originally imagined this as darkly humorous, even campy. But Gilbert played it in a way that was surprisingly powerful: a threat. Gorman didn't laugh. He got chills.

Egor was right.

"Life is for the living, Liv."

His best friend burst out laughing. "Darling, I love you. But here's three things I'm pretty sure are true. One: a cute twentysomething is not going to run away to a Greek island with you. Two: everyone creates their own version of a marriage. If freedom is important to you, invent a marriage with freedom baked into it. Three: Henry is wonderful, and he loves you. You might see marriage as a bad imitation of heteronormativity. But he probably sees it as a safety net for the life your generation fought so hard to get."

A warm breeze rustled through the dusk, sending dead willow leaves floating around them. Gorman remembered when the willow was too small for the patch of new, dark mulch around it. Now, it was as dried-up as the spiderweb-covered pot plants. The liver-spotted skin on the back of his hand. Gorman didn't want to get old. He didn't want to be a dull old man any more than he wanted to lose his sense of self in a partnership. But possibly, there was some truth to what Liv had just laid out.

Liv asked, "Does Henry want children?"

Even though they'd never discussed it, the answer came from somewhere deeper than logic. "Yes."

Liv made eye contact with him deliberately. "Then, trust me: a man like Henry won't wait forever."

The idea sent a peculiar chill up Gorman's spine.

He loved Henry. He loved that Henry fell asleep reading in bed almost every night and didn't wake when Gorman carefully removed his reading glasses. He loved that Henry approached life with a measured and practical thoughtfulness but could still be spontaneous and funny and cut a mean rug on the dance floor. He was trustworthy and hardworking and patient. Kind to children and animals.

Marriage used to be boring. But it was interesting to consider— just *consider*—that getting married, or hell, becoming a *father*, in his mid*fifties* might just be the most radical thing Ralph Gorman could ever do.

45

As much as Clay was enjoying dating Zia, he knew there was something she wasn't telling him. The secrecy wasn't a problem—everyone had their boundaries, and the fact she wasn't broadcasting every waking thought was refreshing. But Clay sensed her wanderlust wasn't the carefree kind that sent twentysomethings cavorting around the world with backpacks and journals. Zia pursued exploration with the mindfulness of someone in a walking meditation.

It niggled him. Still, he was very happy to be back in Manhattan, spending a night at home together, making a *delizioso* lasagna.

While she showered, Clay popped in his wireless earbuds and returned a call to Dave. "Sorry I've been MIA," he told his manager, hunting around for a bottle of wine. "Zia and I have been . . . catching up."

Dave chuckled. "Good for you, man." Then, after a slightly awkward pause, "That's kind of what I was calling about."

Clay paused, one hand on a dusty bottle at the back of the pantry. "Meaning?"

"You want the good news or the bad?"

"The bad." Always. Zia, the eternal optimist, would have opted for the former.

"Michelle's book is coming out."

"*What*? What about the army of lawyers? A bloodbath, with billable hours?"

"Freedom of speech, man. And she never signed an NDA, so . . ."

Clay groaned. His knees buckled, and he sank to the kitchen floor. He could see the tabloid covers now. CLAY BEGGED MICHELLE TO MAKE HIM HER SEX SLAVE!

"I know, man," Dave sighed. "It sucks."

It didn't just suck. It was a colossal violation. As his star rose over the years, Clay had spent a lot of time musing about personhood and celebrity. The more famous he got, the less the rules of society applied to him. Often that worked in his favor—his outsize paycheck, the access he could expect, the best seat in every restaurant, concert, first class, whatever. But it also worked against him. He was more an idea than a person. Something to be used: for power, for money, for a laugh. His identity, and thus his worth, was determined by a scrim around him that was in part created by his actions, and in part created by the culture, and its oscillating tastes and values. Michelle's book would change how society saw him and thus change him, without him taking any action at all. There was something deeply frightening about that reality. That ultimately there were two Clays. The real Clay, and the Clay invented by the desires of others: Illusion Clay. And he was never quite sure which one was in charge of his life.

"What's the good news?"

"Excellent question. The good news is there is a *lot* of interest in your mysterious new woman."

The jerk of panic propelled his head back up. "What? How does anyone even know?"

"Russo, c'mon. New York's a big small town. You can't keep this stuff secret forever."

"Yes, I can." Even to his own ears, he sounded whiny.

"All I'm saying is, Lana"—his publicist—"and I think a well-timed announcement would take a lot of eyeballs away from Michelle's book, and onto you. What story would you rather read: the one about the bitter, bitchy ex, or the one about the happy, hot new love?"

"Neither." Jesus, didn't everyone have better things to do than read about people they didn't even know?

"Well, most people prefer the happy, hot new love. We get you papped, then you bring her to a red carpet. Maybe a spread for *People*—"

"No!"

"You're right: *Vogue.* No, *Vanity Fair*—"

"No, *no.*" Clay was back on his feet, checking the shower was still running. He lowered his voice. "I'm not ready. We're still getting to know each other. She's not even my girlfriend."

"Yeah, cool."

He could all but hear Dave rolling his eyes.

"How long's it been?" Dave asked.

"Three months." That wasn't long. Was it?

Dave went on, sounding annoyingly casual, "And you're not seeing anyone else, you spend all your free time with her, and when you're not with her you kind of talk about her nonstop."

"I don't talk about her—"

"Dude," Dave interrupted. "You do."

The old Clay would've done it. Not parade Zia around like a sideshow, but make things more official. Be seen in public. Tell the truth about his feelings to his family and inner circle. But the new Clay was cautious. There was still that fear, as groundless as it was, that Zia didn't like the real Clay. That she'd fallen for Illusion Clay, the one he had no control over, the one most people genuinely believed him to be. That she'd start to want what that Clay could give her, further erasing the real Clay from the world. He pressed his lips together, willing the strength to trust her. Love her, like she deserved to be loved. But it wasn't there.

And then, there was the other concern. The darker one.

"Say we do it," Clay said flatly. "Would she get hate mail? Twitter trolls? Death threats?"

These were, of course, rhetorical questions.

Dave was silent for a beat. "You have a lot of very supportive fans."

"But it's different for women. Different for people of color. Different if you're not used to it."

And there was no way optimistic, kindhearted Zia Ruiz would be able to handle the tsunami of hatred, of overt racism and sexism, that would try to drown her if they were to go public. It would threaten her faith in humanity. Clay left the house every morning knowing that tens of thousands of people hated him, for no good reason at all. He didn't like it, but it went with the territory. But he couldn't do that to Zia.

"Of course it's a concern," Dave said carefully. "But are you sure worrying about that is not just an excuse?"

He wasn't sure. But he needed more time to figure it all out. He wilted forward in defeat. "We're not ready."

Dave sighed. "We'll work something else out. And, Clay?"

"What?"

His manager's words were tactful. But they were also a warning. "Zia's a pretty cool chick. She won't live in the shadows forever."

46

WE'RE GETTING HITCHED!

vanessa
& leonard

**Friday, August 27, at six in the evening
Harvard Club, New York City**

#NESSALOVESLENNY #LOVEWON

Liv suggested Vanessa keep her father in the loop about all the wedding preparations: the menu, the ceremony, the guest list, the dress. "The more he knows about the day, the more connected he'll feel to it," Liv said. "Hopefully."

But despite Vanessa's efforts, her line of communication was decidedly one-way. Liv's polite voice mails and emails also went unanswered. As the day of the wedding dawned, hazy and humid, Liv felt equally ashamed and angry that her logistical powers weren't enough to guarantee Vanessa's key bridal wish. Weddings were a space outside of normal life. A space where dreams could come true and magic could happen. Liv was determined to create that magic for Vanessa. Intent on proving to herself and her client that she hadn't lost her touch.

The ceremony was set for 6:00 p.m., with doors open to guests a half hour prior. Liv and Savannah arrived at midday to oversee setup:

unpacking personal decor, running through the timeline with the vendors, double-checking the floor plans. It wasn't exactly a modern venue. As Liv put it to Savannah, it was a clubhouse where rich white men could fanboy about late-stage capitalism over a bottle of American bourbon.

The venue's mounted animal heads—including one of an elephant—appeared as earnest odes to colonialism. *Better days*, the deceased beasts seemed to signify. *Better days*.

At exactly 5:30 p.m., General Fitzpatrick was one of the first to arrive, in his service dress uniform. Instead of mingling with Lenny and Vanessa's friends, he loitered in a far corner, a drink in hand.

This would've been Eliot's job. A bit of dick swinging and sexist jokes about bridesmaids and *C'mon, man, do the right thing.* Now the task fell to Liv. She lowered her center of gravity, channeling the cocky confidence of her dearly departed, and swaggered over. "Ahoy there."

His eyes narrowed, not able to place her.

"Liv Goldenhorn. Vanessa's wedding planner."

He returned her handshake reluctantly. The air around him was prickly.

"The club looks fantastic," Liv enthused. "So much history." From every wall, portraits of dead white men judged her best effort at manly. "I heard Teddy Roosevelt bagged the elephant in the Great Hall."

The general snorted. "Old wives' tale." His voice was thick and guttural. Possibly not his first cocktail. "Do you hunt, Mrs. Goldenhorn?"

Not the time to point out it was *Ms.* "I was born on the Upper East Side. Less bayonets, more bagels."

This failed to raise a smile. "Didn't think so. Not really a woman's game."

Which was probably crocheting and childbirth. Time to get "man-to-man."

"Let's cut to the chase. It's your child's wedding day. It would really mean so much to everyone here, especially Vanessa, if you'd honor her desire to walk her down the aisle."

The general bristled. "Do you have children?"

Liv braced herself. "I have a son."

"A little boy."

She knew where this was going, but felt no choice but to answer: "Yes."

"And how would you feel if one day that little boy—who you played catch with and taught how to chop firewood—came home and said, *I'm . . . . I'm . . .*" His voice died on the vine. He couldn't even conjure the words.

"A girl?" Liv finished. Her blood turned hot. "Look, honestly? I'm sure that would be disorientating and confusing. But I love my child, General Fitzpatrick. Not his gender. And whoever he turns out to be, even if it's wildly different from what I wanted or what I'm comfortable with, I'll be on board."

"Really?"

"*Yes.*"

The general took a long slug of his drink. "You have absolutely no idea what you're talking about."

Liv snapped, "Well, that makes two of us."

"Excuse me?"

Maybe it was the talk about Ben, or the fact the ceremony was in twenty short minutes, or maybe it was just the fact that this man was choosing to hurt his daughter on her wedding day over his outdated notion of tradition.

"With all due respect, you're being an asshole. So for Chrissake, just do the damn aisle walk."

The general's voice was pure steel. "With all due respect, go to hell."

The guests assembled for the ceremony. Lenny stood at the altar, smiling nervously and rocking on his heels. Around the corner, Vanessa waited for Liv's cue.

The general was MIA.

Liv raked the seated crowd. She spotted Sam across the room, whom she'd asked to do a sweep of the kitchen. Sometimes guests could be found eating their feelings. But Sam just shrugged and shook his head.

"What'd he say when you talked to him?" asked Savannah.

Liv tightened her hands around her clipboard, inwardly cursing. "I may have lost my cool."

Savannah stared at her. "What does that mean?"

Liv continued searching the guests. "He wouldn't have just left, would he?"

Savannah's face slackened. "*No.* He's going to walk Vanessa down the aisle. He's her *dad.* It's her *wedding day.*"

"I know," Liv said tightly. A small, stupidly hopeful part of herself was expecting to see the general magically appear on Vanessa's arm. Give Liv a nod, maybe even a wry smile.

"We have to find him," Savannah said. "We have to make him see—"

"There he is."

The general was slipping into a spare seat toward the back. Not even the first row.

Savannah blinked. "So, he's not . . ."

"Nope." Liv shook her head, just once. She'd blown it. "Keep it together," she told her horrified business partner. "This isn't about you." Liv gave Vanessa her cue.

The music started. The crowd twisted around, their faces happy and expectant.

Vanessa Martha Fitzpatrick held her head high. Traditions can be observed, updated, or rejected. But it was harder, sometimes impossible, to engage with tradition entirely on your own. With deliberate measured steps, Vanessa began walking herself down the center of the aisle.

47

Liv said it was over. But Savannah Shipley could not take no for an answer.

In the cocktail hour, she found the general at the far end of one of the club's crimson-and-dark-wood bars, nursing a whiskey. She took the seat next to him and ordered one neat, flashing him a smile as bright as the brass buttons on his suit jacket.

He eyed her. "Didn't think girls drank whiskey."

He didn't appear to recognize her. Maybe that was a good thing.

"I'm from Kentucky, sir," she said, leaning into the accent. "We don't drink much else."

"Kentucky, huh?" His voice was still wary. "I'm from Cincinnati."

"I have cousins there! Tell me somethin', is the Sugar n' Spice Diner still the best breakfast spot in town?"

He shrugged, but she could see she'd sparked a memory.

"We used to go after church," she persisted. "Stack of their famous wispy-thin pancakes . . . ?"

"With bacon on the side." He patted his gut with a faint chuckle. "Trying to cut back. Doctor's orders."

"Still, you gotta eat. What'd Mark Twain say? 'Eat what you like and let the food fight it out inside.'"

The general snorted and turned back to his glass.

"Well, I've had a humdinger of a week," Savannah announced.

He took a sip, curious in spite of himself. "How's that?"

Savannah pouted, girlish. "I had a fight with my daddy."

"That's no good." The general's demeanor turned fatherly. "Your old man is always right. You remember that."

"Oh, sir, I know. My daddy's my hero. He taught me to ride a horse and shoot a rifle and I'm still damn good at both."

The general grunted, his gaze softening with nostalgia and an undercurrent of pain.

"Now that I live in New York," Savannah continued, "I worry he thinks I've left him behind. I haven't. I'm just becoming my own person. I think that frightens him." She pressed her hand to her chest, willing a tear. "I love my daddy so much. I just can't imagine him not being part of my life."

General Fitzpatrick circled the whiskey in his glass as if in thought.

Savannah blew out a breath, her smile turning cheery. "But I know we'll make up. Because deep down, we love each other. He just has to *understand*."

"Understand what?"

"That everyone grows up. And it's never too late to say sorry and start again." Savannah held the general's arm, speaking in the hushed tone of two close friends. "In my book: family comes first. Always."

A light went off behind his eyes. "You're one of the wedding planners."

Savannah froze; sprung.

He huffed out an annoyed, if genuine, chuckle. "You almost had me."

"Honestly, sir? I meant every word." Savannah dropped the syrupy charm, replacing it with her best attempt at New York candor. "Look, my dad and I don't always see eye to eye. But he's my *father*. And I'd rather have an imperfect father than no father at all." She felt an unexpected surge of power as she leveled her eye contact with his. "You've got one chance to get Vanessa back. Do *not* fuck it up." Savannah picked up her whiskey and left, daring to hope she'd made an impact.

48

At 7:30 p.m., Liv ushered the guests into dinner in the Great Hall. Vanessa and Lenny took their seats at the head table. But the general's chair, several seats down from Vanessa's, was empty. Liv glanced over the other tables, wondering if he'd missed his name card.

"Excuse me?"

General Fitzpatrick was standing on the stage, a microphone in one hand. Zach, who was supposed to be MC'ing, shrugged helplessly at Liv, mouthing, *He just took it!*

"Quiet," ordered the general, and the room obeyed.

Liv ran through her options. Should she take the mic? Cut the power? Scream, "Look at me, I'm a pumpkin!" and hustle the old man back to the 1950s? Catching Savannah's eye, Liv pointed at Zach and made a warning face. Savannah nodded. She understood that if the old man went rogue, Zach should drown him out.

"My name is General Tucker Fitzpatrick and I'm . . ."

Liv tensed, a sprinter ready for the starter gun. If he said "Adam's father," she'd take him out herself.

The bride was sitting stock-still. Her face was the color of her dress.

Savannah was by Zach's side. The DJ had one finger hovering over his computer keyboard, ready.

"I'm," said the general, "I'm *Vanessa's* father."

Liv let out a breath. It hadn't been easy to say it. But at least he had.

The general rubbed between his eyes. "Although I probably haven't been a very good father the past few years."

Liv swapped a look of disbelief with Savannah. That was the last thing she expected him to admit.

"When I look around this room," the general continued, "I don't see a lot of familiar faces. I don't really know my *daughter's* life here." Again, too much emphasis on *daughter*. But he was trying. "I don't really know my daughter. At all. And that's . . . well, that's my fault."

No one moved. All fidgeting and whispers and wine guzzling had ceased. The room was utterly, eerily silent.

"I was scared, I guess. Of something that I didn't know anything about. Something that seemed very . . . strange to me."

Liv tensed. *Pull it back, old man.*

"But I'd like to get to know you, Vanessa. I'd like to meet you. The real you. If it's . . . if it's not too late." The general's eyes watered. His voice thickened, on the verge of breaking. "Because I'll always be your father. Your daddy." And now his voice did crack. "You look so beautiful, sweetheart. I wish you and Lenny nothing but the best." The general offered a shaking hand. "Would you do me the great honor of joining me for the father-daughter dance?"

Vanessa let out a sob, and rose to her feet.

Liv's eyes welled. It'd been so long since she'd borne witness to this. A moment in which this cruel and terrible world seemed almost good. Almost wonderful. Across the room, Sam was standing at the entrance to the kitchen, wiping away a tear. Liv caught his eye and held his gaze. For a long moment, they were the only two people in the room.

A tiny latch, no bigger than a thimble, sprung open inside Liv's chest.

Vanessa crossed the floor to her father. Zach put on "You've Got A Friend" by James Taylor. The sweet and simple melody filled the hall—"*Winter, spring, summer or fall, all you have to do is call . . .*"—and General Tucker Adam Fitzpatrick danced with his only daughter, the two of them holding each other with a careful, new tenderness.

49

It was well after midnight before Darlene and Zach were able to load out their gear. Ordinarily, Darlene wouldn't need to wait for the end of a wedding before leaving, but she made a lame excuse, and Zach didn't protest.

Having a fake boyfriend was suiting Darlene Mitchell very, very nicely. When she needed help installing some new blinds: Fake Boyfriend. When she wanted someone to go with her to the Cindy Sherman retrospective at the Met, Fake Boyfriend was on hand. When Fake Boyfriend invited her to go see the Yankees—his version of an art gallery—she accepted. Seeing a professional sports game in New York had been on her bucket list for years, and she was surprised by how much she liked it. Or maybe, how much fun seeing it with a fake boyfriend made it. Zach was getting better at being on time for gigs, and he never skipped out on loading out at the end. And it did not go unnoticed that the usual string of frothy blondes he kept in his orbit had either disappeared or were being kept discreetly out of sight. She hoped the former. Of course they hadn't had the exclusivity conversation, because they weren't really dating, but deep down Darlene hoped she was the only person Zach was kissing.

For social media, she reminded herself. For the money.

Photographing themselves for Zach's Instagram—and the rather disturbing likes Zach's mother gave their couple photos—had actually helped maintain a boundary between them. Kissing Zach made her think about Zach—a lot—so Darlene had decided no more spontaneous smooches; only staged ones. She made their affection feel like acting in an advertisement, and that was good. That made it manageable, even as she could tell Zach wanted to throw her against a wall and, well . . .

She'd confessed the scheme to her book club, framing it as a clever plan to make a ton of cash but underlining that obviously, Zach wasn't a serious contender for a boyfriend. They weren't as judgmental as she'd expected. "Do you" was the general mantra; "*And if that means doing him, more power to you, girl.*"

Darlene's boundaries were getting squiggly. The Harvard Club guests had loved her set and Zach had looked so cute and confident behind the decks and, hey, weddings really did put you in the mood for love . . .

They piled the equipment into the rental car and came back up for one last sweep of the Great Hall. Incredible how a space could be transformed by a flash mob of love and fun and dancing. Darlene drifted onto the empty dance floor, tipping her head to take in the chandeliers. Zach took her hand, twirling her in a circle. She giggled, tired and punch-drunk. "What are you doing?"

He hooked his arm around her waist, taking her right hand in a waltz position. "Dancing."

She laughed as he spun her around the floor, awkwardly, out of step, two silly rag dolls. Then he tugged her into a dark corner. His hand lingered close to her ass.

"Zach!" She glanced around. "We're still at work." But it was only a half-hearted protest.

He pressed her against the wooden wall. "Damn, Dee. You looked *sexy* tonight."

The smell of his skin made her mouth water. His arms felt strong beneath the fabric of his shirt. "This isn't professional."

"Dee, everyone already thinks we're together."

She could feel the urgency in his every cell: to take her, to kiss her. "What, for another photo?"

His voice was low and delicious in her ear. "No. Because I want you, Darlene."

The words ran over her like a harpist caressing her strings. It was too much: his blue eyes, and beautiful mouth, and the way he was looking at her like she was the most gorgeous creature he'd ever seen. She wanted this boy. More than anything. Her words came in a breathy pant. "Kiss me."

Zach Livingstone kissed her like the world had exploded and they were the last two people left on earth. Urgent and desperate but also sweet, also tender. His hands cupped her jaw, warm thumb pads brushing her cheekbones. His kiss was like hearing her favorite song: the hot whoosh of affection; the calm, deep connection; the way it soothed the anxious part of her soul. They were both smiling, and Zach laughed, maybe out of sheer joy or surprise. Darlene pulled him back to her, her hands grabbing his collar, his shirt, unable to get close enough. Everything inside her was flooding, breaking, and she was deliciously, deliriously *gone*.

"Has anyone seen the band?"

Savannah Shipley's voice stopped them cold. They sprung apart.

"There you are!" Savannah waved and bounded toward them. "I have your tips!"

"You are a goddess." Zach grinned and plucked his envelope. He'd transformed so quickly from passionate lover to easy-breezy Zach. Dating-round-the-clock Zach. Very-into-white-girls Zach.

"Stellar effort tonight," he said to Savannah. "I think you had something to do with the father-daughter dance lovefest?"

Savannah laughed, launching into the story. Zach's eyes stayed glued on her.

Something scalding and sickening twisted around Darlene's organs and squeezed like a python.

Jealousy.

So feverish it took her breath away.

Maybe he was charming the nice wedding planner who hired them. Or maybe Zach was just a manslut. He might act like he had real feelings for her. He might even really think it. But if she gave herself to him, would the air go out of the fantasy? She was almost thirty. He wasn't even the age his parents believed the human brain finished developing at. He wasn't trustworthy. He was a trust fund baby.

Zach watched Savannah leave, her ass round as a peach in her tight black skirt. He turned back to Darlene with a roguish grin. "Where were we?"

Darlene fortified herself and brushed past him. "Leaving."

50

Zia arrived at Clay's to find him sprawled on the sectional overlooking the Hudson River, working on his laptop.

"Hey gorgeous." He smiled. "How was the wedding?"

"Beautiful. Inspiring. The bride's speech was so moving." She plopped down next to him and kicked off her shoes. "I'm still kind of wired. Think we could sneak out to a bar or something?"

"There's plenty of booze here." He arched an eyebrow, half joking. "This way, I have you all to myself."

It turned her cold. Her body and heart closed like an anemone.

"What? What's wrong?"

Her first instinct was to leave. She met his concerned gaze. "Can we talk?"

Clay closed the computer. "Always."

Zia took a few grounding breaths. She'd told the story many times, under many different circumstances. It got easier. But it never got easy. "Right after college, I met an amazing man who I thought I was going to marry. His name was Logan."

She watched Clay absorb that, yes, this was the piece of her past that was missing. His gaze was entirely focused on her. "I'm listening."

"He was successful, handsome, charming. I was waitressing—this was way before I started working for Global Care. Logan and his coworkers used to have lunch at a restaurant I worked at in the financial district. The first time I waited on him, he asked if I had a boyfriend. I said no, and he said, 'Now you do.'" Zia shook her head, still baffled by his confidence. "I kind of laughed it off, but he was persistent. He took me to Eleven Madison Park for our first date. I'd never been to a place like that. The food, the service. The bill. Which, of course, we didn't split. I never paid for anything. He didn't let me."

Clay shifted, as if ready to hold her but careful to give her space.

"I was living with my sister and her kids," Zia went on. "So when he said I should move in with him, y'know, it made sense. So I did. And that's when things started to get bad."

"Bad, how?"

"Logan was incredibly controlling," Zia said. "What I wore, what I ate, how I spoke, who I spoke to. And he was incredibly jealous. He tracked my phone. If I was ever anywhere he didn't know about, he'd get so mad. One time, I ran into a friend from my neighborhood and we grabbed lunch near his place. Afterward, it started to rain, so I ran up to get an umbrella from his apartment. Out of nowhere, Logan shows up and just starts laying into him."

Clay looked horrified. "Jesus Christ."

"It was a nightmare." Zia rubbed her arms, her muscles tensing. "I knew I should leave him, but when you're in an abusive relationship, you lose sight of what's normal. You forget what's normal. He kept telling me it was because he loved me, and I believed him. So when we'd fight and"—she drew in a shaky breath—"he'd hit me, again, I just thought that was normal. That love was complicated, relationships were hard, and it was my fault for setting him off."

Clay made a noise: a low, pained sound.

"And so one night, I watched a documentary about people who volunteered at an elephant sanctuary in Thailand. New York was the only city I knew; I'd never even been to Boston. I suggested we take a trip together. Logan traveled for work all the time, and I'd always just be stuck in the apartment. He said no. But I couldn't let it go. Logan knew all my passwords, so I started a secret email account on a laptop I bought myself. Researched tickets, hotels. I guess I was planning my escape."

Clay looked like he was holding his breath. His entire body was taut.

Zia kept her voice even. "Logan found my laptop. He locked me in my walk-in closet. And left. I was in there for three days. My sister called the cops, thank God. When they found me, I was almost dead from dehydration. I never saw him again, except for in court."

"Did he go to jail?"

Zia shook her head. "Suspended sentence."

Clay's voice was shaking. "He could've killed you."

"He could've. But he didn't." Zia exhaled, letting the memory go. She was here, in New York, with a man who cared about her. "That was seven years ago. I've been to therapy; I've done a lot of work on myself. I don't date assholes anymore. I know there are good guys in the world." Her past had shown her a reservoir of strength she didn't know she had. The ability to persevere. To survive. To forgive. And, to stand up for herself.

"You're a good guy. But I can't belong to you." She touched Clay's face, feeling the dark stubble shading his chin. "Baby, I don't want to be a secret anymore. Being a secret makes me feel trapped. Like you're not serious about me. But I'm serious about you. And if you don't want that, that's okay. Really. We've had a great time together, an amazing time. But if this isn't serious for you, I gotta go."

Clay nodded. His voice was quiet, his words measured. "When we met, I wasn't ready to trust someone. I remember thinking that if I didn't have someone, no one could betray me. But that's no way to live. Relationships are a risk. Life is a risk. And there's no one I'd rather do it with than you." He shifted closer. "We've always been honest with each other. And what I'm honestly thinking right now is this: If I let you walk away, I'll regret it every minute of every hour of every day for the rest of my life." He sounded sincere and resolute, his gold eyes burning. "I feel what you feel. I'm in this. I'm with you."

Zia's heart was doubling, tripling in size. "That makes me so happy."

"You make me happy, Zia. When I'm with you, I feel like myself, and it isn't a bad thing."

She smiled, and he pressed his forehead to hers.

"Goddamn," he murmured. "How'd I end up with such a gorgeous girlfriend?"

Girlfriend. There it was, the first time. And even though it wasn't a moniker Zia'd been especially fixated on, now that she had, she never wanted to give it back. She lifted her eyes to his, wanting to make sure he knew what he was saying.

His grin back was a little goofy. "Sorry it took so long."

"No apology necessary."

"Ah, my girlfriend is the coolest."

"I think you'll find that honor goes to my boyfriend," she told him, feeling a bit goofy herself.

"Boyfriend," he repeated. "I like the sound of that."

So did she. So, so much.

Which meant it was time to tell her sister about Clay.

51

Sam stacked a dozen boxes of leftovers and a fat slice of wedding cake for Ben in Liv's fridge while she paid the babysitter. Usually, Eliot would've left a local wedding like Vanessa and Lenny's hours ago, to put their son to bed and save a hundred bucks on childcare. Tonight, Liv handled it on her own.

Sam closed the fridge door quietly.

"Thanks so much," Liv whispered. "Sure you've got enough yourself?"

"Car's full," Sam whispered back. "Love it when clients don't want leftovers. Dottie'll be thrilled."

The day they'd met, when she'd mistaken Sam for a Fresh Direct sex pest, the air had just started to warm up. Now, as they lingered on the front steps of the brownstone, it was humid and heavy with night-blooming flowers.

Sam put his hands in his jeans pockets. "So, I had fun last week."

"At the movie you fell asleep to?"

"Hey, I just don't buy a cop whose only job is shooting bad guys and saying things like, 'Not on my watch.'" Sam raised his hands. "Where's the paperwork? There was zero paperwork!"

Liv laughed. "It was pretty bad."

"But good company."

"Yes. Very good."

Liv and Sam had been on four dates since their first dinner together. Four very nice, PG-rated dates. Strange that it took almost fifty years and one dead husband to be taken on an actual date. One with twilight strolls and dinner reservations and planned fun. She and Eliot didn't "date." They got drunk and screwed, or "hooked up," as it was now called. She and Sam had not yet "hooked up." They hadn't even kissed. That was all she could handle. As Liv put it to him on their second date (salted caramel cones from Ample Hills, and a walk around Fort Greene Park), no reckless romance. No expectations, no grand declarations. This was dating as a widow. As a mom. And while the purpose of this was to create boundaries as wide as a six-lane highway, it was only partially successful. Because Liv liked Sam Woods. She liked that he thought cop movies had logic flaws. She liked that he knew when fruit was ripe. She liked his old T-shirts and his big hands. She liked that he was both careful and easy with her son. She liked his kind, crinkly brown eyes. She liked that spending time with him felt unhurried and simple and that they could talk about anything and didn't have to pretend to be perfect people, people without a past, because they'd both been hurt and that was okay.

And liking Sam Woods scared the bejesus out of Liv.

On one of their dates, strolling the Brooklyn Heights Promenade, they passed a bride and groom being photographed. *Sweetheart neckline doesn't suit her*, Liv thought. *And he's got about a gallon too much hair gel.*

Apparently, this was not what Sam was thinking. "Think you'd ever do it again?"

"What—get married?" Liv looked at him like he was mad. "I'd rather be flayed alive."

Sam tipped his head back and laughed. "You don't mince words, Olive Goldenhorn."

They found a bench overlooking the East River. "Don't tell me you would. I'm not saying this to be mean, but your marriage was pretty much a disaster."

"No, it wasn't," Sam said mildly. "Not entirely."

"*Three years.* She was cheating on you for—"

"I know, I know. But the way I see it, Claudia and I had ten good years, and three bad ones. Ten when she was honest, three when she wasn't. Ten's more than three. And you said things with Eliot were bad for only a few years, toward the end. But you were married for over two decades. Just because a marriage ends doesn't make it a failure, or bad. I don't think of marriage that way—good or bad."

It was a healthy reframe; Liv understood that. "I see your point. But you're more hopeful than I am. I'm done with it. When I was younger, I thought it was about the *quality* of the love. If you loved each other enough, and it was good enough love, marriage would work."

"Now?"

"Better the devil you know. Marriage sucks. Being single sucks. Pick your poison."

Sam looked at her like she was an errant school kid squandering her natural ability. "So you don't believe in love?"

"I believe it exists. I see it every day: couples high on hormones, whose greatest test has been moving in together. But, it's a delusion. And I'm done with being deluded."

"That's a shame."

"You want to get married again."

He shrugged. "Sure."

"Of course you do. You're a great dad with a cool job and who gets better looking with age, thank you patriarchy. You'll probably end up marrying a twenty-year-old Pilates instructor who thinks Botox is a great investment and doesn't know she's supposed to come too."

Sam cocked his head at her, a pleased smile on his lips. "You think I'm good-looking?"

And because he found the one positive thing in all her prickly words, something warm and wonderful rolled over her, sloughing off her bitterness like a layer of dead skin. *I really like you. Shit.*

Now, standing on the brownstone front steps, late on a Friday night after the Fitzpatrick-Maple wedding, Sam's eyes met hers. "I, ah, got you something. It's in the car."

Liv's heart hiccupped as he opened the passenger door. Maybe it was just cheap candy. She hoped it was just cheap candy. She definitely hoped it wasn't diamond earrings or, God forbid, a set of house keys.

Loping back up the steps, Sam handed her a brown paper bag. Too big for jewelry or keys. She peeked in the top. Cherries. A memory of asking him about them at Whole Foods, weeks ago, resurfaced. *They're not quite at their peak yet. But I'll keep an eye out.* He'd remembered. She laughed. "You are too good, Sam Woods."

"Just trying to impress you, Liv Goldenhorn."

"It's working."

Their smiles faded into something more serious as they stood, gazing at each other on the brownstone steps. Oof, he was cute. She'd like to kiss Sam Woods. Yes. That's exactly what she'd like to do.

Sam cleared his throat. "So, I'd quite like to kiss you right now, and I know I shouldn't ask because that isn't manly, but I guess I *am* asking because I don't want you to—"

"Shut up," she said, tugging his T-shirt so that their lips met.

It was not a perfect kiss. It was awkward and too quick and Liv was still holding the bag of cherries, which sort of smushed between them. But it was still electrifying. Liv hadn't kissed anyone except her husband for more than twenty years. Kissing Eliot was like speaking English. Kissing Sam was like suddenly realizing she was fluent in French. It left them both shy and breathless and smiling self-consciously.

"That was . . . ," Sam began. "You know, I can do better at that."

"Me too," Liv said. "I'm actually very good at that."

"Guess we're just a bit out of practice."

"Well, we can try again sometime," Liv suggested.

"I'll hold you to that." He checked the time. "Shoot, I gotta go." He ran down the steps, then ran back up them again. This time, he didn't ask for permission as he kissed Liv confidently on the mouth. Such a different mouth from Eliot's. Solid and warm. *Ooh là là.* Her hand touched his cheek as he pulled back.

"Better," he said, certain.

Liv watched him drive away feeling like a swoony teenage girl. She selected a dark red cherry and popped it in her mouth. Summer exploded on her tongue.

52

The following Monday, Savannah arrived early to In Love in New York, using the key Liv had cut for her. The brownstone was silent— Liv would still be dropping Ben off at day camp. She opened the blinds, made a pot of coffee, and set about responding to the email inquiries that'd come in over the weekend. *Yes, we'd be thrilled to help you throw a Star Wars–themed wedding on May the 4th.* But it was all on autopilot. Savannah's mind was back in Bushwick, on a certain brunette with a gap-toothed smile.

After they spoke at the restaurant, Honey shared her personal Instagram with Savannah. Savannah didn't know what was more surprising—that Honey was gay, or she had a private account. This small corner of the social media universe revealed the real Honey Calhoun. The Honey who drank coffee out of Pride-themed mugs and binged *RuPaul's Drag Race* and hung out at girl parties and gay bars. Savannah assumed hardworking Honey spent every waking hour at the restaurant. But no, every now and then, her Stories showed her doing shots with women with green hair and nose rings, Hayley Kiyoko pumping in the background. It looked cool. Sexy and slightly intimidating.

Not that Savannah had a lot of time to party herself. They were still in high season: In Love in New York worked every Friday and weekend as day-of coordinators, while meeting new clients readying to marry the following year. Savannah didn't want Honey to think there was anything off between them after coming out to her, so she made an effort with texts and popping by 'Shwick Chick when she could.

But something had changed between them. Their usual ease had sharpened. When their hands bumped as they reached for the hot sauce, electric heat scissored through Savannah. Their eye contact wasn't casual. Everything felt . . . loaded.

Because of what Honey had said: *I only liked it because everyone else did.* She wasn't talking about Alabama football; Honey had questioned Savannah's sexuality. At first, this made Savannah angry. Wasn't questioning your sexuality something you did yourself? What right did Honey have to make assumptions about her? She didn't know her! She was not gay, or queer, or bi, or *whatever*—she just wasn't!

But after the sting wore off, Savannah realized being mad was easy. Being self-reflective was harder.

Eliot wasn't a typical alpha male—he looked nothing like the man in the center of her New York vision board. Maybe there was something queer, in both senses of the word, about her attraction to him. A departure from what girls like her were supposed to seek out. Yes, she'd thought about kissing girls, who hadn't? That was just ordinary sexual curiosity. Maybe she wasn't 100 percent straight: no one in Brooklyn seemed to be, so being 90 percent straight—85 percent straight—made her pretty much *normal*. Maybe she could kiss a girl: big deal. She was young; it was the twenty-first century; she was living in New York City for crying out loud!

But she couldn't imagine having sex with a girl. It was hard enough accepting her own vagina. The idea of doing the things one did during sex with another vagina seemed a bit . . . icky. So she couldn't imagine having a girlfriend. Or a wife. Definitely *not* a wife; it just sounded weird thinking about it. *She* was going to *be* a wife: she would not *have* a wife. That'd be like living upside down or eating breakfast for dinner.

There was nothing wrong with being gay . . . for other people. Try as she might, Savannah couldn't shake the idea that being a little bit gay was like being a little bit terminally ill. Her parents were sympathetic for gayness in the way people were sympathetic for cancer. Brooklyn Savannah was open to the idea that, hey, maybe her sexuality wasn't so black-and-white. Southern Savannah was terrified of the shades of gray she was starting to sense in herself.

She had so many questions. How did two women even be in a relationship together? She knew it wasn't about "one being the man"—or maybe it was?—but didn't men and women sort of balance each other out?

Or did the right partner balance you out? Maybe gender had nothing to do with it at all.

She needed more intel. As she heard Liv opening the front door, Savannah tapped open her to-do list and made a note. *Look into L stuff: books/bars etc?*

"Morning!" Liv sailed in, offering her a cherry from a paper bag.

"Yum." Savannah plucked a couple. "Love cherries."

"Me too."

"You're in a good mood."

"Am I?" Liv said, curiously coquettish.

They fell into their Monday routine, catching up on each other's weekends and that day's meetings and bigger items in the week ahead, while sifting through the mail and munching more cherries. Liv opened a card that had arrived hand-delivered. "It's from Vanessa." She read aloud. "'Dear Liv and Savannah, Thank you so much for planning our dream wedding: it truly was the best day of our lives. A special thank-you for all your help with my father. I'm thrilled to say Lenny, my dad, and I are planning to spend this Christmas together for the first time.'"

Savannah's heart ballooned. Vanessa's happiness reflected back on her, and she basked in it like sunlight.

"'A wise woman once said,'" Liv continued, "'*The quality of our lives is defined by the quality of our relationships.* You have helped make my life richer and more meaningful. I am forever grateful.'"

The two women Eliot Goldenhorn had posthumously brought together were both damp-eyed. Savannah squeezed Liv's arm, holding it for a long moment. It didn't feel weird. It felt warm. Entirely natural.

Nothing made Savannah Shipley feel as good as helping other people feel accepted and loved. It sounded cheesy, but love didn't have a sexuality or gender. Or an agenda.

It was just love, wasn't it?

PART THREE

IN LOVE IN THE HAMPTONS

53

Summer stayed long and slow in New York, the dog days of August giving way to a luxurious September. Leaves the color of pumpkin soup scattered across the sidewalks. Seasonal menus switched heirloom salads for hearty terrines. Plaid appeared in every shopfront window, and it began getting dark at a reasonable hour. Fall, that season of crisp air and apple crisp, was on its way.

Savannah Shipley no longer felt like a bumbling newbie. She'd become accustomed to calming bridal anxiety and anticipating month-out meltdowns. Panicky 2:00 a.m. emails such as *Looks like rain and I am FREAKING OUT* and *Need to change the seating plan again (!!!)* could be handled with increasing ease. She'd borne witness to couples in love and couples in a fight and couples who really just wanted the whole damn thing over with. Weddings were the first real test a couple would endure: a trial by fire. At one stage, one partner (and yes, usually a bride) would come to an emotional realization that this wedding "just wasn't *me.*" It was too big or too small. A church should be a field. A Carolina Herrera gown should be a BHLDN dress. A jam-packed three-day weekend should be a simple evening affair. At first, Savannah tried to make the changes the bride requested. But after getting off the phone with a woman convinced that her Italian destination wedding should be in her parents' backyard in Michigan, Liv explained it as such: everyone learns about planning their wedding *while* planning their wedding. If they could do it all again, of course they'd do it differently, but that wasn't possible. Additionally, what most brides didn't realize was, while their wedding was culturally sanctioned as *their* day—it wasn't. It was the couple's day. A wedding could never be one person's vision. And that was more difficult than wives-to-be anticipated.

And Liv Goldenhorn had seen it all. The more worked up the bride got, the calmer Liv became. She could play therapist or bad cop or soothing maternal figure. Her approach oscillated between ritual and making it up as she went along, and the result made the process feel energized, even when things got messy. Planning a wedding was widely believed to be exciting, romantic, and fun, when in reality most couples found it complicated, tiring, and incredibly stressful. Overall, Savannah was astounded just how far planning was from the glossy perfection she'd grown up salivating over in bridal blogs and *Martha Stewart Weddings*. Those pictures were to planning a wedding what porn was to sex. At best, in the same ballpark; at worst, a highly unrealistic simulacrum that created unrealistic, damaging expectations.

Yes, Savannah Shipley was learning the ropes of wedding planning. But the arrival of Imogene Livingstone and Mina Choi for one of their last in-person meetings before their late September wedding knocked her right off her perch.

Because the two brides-to-be were just so . . . *gorgeous*.

The family resemblance between Imogene and her brother, Zach, was clear: the wide, charming smile and huge blue eyes that sparkled beneath thick brown bangs. Mina was just as stunning, tall and poised, with a sheet of glossy black hair and a self-possessed disposition. The couple held hands loosely. While Liv went over the final run of show and setup needs, Savannah couldn't take her eyes off the way Imogene's thumb moved up and down slowly over Mina's knuckle. Up and down. Up, and down . . .

"*Savannah*."

Liv was gesturing at her, one eye on her phone, telling the brides they'd be right back. Out in the hallway, Liv explained that Ben had a tummy bug: she had to pick him up from school. "Back in a jiff. You got this, right?"

Liv had never left Savannah in charge of a meeting before. "Of course!" Two hands, interlocked. Soft hands. Long, delicate fingers. "Just, um, remind me where we were up to?"

But Liv had already hurried out the front door.

Back in the home office, Savannah gave the two women a bright smile. "Liv's had to step out." The spreadsheet was still open on Liv's laptop. She closed it and opened a notebook. "So: where did you two meet?"

Mina's eyebrows pincered. "We already went over all this—"

"At law school." Imogene was as natural a raconteur as her brother. "In a study group. Which I quickly downgraded to a study *duo*. That only met late at night."

"And was it fireworks right away, or were you friends first?"

Mina said, "I want to make sure we get the order of the speeches settled—"

"Fireworks for me." Imogene leaned back in her chair with the ease of a talk show guest. "Nothing for Little Miss Cool over here. I swear, I was spinning plates and tap-dancing for *two years* to get her attention!"

"It was one year." Mina's smile was dry but amused. "And it wasn't as if I didn't notice you. I just had a . . . complication."

"Boyfriend," Imogene supplied. "I invited her over for an *L Word* marathon—the reboot hadn't come out yet, so we're talking vintage *L Word*—and after a *lot* of tequila—"

"I have to be back in court in half an hour." Mina's voice was efficient. "Can we stay on track, please?"

"Yes." Savannah made a mental note to watch *The L Word* as soon as humanly possible. "Of course."

But while Savannah was asking how long they wanted the welcome drinks to go for, what she really wanted to know was how long Mina had a boyfriend for. If Imogene had ever had a boyfriend. How they identified. What their parents had said. She really wanted to know that, but they'd probably think she was implying gayness was a parental disappointment. She was in the middle of a meeting; she couldn't ask them anything. *Stop thinking about asking them something!*

Especially the question that kept popping into her head: *How did they know?*

Eventually Mina announced she had to get back to work. Minutes later, Mina and Imogene were outside the brownstone, waiting for a Lyft. Savannah lingered by the three-corner bay window, watching the way Imogene's hand grazed the small of Mina's back. The way Mina turned to her, giving her a soft, private smile. The way their lips met, loving and passionate, mouths open and—

Savannah realized she was spying. Creepy! She backed away from the window so fast she tripped. She was pretty certain spying on couples making out was not part of the In Love in New York offerings. And yet . . . she wanted to see.

She was back at the window.

Savannah had seen two women kiss before. But not two women like Imogene and Mina. Not in a way that made her feel like what she was seeing was possible, maybe, for her too. Their hands on each other, their long hair brushing the other's cheek. For one brief, resplendent moment, Savannah stopped feeling afraid and uncertain and so completely confused. Their kiss was a bell, ringing loud and clear, echoing for miles around.

The Lyft pulled up. The brides hopped in. Savannah sank back onto the pink sofa, fanning herself, the heat of the entire summer simmering under her skin.

54

Some people treated yoga like a religion, but for Darlene, it was just a workout. An efficient and effective way to stay toned and give her anxious brain some well-deserved downtime. Except lately it wasn't an hour of sweaty *asanas* followed by a mini nap with a bunch of barely dressed strangers. It was just time, more time, to think about Zach. Correction: to feel a vast array of powerful emotions solely inspired by Zachary Livingstone. Crow pose had nothing on this.

Kissing Zach at the Harvard Club triggered a tsunami of obsessive thoughts and wild affection. For the first time in her life, Darlene Mitchell was horrified to find herself lovesick. And yes, it was a sickness. It was crippling. Against her will, Zach had taken control of her mind.

She replayed every sweet and sexy moment over and over again: kissing him outside Babbo, on her sofa, by his parents' pool. Doing gigs, writing a song, playing canasta, singing along to Salt-N-Pepa, running her fingers through his hair, feeling his heartbeat match hers. What she could not handle was the idea of anyone else doing those sorts of things with Zach. The thought of Zach kissing another woman was nightmarish. It actually hurt.

And Darlene could not physically or emotionally handle the reality that in giving herself to Zach, she was giving him the chance to destroy her when—and it was a when, not if—he kissed someone else.

If that was love, she didn't want it. Couldn't take it.

It needed to stop.

She needed to stop it. To get back in control of her brain and her heart and her life. To be the smart, rational person who focused on getting someone to listen to the half dozen new songs she'd been working on, in the rare moments she could concentrate.

And so, after yoga, when Zia asked her how things were going with the Brit in question, she answered honestly. "Fine. But I'll be glad when it's all over."

They were sipping cups of mint tea on one of the communal sofas in the yoga studio's foyer, still in their workout clothes. Next to them, other yogis chatted and checked their phones.

"I thought you really liked Zach," Zia said.

"I do," Darlene replied carefully. "And because I do, and because I'm not actually his girlfriend, I think we need some more boundaries."

"More boundaries?" Zia teased. "I didn't think you had any."

Fair point. "Obviously we're going a bit method on all this."

"Yeah, you're crazy into him, and he's crazy into you."

"But that might not last." Darlene drew breath, aiming for even and objective. "Zach is . . . distractible. If we focus on seeing the contract through and only being a couple when we absolutely have to, then I get to make my EP, and Zach gets his trust, and we haven't made a lot of false promises to each other."

"Sounds very sensible." Her roommate sipped her tea, looking doubtful. "But I also think Zee-Bot is pretty great. He adores you, and he's so open about it." Zia narrowed her eyes. "Is that really all that's going on?"

Darlene pressed her lips together and nodded. The only thing worse than feeling like Zach Livingstone could crack her like an egg would be anyone knowing it. "How's everything going with your boyfriend?"

Zia sighed. "Good. But we have our issues, too."

Darlene made room for two young women dressed in matching leopard-print Lululemon, scooting closer to Zia. "Like what?"

"I know Clay cares about me. I'm his girlfriend, it's all official. But we haven't made any progress on going public."

"Why not?"

"There's always some reason why now isn't the right time. And being someone's secret is really, really hard." Zia ticked off her fingers. "No public dates, no public affection—we don't even leave the apartment at the same time. I can't go to any of his events or visit him on set. Haven't met any of his friends, apart from his manager. I haven't even told my sister about him. Not that that's going to be easy. Actually, not having to tell her is the one silver lining of still being a secret."

"Why?"

"My sister is broke. Broker than usual, and I have no idea why. I have a feeling she'll be jealous. And mad I haven't told her sooner." Zia slouched further in the sofa, picking at her cuticles. "It's like we're having an affair. Like what we're doing is wrong."

Darlene liked Clay. But as Zia's words sank in, she realized she liked the *idea* of Clay, an idea that was muddied by her own feelings about fame and talent and success. "How much time does he need?"

"Unclear. He's leaving for a six-week shoot in Brazil in a couple of weeks. So probably not before then."

"*Six weeks?* That blows."

"I'll miss him. But I really believe in this film." Zia pulled herself upright. "The script is so smart, so intense. He could win an Oscar for this, I swear."

Zia explained the film was adapted from a recent bestselling memoir of the same name, *The Jungle of Us.* Two coworkers at an environmental nonprofit get lost in the Amazon for four months, with no food, no map, no survival skills, nothing. The coworkers, both male, also used to date. In the end they both survive and end up back together. At once, it was an action-packed survival story, a gripping psychological drama, and an inspirational love story. It even wove in environmental themes about deforestation, illegal wildlife trade, and—Clay's passion—climate change. Zia read the script before Clay, and it reminded her of the time she got lost in the jungle in Southeast Asia, albeit only for one night. She pushed for him to accept the part. After he committed, Matt Damon attached to play the other lead, and the budget doubled. There was already a ton of buzz.

"Wow." Darlene was stunned. "Have you met Matt Damon?"

Zia chuckled wearily. "No. I haven't met anyone." She shifted closer and lowered her voice. "I'm starting to feel . . . not triggered. But not *not* triggered. You remember my asshole ex, right?"

Darlene nodded. Zia'd told her about Logan last year.

"He cut me off from my friends and family, too. And while this is different, it's also not. I'm really starting to see that a relationship can't survive in a vacuum. You need the support of your tribe to help it grow. To support it. Validate it."

"I'm sure Clay would understand that. Maybe you need to give him a deadline."

"Maybe." Zia looked unsure. "Ugh, this is so tough. Can we go home?"

"Absolutely." Darlene gathered up their cups. "I'll buy us a pizza. Then maybe you can listen to my new songs and give me some brutally honest feedback."

"Perfect," said Zia. "But spoiler alert: I'm probably going to love every single one of them."

They shouldered their yoga bags and stepped out into the overcast, humid evening, heading for the subway.

55

Unlike Gorman, Henry Chu had a practical approach to problem-solving. Noisy neighbors? Go talk to them. Pothole in the street in front of the shop? Take it up with city council. So when his partner of seven years started spending all his time with a younger man in the apparent name of art, the solution seemed simple.

Gorman stared at Henry, aghast. "What do you mean, you've invited Gilbert over for dinner?"

Henry wiped his hands on his apron. "I mean just that. He'll be here at seven."

Affairs, Henry was aware, thrived in darkness. In secret. If Liv had overseen Eliot and Savannah's affair, things might've turned out a lot differently. In meeting Gilbert, Henry intended for everything to get out in the open. Henry could clarify his needs, and if it came to it, they'd establish the boundaries for Gorman and Gilbert's sexual relationship. Possibly—hopefully—the excitement Gilbert stoked in Gorman's mind would disappear, just as the fear of the boogeyman vanishes when the dark becomes light.

The doorbell rang at 7:22 p.m. Gorman was on his second martini, clearly nervous.

Henry was expecting someone cute—Gorman had good taste. But even Henry had to admit, the young man standing on the doorstep was exceptionally good-looking. Buff and sandy-blond with a cute, chipper grin.

Gilbert stepped inside. "Sorry, just realized I didn't bring anything. So rude!"

"Don't worry about it," said Gorman at the same time Henry said, "No, no, it's fine."

Gilbert unzipped a windbreaker to reveal a T-shirt that read *Supergay!* in rainbow letters, taking in the apartment with wide eyes. "Omigod, I love your place. It's massive!"

"Crostini?" Henry extended a tray at the same time Gorman said, "What would you like to drink?"

They made it through appetizers, then sat down to dinner. Gilbert praised the food, and the flower arrangement, and Henry's haircut. By the time they moved on to dessert, Henry's nerves had settled. He could see Gilbert's allure—beyond his physical appeal, the young man gave the impression of being slightly in awe of everything around him, while simultaneously exuding unaffected confidence. Gilbert wanted to know all about Henry's life, from growing up in Flushing to opening a flower shop in gentrified Brooklyn. Gorman was atypically quiet as Henry answered Gilbert's many questions, even as Henry tried to draw him into the conversation. Poor Gor was probably used to being the sole object of Gilbert's flattering fascination.

They retired to the living room. Henry put on a Patsy Cline record and splashed brandy into three glasses. Gilbert curled up on the carpet going through the record collection. Gorman and Henry sat on the couch, watching him.

"Ooh, Sam Smith." Gilbert flipped the sleeve over. "Love them."

Henry felt pleased. That was his. "You have good taste."

"Obviously," Gilbert joked. "I'm doing your husband's play."

"Oh," said Henry, "we're not actually . . ."

"Married," Gorman finished. "Or, um, monogamous."

Henry gave Gorman an unimpressed look. Not the most elegant way to bring it up.

Gorman returned it with a tiny shrug.

"What about you?" Henry turned back to Gilbert, whose attention was a little too deliberately on the records. "Boyfriend?"

Gilbert shook his head. "I basically just got here, you know? So I'm just, like, having fun. This is really good brandy, by the way," he added, finishing his glass.

"Let me top you up." Henry took his glass, heading into the kitchen. Alone for a moment, he placed both hands on the counter, regretting drinking so much during dinner. His head was swimming, and he was half expecting to return to the sight of a shirtless Gilbert poured into the lap of his partner. Which felt one part exciting, two parts bewildering, and ten parts awful.

I'll say this for monogamy. The rules are much simpler.

A noise behind him.

Gilbert, coming at him fast and hard like a gay Terminator. Gilbert's mouth was on his, kissing him.

"Oh—ugh!" Henry stumbled back against the corner.

Gilbert looked horrified. "Sorry. Omigod. I thought—"

"Sorry." Henry touched his mouth, the kiss lingering on his lips. "I didn't mean—"

"Sorry." Gorman appeared in the doorway. "What's going on?"

"I thought," Henry managed, "we thought you were interested in . . ."

"Me," Gorman finished, mortified.

"Oh gosh, no," Gilbert said in a rush. "No offense, but you kind of remind me of my dad."

Gorman's cheeks turned hot pink.

"But if you guys are open," Gilbert continued, "Henry . . . ?"

"Me?" Henry felt like the underdog nominee whose name had just been read onstage.

"Think about it." Gilbert started hurriedly backing toward the door, only pausing to slip on his windbreaker. "Thanks for dinner, it was yum. See you at rehearsals next week, Gor." The front door banged shut behind him.

Gorman's shoulders slumped. He removed his kerchief and wiped his forehead. The rejection had clearly stripped him of confidence, leaving him looking less vintage, more secondhand. "Well, that was humiliating. What are you laughing at?"

"I don't know." Henry wiped a tear from his eye, unsure if it was from hilarity or grief. "I think I'm in shock."

"Obviously, you're not going to do it," Gorman said. "Him, I mean."

"Why not?"

Gorman blinked. "Because . . . Well, because . . ."

Henry picked up his brandy glass. *One more nightcap before bed? Why not.* "Like Gilbert suggested: I'll think about it."

56

There were many differences between dating in your midtwenties versus your (very) late forties. For one, transparency. When Liv and Eliot started hanging out, spontaneity was king and caring was deeply uncool. Both parties outdid each other in portraying who cared less about whether the relationship would "be anything" as the twin forces of lust and anxiety writhed around each other like battling serpents. But Liv and Sam had to make plans weeks in advance, negotiating the demanding schedules of their kids and work and therapy sessions and grocery runs. The mystery was muted. At first Liv wondered if this would make it less exciting. But her bandwidth for exciting was limited, and really, *exciting* was just another word for "tense." Transparency was calming. Liv needed calm.

Another difference was pace. They had not yet had sex. When Eliot died, Liv honestly believed she'd never have sex again. Whenever she wanted to feel bad—and that want came often last winter—she'd remind herself of the painful prophecy and dig the knife a little deeper: *You are alone. You will always be alone.*

Now, her body was starting to thaw. She liked kissing Sam. Very much. He was bigger than Eliot but gentler, less urgent. If Eliot was a lithe and wily cheetah, Sam was a solid, self-assured lion. As the late-summer air took on the texture of fur, tenderness gave way to passion and a primal, driving need that left them panting and hungry and unfulfilled.

"Do you think we're . . ." Liv did the top buttons of her shirt up, another fumbly make-out session cut short by Ben calling from his bedroom after a bad dream. ". . . um . . . ready—"

"Yes," Sam said. "A thousand percent."

Liv laughed at his certainty. "Okay. Let's find a date."

Sam made a low noise and pulled her close for a kiss. Not his usual good night kiss. A searching, openmouthed kiss that included one thumb brushed over a decidedly erect nipple.

Oh, yes. Liv's sex days were not over yet.

They made a plan. For a weekend when Claudia had custody of Dottie, and Ben could sleep over at his grandmother's. A plan with enough time for Liv to fit in a few workouts and buy impractical lingerie and raze the jungle sprouting between her legs. Liv purchased the underwear online, squinting at the tanned leather stomach of the child-model in an effort to picture it on her own, normal body. Working out was harder. Gyms were made for people under forty who were already in shape. Liv wanted a toned tummy, but her greatest ab workout was sneezing.

"Come for a run with me!" Savannah jogged in place in the office doorway, a headband keeping a tight blond ponytail off her face. She was wearing a lot less makeup these days. It didn't just make her look prettier. It made her look more confident, somehow. "It's lovely out!"

Day after day, Liv found an excuse—emails to send, vendors to call. But as Sex Date crept closer, and Savannah kept pestering, Liv finally broke down. She unearthed sneakers that hadn't been worn since Obama was president and joined Savannah for a very slow, very difficult run-walk.

"I'd forgotten . . . how hard . . . this is," Liv managed between pants. Her face was on fire.

Savannah kept pace with her. "It's just practice, Liv! You're doing great!"

"I want . . . to die."

Savannah laughed gaily. "I had a thought about Eliot. Something that might help you get to the bottom of why everything worked out the way it did. Why don't you try asking Google for his Gmail password?"

Liv pictured scaling a mountain to find a socially awkward thirty-year-old in sneakers at its peak: *Please, Mr. Google, I'm old: help me?* "Sounds hard."

"Not really." Naturally Savannah had already researched exactly how this was done: copy of the death certificate, proof of an email exchange between Liv and Eliot. "Maybe there'd be something in his in-box that would explain the will."

It was not a prospect Liv coveted: reading Eliot's flirtatious messages to a naive Savannah, sandwiched in between the terse updates to his wife.

"I can do the application," Savannah offered.

"Fine," Liv puffed. "Ooh. I think I have a stitch." They'd gone two blocks.

The days fell away:

Sex Date was next week.

Sex Date was tomorrow.

Sex Date was *tonight*.

Liv woke with a palatable feeling of dread. *Snap out of it*, she told herself. *This is supposed to be fun! Relax!*

But she couldn't. Fear hung around her like a watchful black crow. No matter how busy she made herself with washing the sheets and applying various serums and dropping off Ben at her mother's, the dark bird was there. Judging her jiggling belly and post-childbirth vagina, which felt roomy enough to house an entire murder of crows. What if it wasn't as good as sex with Eliot? What if it was better? What if she couldn't get into it, or got too into it and said, "I love you!" when she really meant, "I'm coming!" She knew she needed to calm down and be an adult about the whole thing. But sometimes being a calm adult was really hard, and it was a lot easier to be a panicked non-adult.

As the sky darkened, Liv slipped into a robe, then jeans, then back into the robe. Mild panic upgraded itself to borderline terror. She needed something to take the edge off.

She couldn't remember who'd given her the joint: it'd appeared in the foggy non-time immediately following Eliot's death. Liv was an uncommitted weed smoker in her youth, but stopped altogether while trying to conceive and never got back into it. Back then, everyone smoked limp little joints that got disgustingly damp at the filter when passed around. But this elegantly rolled object looked factory-perfect and made getting baked seem extremely sophisticated.

Liv lit it and took a tiny hit. Easy enough. She poured herself a glass of wine, which disappeared in no time, so she poured herself another. That was one of the pleasures of drinking at home—a country club pour every time. But the wine barely made a dent in her nerves, and the weed, well, that didn't seem to be working *at all*. Sam would be there in less than thirty minutes, and she was still jumpy with nerves.

Screw it.

She took a longer, deeper drag, and then one more for good measure, enjoying the way it burned her throat and made her eyes water. That meant it was working.

Relax, she instructed herself, bringing the wineglass to her lips. *Relax*.

57

The Strand bookstore on Broadway was packed and buzzy by the time Darlene and Zach arrived. Zach hadn't RSVP'd, but after he turned on the charm for the woman with the clipboard, the sold-out event wasn't sold-out for him. Oddly, Darlene seemed irritated by this.

The book launch wasn't a date. It was a punishment. And Zach had no idea why.

Things with Darlene had gotten a little . . . cool. It might be his dumb paranoia, but she seemed to take a giant step away from him after The Kiss That Mattered. The first kiss they hadn't documented for social media (and what a handy excuse that'd turned out to be). The first kiss where he let her have him, all of him, every desperate, driving, needy part of him . . . but then she'd backed off. Not disappeared, they were still in their stupid fake relationship, which he was both annoyed by and thankful for. But she was no longer asking him to kiss her, with those blown dark eyes and pink parted lips. Instead, he'd begged to be her plus-one for a book launch. Not just any book launch. Awful Charles's book launch. Her ex.

"He's in conversation with *Rachel Maddow*," Darlene had said, after Zach spotted the invite stuck to her fridge.

"The tennis player?"

"No! The journalist. On MSNBC. You definitely know her."

Zach maybe knew her. "I didn't think you were still in touch with Charles."

Darlene had shrugged, grabbing a bowl of the shrimp lo mein he'd brought over. "I ran into him. He invited me. I said yes."

"Why?"

"I can't spend all my time with you."

"Why not?"

"Because we're not actually a couple." Her voice hitched before she regained control. "It's healthy to have a wide circle of intellectually stimulating friends."

Who happen to be your ex. So here they were, front row, in seats reserved with Darlene's name, which she was obviously impressed by. On the stage were two chairs, a fifteen-foot projection of the book cover—*Mistakes Were Made: The Paradox of the Working-Class Revolution*—and a photograph of Awful Charles boasting the confidence of a pop star in the pasty body of a garden gnome.

"Look, there's Jon Favreau," Darlene whispered, side-eyeing a handsome dude in a suit. "And, omigod, is that AOC?"

More people Darlene knew that he didn't, perfect.

His beautiful bandmate was a Virgo, and Virgos were cautious with their feelings, unlike his Libran self. Libras were suckers for love, and yes, Zach'd had his fair share of bedfellows. But he never felt comfortable letting those women know the real him. They saw fun Zach, good-time Zach; vacation flings, nothing real. Darlene knew him better than anyone: as a musician, a son, a creative collaborator. She knew all his flaws. He cared about her. Respected and trusted her. But he got the feeling her tight jumpsuit and natural curls weren't for his benefit tonight. The look she gave his wrinkled button-down was almost derisive. Zach searched the room. "Don't tell me there's no bar. Aren't all writers alcoholics?"

"Charles is sober."

"Ugh." Zach grimaced. "Of course he is."

Darlene narrowed her eyes. "Which I actually really respect."

"Oh, yeah. Me too."

"But there'll probably be wine at the dinner afterward," she added, patting his arm.

Zach slouched further in his seat. Now, there was a *dinner* he'd have to attend full of brilliant, bookish people like Awful Charles and Jon Favreau and AOC—people who made him feel as insightful as a loaf of white bread. He grabbed Darlene's hand and tugged her toward him, feeling needy. "Why don't we skip it? There's a good little wine bar up the street. We could get high, play footsie under the table."

Darlene extracted her hand from his. "I told you we're here as *friends*."

The word slapped him across the face. "Why do you keep saying that?"

"Because," she replied coolly, "it's the truth."

Zach fought the impulse to scream. When would Darlene admit that they were made for each other, that they were falling in love? She could have his money, all of it. Darlene was his future, and the trust was only important in that it'd enable them to be together as much as possible. Why was she insisting they were "friends"?

Maybe because, for her, it was just about the money. Maybe she wasn't feeling the feelings he was feeling at all.

The lights dimmed. Awful Charles and Rachel Maddow came on-stage to rapturous applause. Charles was preening, activated by the crowd, which Zach found both familiar and sickening. "Wake me up when it's over."

Darlene looked unimpressed. "You might want to rethink the whole anti-intellectualism thing, Zach. It's not very attractive."

Zach deflated like a sad balloon. That was it: whatever attraction she'd felt had worn off. She'd realized that being open-minded and kind and all those other nice things she'd said that night when she defended him in front of his family *just wasn't enough*. His insecurity sickened him—he knew it was about as appealing as the "whole anti-intellectualism thing." But he couldn't control it.

Zach's heart tore at the edges as Darlene trained her gaze on Charles.

58

Savannah flung open her front door, feeling like a wind-up toy let loose. "*HI!*"

Honey instinctively swayed back. "Hi."

"Come in, come in. Gosh, you look so pretty. Is it too hot in here? I can turn up the AC, I just can*not* seem to get the temperature right!"

"It's fine." Honey's expression was bemused. Her summer tan had faded the spray of freckles across her nose. Savannah had the urge to touch them, connecting each dot, one by one. Honey frowned at her. "Do I have something on my face?"

"What? No. Ha! So good to see you." She launched herself at Honey for a hug.

"Ow." Honey wriggled. "Little much."

"Sorry." Savannah leaped back, embarrassed. "Just happy to see you! It's been so long and I—" *Am nervous and excited and scared and* everything *because I think I want to kiss you and I have no idea how!*

"Savannah." Honey's brown eyes were gentle and possibly tinged with mirth. "Calm down, okay? Why don't we have a drink and put the movie on."

"Yes. Of course. Great idea." Savannah restrained herself from offering five more affirmations.

Honey had traded jeans and a T-shirt for cutoffs and a T-shirt. Savannah had decided on a short summery romper, with just a touch of lip gloss and blush. It was too hot for much more.

Honey poured two glasses of the rosé she'd brought and asked if Savannah's roommates were home. Arj was working, Leonie was visiting her parents in New Jersey, and Yuli was working on his latest young adult novel in a coffee shop.

"Just us," Savannah said, as if this was a coincidence and not a well-executed plan.

"Great." Honey's tone was so noncommittal, Savannah couldn't read it at all. Their conversation from last month sounded in her mind: *I don't want to get my heart broken by a straight girl.*

But what if I'm not straight? is what Savannah wished she'd said. *How do I know?*

Savannah Shipley had accepted that, yes, she was definitely very interested in kissing a girl. Specifically, Honey. But she'd invested her entire romantic life in the steadfast belief—the knowledge—that one day, she would marry a man. Just like everyone else around her. And dismantling that idea was as overwhelming and impossible as asking one to demolish a house with a teaspoon. The foundations were too solid. The structure was too big.

And yet, there was: *I only liked it because everyone else did.*

Her New York vision board, with its central clipping of a hot guy in a tux, had been stuffed under her bed for weeks.

Honey sat on the sofa. "What are we watching?"

Panicked, Savannah doubted her choice. It was undeniably an offering. The first tap of that teaspoon against solid brick. "I thought we could check out a show called, um, *Feel Good.*"

Honey almost did a double take.

Savannah busied herself with pouring cheese puffs into a bowl. "I don't know, it sounded fun, but we don't have to if you've already seen it."

Honey curled up at the far end of the sofa. Her eyes rested on Savannah curiously. "I saw it. But I'll watch it again."

Savannah's phone vibrated. *Dad Calling.* She felt a flicker of guilt. But she wasn't doing anything wrong. She turned her phone off. "Let's do it."

Feel Good was about a Canadian comedian living in London named Mae Martin who started dating a girl called George, who'd never dated another girl before. They were kissing in the first ten minutes and then they moved in together and then it came out that Mae used to be an addict but that didn't matter because Savannah was already in love with Mae, and George, and the idea of Mae and George together. It was familiar and alien, and Savannah was experiencing a disorienting whiplash of recognizing a version of herself in George, a fictional character from a different world. With different rules.

When the episode ended, she immediately pressed play for the second one. Then the third. Then the fourth.

"Savannah?"

"Huh?" Savannah startled, finger on the remote.

Honey stretched, looking amused. "Can we take a break?"

"Oh. Sure." Savannah checked the time and blushed. "Sorry."

Honey rose to get the wine from the fridge. She poured them both a glass, emptying the bottle. "I take it you're into it?"

Savannah nodded, the words spilling out in a rush. "Holy mack, it's amazing. It's funny and smart and obviously, um, sexy. I really like George and Mae is just so *hot*. She's like a pretty boy and a pretty girl and I'm *really* into it."

Honey laughed. When she sat back down on the sofa, it was closer to Savannah. Her cheeks were flushed from the wine. She propped her hand up with her head, her fingers buried in her dark curls. "Do you think she's your type? Or are you just into girls, in general?"

Savannah inched closer. It felt like sharing a secret. An illicit, exhilarating one. "Maybe . . . girls in general?"

The sky had darkened over the past few hours, and now it was night. All the lights in the apartment were off. The only light came from the TV, paused on the credit roll. Honey's voice was soft. "Girls like me?"

Savannah's gaze dropped to Honey's mouth. Her rosebud lips, plump and parted. She wanted to feel them. Touch them. Savannah nodded, her voice both small and, somehow, enormous. "Yes."

Honey shifted closer. Her eyes were questions as she reached for Savannah's hand, taking it in hers.

Their fingers met. Electricity jolted up her spine. Savannah was so overwhelmed, for one horrifying second she thought she might cry. Then the feeling settled, blooming into something more manageable, and they were holding hands. Just like Imogene and Mina. She was holding Honey's hand.

But she wanted more.

The air between them sparked with possibility.

She leaned toward Honey, closing the distance between their mouths. Honey did the same. This was it. It was happening. She could feel Honey's breath. Savannah's heart was beating wildly, slamming her rib cage with an undiscovered ferocity. Everything inside her was urging her forward, forward, forward until Honey's lips met hers and they were kissing.

They were kissing.

And all of a sudden, everything made sense.

Every love song made sense.

Every romantic movie made sense.

Every poem, every painting, every Taylor Swift lyric, everything in the entire world made sense because this, *this*, was how it was supposed to feel. How love was supposed to feel, how kissing was supposed to feel. This was what everyone was talking about.

It was a sweet kiss, a sexy kiss, the first kiss where she wasn't thinking about if her breath smelled or how much tongue she should use. It was simply the most natural, most easy, most thrilling act of her entire life.

When she pulled away, her eyes were wet. Honey stroked her face, a smile turning worried. "What's wrong?"

Savannah pressed Honey's fingers into her cheek and shook her head. "Nothing," she managed. "Nothing's wrong at all."

Because everything was finally right.

59

Sam hurried up the steps to the brownstone. He was almost an hour late. His ex-wife, Claudia, had come down with the flu, so he'd asked Claudia's sister to sleep over and babysit. Dottie loved her aunt, but since the divorce, his daughter had become sensitive to broken promises and changes to routine. It'd taken bribes of ice cream and a princess costume to allow Sam to leave for an "overnight work trip," and even then he felt extraordinarily guilty. On top of everything, he was lying to his child, even if it was for a good reason.

Sam liked order. While happy to improvise in the kitchen, he preferred the satisfaction of following set rules to produce an expected outcome. But there was no recipe for this, the divorced-dad-dates-a-widowed-mom dish. This was life: messy, chaotic, and never quite turning out how you anticipated.

He'd been keeping Liv in the loop over text. Her last few messages had been a little . . . strange.

Sam, 6:50 p.m.: Issues with Dottie: I'm going to be a bit late.

Liv, 6:58 p.m.: No problem!!!!

Sam, 7:25p.m.: Working on it. So sorry.

Liv, 7:35 p.m.: I'm good!!!! Ha ha, LOL. 😉

Sam, 7:45 p.m.: Okay, finally en route! Be there by eight.

Liv, 7:47 p.m.: !!!???!!! WOW. I feel

Liv, 7:48 p.m.: Srry sent that too

Liv, 7:49 p.m.: IM RELAXED!!! 😊 😊 😊

Sam, 7:50 p.m.: You okay?

Liv, 7:55 p.m.: HA HA HA!

Inside the brownstone, he could hear Fleetwood Mac. The soft, rocking blues took him back to being long-haired and loose-limbed, pre-children, pre-marriage, even. A time without consequences, when the future was nothing but possibility and pleasure. Sam took a moment to ruffle up his hair and then unruffle it. He'd slept with a few women since his divorce, but not someone he really liked. There'd been a moment when they first met, her waving a banana, when her bathrobe had gaped open and he'd almost glimpsed a nipple. He'd thought about that moment many times. Liv was complex, sometimes prickly, sometimes even mean—and he liked it. It felt dangerous. And he had a suspicion she'd be a little hellcat in bed. Not that they would definitely have sex tonight: they were taking it slow. No matter what happened, they'd have fun.

And, hopefully, they'd have sex.

Sam rang the doorbell.

From the other side of the door, uneven footsteps approached. Then, nothing. "Liv?"

A muffled squeak sounded from the other side of the door, followed by a giggle.

He smiled. "Hello?"

The door yanked open. Liv was wearing a black silk robe over a pair of jeans. Her hair was wild. Her lips were painted dark red. The effect was witchy and a little weird. Not unappealing. She planted her hands on either side of the doorframe. "Hello." Her voice was husky. "Mr. Sam."

A rill of excitement pulsed through his body. This was a Liv he hadn't seen before. The fact that this complicated, alluring woman could keep opening up to him was thrilling. "Hello," he replied, "Ms. Liv."

She threw her head back and laughed.

Sam chuckled along, double-checking that what he'd said wasn't actually that funny. Was something off? Or was she just nervous like he was? He followed her inside. "You seem very, ah, chill."

"I am." She sounded drifty and full of air. "I'm chill. Chill as a cucumber." She spun around, putting both hands atop her head like a little hat. She made her voice high and squeaky. "Hello, I'm a cucumber. Put me in salads."

"Okay . . ."

Liv swept into the living room and started dancing to "Dreams." Well, dancing wasn't the right word for it. *Flailing* was more accurate.

A half-empty bottle of red wine sat on the coffee table. Next to it, half a joint.

Oh.

"Hey babe, have you been smoking?"

"A little." She blinked slowly. "A lot?"

Fortunately you couldn't overdose on weed. But the combination had clearly pushed Liv over her limit. Sam picked up the joint and the wine bottle from the coffee table. Liv watched them go, saying, "Nooo," in a small, sad voice.

Sam stowed the bottle of wine he'd brought in the pantry, corked the open bottle, and poured a glass of water. "Drink this."

Liv took a sip and made a face. "It's water."

"Yup."

"Yuck." She turned her face away from it, like a child refusing brussels sprouts.

"Please? For me?"

Sighing as if this was the single most annoying thing that'd ever been requested of her, Liv took a few gulps. She leaned back into the sofa, propping her head up in a sloppy approximation of sexy. "Why don't you show me that cucumber in your pants, Sammy?"

"Oh, boy." Sam laughed. "I don't think so. Not tonight."

"But we have a sex date," she whined. "I got a wax. It *hurt.*"

Sam inhaled, oscillating between concerned and amused. "That's very thoughtful, sweetie, but you're a little out of it."

Liv launched herself at him, her fingers diving for the top of his jeans. "I wanna see it."

Sam skidded back. "No, Liv."

"I wanna see your cucumber!"

"No, baby."

"*Yes!*" She fought to undo his top button.

"*No!*" Sam wrestled her eager hands from his fly, his voice gentle but firm. "C'mon, darling. It's time you went to bed."

With much effort, Sam managed to get Liv into bed and drink another glass of water. "You'll thank me in the morning," he said, moving to turn off the light. The paintings on the wall were bold and interesting, and the bed was a king. It was a bedroom he'd, ordinarily, enjoy having sex in.

"Sam?" Liv's voice was already thick with sleep.

"Yes, babe?"

Her eyes were closed. He was ready for some unchecked confession. Maybe *I like you. I really like you.* Maybe *Thank you.* Liv's voice was gentle in the near darkness. "I just farted."

He pressed his lips together so as not to laugh and switched off the light. "Good night, Liv."

60

The after-party dinner for Charles's book launch was at a nearby restaurant, in a private dining room lit by undulating chandeliers. Zach was pleased to see the long table held at least sixty name cards. Perhaps he and Darlene would be seated far away from Charles and they'd manage to have something of a pleasant dinner date. No such luck. Charles was seated across from them. Darlene was seated next to Jon Favreau. The name card for "Zack L"—handwritten, probably because he didn't RSVP—had him next to Darlene on one side, and Rachel bloody Maddow on the other.

"Lucky you." Darlene snuck a peek at Charles and ran her tongue over her bottom lip.

That was *his* nervous habit: Darlene did that when she got cute and shy around *him*.

"Yes," Zach replied tightly. "Lucky."

Bowls of salad were placed on the table. Zach racked his brain for a good opening line for Rachel. He'd mixed with plenty of impressive people in his life, and ordinarily felt comfortable in pretty much all social situations. But tonight was different: Darlene's indifference had undermined his usual social ease. And he didn't understand political stuff in the way he understood music or sex or humor; things you felt rather than things you knew. "This salad's really good," is what he landed on.

Rachel's smile was mild. "Delicious."

"People think salad is easy, but it's not. You've got to get the right ratio of dressing to greens." What was he doing? Why was he talking about salad? "Too little and it's not very flavorful, but too much and it gets wet and, um, soggy."

Rachel frowned. He could see her wondering if he was a lunatic. "Soggy?"

Don't say soggy again. Don't say soggy again. "And different greens get soggy *differently*. Arugula: now, that'll get soggy. Kale, not so much on the, um, soggy . . . front."

"Charles." Rachel turned her attention to him. "I've been thinking about what you said on false consciousness."

Zach's face heated. *Idiot.*

Next to him, Jon Favreau was making Darlene cackle with laughter. Ordinarily a lovely sound, but right now it screeched like nails down a blackboard. How soon till this nightmare could be over? Every passing minute underlined the fact that he didn't belong here at all.

"So, Zach." Charles was speaking to him across the table. "Didn't think this sort of thing was up your alley."

Screw you, mate. He knew Charles thought he was a Zoolander-level idiot: a lot of less attractive men did. "I enjoyed it very much." Actually, there were parts of the conversation that he enjoyed, when Charles wasn't posturing and generally being a cocky knob. The debate had the lively, unpredictable feel of improvised jazz.

Charles took a sip of water. "So I assume you're still Darlene's bandmate?"

"That's right. Bandmate." Zach gave Darlene a smile that tottered over the line between platonic and secret passion.

She returned it like a bad throw.

Charles watched the whole exchange with open alarm. His mouth hardened. "I'm curious, Zach. What was your take on the debate in my book?"

Zach felt a small slap of panic. "Considering I'm at the launch, I haven't quite had the chance to read it yet."

"Sure," Charles said. "But why do you think the working class vote against their own interests?"

To his horror, Zach sensed Rachel Maddow leaning closer, curious as to his reply. "That's a very complex issue. That I'm not really qualified to have an opinion on."

Charles nodded slowly. Mockingly. "No, you're not really the political type, are you?" He returned to his dinner, slicing into his fish.

"How many people googled 'What is the EU?' after voting in Brexit? Millions, wasn't it?"

Zach had voted for Britain to stay in the EU. And he knew what the European Union was, Christ. Charles might be a progressive, but he was also a bit of a bully who loved the sound of his own voice.

"Racism," Charles continued, voice swelling like a politician, "is just as much of a problem in the UK as it is here. Right, Darlene?"

Darlene blinked. "I know more about racism in *America*," she said, with what Zach felt was admirable control. "Which, considering Black women make thirty-nine percent less than white men, is obviously alive and well."

"Spoken like a true Princeton grad." Charles's smile read as patronizing.

Zach didn't get the sense that for Charles, Darlene-as-girlfriend was proof that he could "date up" in terms of her hotness; rather, that he could date across racial difference—and he wanted everyone at the table to see it. And that was so mind-blowingly *foul*.

The conversation appeared to have come to an end. But Zach was surprised to realize he wasn't done. "Obviously racism is an issue in the UK, and here, and everywhere," he said. "But the leave vote wasn't all about immigration. It was a protest vote. Like Trump."

Charles snapped to attention, stunned that Zach had dared offer an opinion. "What's that about Trump?"

Instantly, Zach doubted himself. But it was too late now. "Well, his election was a protest vote. Wasn't it?"

Charles raised his voice. "Donald Trump is an ignominy who should be erased from the pages of history."

Zach almost laughed. "What, like, censored? Careful, Charles, you'll be burning books in a minute."

A flash of anger passed Charles's face before it was hidden with noble posturing. "Brexit was about race, and class, as was Trump."

"Obviously," said Zach. "But you make it sound like people were stupid for voting for them: *Against their own interests*."

"Not knowing what the EU is after you vote to remove yourself isn't just stupid, Zach," Charles said. "It's disrespectful, dishonorable, and unpatriotic."

"Sure," Zach said, "I agree with that too, I think. And look, I am definitely not working-class. But I played music in London, right, I played, and drank, with lots of guys from the north. And it's really bloody rough up there."

"Rough like how?" Darlene asked.

"No jobs, loads of drugs, really dangerous," Zach said. "They see what it's like for the elite, like me, and you, Charles, and everyone at this table, and they're pissed. And rightly so."

The people around him were all listening. Including Rachel.

"And so, yeah," Zach said, "some of them voted to leave."

"These are friends of yours?" Charles said. "People who supported one of the most racist cultural shifts in modern memory?"

"I think Zach said they were his colleagues," Darlene said. "But does it matter if they were also friends? We're always talking about how we need to hear all sides; get out of our bubbles."

"And I'm not saying I condone it," Zach said, "I'm saying I understand why people voted for Trump or for Brexit, not as a mistake, but as a . . . flex. A firing shot."

"Even if they are shooting at the wrong target," Darlene said. "The right-wing media—"

Charles addressed Zach. "People voted for Trump because—"

Zach spoke over Charles. "She wasn't finished." The thought of punching Charles in the face flashed briefly, enjoyably.

"The right-wing media," Darlene repeated, "does a pretty good job of convincing people that immigrants and people of color are taking their resources, rather than the top one percent in the US who own forty percent of America's wealth."

"Totally," said Zach. "Yes. And, to be honest, I think it's a patronizing liberal fantasy to think it was all a big mistake. These people need help and respect, not to be gaslit about their own intentions."

Next to him, Rachel Maddow nodded.

"Well, maybe you should write a book about it," said Charles. "Oh, wait, you're a musician, not a thought leader."

"Is that what you are?" Zach feigned surprise. "All this time, I've been going with 'pretentious know-it-all.'"

Someone choked out a laugh. Charles pressed his lips together. With enormous effort, he turned to the person next to him and struck up a conversation.

Darlene gave Zach a look. Before he could figure out if she was amused or annoyed, Jon Favreau was in her ear again.

Rachel Maddow leaned toward Zach. "You're obviously not a fan," she murmured. "What brought you here?"

Zach glanced at the now-distracted Charles and Darlene. "Matters of the heart, Ms. Maddow."

To his surprise, she looked intrigued. "Spill."

61

Liv awoke feeling like a notch below fetid-swamp-monster. Her tongue was a secondhand shag carpet. Her brain was in a vise that was tightening. Sunlight barged rudely through the curtains. It was late. Very late.

"Ben!" The word, a choked gasp. School. Ben. Late. She jerked herself upright, flinging a hand, knocking a glass. It fell with a tiny smash.

It was Sunday. And Ben . . . Ben was at her mother's.

Last night flooded back in a sickening rush.

Sam.

Sex Date.

Weed.

Cucumber.

Oh *no*.

Her bedroom door creaked. "Morning, sleepyhead."

Liv crawled back under the covers, praying for a trapdoor. She heard Sam pick up the bits of broken glass, then sit down next to her on the bed. "How's the head?"

She could barely look at him. Her words were croaks. "Just . . . tell me I didn't."

"Didn't what?"

Thrash around to Fleetwood Mac? Cackle like a maniac? Demand you show me your cucumber? She cracked an eye at him. He looked Sunday fresh. Where had he slept? The couch? Ben's room? Oh *God*. "Any of it."

He chuckled. "Yeah, you were a bit out of it."

"I was catatonic." Her stomach took this opportunity to rumble loudly. This was all about as sexy as a Pap smear. "What time is it?"

"Time for breakfast. Stay right there."

There was zero chance she could do anything else.

Sam delivered breakfast in bed. Hash browns and eggs and bacon. Hot and salty and delicious. When Liv was in her twenties, she could knock back a bottle of wine and wake up feeling fantastic. Now it took two cups of coffee, an aspirin, and a long hot shower for her headache to finally subside. She came downstairs in a robe. Sam was in the kitchen, cleaning up. A repeat of the first day they met. Except this time, she knew the man wiping down the chopping board. And she liked him so, so much.

They settled on the couch, Liv's feet in his lap. It wasn't yet noon. Ben wouldn't be back until dinnertime. "So," Sam said. "What was all that about?"

"Oh, I just like to get shitfaced before I do it," Liv deadpanned, and Sam laughed. "No, I am really sorry. I was nervous. Guess I overcorrected."

"I was nervous too," Sam said. He was massaging her feet. It was making her feel tingly. "It's been a while, and I wasn't sure if the, ah, pocket rocket"—he gestured at his lap—"would still be fully functional."

"It certainly seems to be working. All those nights on your couch . . ." Her smile was suggestive.

Sam grinned back, his eyes tracing the body hidden beneath the robe. "There have been a few admirable launch missions."

"Very admirable indeed . . ."

Perhaps Sex Date was not over yet.

Liv crawled over the sofa to him. She straddled him and kissed his mouth.

"Hello," Sam said, surprised, but pleased. He glanced at his lap. "And, hello. Houston, we have liftoff."

Liv giggled.

"Too many space jokes?" Sam asked.

"Never," she said, and kissed him again. This time he kissed her back, one large hand on her jaw, the other on her back. She was still hungover, but in a way that made her lazy and languid. Able to relax into the unfamiliar-yet-familiar feeling of making love. She took Sam's earlobe between her teeth. "What time do you have to get home?"

"Dottie's at a birthday party with her aunt."

Liv tugged her robe open.

Sam's eyes glazed as he focused on her breasts. He flipped Liv onto the couch, his mouth on her neck, his body on hers. His full, delicious weight pressed her into the old sofa. Liv closed her eyes and thanked her lucky stars. What was she so worried about? This would be *easy*.

"To infinity," she murmured, "and beyond."

62

"What's up with you?"

Zia blinked at her sister. Layla was staring back with narrowed eyes. Dark circles cut under them. She looked more tired than usual. *Tell her. Just tell her!*

Her niece and nephew were weaving, whining, wanting attention. The television was on, blaring Sunday cartoons. Layla persisted. "What, you have a fight with Tom or something?"

"Actually, yeah, I did want to tell you something about, um, Tom." They still hadn't gone public, but Zia knew she was using this as an excuse not to be honest. Maybe Layla would be happy for her. Excited to meet a guy who really cared about her. "The thing is—"

Mateo rocketed past, slamming into a side table, knocking a lamp. It fell to the tiles, smashing to bits. Layla leaped to her feet. "Jesus, what the hell!"

Mateo mumbled sorry. His cast had come off the week before, and he was making up for lost time.

Layla stomped on the pieces, furious. "That's great, Matty. That's just great!"

"Calm down." Why was her sister getting so worked up? "We'll get another one."

"As if I can afford that," Layla muttered.

Zia swept up the broken pieces and dumped them in the trash while her sister poured a very full juice cup of very cheap wine and sent the kids to the bedroom they shared with her. Layla massaged the joints in her hands, grimacing. "So, what about Tom?"

"Oh, it can wait."

"I'm working doubles all next week."

"Okay. Okay." Zia muted the television. Sweat had broken out under her armpits and on top of her lip. She didn't expect to be this nervous. "So, this is kind of a crazy story, actually. Tom's name isn't actually *Tom*."

"What, are you banging one of my exes?"

"No! God, no, Layla. It's, well, I'm kind of dating"—*say it. Say it!*—"Clay Russo."

Layla blinked. Frowned. "Is that Pablo's cousin?"

"No, Clay Russo. He's an actor, and an activist."

"I know who *Clay Russo* is."

"Well, that's who I'm dating. Not a gardener," she added dumbly.

Layla looked confused. "Ha ha?"

"It's not a joke."

"I think I'd have picked, like, Jesse Williams. Dude's fine." Layla sipped her wine, bored of the bad joke.

"I'm not making it up. We met at a wedding back in May. He was a guest. We hit it off. It's been on the down-low but now—"

"Zia—"

"He's my boyfriend, and I want you to meet him and—"

"Zia, whoa!" Layla put down the cup, her expression transforming into real concern. An old tenderness emerged, the one born in the aftermath of the Logan breakup and court case. "You sound like you really believe this."

At a loss at what else to do, Zia got out her phone. Layla watched her unlock it, and tap open her photos. They still didn't take any couple pictures, but the other night they'd drunk a lot of cabernet and made a mess in the kitchen. Zia had tipsily snapped Clay covered in pasta sauce, laughing hysterically. She showed the only picture she had of Clay to her sister. "See? That's his kitchen."

Layla peered at the photo. "You get this off the internet?"

Zia exhaled, frustrated, pointing at the picture. "That's my tote bag. Sis, I'm telling the truth."

Layla's face started to go slack. Her eyes flicked from the picture to Zia, back and forth. "You're dating *Clay Russo*. For real?"

"*Yes.*"

"Swear on *Abuelita*'s grave. Swear on my kids' lives."

Zia looked her right in the eye. "I swear. He's my boyfriend, but we're still not public. Which sucks, actually, because—"

Her sister started to cry.

"Layla!" Zia scooted closer, alarmed. Of all the reactions she expected, this wasn't one of them. It must be the shock. Zia rubbed her back as her sister began weeping. "Layla, honey."

"*Gracias a Dios, gracias a Dios.*" Her sister was rocking back and forth. She was laughing. "I prayed. I prayed for this."

"For me getting a boyfriend?"

"No." Layla's laugh was a little manic. "Oh, Zia. This fixes everything."

Zia's skin cooled. "Fixes what?"

"Zia." Her sister wiped her nose with her sweatshirt sleeve. She looked ecstatic. "A few months ago, my insurance stopped covering my Humira. Do you know what that is?"

"The medication for your arthritis?"

"That's right. So now it costs, like, five freaking grand. Every *two weeks.*"

Zia gasped. The bill she'd seen in the trash. It wasn't for Mateo. It was for Layla. "What? Why didn't you tell me?"

"Oh, honey." Layla kissed her sister's hands. "You already give us so much. And you don't have an extra five grand. But now . . ."

"Now?"

Layla's eyes were fever bright. "C'mon, Zia. Ten thousand a month is nothing to guys like that. *Nothing.*"

Zia couldn't believe what she was hearing. "I can't ask Clay for money, Layla. I'll help you as much as I can, I'll pick up extra shifts, but—"

"Look at that kitchen!" Layla erupted, pointing at Zia's phone. "That place costs a million bucks!"

Try ten million. Zia's heart was racing. She shook her head, trying to get ahold of the situation. "How much do you need?"

Layla licked her lips. "Like, fifty grand? To pay off my credit cards and make it through this year."

Panic coursed through Zia's chest. She pictured asking Clay for fifty grand. *Hey babe, so I told my sister about us, and she was wondering if there was any way—* Zia shut her eyes, mortified. "It's just, he has a thing about being used, and—"

"He has a *thing* about being *used*?"

"Layla, I can't ask Clay to give me fifty thousand dollars! Do you have any idea how insane that is?"

"Then, 'borrow' a leather jacket and I'll put it on eBay. I know what those things can cost, I read about it in—"

Zia shot to her feet. "You're unbelievable."

"No, you're unbelievable." Layla was on her feet, too. "That you'd choose some rich boy over your own *family*."

The guilt trip hit Zia hard. "I'm not choosing him over you! I just can't ask him for money!"

"I'm in *pain*. Every day!"

"Layla, Clay isn't a free ATM!"

"Why the hell not?" Her sister was wild-eyed. "I can't believe this is an argument. You're so selfish, Zia. You've always gotten everything, and I get *nothing*."

"I can't listen to this." Zia grabbed her bag and stormed for the front door, tears in her eyes.

"Yeah, off you go," Layla taunted her. "Run away like you always do. You don't care about anybody but yourself."

Zia shut the front door with a bang, tears rising up in her like a geyser, ready to blow.

63

When Savannah was eleven, she was obsessed with a book series called the Sweetwater Girls. They told the story of three sisters: the spirited, ambitious Hope (aged fourteen, brunette); impulsive troublemaker Faith (fifteen, redhead); and bookish, beautiful Grace (sixteen, blonde), who lived in the geographically ambiguous lakeside town of Sweetwater. The books revolved around the girls' love lives and friendships and school dramas, stuffed with cliffhangers and emotion, and racy enough to feel illicit. Savannah had her first orgasm after Grace let local bad boy Chase Daniels touch her breast (the eldest sister had bumped her head and experienced a complete personality change; this dangerous medical phenomenon would be reversed after Grace bumped her head again). There was no greater thrill than opening the pages of, say, #23 *Hope for Class President* or #107 *Grace's Two Loves*, and losing herself in the perpetually sunny world of Sweetwater and its three beautiful sisters. For over a year, it was a singular focus, a fiction addiction of the highest order. When Savannah grew out of the series, she never again found a passion as wholly consuming, pleasurable, and engrossing as the Sweetwater Girls.

Until she kissed Honey.

Honey and Savannah didn't leave Savannah's bedroom for one hundred years. At least, that's how it felt. Cool Leonie referred to it as *love soup*: the sensation of being completely submerged in another person. Savannah was in the soup, and it was delicious.

It wasn't until Savannah kissed a girl that she realized how much she needed—craved—softness. Softness of skin, of lips, of hair, of voice. How much she'd been trying to enjoy masculine hardness because that's what she was supposed to like. And now a *galaxy* of possibility had opened up. And it all started with one gorgeous brunette who was permanently sequestered in Savannah's twin bed. A brunette with Hope's independence, Faith's sass, and Grace's inner goodness.

"I'm so into you," Savannah kept repeating, as they rolled on top of each other. "I'm just *so* into you."

"I told you," Honey would giggle. "I knew it."

Now, early on a Friday evening, Savannah admired how cute Honey looked, dressed only in Savannah's Kentucky Wildcats T-shirt and boy-short underwear, as she peered into the fridge. "What are we going to eat? If I eat any more pizza, I'll turn into a pizza."

"I know," Savannah groaned. "I need to buy groceries. I've been . . . distracted."

"We could go out."

Out. Savannah was struggling with going—or really, being—out.

They had gone out a couple of times, to get pizza or happy hour wine. But Honey wanted to hold hands and make out, and while Savannah pretended she was cool with that, she wasn't. It felt like too much. Like they were on display. Holding hands with a woman in public, having a *girlfriend*, marked her as different. Outside the norm. And on top of all that was her faith. She was pretty sure her God loved her, and accepted her for who she was, without caveat. But she wasn't absolutely sure. The hipster churches in Brooklyn were open-minded. The regular churches in Kentucky were way more traditional. And the idea of being alienated from society or her faith because of who she was dating made her feel afraid. Which is why it was easier not to think about either.

Savannah followed Honey into the kitchen. "Can't go out. Too far from bed."

Honey laughed and hopped up onto the kitchen counter. "Let's go away for a weekend. My friends are dying to meet you. You'll love them; they're hilarious."

Savannah had read that lesbian relationships move fast. But this was warp speed. "You told your friends about me?"

"Of course. I was thinking it was time we were 'Insta official.'"

Honey said it like it was a joke. But Savannah knew she wasn't joking. Apparently her entrepreneurial spirit also extended to relationships.

"Hey, do you remember," Honey said, "when we first met, you asked me when New York started feeling like home?"

Savannah was too nervous over where this was going to do anything other than lie. "Um, yes?"

"It felt like home when I met you." Honey looked deep in Savannah's eyes. Too deep. Way, way too deep.

"I'm starving," Savannah blurted. "We need takeout—Thai food sound good?"

She was across the street and ordering chicken pad see ew before she knew it. God bless New York: a million dinner options from around the world on a single block.

They hadn't discussed Savannah's sexuality. Honey seemed to believe it was now a moot point, as relevant as discussing alien conspiracy theories after being sucked up by a silver spaceship. But Savannah didn't bring it up because, ultimately, she had no idea what all this meant. Yes, she liked Honey. But was she gay? Bi? Queer or questioning? Into all women or just into Honey? Was it an experiment? Or something more permanent?

She was starting to understand that sexuality existed on a spectrum. But figuring out where she fit on that spectrum felt like seeing color for the first time and instantly being asked to pick her favorite. Honey was gay, and the way she felt about sex with men was the way Savannah felt about wearing flannel: hard pass. But Savannah couldn't say with absolute certainty she'd never have feelings for a guy *for the rest of her life*. She knew she didn't need to define herself, and even if other people wanted her to, it wasn't any of their business. But the fact remained that for reasons she could name and reasons she couldn't, she wasn't comfortable moving at the same pace as Honey.

Savannah retraced her steps to the loft feeling apprehensive about the coming conversation. But as she approached the front door, that apprehension distorted into something weird and disorienting. There were voices inside that weren't her roommates or their friends. As she turned the key in the lock, Savannah had the surreal feeling she was stepping back into her old apartment in Kentucky, falling through layers of time and space.

The two people standing inside turned and beamed at her. "Hi, Pookie!"

Her parents.

Were in New York.

With Honey. Who they'd been talking to. Her mom was wearing sneakers and a Patagonia vest, even though it was eighty degrees. Her dad was in a Hawaiian shirt. Savannah's heart started thrashing about in her chest. It took her several seconds to remember how to speak. "M-Mom. Dad. Wh-what are you doing here?"

"Visiting you!" Sherry was smiling so hard her eyes were slits. "You said it was a great idea!"

Savannah recalled an email from weeks ago: *Dad found a last-minute deal from Louisville to NYC! Should we take it?* She'd barely skimmed it, whipping off a distracted reply: *Sure, whatever, great idea.* They'd never followed up. She'd assumed it was a pipe dream.

"This is a fun neighborhood, huh?" Terry glanced out the window and frowned. "Very cool."

"Yes, it's very . . . urban, isn't it?" Sherry added.

Honey crossed her arms. She'd put on a pair of Savannah's sweats. She looked like she did when serving drunk douchebags at the bar—outwardly pleasant, inwardly steely.

Terry was looking around the loft like he wanted to torch it. "You said four people live here?"

"We were just chatting with Honey," Sherry said, turning to her. "Now, do you live here too?"

"No," Honey said, looking at Savannah.

"This is my . . ." Savannah stared back at Honey. She imagined saying *girlfriend. This is my girlfriend.* Her parents wouldn't even hear that, they'd hear *girl friend,* and she'd have to correct them, *No, Mom, this is my girlfriend, this is someone I'm dating.* She imagined the silence. Twin blank looks. The *Is this a joke?,* the *I'm sorry, what's happening?* The shock. The confusion. The nervous laugh, the sudden need to sit down. And then, as the truth of what she was saying sunk in, the horror. Not so much that she was dating a woman, although it certainly would not be good news. The horror that over the course of the six short months since she'd left her home state, their only child had turned into someone they didn't even recognize. Didn't even know. Or—and possibly, this was worse—that she'd been lying to them. For years. Willfully deceiving them about who she was. "Friend."

Honey blinked. Just once.

Sherry addressed Savannah. "We booked a hotel in Times Square, so I guess we'll just get a cab? We're only here for the weekend, but I thought we could see a Broadway show and Dad wants to see some baseball—"

"Is the front door fireproof?" Her dad was opening and shutting it.

"—and we want to do the Hop On, Hop Off bus." Her mom blew her nose. "Do we have to buy tickets for Ellis Island?"

"I gotta go to work," Honey lied, backing toward the front door. "Nice to meet you guys. Enjoy New York." Her warmth was entirely professional. "Bye, Savannah."

"Wait," Savannah said, but she was gone.

And so instead of lazing around in bed with Honey all weekend, Savannah found herself touring her parents around the city. It was both Terry and Sherry's first time there. They were good sports about it, but Savannah could tell they found it chaotic, crowded, and completely charmless. Their jokes—"There sure is a lot of garbage here!" or "I had no idea you could charge that much for coffee!"—were thinly disguised criticisms. Her dad liked the baseball, and her mom thought Central Park was pretty, but the trip asked more questions than it answered. Specifically: *Why do you like it here?* Her love for the city was a disappointment. Savannah had always believed her parents to be open-minded and permissive—they'd never pressured her to pick a specific major or told her how to dress. But now she understood they did have expectations of her life, as it related to them. And having a daughter with a girlfriend who lived in New York City was definitely not part of their parental fantasies.

As Savannah rode with them in a taxi to the airport on Sunday night, her mom squeezed her knee, thanking her for showing them the famous New York City. "But you must be looking forward to coming home."

Savannah pictured spending the rest of the evening in bed with Honey or even just hanging with her roommates and a lot of boxed wine. "I am," she admitted.

Her mom smiled, relieved. "Us too."

They'd mixed up the meaning of *home*.

*   *   *

It took an entire week to lure Honey over. When she finally showed up, the usual ease between them was gone. They watched an old episode of *Schitt's Creek* in bed on Savannah's laptop, but when neither of them were laughing, Savannah knew something was really wrong. She closed the computer. "Are you mad at me?"

Honey frowned. "Of course not."

"You're acting like you're mad."

"I'm not." Honey drew her legs up to her chest. "I just had—I'm having—some feelings. Feelings I didn't really expect to have." She twisted a curl tight around the tip of her finger. "Look, I get the parent thing. You're not about to tell them we're together. It's brand-new, it hasn't even been a month: I get it."

"But?"

"But, I was in the closet for so long, Savannah. And I can't go back." She hopped off the bed to pace Savannah's room. "I've been thinking about this all week, and here's where I'm at: I need to be out. Totally out. I want to meet the parents, and tag my girlfriend on Instagram, and hold her hand in public, and one day in the not-too-distant future get married to someone in a dress. And I know that's a lot to lay on you. But I know what I want, and I know what I don't want. I can't be your *friend*, Savannah. Your 'gal pal,' your 'traveling companion.' Not for very long, anyway."

Savannah's pulse sped up, panicky. This sounded like an ultimatum. "It's just . . . this is all so new: I don't know what I am—straight and a little bit gay. Gay and a little bit straight." She paused. "I mean, probably that one, but I'm not totally there yet."

"You don't need to label yourself," Honey said. "That's kind of the slogan of our generation."

"It's not about labels," Savannah said. "It's about knowing myself. I'm still figuring out who I am."

"I get it," Honey said gently. "But I know who *I* am. And that's super gay, and super into you. So either we're doing this, or I might have to seriously think about finding someone else to fall for." Honey looked at her evenly and with absolute certainty. "Someone who's ready to love me back."

64

Zach dumped a pile of books on the café table. Imogene's tea sloshed over the edge of a thin China rim. "What the—"

"Did you know that every two days, we create as much information as we did from the dawn of civilization up to *2003*?" Zach pulled the earbuds from his ear. "We've never had so much bad information, and a serious threat to American democracy!"

"I did know that, actually." It was a sunny Sunday afternoon in the West Village, and the siblings were meeting for tea to discuss Zach's best man speech, i.e., ensure he didn't just wing it. Zach's sister sifted through his stack of books: *Lit: Race Relations in America Today*, *Capitalism vs. Marxism: New Ideas on Old Systems*, a collection of essays by Roxane Gay. "Oh, *Mistakes Were Made: The Paradox of the Working-Class Revolution*. I just read the review in the *Times*."

"How was it?"

"Spicy."

"Ha." Zach shoved Charles's book to the bottom of the pile. "Do you listen to political podcasts? They're kind of amazing, I'm learning *so* much—" He broke off, noticing a woman with a stroller struggling to open the café door. He hurried to open it for her, then pushed two tables together so she'd have enough room.

Imogene watched her brother sit back down with amazement. "So, you listen to podcasts *and* you open doors for people now?"

"I'm part of the problem, Genie. I'm trying."

Imogene folded her arms. "This is about Darlene."

"How'd you know?"

"Because people only make radical life changes when they're in love or dying, and you're obviously healthy as a horse."

Zach shifted in his chair, suddenly feeling very British. "Well, I think *love* might be jumping the gun, Genie—"

"Zachary!" Imogene shouted. "You're in love!"

"Okay, yes, fine! I might be in love." Zach pushed his hair out of his eyes. "I *am* in love."

He had never spoken the words in any situation that wasn't post-coital or influenced by a psychoactive drug. "I'm in love." The realization filled him completely, like a soaring, shining aria reaching its fantastic peak. "I'm in love." He laughed out loud. "I'm—"

"Becoming a tremendous bore and a disgusting navel-gazer, so yes, you are obviously in love." His sister raised her teacup in salute. "Congratulations. Mum and Dad will be thrilled. I think daring Darlene's made them both more woke."

"Don't say *woke*, Genie, you sound like a colonizer. And look, don't go setting a registry up for us yet. It's all a bit . . . complicated."

"Meaning?"

After she swore an oath of secrecy, Zach told his older sister everything: the contract and $25,000. The fake relationship and the real feelings.

"I knew it." Imogene sounded equally charmed and satisfied. "I tried to get her to shit talk you at that dinner where you won at canasta. Called you a train wreck."

"I *am* a train wreck," Zach moaned.

"She didn't bite. She defended you. I *knew* there was something going on."

"There is. I'm in love, as we've established." Zach gazed mournfully at his sister. "What do I do?"

"Isn't it obvious?"

Zach popped a sugar cube in his tea. "Kill Charles in his sleep and wear his corpse as a cape?"

Imogene grabbed her little brother's shoulders with both hands. "Tell her the truth, you prat. Tell her that you love her."

"What . . . now?"

"No, wait until she's back with Charles, or gotten famous and started sleeping with groupies." She swatted his arm. "Yes, now."

Zach pictured it: Darlene recoiling in horror. "What if she doesn't feel the same way?"

"Then you see out the rest of your ridiculous contract, pocket the trust, and find a new singer to work with."

It was Zach's turn to recoil. "I don't want to find a new singer to work with."

"You should've thought of that before you stuck your tongue down her throat." Imogene gestured about airily. "Love is a many-splendored thing, but it's also a total bastard. It'll chop your heart out and eat it for breakfast, and you do *not* want to feel that way every time you play a wedding with the woman you one day want to see walking down the aisle toward you. If it's not going to happen, better to know now and maintain a shred of your ever-diminishing dignity."

Christ on a cracker: Imogene was right. He needed to tell Darlene the truth about his feelings. And if she didn't return them, he'd have to cut ties, losing his bandmate, his girlfriend (albeit fake), *and* his friend (maybe his *best* friend?). Why was she being so distant? She still wasn't returning any of his texts. Maybe he'd embarrassed himself with Rachel Maddow. He did end up getting pretty drunk with her, but only because it was pissing Charles off so much.

Zach slumped in his seat, barely able to get the words out. "What if she thinks I'm not smart enough?"

"She'd be right." Imogene realized he wasn't joking. "Oh, Zook, don't be silly. You're incredibly bright."

"Not as bright as Darlene."

"I'm not as bright as Mina. And she still loves me. Difference can be a turn-on." Imogene sipped her tea. "My future wife drinks *coffee*." She lowered her voice. "And I'm kind of into it."

Zach gazed out at the street, at all the people walking dogs and pushing strollers, leading normal, happy lives. He'd been one of them, not that long ago. Oblivious and carefree. But now everything felt complicated and high-stakes and horrendously *adult*. "I've never been on this side of it. Never had my heart broken."

Imogene flicked his earlobe. "Character building. But here's hoping she feels the same way."

Zach gathered up his pile of books and got to his feet. "Only one way to find out—"

"Hang on." Imogene grabbed his sleeve. "We've still got to work-shop your best man speech."

Love may have changed Zach's heart, but it hadn't changed his personality. He'd completely forgotten he was there to fulfill a responsibility.

"Right," he said, sitting back down. "I've got loads of ideas for jokes, and they're all absolutely filthy."

65

Darlene didn't mean to end up in Charles's Brooklyn neighborhood. But when choosing somewhere to get a manicure for Imogene and Mina's wedding, she did go slightly out of her way to visit the place in Cobble Hill where she was a regular when she and Charles were dating. A rainstorm passed while her cuticles were being cut. When she stepped outside, a rainbow arched, and the damp air felt hopeful. She wiped off a bench and returned a call to her father. They dove into a meaty conversation about two good articles they'd both read recently (a profile on Elon Musk; the history of the Black press). But when he asked how music was going, instead of listing off some recent wins as per usual, she found herself a bit tongue-tied. Her father asked if something had happened with Zach.

"No, no," she replied automatically. Then she paused. She did want to get closer to her dad. And that meant being honest. Opening up. "Actually, yes. We . . . crossed a line."

Silence. Darlene winced, waiting for his reply.

"Okay," he said slowly. "If you're saying what I think you're saying . . ."

"I guess I am."

More silence. "Well, I support you no matter what, but I would prefer it if you dated someone . . . more like me."

Darlene sat bolt upright. She knew he didn't mean an academic. "Oh. Well, we're not actually dating." Which sounded like they were just hooking up. "We're not anything. Don't worry, Dad. I gotta go. Talk to you soon." She hung up, certain she'd played that all wrong, feeling disappointed, annoyed, and guilty over her father's response.

To calm herself down, Darlene treated herself to a large decaf iced coffee, and the arts section of the paper. Then she popped into

Books Are Magic, the independent bookstore on Smith Street. Browsing the airy, prettily arranged store relaxed her further. Charles had recommended some new titles in his Q and A. She'd just found one, *Capitalism vs. Marxism*, and was skimming the back cover, when her phone vibrated.

Zach.

So strange the way her feelings had roller-coastered over this boy. A year ago she'd be wary, ready for him to offer an excuse or let her down. Three months ago, his name would elicit the same panicked thrill as a bungee jump. Right now, it was a mix of both. She didn't know if she could trust his affections, or hers, or if their fake relationship was in any way real. If they were truly compatible, if a relationship would survive their respective families, if she even wanted that. But she couldn't deny the way her heart picked up when hearing his name and picturing his face. He wasn't perfect. But he was hers. According to the contract, she reminded herself briskly.

"Hi, Zach."

"Hey! Hi." He sounded flustered. "Wasn't sure if you were going to pick up."

She pictured him running a hand through his hair, dressed in a soft white button-down in need of an iron. It'd been days since she'd heard his voice. The accent was still cute. "What's up?"

"Look, I'm sorry about the dinner with Charles."

"You don't need to be sorry. I thought Charles was being a little unkind."

"Yeah, he's a poncey prick," Zach muttered. "But I'm sorry if I did anything to make you not reply to any of my texts . . . ?"

"Your texts weren't about work. They were *Monty Python* GIFs." Which truthfully had made her laugh. "Just trying to keep it professional."

"Right. *Professional.*"

She couldn't tell if he thought this was funny or infuriating.

"Can I take you out for dinner?"

"Well, I'll see you Friday," she replied, a bit surprised by the request. "You're still driving us to the Hamptons for your sister's rehearsal dinner, right?"

"Yes, but could we have dinner first? Tonight? Me in a suit jacket, you in a dress. There's something I want to talk to—tell you—about."

He sounded nervous. No, excited. He wasn't going to *say something* was he? As in, about them? Darlene's chest fluttered hard. She meandered toward the back of the bookstore. "We can have dinner."

"Brilliant. Excellent, fantastic, great. Do you want to meet at—"

"Charles!"

"Charles's . . . event? God no, that would be dystopic for me."

"No, Charles is here." Right in front of her, in the bookstore. The humidity turned his ginger curls to ginger frizz. "I'll call you later." Darlene dropped her phone in her bag. Now she was the one who was flustered. "Hi!"

"Hello, Darlene. Looking gorgeous, as always."

"Gosh, I feel like I'm talking to a celebrity." Darlene touched her cheek, unexpectedly nervous. Charles always made her—possibly everyone—feel slightly on edge.

"Well, I did just get invited on *The Daily Show*," Charles simpered. "What are you doing here?"

"Looking up some of the titles you recommended. You?"

"Signing books." Charles indicated the copies on the front table, before turning back with a complex expression. "You have to put me out of my misery. Please tell me something isn't going on with you and *Zach*."

Thank God Charles unfollowed her when they broke up, and he definitely didn't follow Zach. He likely hadn't seen all the pictures Zach had tagged her in. "It's complicated," was the simplest, truest answer she could conjure.

Her ex-boyfriend grimaced. "It's just so frustrating."

"What is?"

"Zach Livingstone is a human blow-up doll!" Charles spluttered. "Look, I get it: pleasures of the flesh, et cetera—but if one day I get an invite to your wedding, it's pistols at dawn. I mean it!"

Even broken up, Darlene had a powerful urge to impress Charles. It reminded her of typical conversations with her father, the satisfaction of a flowing, erudite conversation with someone she found authoritative. Ultimately, it was why she and Charles didn't work as a couple, but still, the old instinct flared. She racked her brain for the cleverest way to return his shot. "Don't worry: I'm completely clear-eyed about Zach Livingstone. *Thou hast no more brain than I have in mine elbows.*"

Charles rewarded her effort with an extremely rare giggle. "Shakespeare truly was the master of insults."

Darlene flushed hard with his approval. It made her feel light-headed and reckless. "I'd sooner marry a donkey than date Zach Livingstone!" She regretted the cruel boast as soon as it leaped from her lips. It was mean, but more so, it was in no way true.

Charles snorted laughter. He caught the eye of the person at the front counter and pulled himself together. "Must be off."

She gave him a quick hug. "Thank you, Charles. For always seeing the best in me."

He gave her a pleased grin, and headed off, calling back over his shoulder. "Remember: pistols at dawn."

Darlene forced a laugh and tapped her elbow. But when Charles looked away, her smile dropped. That hadn't felt as satisfying as she hoped it would.

Did Charles see the best in her? He rarely complimented her. And when he did, it was usually about her looks, never about her intelligence. She'd always cast Charles as her teacher, and she, the willing student. She could see now she'd put him on too high a pedestal.

She thought about the Cindy Sherman exhibition she and Zach went to a few weeks ago. There'd been a long line, which would usually irritate or simply bore Darlene. Zach didn't mind at all, striking up a spirited conversation with the couple in front of them, middle-aged tourists from Germany. Charles never talked to strangers, a.k.a. "the great unwashed." Zach connected with them effortlessly: he liked strangers. Sure, Zach had never heard of Cindy Sherman, someone Charles could offer a top-of-mind bio on in his sleep. But Zach made the wait, and the whole day, fun.

And she got to teach him about Cindy Sherman.

She got to teach Zach about a lot of things. And his willingness to learn relaxed her in a way learning from Charles never did. Being with Zach made her feel . . . happy. Being with Charles made her feel anxious and needy. She rarely felt anxious around Zach; at least, not before they'd started making out. As much as Charles taught her, she never felt like they were equals.

I feel like an equal with Zach.

Sun streamed through the bookstore's skylight, warming her skin. And suddenly, it all became clear.

They were falling in love.

No.

She was already in love.

That was it: so plain and simple it was a mystery how it ever hadn't been so.

She loved Zach Livingstone. And he loved her. *Of course he did.*

The realization bloomed electric inside her, filling her limbs until she was high and floating and giddy and silly. She loved Zach. They *loved* each other. Since their first kiss he'd never given her a real reason to suspect he couldn't be trusted: that was all in her head. Darlene was struck with a desperate desire to run after Charles and redo the last minute of their conversation—but it didn't matter. Charles was her ex, and what he thought of her and Zach was of no consequence at all.

His summer-blue eyes. His flop of hair and crooked grin. It was all hers.

Mina and Imogene's wedding was this weekend. What a perfect place to declare their feelings, and finally consummate a love story that'd been building for two long years.

I love you, Zach. It's you. It's only, always, you.

Feeling queenly, Darlene put on her sunglasses and stepped out onto Smith Street.

And it was only now, four miles away on the island of Manhattan, that Zach Livingstone did what Darlene had failed to do when she bumped into Charles.

He hung up the phone.

For a long moment, he sat on the end of his bed, staring at the carpet.

Speechless.

Unable to breathe.

I'd sooner marry a donkey than date Zach Livingstone.

A freight train slammed into him, throwing him a hundred feet, crushing every bone in his body. He ended up on his bedroom floor in a broken heap, choking in gulps of air. *Now I know,* he thought, head cradled in his hands. *Now I know what heartbreak feels like.*

66

Liv and Sam were in firm agreement not to tell their children they were dating. All the holier-than-thou parenting blogs shrieked that whatever time frame one had in mind was far, *far* too soon, and a too-early introduction would permanently and egregiously damage the child in question. Before becoming a mother, Liv found the idea of caring what other moms thought of her parenting style downright absurd. Let alone moms on the internet she'd *never even met*. She still felt that way, but also, secretly, she wanted the judgy internet moms' approval. She didn't want to screw up the introduction, or Ben. Part of her worried she'd already screwed him up, what with his father dying, her imperfect parenting, and her own expectations. Ben's birth was hard-won, and at first, she was looking forward to a son who was as funny and charismatic as his father. But Ben was serious and sensitive. It took effort to release those expectations and get to know the independent little human who might not roll with the punches of meeting Mom's new boyfriend.

And so, she and Sam were a secret, skillfully skirting their children's lives like a well-trained concierge. This was for the kids' benefit . . . but it was also kind of fun. The sneaking around and stolen glances gave the relationship extra heat. And, somewhat disturbingly, was an insight into her own husband's liaison with her business partner. In the meat-and-potatoes world of adult tedium, affairs were sweet and sticky dulce de leche.

Benny had met Sam, and so the occasional run-in was permitted: Sam was a coworker, just like Savannah. The two liked to throw a baseball under the willow tree or make dinner together. Taco pizzas or sloppy joes were Liv's son's favorite meals to cook with the gentle, patient chef. After a while, Ben started bringing him up in conversation: *Sam said bananas float in water. Sam thinks the Mets have a real chance this year.* Sam was one of twenty invited to a Friday night Shabbat, and not just because he offered to make beef brisket.

But Liv had never met Sam's daughter, Dottie. Sam talked about her but hadn't offered to show pictures. Sam's ex-wife had a firm *no kids on social media* policy, and so his five-year-old was absent from the ghost town that was his never-updated Facebook page. Liv assumed that sharing this part of his life with her—arguably, the biggest and most sensitive part—was something he wasn't ready for, or felt she wasn't ready for. So she was more than aware of the significance when, one afternoon, Sam leaned back into the old sofa they'd first made love on and said, "Would you like to see some pictures?"

Liv's heart leaped straight up in the air. "I'd love to."

And only now, as Sam started fiddling with his phone, did the reality of a future together suddenly come into full view. A blended family. The four of them, under one roof. Would they live here in the brownstone? Sam in the bedroom she'd shared with Eliot, Dottie in the guest room, guests on the sofa? Would Sam be okay with raising Ben Jewish, would they have to start doing Christmas, what would Ben think of that? It was far, *far* too soon to think about any of this, and the too-early introduction of all the questions gave Liv a faint headache. *Oh shit*, she thought, lightheaded, as she accepted the phone Sam handed her. *Am I about to meet my . . . stepdaughter?*

A rush of hot-cold swept her body. She closed her eyes and inhaled a grounding breath. Then she focused on the picture on Sam's phone, both panicked and excited by what it would present.

Liv had never found other people's children as awe-inspiring as her own. Before becoming a parent, babies appeared to be squirmy, starry-eyed drool machines. Ben, on the other hand, well, Ben was a *delicious* and *perfect* baby, king of the babies, the best baby in the world! . . . But this sudden change of mind did not extend to every baby. Her child was magnificent. Other children were fine.

And then Liv Goldenhorn set eyes on Dottie Woods.

A new part of her heart, hitherto undiscovered, unlocked.

In the picture, a blond-pigtailed girl was mugging at the camera. She was wearing a yellow slicker, mid-stomp in a puddle. Her chubby face was streaked with mud. She was supremely, ecstatically happy.

Dottie Woods was perfect.

She also had Down syndrome.

"We found out when Claudia was pregnant. We could have . . ." Sam drifted off. "We didn't."

All at once, Liv wanted to know every single thing about her—did she have a favorite movie, who were her friends, what was her night-time routine? Was she shy or gregarious? Cautious or a whole ball of trouble?

What did it mean to have a child with special needs?

Sam's voice became wobbly in the near distance, telling her what an awesome kid Dottie was and that Down syndrome didn't define who she was. "Her smile lights up the room. She's just a typical little girl."

A long-dormant desire awoke fast and hard, like someone breaking the surface and gasping for air.

I always wanted a daughter.

Liv started to cry. It took her completely by surprise. Sam was just as alarmed. "What? What's wrong?"

Liv couldn't answer. She put her head in her hands and wept.

Sam made a worried noise and shifted closer, willing to wait for an explanation. She pressed her face into his flannel shirt. The smell of his fabric softener—that clean, sweet, domestic smell—calmed her. The reasons for her emotion started to bubble up.

Because she had not had a daughter of her own.

Because her marriage had failed and Eliot was gone.

Because she loved her son so completely.

Because she was falling in love with the man next to her.

Because she was going to fall in love with this little girl and every-thing would change and nothing would ever be the same. And that was going to be hard, so hard, so mind-blowingly hard.

But it could also be good. It could also be so good.

"Liv," Sam tried again. "What's wrong?"

She looked deep into his caramel-brown eyes, pressing her hand against his cheek. The truth was the impossible made real. "I'm just . . . so . . . *happy.*"

67

Zia wrestled with discussing the money Layla needed with Clay. While it might be possible to ask one day, it was impossible now.

The Jungle of Us's biggest financier had dropped out. There were problems with shooting permits in Brazil. The writer was lagging on the latest draft, the studio was getting cold feet about an important gay sex scene: the list went on. As one of the executive producers, Clay was doing everything he could to help put out the fires. And on top of all that, the conversation Zia and Darlene shared in their yoga studio had been placed as a blind item. *Which sexy movie star is keeping a yoga-toned girlfriend secret from his many fans? Our spies say this dark-haired beauty is begging her jungle man to commit!*

Zia read the gossip blog three times before the words sunk in. "But that was a private conversation!"

Clay swept his hands through his hair. He'd been in fourteen-hour rehearsals and punishing training sessions for weeks. "Doesn't matter."

A vague memory of two girls in matching leopard-print Lululemon came into focus. They'd *spied* on her? "I was talking with Darlene. I was being careful."

"Not careful enough. I just—" Clay released a frustrated breath. "Look, it's not a big deal . . ."

Zia dropped the phone on Clay's kitchen countertop. Shame twisted her stomach. "Then why are you upset?"

"Because you need to be more discreet, Zia! Privacy protects us both."

"I *was* being discreet."

"No, you weren't."

"I need to be able to talk to my friends about my boyfriend!" Zia raised her voice without meaning to. "That's *normal*, that's what normal people do."

"I guess we're not normal, then."

"Well, it's starting to feel really, really wrong."

The silence that filled the penthouse had the weight of concrete. Zia's heart pounded beneath a too-tight new bra. This was supposed to be a relaxed and sexy night.

Clay put one hand on the kitchen counter carefully. His voice was guarded. "What are you saying?"

It felt like an invitation to break up: *I'm saying this isn't working. I'm saying this is over.* Is that what he wanted? Was *he* breaking up with *her*? No. They were not breaking up over one little mistake. Clay was leaving for Brazil in two short days: this was not the time to negotiate new rules, or God forbid, take a break. He was stressed and sleep-deprived and ultimately, what he'd said earlier was right. This wasn't a big deal.

Zia summoned compassion and clarity, and picked up his hand. "I care about you."

He lifted his eyes to hers. Those golden eyes she knew so well. His walls were gone. "I care about you, too."

"I'm sorry. I'll be more careful."

"I'm sorry, too." He dropped his head, wincing. "I know I'm a pain in the ass. I know this sucks for you. I just . . . have issues."

"I know." She touched her forehead to his, trying to realign.

"After this film . . ." He shook his head, seeming overwhelmed, like he couldn't even imagine life after this film. "I want us to work. I do."

And even though Zia knew their power balance was off and didn't know if Clay would ever realize his need for privacy was just a way to keep her emotionally at bay, she replied truthfully, "I do, too."

"I do have some good news." He looked almost sheepish. "Michelle's book isn't coming out."

The book by his ex-girlfriend. The tell-all, the exposé. "That's amazing! What happened?"

"Publishers dropped it. I think my team made it clear we'd sue and they didn't want the hassle."

"Baby, that's great news." She kissed him, and then kissed him again, and again, until his body woke up and they stopped talking.

Softness gave way to the passion they'd always had and could access as easy as whistling. They had sex on the kitchen floor. Zia straddled him, rocking her hips fast and hard to make herself come. In this moment, she felt strong and vital and completely in control.

But it was just sex.

Early the next morning, Zia's head filled with questions as she watched Clay sleeping on the other side of the bed.

What did they have? Was it real? Was she making the necessary compromises every relationship requires, especially one as complex as this? Or was it too heavily weighted in Clay's favor? He was wealthier, more powerful, male. They felt equal making dinner, equal curled up watching old movies. But were they equal? Was the fact she was in charge in the bedroom just a sexy distraction that excused their real-life inequity?

Was he giving up as much as she was?

Was he hers in the same way she was his?

Beneath his eyelids, Clay's eyes flickered, dreaming. Her body had grown accustomed to him: his smell, his touch. They were often thinking the same thing at the same time.

Zia's ability to be a chameleon had its upsides. But she also had a tendency to mold herself to the people she was with.

Clay had his needs, and she had hers. It couldn't be all on his terms. Moving slowly so as not to wake him, she reached for her phone on the nightstand. Held it above the bed. In the rectangular screen, two lovers were tangled naked in Clay's gray sheets. Sculpted and softly lit by the sun that was just starting to warm the enormous bedroom, as golden as the necklace that always circled her throat. She captured the image silently, twin feelings of relief and rebellion twisting through her. This was how she'd hold him close for the next six weeks. This was how she would keep them alive: this memory, this moment.

A secret, like so many others.

After they said their goodbyes, Zia rode her bike to Astoria, picked up Mateo and Lucy from day care, and walked with them back to the apartment. By the time her sister got home from work that night, she'd deep cleaned the entire apartment and had a chicken tagine simmering on the stove. Zia was on edge, hoping her sister wouldn't choose easy anger over something more reasonable. But when she apologized, Layla couldn't meet her eyes, even though she said she was sorry too.

"He's in rehearsals till late then leaving for six weeks in Brazil first thing tomorrow," Zia told her. "Maybe when he gets back, I can bring it up."

"Six weeks?" Layla's expression turned poisonous, and she turned away.

Her sister's tiny bathroom was filled with faded bath toys. A far cry from the waterfall shower and clawfoot tub Zia had gotten used to. Now that she wouldn't be back there for a month and a half, it seemed like a dream. Like the idea of her and "famous movie star" Clay Russo was a bizarre delusion. At least she had the picture. And the necklace. Six weeks wasn't so long. Maybe she could use the time to plan a trip for them—somewhere off the grid that allowed them to do volunteer work; give back to a community in a real way. She needed to get back to herself, her dreams, her passions, her values. Maybe the time apart would be a blessing in disguise.

She splashed her face with water, wondering if the face in the mirror was someone who could always live in Clay Russo's shadow.

Something inside her recoiled, whispering, *Run.*

68

Gorman watched Henry watching Gilbert on the stage of the HERE Arts Center.

In the months prior, Gorman imagined the opening night of *Tears of a Recalcitrant Snail* in extremes: wild success or abject failure. The one where there's a line around the block for a sold-out show and reviewers fighting over press tickets. The one where the only audience members are him, Henry, and somebody's aging parent who falls asleep. Reality, of course, fell somewhere in the middle. It was a sold-out show, but it was a small theater. Reviewers weren't fighting over tickets, they were sitting in the second row, and there were three of them. No one fell asleep.

Technically, the show went well. No missed cues, no flubbed lines. There was an electricity onstage that'd been missing in the previews. But Gorman couldn't focus on the action. He was focused on Henry. The calm solidity of his profile. His hands folded neatly in his lap. His even, watchful attention.

"We'll talk about it," Henry had said, "after the show."

It being sex with Gilbert.

Maybe it was because he'd forgotten what it was like for Henry to sleep with other people, or maybe it was because the concept of marriage had started to seem less suffocating, and more like a first draft he could work with. Whatever the reason, Gorman didn't like the idea of Henry and Gilbert. Not one little bit.

There was a standing ovation at curtains. The cast pointed their collective arm at the sound booth, then the director, then Gorman. Henry whistled through his teeth. Gorman inclined his head like the queen acknowledging her loyal subjects. He was supposed to be relishing this moment; he'd fantasized about it his entire life. But he was only aping his role as grateful, humble wordsmith. All Gorman could think about was if Henry liked Gilbert, and how monumentally awful that would be, and honestly, it was incredibly annoying.

"What'd you think?" Gorman asked as everyone started hunting around for their coats.

"Babe, it was brilliant!" Henry sounded genuinely enthusiastic. "A lot funnier than I was expecting, and the scene where Egor comes out to his mother?" He shook his head in awe. "I got chills."

"No," Gorman said, feeling oddly urgent, "what did you think of Gilbert?"

Henry looked surprised, but then everyone was up and crowding toward the small playhouse bar. Someone pushed a drink in his hand, wanting to talk about the play.

"Henry," Gorman tried again. "What did—"

"Gor!" Henry laughed. "It's your night." He indicated the throng of people around them, their gazes fixed on Gorman. "Enjoy it. That's an order."

Because Henry was usually right about most things, Gorman put the issue aside and found himself the center of a large, lovely circle of praise and adoration. *So funny!* and *My mother was exactly the same*, and *I can't believe I'm talking to the playwright!* The validation filled him up like helium, expanding him in all directions. It was summer in Paris and box seats at the opera and cocktails by a pool with a view of the Pacific.

As the bar called last drinks, Gilbert popped up in front of him, flushed and happy. "We're gonna go dancing." He indicated a trio of the younger actors. "You and Henry have to come."

Gilbert had never invited him out dancing. It was *all happening*. Gorman expected Henry to wrinkle his nose—dancing, on a Tuesday?—but his eyes widened and he nodded eagerly.

They all ended up on line for a West Village club Gorman had never heard of. A rumor skipped up the queue it'd be an hour wait. Gorman dimly recalled waiting this long when he was Gilbert's age. Gossiping and smoking hand-rolled cigarettes with his catty, gorgeous friends, feeling anxious and expansive about the night ahead. Tomorrow wasn't a concern back then. But that was a very long time ago.

In front of them, Gilbert sucked on a JUUL, billowing out saccharine-flavored smoke. He offered it to Gorman and Henry. They both shook their heads and exchanged a private smile. *Kids.*

Henry slipped his arm through Gorman's, snuggling closer. "So, what's your next play about, handsome?"

"Oh, I don't know if I'll write another one." *Lightning only strikes once, right?*

Henry elbowed him. "What? You have to!"

"Do I?"

"Don't you want to?"

Gorman felt oddly shy. The whole night was still so unbelievable. "Yes."

"Then we'll make it happen."

"What about the shop?"

Henry's eyes were soft and full of pride. "The shop makes me happy. This makes you happy." He shrugged. "We'll figure it out."

Gorman swelled with gratitude. He kissed Henry on the mouth and inhaled his shampoo: basil and lemon. He never got sick of that smell. He liked it every time.

The line shuffled forward, but there were still twenty people in front of them. What were they waiting for? A noisy club playing songs he didn't know, selling overpriced drinks, full of people three decades younger than him? Gilbert dancing with Henry? Kissing Henry? Taking Henry back to some poky little studio? "Do you really want to go to a club, Choo-Choo?"

"Not especially," said Henry, "I thought you wanted to go."

"Let's go home." Gorman took Henry's hand. "I only want to be with you."

69

The next morning, Zia took her time cycling home from her sister's, relishing the feeling of fresh air on her arms and in her lungs. Whenever she and Clay took a car, it was a monstrous black Suburban with tinted windows, entered and exited in an underground parking lot. Being on a bike felt like flying. Clay would be at the airport by now and already, she was enjoying the mental break. She picked up some groceries from the bodega, and on a whim, a bright bunch of flowers for Darlene. She locked up her bike, sidestepping a couple of tourists with bulky SLR cameras, heads buried in their phones. *Look around you*, she wanted to tell them. *The world is beautiful—you're missing it.*

She unlocked their front door and bumped it open with her hip. She'd cook tonight and catch up with Darlene. Maybe a sheet mask, a podcast, paint her toenails red—

"Zia!" Darlene thundered down the hallway from her bedroom in a panic. "I called you a million times!"

Zia dropped the bag of groceries on the floor, her adrenaline spiking. Her mom. Layla. Darlene's parents. Zach. "What, what's happened?"

Darlene shoved her phone in Zia's face. "I knew you wouldn't have—you didn't, right? It's everywhere, just now, like, five minutes ago."

Darlene's phone was larger than her own. Which meant the picture of her and Clay—the picture she'd taken yesterday morning—looked even more luminous. Even more gorgeous. It was closer cropped and color corrected to enrich the golden-morning light slanting over their forms. Impossibly, she met her own eyes, as the Zia on the screen stared directly at her. Her breasts were wrapped tight in the gray sheet, looking large and voluptuous, her legs tucked to one side. Next to her on the bed, Clay was still fast asleep.

Still completely naked.

Horror jammed itself in her chest and split her open.

Zia had only been half aware of the fact Clay's penis was visible in the photograph. They often slept naked, and his impressive form had become familiar to her, no longer eliciting the same giddy excitement it did months ago. But now, Clay's penile presence was horrifically underlined. A black star was placed over her boyfriend's nether regions, its size indicating Clay's own.

But this couldn't be on Darlene's phone. Because that meant . . .

Zia stabbed at the screen, swiping frantically until a gaudy celebrity gossip website popped up. *Exclusive! Clay Russo and sexy new girlfriend Zia Ruiz get steamy at home!* Sound fell away as Zia scanned the article, only registering snippets. *This exclusive picture . . . the star's impressive, er, physique . . . Ruiz, 27, met at a wedding she was working at . . . clearly a scorching hot new couple!* At the bottom of the article were social media share buttons. Published seven minutes ago, the article already had 23.4K Facebook shares. As Zia watched, the number changed. 23.5K.

Twenty-three thousand, five hundred.

People.

Had seen that picture.

Everyone had seen that picture.

Clay was naked in that picture.

Someone grabbed her arm. Zia stifled a scream. She was in the apartment, the apartment she shared with Darlene. Darlene was yelling. "Tell me you didn't sell this picture of Clay, Zia!"

"No, no!" Zia scrabbled in her bag for her phone. Adrenaline jacked her system, making everything sped up and frantic. "No, this is a mistake, I have to call someone, a lawyer, I need a lawyer—"

"Who sent it then?" Darlene asked. "Clay?"

Clay would see this. This *violation*.

Someone pounded on the front door. A rough male voice. "Hello, Zia? Harry Garbon from the *New York Post*, how long have you and Clay Russo been an item?"

Zia and Darlene stared at each other, both breathing hard.

Harry Garbon continued. "Any comment on the allegations you're just using him for money?"

Darlene was at the window. "There's photographers outside."

A half dozen men, including the two "tourists" with SLR cameras Zia'd passed, were milling on the street below. Catching sight of Zia peering down at them, they started shooting and calling her name. Zia let out a cry and stumbled back.

Harry Garbon pounded on the door. "All I need is a picture, honey, one picture."

Darlene beelined for the door and made sure it was locked. "No comment," she stated. "This is private property: I'm calling the police." She pulled Zia down the hallway, into her bedroom.

Zia felt like her body was shutting down. "They know. They all—that picture. I didn't . . ."

"So who leaked it?"

Zia squeezed her eyes shut. The truth was excruciating. Not just because of what it meant for Clay.

Layla had been acting funny all morning—pissy and defensive and then when Zia was saying goodbye, oddly contrite. Zia dug for her phone, as always, on silent. There were fifty missed calls. Dozens of messages. A front-of-house manager she used to work with years ago: *Zia!!! OMG you and Clay!!!! Congrats girl, he is HOT!!! Please come in anytime, Chef would love to—*

Zia deleted it. As she did, another popped up, a volunteer she'd befriended in Cambodia. *Holy shit!! Ha ha ha I knew you when. Looks like your bf has a massive cock* 😜.

Zia thrust her phone at Darlene. "Call my sister."

"This is gonna be okay, Z, I promise."

"Just call her!" Why had she taken the photo, why hadn't she deleted it, why hadn't she called Layla out on acting weird. *Why—*

Layla picked up.

Blood roared in Zia's ears. "Tell me it wasn't you."

There was a painful silence. "Zia, I didn't mean for—"

"*No.*" Zia bit her hand to keep from screaming. "Why? How could you?"

"It wasn't meant to . . . It was an Australian website, they said you wouldn't even know—"

"Layla!" Zia shouted. "Why the hell did you sell a picture of me and Clay? That you *stole* off my phone?"

"You're so wrapped up in him! You barely have any time for us anymore—"

Zia hung up, unable to take it. Her own *sister*. "I have to call Clay." She knew Layla knew her passcode—why hadn't she changed it after she told her about Clay?

"Hey, it's Clay. Leave a message."

Zia hung up and threw the phone on Darlene's bed. "Shit. *Shit*."

She could call Dave, maybe he'd be with Clay, at the airport, on the plane already? She had to see Clay, had to explain—

"What Layla did is illegal." Darlene was reading off her phone. "It's illegal to sell a picture you didn't take, especially one like that. She must've lied or forged your signature or pretended to *be* you. Layla could get in a lot of trouble for this."

"Well, maybe I'll sue my sister," Zia snapped sarcastically. "My broke-ass sister with two little kids, maybe I'll send her ass to jail." She picked up her phone—*Zia, hi, this is Phoebe North, deputy editor of US Weekly*—and called Dave.

He answered on the first ring. His voice was atypically brisk. "Don't make any comment."

"Dave! Thank God. I didn't sell it, I swear."

"Where are you?"

"At home."

"Stay there. Don't answer the door."

"I need to speak to Clay."

A pause. "That's probably not a good idea."

"Shit, Dave, I need to speak to my boyfriend! Is he on the plane, where is he?"

Silence.

"Where are you?" Zia was shouting. "Where is he?"

"We're at his place—"

"I'm coming."

She grabbed the largest hoodie she owned and bolted for the front door. The untouched photo, the one without the black star, was probably online too. It'd likely live on the internet forever, always one Google search away: *Clay Russo nude*. Clay didn't even bare his butt in movies. The word *viral* took on a whole new meaning.

Infection. Spreading and multiplying beyond control, utterly un-stoppable.

Clay would be humiliated, on a global scale. The pain of it squeezed her chest and lungs, making it hard to get a good breath. It felt like terror.

And it was 100 percent her fault.

It was a mistake to leave the apartment without a plan, and on her own. The small group of male photographers swarmed her, yelling questions and accusations: *Zia, is it true about you and Clay Russo? What's he like in bed?* She made it to her bike, but between the chaos around her and tears in her eyes, she couldn't work the lock. Some-one yanked the hoodie off her head. She almost screamed.

"Zia!" Darlene called from her window, pointing at an idling car. "I called you a Lyft!"

She fought her way into the back seat. In the rearview mirror, the driver examined her. Trying to figure out if she was a celebrity. *No, but I sleep with one, and now everyone knows.* She pulled the hoodie low and texted Darlene to change the address to Clay's apartment.

There, more photographers were waiting, but an experienced doorman held them back. The marble foyer felt huge and quiet as a crypt. A fairly famous young actress who owned a condo in the com-plex watched her scurry inside. She was someone Zia made friendly small talk with while sunbathing on the building's roof. Now, a slight look of suspicion narrowed her eyes.

The doorman called up. Zia prayed not to be turned away. Thank-fully, she wasn't.

The elevator doors opened into Clay's apartment to reveal a brusque-looking woman Zia recognized as Lana, Clay's publicist, flanked by two younger women, a guy in a suit, and Dave, all huddled around the kitchen island, which was covered with open laptops. A tinny voice was speaking from a phone. ". . . absolutely a violation of statute and total invasion, even for Clay's reduced expectation. We're still figuring out if it constitutes revenge porn, but it may not even matter if—"

"Hang on, Kien." Dave cut the voice off.

Five sets of eyes landed on Zia. Five people whose entire jobs were now managing her epic, unforgivable screwup. She felt exactly ten years old.

For a long moment, no one said anything. Then Lana pointed at her. "I need to talk to you."

Clay walked in from the bedroom, dressed in black jeans and a black sweater. As soon as he saw Zia, he pulled up short. "What's she doing here?"

Coldness slammed Zia in the chest. *She*. She'd been reduced to *she*. Dave hesitated. "I let her in."

"Can we talk?" Zia begged Clay. "Please?"

Everyone looked at Clay. He ran a hand through his hair, his mouth tight. "Yeah, sure," he said eventually, in a way that sounded like, *May as well get this over with.*

Clay shut the doors to the windowless media room. A C-shaped leather sectional faced a TV screen the size of a dining room table. His man cave. His space. Zia shivered. Even in the hoodie, she was freezing.

Clay faced her with an expression she hadn't seen before. Disbelief. Derision. He spread his arms wide, showman-like. "What the hell, Zia?"

Instinctively she moved toward him, needing contact. "Clay, I'm—"

He raised both hands and took a step back. *Don't. Touch me.*

She stood in the middle of the room, wringing the bottom of the hoodie. Tears streamed down her cheeks. "M-my sister—"

"Your sister, posing as you, sold the photograph for fifty thousand dollars, yes, we know." His voice was curt. This Clay wasn't kind and gentle. He was powerful, and he was pissed. "Why did you take a photo of me naked?"

"I'm sorry. I didn't mean to . . . I didn't think—"

"Are there others?"

"What?"

"Other pictures?" he clarified impatiently. "How many others are there, and does she have them?"

"No." Zia shook her head, stunned at the question, which, of course, made perfect sense. "No, that was . . . there's no other photos like that."

His eyes were narrowed, arms folded over his chest. He wasn't sure whether he believed her. "So, what: you wanted to sell it and your sister got there first?"

"What? No!" She took another step forward.

Clay's hands shot up again. "Don't come near me."

Anger lashed through her. "Jesus, Clay. I'm your girlfriend, and I took a picture of us. A picture for *me*. My sister *stole* it. I didn't *show* it to her. You were leaving for six weeks—I wanted something to remember us, to keep us safe."

"Safe? You wanted to keep us safe?" Clay was shouting. "*My cock is on the internet*. Forever. Do you have any idea how degrading that is? Anyone can see my *penis* anytime they want. That's a *sex crime*."

Zia started crying hard, overwhelmed with revulsion and humiliation. She was a *survivor* of an abusive relationship. But Clay was right: this *was* a sex crime. "I'm sorry. You don't know how h-hard it's been." She was shaking. "You keep me so far away."

"We're together all the time!"

"But I can't talk about you to anyone; I can't go anywhere with you. We never talk about the future. I make myself constantly available for you. I plan my life around you, your needs, your schedule, your rules. You have complete control over me." And only as she said the words out loud did she realize how true they were, how she'd repeated the same pattern: let a powerful man call the shots, telling herself it was okay because they were in love.

In love.

They hadn't said it to each other yet. But she *did* love him, and she thought he loved her, and what an awful time to fully realize it all. "I needed to take something back. So, I took a picture. For me, just for me."

"A picture that now the whole world has seen." Clay sat on the back of the sectional, his eyes burning with suspicion. "It just seems kind of . . . calculated."

Zia tried to swallow. There was something nightmarishly recognizable about all this: being distrusted, being accused. "Calculated?"

"Yeah. You always say family comes first. I bet fifty grand really helped your sister out."

The ugliness of it made her gasp. Her shame boiled into outrage. "You don't believe me? I'm telling you the truth, Clay. I've *always* told you the truth."

He looked back at her with cool eyes and the fact he was still trying to figure it out made her want to break something. When he spoke, his voice was low and quiet. "Zia, I'm sorry. I can't do this."

"Do what?"

"I need to be around people I can trust. I don't trust you anymore."

It was so painfully absurd, she almost laughed in disbelief. "You're breaking up with me?"

"I'm sorry. But this is goodbye."

The smile he gave her was sad and full of remorse. And, final. Without another word, Clay turned and walked out of the room.

MR. AND MRS. MARK LIVINGSTONE
REQUEST THE HONOR OF YOUR PRESENCE
AT THE WEDDING OF

Miss Imogene Elizabeth Livingstone

AND

Miss Mina Yoona Choi

SATURDAY, THE TWENTY-FIFTH OF SEPTEMBER
AT THREE O'CLOCK IN THE AFTERNOON
LIVINGSTONE ESTATE
WATER MILL, SOUTHAMPTON

Black tie requested
(Bring your dancing shoes)

Once Darlene allowed herself the pleasure of fantasizing about a future with Zach, it was hard to stop. So easy to imagine.

It'd start with sex in a plush Hamptons hotel room. In a mountain of pillows, his body on top of hers, her legs wrapped around him, undulating in rhythm, their eyes locked on each other. "I love you, Zach," she'd gasp, close to climax.

"Oh, Dee," he'd sort-of-groan-sort-of-moan. "I love you too."

Moving in together, white bridal tulle, fat brown babies: it was all impossibly *possible*.

But there was no two ways about it: her fake boyfriend was acting very strangely.

Darlene phoned Zach back after leaving the bookstore in Cobble Hill, to finish setting up the dinner he seemed so jazzed about. But the call went to voice mail and only after messaging him twice did he text back that he was leaving for the Hamptons early and they'd meet at the wedding. He didn't even drive her up.

It was one thing for him to be distant and distracted at the rehearsal dinner, an eighty-person affair at a restaurant in Southampton. Both the Livingstones and the Chois had planefuls of extended family in town, and Zach was expected to charm and circulate and take selfies with distant cousins. But when he elected to stay at his family's home and not with Darlene in her nearby hotel, she felt confused and disappointed. It was supposed to start in the hotel. She'd booked one with two beds, but she was under the impression they both knew what would happen. Sort-of-moans-sort-of-groans. *I love you, Zach.*

But now he was backing out.

The rehearsal dinner was over, but the night was still young. Zach caught the eye of someone over her shoulder and called out an inside joke Darlene didn't get. He turned back to her perfunctorily. "I'll sleep on a couch. Just feels like I should be with my family."

A couch? Zach's hardiness when it came to sleeping rough was on par with the princess and the pea. Something rotten was curdling in the back of her mind. Something she wasn't ready to look at. Disappointment, bordering on nerves, leaked into her bloodstream. "Well, what about the after-party everyone's talking about? Should we go?"

"Oliver, you ponce!" Zach called to a disheveled boy about his age. "You're not even pissed, ya girl!"

"Screw you, mate!" Oliver barreled over and hauled Zach into a headlock. They roughhoused like children, almost knocking Darlene over.

Zach addressed Darlene from the headlock, his face at Oliver's hip. "See you tomorrow, 'ey, love?"

"Yeah, love, see you tomorrow," mimicked Oliver. They broke into giggles before shoving each other and hailing a passing taxi.

Darlene tried to enjoy having a huge hotel room all to herself by drawing a bath and putting on some music. Zach had gotten a bit drunk and was excited to see old friends, that's all. Tomorrow, the actual wedding, would be different.

It had to be.

The day dawned crisp, but by midafternoon had warmed to the midsixties. The shuttle dropped guests at the side garden, which led out to pre-ceremony drinks in the football-field-size backyard. Darlene was in one of the first groups to arrive. She felt proud of how she looked. Zach had seen all the dresses she usually wore to black-tie weddings when they were performing, so she'd gone to considerable effort to borrow a new one for her very first black-tie wedding attended as a guest. The gown was floor-length forest-green silk. Strapless, with a full skirt that rustled when she walked. She'd gasped when she saw herself in the hotel mirror. Now, she was eager for Zach to have the same reaction. She approached a server with a tray of appetizers and was stunned to see it being proffered by Zia. Her shirt was slightly wrinkled. She looked like she hadn't slept in days. Darlene dragged her to the party's edge. "What are you doing here? You did *not* have to work today."

Zia's voice was flat. "Being alone is worse. And I need the money."

Darlene softened, wanting badly to help fix the mistake Zia had made.

The Jungle of Us had to delay their shoot date in order for Clay to work damage control on various late-night shows, where he endured a lot of bad jokes with a big smile. Only those who knew him best could see how much it hurt. This narrative recast the photo as stolen from a hacked cell phone and Zia as a former fling from months ago. Zia was able to convince Clay's legal team that it wasn't her intent to post the picture, an act which would've constituted revenge porn, a class A misdemeanor in New York. Thankfully, this refocused the legal team's efforts away from her and her sister and onto suing the site that bought it.

And Clay was four thousand miles away in Brazil.

Darlene touched her friend's arm. "You're not serious about running off overseas again, are you?" Zia had mentioned taking another volunteer coordinator position, somewhere far away from everything and everyone. "I've just gotten used to having a roommate."

Zia looked blankly around the party. A sea of men in sharp suits and women in sky-high stilettos or dresses all the way to the floor. "There's no future for me here."

Zach's mother, Catherine, caught Darlene's eye, gesturing for her with the wave of a diamond-encrusted hand. "Go easy on yourself," Darlene told Zia. "I love you."

"I love you too," Zia replied. "I just wish I was saying that to . . ." Her words wilted and died.

The backyard started to fill. Fifty guests became one hundred, then two hundred. It was both Korean and Hamptons custom to have a sizable guest list. Darlene was no longer playing the role of devoted girlfriend—she felt like she *was* Zach's girlfriend, proud of his accomplishments, grateful to be connected to him. She chatted briefly with Liv, noting how much happier the wedding planner was looking lately. Savannah did not seem as rosy-cheeked. Darlene spotted her gazing at a quartet of cool, gay lady couples, before snapping to, and hurrying inside.

Just as Darlene was starting to think she wouldn't see Zach until the ceremony, the patio door slid open, and there he was. Her jaw dropped. "Holy Livingstone."

Zach in a tux? Simply spectacular. Tall, dark, and mouthwateringly handsome. He was James Bond, an ad for Rolex, an argument for dual citizenship. The three-piece tux was the same blue as his eyes. It made his shoulders look square, and his body look strong. His typically floppy brown hair was swept back off his face, exposing clear skin and cheekbones Darlene didn't even know he had. The entire effect made him look like Prince freaking Charming. How had she ever doubted it? She was, and perhaps always had been, hopelessly, crazily, wildly in love with this boy. This funny, sensitive, surprisingly sweet boy. Her fake boyfriend. Her real heart.

He hugged a svelte blonde in a tight red dress and kissed her hello. Darlene worked hard to let the wallop of jealousy pass—it was nothing; it was a wedding. After the blonde left, he finally caught Darlene's eye. And yes, *there* was the reaction she was hoping for: the pulse of his eyes and slackening of his mouth as his gaze dragged up and down her dress. She approached, dopey with desire, lifting her mouth to his. Somehow, her lips landed on his cheek.

Zach stepped back, putting a foot of air between them. "Hey. You look great."

Great? Not beautiful, not gorgeous? Where was tongue-unfurled you-look-*sexy*-Dee Zach? "You look fantastic." She moved closer, putting her hand on his chest. "Can we talk?"

He resisted. "I have people I need to say hello to."

Ignoring this, she tugged him away from the other guests, to the end of the patio. Her heart was pounding, terrified at the prospect of uncut, emotional honesty. But she couldn't put it off any longer. "Zach."

"Darlene." His voice was crisp. "There's something you should know."

"Me first, please. Look, I know neither of us expected this. But these past few months have been—"

"Zach, sorry—what bathroom should I use?" The svelte blonde in the red dress was back.

Zach lit up like a Christmas tree. "Bitsy! You know it's bad form to do coke before the ceremony . . . and not invite me." He moved toward her, away from Darlene.

Darlene tried not to think it. But here it came: Bitsy was exactly Zach's type.

Bitsy laughed and whacked him with her clutch. "Don't be silly, Zook. I just want to know if I can use the one in Imogene's room, or if she's in there getting ready."

Zach looped an arm around Bitsy's shoulder, drawing her to his chest. "If she is, there's a good chance a lot of drunk bridesmaids are by her side. So maybe I should come with you."

Bitsy laughed again and extended a hand to Darlene affably. "I'm Bitsy. Family friend."

"Family favorite," Zach amended. "This is Darlene. We . . . work together."

What? Was he drunk? High? She stared into his completely clear eyes. "And, I'm your girlfriend," Darlene added. *Right?*

"Oh." Bitsy sobered, confused.

Both women stared at Zach.

Zach laughed, as if Darlene had done something hilariously stupid. "In name only." He shot Bitsy a devilish smile. "Can you keep a secret?" And then Zach proceeded to explain the whole damn scheme to a titillated Bitsy—the contract, the $25,000 paycheck, the trust. It was like watching actors in a Broadway play break the fourth wall and start discussing the denouement with the front row. "So, we only have a few more weeks of pretending to like each other." Zach looked oddly, almost scarily, cool. "To be honest, it'll be a relief when it's over."

Bitsy gave Darlene a scandalized smile. "Oh my gosh. It's so *Pretty Woman* of you."

The words hit Darlene deep in her stomach, adding to the sick wave of confusion. She couldn't even pretend to smile back. "Zach, can we talk?"

"Congresswoman!" Zach brushed past her to extend a hand to a distinguished-looking Black woman in a blue gown. "I've been meaning to chat with you about your recent climate change bill. It's an absolute cracker, but does it go far enough reducing emissions from steel? Convince me!"

What.

The hell.

Was happening?

The ceremony was lovely, but Darlene didn't hear a word. The dinner was delicious, but Darlene didn't taste a bite. The DJ was excellent, but Darlene was too busy watching Zach get stupendously smashed, flailing around the dance floor like a sentient scarecrow, to hear a single note. Every time she tried to corner him, he found a way to cold-shoulder her or, worse, flirt with another woman, right in front of her. She'd be furious if she wasn't so flummoxed. What had changed? Surely Zach hadn't just woken up and decided he wanted to go back to his old bachelor ways, apropos of nothing? A large part of her wanted to leave. Head back to the hotel, become close friends with the minibar and fire up Tinder or something equally reckless.

But a larger part—the part that, for better or worse, still cared about this man—needed to figure out what was going on. To parse the meaning of *that* moment from his best man speech: "It's a small miracle to find someone who will love you, and accept you, for who you are. Who you can trust, completely."

She swore he looked right at her, his eyes ice-cold.

She found him at the bar by the pool. His once-immaculate suit was destroyed—jacket gone, bow tie askew, shirt halfway untucked. His previously neat hair was back to being tousled and undone. He was laughing with a hot female bartender. Darlene took the spot next to him and folded her arms.

He took her in, blinking slow and disdainful. "I'm busy."

"I'm not leaving until we talk."

"For Chrissake." He rolled his eyes. "Take a hint."

Darlene didn't move.

"Fine." He twisted to face her. His sneer was gone. In its place was pain. "I heard you. Talking to Charles. In the bookstore. You left your phone on after I called you."

The rotten thing in the back of her brain oozed all over her. Sound fell away. "What did you hear?"

Zach cleared his throat, darkly dramatic. "*I'd sooner marry a donkey than date Zach Livingstone.* And a really clever line from William Shakespeare." Zach picked up a half-empty glass of champagne and drained it. "He sounds interesting. I'll have to look him up."

Darlene's mind went static with horror. She grabbed his arm. "I didn't mean that."

He removed her grip. "But you said it."

"I didn't mean it," Darlene pleaded, desperate and horrified. "I was trying to impress Charles."

Zach didn't look angry or bitter. He just looked crushed. "But you said it."

"Zach!" Bitsy was approaching, somehow still looking like a Sunday picnic.

Zach's emotions wiped from his face, transforming to simple happiness. It was eerie how quickly he could throw up a wall, play the joker, the fool. Darlene had challenged his family to see Zach in a better light right here at this house, only two months ago. She'd defended him, and in return, he'd been a loyal friend. And this was how she'd repaid him: dragging his kind heart through the mud to impress her pretentious ex. What a pathetic thing to do, and oh God, he'd had to sit with that for the week leading up to his sister's *wedding*. She'd do anything to make this right. But before a single gesture or sacrifice became clear, Bitsy was at the bar and Zach was all over her like a rash.

"Darling," he purred, one hand around her waist. "You are upsettingly sober."

Bitsy's smile was bright as she leaned into Zach. "Can't have consensual sex if I'm blackout."

They both laughed like lovers conspiring. It was a punishment, and it was working. But even now, Darlene could see the difference in Zach's seduction of Bitsy versus herself. There'd always been a vulnerability in Zach's eyes when they were together, belying the depth of feeling he had for her. With Bitsy, he was back to being a game show host.

"Zach," Darlene said. "Can we *please* talk?"

"Go, enjoy the party, Mitchell. There's loads of really smart people here." He walked his fingers up Bitsy's bare arm. "You're so brilliant, Bits. How much do I have to pay you to snog me?"

Bitsy curled into him, delighted. "Darling, I am completely free of charge."

The only way to stop this was with honesty. As much as everything inside her was wincing, saying *No, no, don't do it,* Darlene willed the words to leave her lips. "Zach, I have real feelings for you."

Bitsy glanced at her. "What?"

Darlene moved closer. "I care about you, Zach. I like you. A lot." She gazed desperately at Bitsy, willing girl code. "Please. Five minutes."

Bitsy took one look at Zach's expression and backed up. "I am not about drama or being used to make someone else jealous." She stepped past Darlene, pausing to murmur in her ear, "Just so you know: Zach is adult Disneyland. Get tested."

And even though it was meant to be a warning, it just made Darlene see Zach clearer—as someone who treated his insecurities with casual sex because he didn't think he deserved anything better.

Darlene drew him away from the bright lights and shouted conversations, toward a copse of red maple trees on the far edges of the backyard. The party was just a smudge in the middle distance; they were alone. An owl hooted. An unseen animal rustled in the undergrowth. Shadows pooled over Zach's face as he slugged from a bottle of red wine that spilled down his shirtfront like a gush of blood.

"What I did was wrong, Zach," Darlene began. "I'm sorry, I'm so, so sorry. I was trying to impress Charles by being mean about you. He's always made me feel intellectually inferior, and I still feel insecure around him. Being mean was immature and cruel. What I said was a lie, Zach. I was lying."

"Am I just a joke to you? Stupid Zach Livingstone, just a clown who's always on call—"

"No! No, Zach—"

"A donkey?" His voice rose, furious and devastated and ringing with passion. "A fucking *donkey*?" Zach threw both arms wide. Red wine arced in the air, splattering to the earth. He was shouting. "Jesus Christ, I *worshipped* you. I was so absolutely, *ridiculously* in love with you. For months. Bloody *months*." His expression was raw pain. "But now all I see is someone who thinks I'm an idiot."

"But I don't think you're an idiot."

"I don't get it. I don't get any of it." He jammed the heel of his hand into his eye, rubbing hard. "Why'd you ghost me after the Harvard Club? You were feeling it, I know you were, then poof! You clammed up. Why?"

"I needed some . . . boundaries."

"Why?" He was frustrated, shouting at the stars. "Talk to me, tell me how you're feeling, *God*."

"I didn't know if I gave in and let myself—let us—be something, that you wouldn't just, like, run off with some other girl in a few weeks."

"What the hell did I do to make you think that?" He was so close she could smell the red wine on his breath. "You were all I could think about. It was only *you*. And then you go and say—*that*. To *Charles*."

"But I *didn't mean it*." Her heart was jackhammering in her chest. This wasn't how she imagined saying it. But now, it might be the only thing that could save them. "Zach, I . . . I care about you."

Nothing. Silence, but for the throbbing bass of the distant speakers. Zach went still, suddenly alert. His eyes darted back and forth between her own. "Care?"

"Yes." She nodded. A tear slipped down her cheek. "I care about you a lot."

"Care?" He repeated it like he knew it was code for the word she couldn't say, even now. "God, what is wrong with you? Why can't you talk about your feelings?"

"Because I'm not you, Zach!" Darlene exploded with guilt and anger, her defenses blasting apart. "I don't get to be you. I don't get to waltz through life. I don't get to make mistakes. I don't have a safety net. My life is really hard, in a million ways you will never understand, and I screwed up. I screwed up, and I'm sorry."

Zach listened, astounded. Shame-faced. He nodded, rubbing his forehead. "Fair. Yes, of course, that's bloody fair." Then his hand fell to his side. "So how does making me second-best to Eeyore fit into that?"

"I don't know. It doesn't. I just need you to know that despite everything, I had—*have*—very . . . strong . . . feelings for you."

Zach stared at her. Really stared. "Do you love me, Darlene? Is that it?"

Yes, *that was it.* And he needed to hear it. But no words left her lips. She wasn't from a lovey-dovey family, she couldn't parse this alcohol-soaked fight they were having, this wasn't the way you said things like this. Fear, anger, and sadness muted her truth. Like it so often did.

Zach wiped his mouth with the back of his sleeve, looking undone and messy and tragically romantic. "So, what—was this all about the money?"

A whip of anger cracked through her. "No, it's not about the money, I don't want your money, and fuck you for telling Bitsy. She basically said I'm a call girl." The truth of it boiled in Darlene, and she became more furious. She was making it worse, but she couldn't stop. "I guess because I didn't drop my pants for you right away like the *one million* girls you've banged in New York, you *purchased* me. Do you have any idea how messed up that is? God, in what world did I ever think you'd change? You're nothing more than a privileged little boy too scared to stand up to his own parents."

Something inside Zach's face collapsed. He sagged, wincing, like he'd just been punched in the stomach. Then he took another slug of wine, half of it splashing down his chin. "Wow. Tell me what you really think."

Regret consumed her. She was supposed to be making things better. "Shit, I'm sorry."

"Don't be. I quit."

"You quit what?"

"Us. This. Our band. You and me." He started stumbling back toward the party, "I'll mail you the check."

"Zach, wait. I didn't mean—"

He yelled over his shoulder, each word bitter and hard. "But thank you so much, Mitchell. For always seeing the best in me."

The farewell she'd given Charles in the bookshop. But it had never been Charles who saw the best in her. It was Zach.

71

Liv, Sam, Ben, and Dottie thundered up the steps of the brownstone, squealing and thoroughly soaked. The afternoon storm had come out of nowhere.

"Oh my gosh!" gasped Liv, as they flung open the front door. "We're drowned rats!"

They made puddles on the hardwood floors as they trooped inside, all talking and laughing at once. Sam toweled off Ben's hair and carefully wiped his glasses while Liv fashioned a cozy dress for Dottie out of an old pink T-shirt.

"Pink's my favorite color," Sam's daughter told Liv.

"Last week you told me blue was your favorite color," Liv replied, tucking a lock of blond hair behind Dottie's ear.

Dottie grinned as if caught out in the most fun lie possible. "It's *also* pink."

"You can have two favorites," Liv told her, kissing the top of her head. "You can have as many favorites as you like."

It hadn't always been this easy. In fact, this might very well have been the first easy day.

Ben had taken relatively well to Sam being Liv's boyfriend. "I already guessed." There'd been a few rough patches, but overall, her son was doing much better. Sleeping through the night, more confident with strangers. Dottie had taken more work. She wanted to know if Sam and Liv were going to get married, if Liv was going to move in, if this meant she would see less of her real mommy. They worked through her questions and concerns, but Dottie hadn't allowed Liv to play with any of her toys until recently. Consistency and patience had been the key. An interest in fairy costumes didn't hurt. Slowly, the kids got used to a new routine of dinner together when Dottie wasn't with Claudia, who had an empathetic smile and an easygoing parenting style Liv admired.

And then today—today had kind of been perfect. They fed ducks in the mucky park pond, played a boisterous game of tag among the piles of yellowed leaves, then set upon one of Sam's elaborate picnic lunches. Ham and gruyere sandwiches, ginger lemonade, and, the big surprise, a double chocolate cherry cake, with five candles. Liv blew them out in one blow.

For years, she'd been ambivalent about turning fifty. For most of this year, she'd been downright dreading it. She'd no longer be young. Things would get more difficult; healthwise, careerwise, wrinkles-and-flappy-skin-wise. But as she sat on the plaid picnic blanket in the brisk autumnal air, rugged up and laughing with the ones she loved, Liv wasn't thinking about what was ending. She was enjoying what was beginning.

Now, back home, the brownstone was a cacophony of hot showers and changes of clothes and *Who wants hot chocolate?* and *Me, me, I do!* It reminded Liv of years ago, when they'd have the cool neighborhood parents and their kids over for Phone-Free Fridays. The little ones hanging from the willow tree in the then-landscaped backyard, the adults cracking open beers to talk national politics or neighborhood gossip. When Eliot was at his best and things between them seemed pretty good. When it was a home, not just a house. When they were a family, not just the two of them, unmoored and trying to find their way. Now, watching Sam help the kids get into their pj's, she recognized that *family* and *happiness* could be rare, transitory states, not guarantees. It made her value them even more.

The overgrown backyard was getting pelted with rain. Sam peered out, folding his arms. "You know that willow tree's got to come down."

It felt like proposing she get her teeth yanked out and replaced with dentures. "So you've been saying."

Sam rubbed his neck. "No, you seriously need to get it out. It's hurricane season and—"

"I know." She pulled him away. "Why don't you go microwave some popcorn."

"Real men don't microwave. We make it from *scratch*." He headed into the kitchen. Liv stayed by the patio doors. The willow was dying. But what Sam didn't know was she and Eliot planted that tree. The year they got married and bought the brownstone, over two decades ago. It'd been there for all the milestones: Ben's birthdays and sitting shiva for her father and sticky summer evenings watching the green-gold fireflies blink on and off, like bits of floating magic. Even though their marriage had ended, the relationship held more good memories than bad. The weeping willow, that big, messy Muppet of a tree, had been there for all of them.

And it was her house and her tree, and it was staying.

After everyone was dry, they settled in to watch a movie. *The Wizard of Oz* had just started on cable. Dorothy meeting the munchkins, her whole world in Technicolor. Sam grabbed a handful of popcorn. "I love this movie."

"Me too." Liv draped a woolen blanket around their knees and kissed him on his deliciously salty mouth.

Ben and Dottie affected disgust. "Ewww!"

"Oh, stop it," she said, poking them until they giggled.

By the end of the film, Ben and Dottie were curled into their respective parent, rosy and boneless with sleep. Liv snuggled next to Sam, his long arm draped around her.

"I love this," he murmured.

An old movie and hot chocolate and their children safe and warm and happy. Everyone safe and warm and happy. "I love this too."

He shifted to face her, his eyes turning soft and serious. "Happy birthday, baby. I hope you had a good day."

"I had the best day."

Outside, the rain roared. It didn't unnerve her. Because the man next to her would be the single standing house after a storm that razed the entire street. His words were quiet, but sure. "I love you, Liv."

She'd known this was coming. In the weeks and months prior, she was worried the words might make her feel anxious or guilty. When she'd spoken her wedding vows to Eliot Max Goldenhorn, she'd promised to love him, and only him, always. She'd never even considered loving someone else. But life had other plans. Now, she was here, with another man, and her child, and his child. All together, filling her with a contentment and ease she barely believed was possible. And so she'd be damned if she didn't tell him God's honest truth. "I love you too, Sam."

Dorothy clicked her ruby red-slippers, sending her home, to the people she cared about.

But Liv was already there.

Later, after Sam and Dottie had left and Ben was asleep in bed, Liv was stacking the dishwasher when she heard movement in the front office.

Savannah was at her desk, working. Damp blond hair fell around her face like a curtain.

Liv yawned. "What are you doing here so late?"

"Tying up some loose ends from the Livingstone-Choi affair," Savannah replied, vague.

"God, that was a lovely wedding." Liv leaned back against the doorframe, hands in her dressing gown pockets. "The pictures are gorgeous."

Savannah's head snapped up. "The pictures are in?"

A minute later, Liv was clicking through the selects. She paused on the first kiss. A dynamic, fantastic shot. Multicolored confetti flying against a cerulean sky. The front row of family on their feet and cheering. Both women locked into a romantic, passionate embrace. Liv smiled. "That's a framer."

Something splashed on the keyboard. Liv whipped her gaze to the ceiling. "Jesus, was that a leak?"

Savannah sniffed. "Liv," she said, in an oddly strained voice. "I have something to tell you."

Leaks were expensive. And even though the business was back up and running, Liv had definitely not budgeted for a new roof. "Hmm?"

"I'm . . . I mean, I think I am . . . a little . . . or maybe a lot . . . gay."

"Oh. Cool. Yeah, think I was starting to get that vibe."

Savannah had never been wowed by any of the grooms. And overly wowed by the brides.

"I did the whole college lesbian thing for a minute," Liv added. "Didn't pan out." She squinted at the ceiling. "You haven't noticed any water in here, have you? It hasn't rained in a while, and I might've missed—"

Savannah burst into loud, hysterical tears.

Oh. Not a leak.

Liv made peppermint tea. She'd never had to slip into the role of counselor and confidante with Savannah. Six months ago this would've disgusted her. Now, their knees were touching as they sat side by side on the pale pink sofa. Savannah unleashed: never meeting the right guy, always having *very close* female friendships, *Feel Good* and her parents and Honey and Honey's ultimatum.

"I like her. A lot. But I don't think I'm ready to be someone's girlfriend, and that's what she wants. What she deserves."

"In a relationship, timing is everything," Liv said. "Maybe the timing just isn't right. It's not easy, doing what we do," she added. "Working every day with other people's dreams, making them real. Finding love yourself and sustaining it long-term, when there's absolutely no script—that's hard."

Savannah's face was wet. "Be honest. Do you think I'm . . . That this is all . . . kind of . . . strange?"

"Strange?"

Savannah's gaze dropped to her tea. The words were a whisper. "Wrong."

The wave of desperate, maternal love took Liv by surprise. She lifted Savannah's chin up so she could speak to her directly. "There is nothing weird or wrong about who you're attracted to, or who you love. Heterosexuality is just more *common*. It's not more *normal*."

Savannah smiled sadly. "I don't know if my parents would agree with that."

"Exactly. You don't know. After you tell them—if you choose to tell them—you'll find out." Liv put her tea aside to focus on Savannah. "But remember this: telling people things that they might not expect to hear, but that are true about you, is a way for them to deepen their relationship with you. To know you, and love you, even more. And speaking as a mom"—Liv's throat thickened—"that's honestly the best gift my son could ever give me. To let me in like that, and allow me to love him even more fully."

She found herself reaching out to hug Savannah. For a long moment, Liv held her as she cried softly.

Liv could never have imagined that the overly made-up young woman handing her a copy of Eliot's will outside the brownstone would end up here, in her arms, weeping about being a little, or a lot, gay. And for Liv to really, really care about that.

PART FOUR

IN LOVE IN NEW YORK CITY

72

The week before Halloween, the wizards at Google finally sent Liv Eliot's email password. *Benny123*.

For five long days, Liv avoided it all. The Pandora's box it might open felt like someone had put her spine on ice. And so Liv made Savannah do it.

"Just look through the last few months or so," she instructed her. "See if there's anything I should know about."

Savannah hesitated. "I'm not sure that's something I'm comfortable doing, Liv."

A punch of dread tightened Liv's throat. "Well, I can't. So I need you . . ." She fluttered her fingers at the laptop.

Savannah entered the password. She scrolled and tapped for a few minutes, moving methodically through pages of junk mail. Then she frowned.

"What?" Liv was hovering, unable to stay away.

It was their attorney, emailing Eliot the updated will. Two weeks prior to his death. It was the last line of his otherwise formal email that'd caught Savannah's attention. *I am sorry to hear of the reason for the requested change and truly wish you all the best.*

Liv read it, and read it again. "Did he mean, like, our marriage?"

Savannah pressed her teeth into her lower lip, thinking. "What other reason might there be?"

Something strange and frightening edged into Liv's mind.

She searched Eliot's in-box for their doctor's name.

Three appointment confirmations. Three appointments she definitely did not remember Eliot attending: she had to bug him to get a checkup. Nothing more from the doctor's office in his email. No further clues.

Liv sat back in her chair. Her fingers were numb.

She'd never gotten a copy of Eliot's autopsy.

It had to be requested from the medical examiner's office, and at the time, it seemed pointless. It was a garden-variety heart attack—what else was there to know?

I am sorry to hear of the reason for the requested change.

Liv watched herself with calm detachment as she followed the steps to officially request Eliot's postmortem exam. Days later, she was alone in the front office when she received an email with an attached PDF. It was a cloudy Friday afternoon. Savannah was doing some returns. Ben was at school. The house was very quiet.

Too nervous to sit, she paced the front office, willing the courage to click the PDF open.

The patient was a forty-nine-year-old Caucasian male . . .

Liv inhaled a jagged breath and looked away. It took her a few minutes to ground herself and return to the report. She skimmed the cold prose, fast, too fast.

heart showed asymmetric as well as concentric hypertrophy
blood vessels were fixed in 10% formalin
hypertrophic cardiomyopathy.
patient was high risk for sudden cardiac death

Liv sank, legless, into the pale pink sofa.

High risk. Sudden cardiac death.

In the coming hours, Eliot's past would catch up to the present. His strange behavior in the months prior to his death would all make a horrible new kind of sense. The furtiveness. The whiplash between overly doting and prickly distance. The doctor's appointments. The affair.

Eliot had been careening through life with a ticking time bomb for a heart. And he knew it.

73

The audience at Zinc Bar was shoulder to shoulder as Darlene began the trusty set closer. "'*They tried to make me go to rehab, I said,* No, no, no.'" And while the students and the tourists and the locals sang along, swaying with their glasses of inexpensive wine, something was missing.

Electricity.

Chemistry.

Zach.

Zach was missing. No one was dancing on tables or making out or doing shots. The Dionysian energy he brought to this, to everything, was gone.

Darlene finished the song. The capable if not particularly charismatic session musicians took a quick bow. The audience clapped. They didn't cheer. Or holler. Or stamp their feet. Darlene couldn't blame them. It was painful to admit, but it was true: Zach made her a better musician. He made her a better person, period. But he'd disappeared. Removed himself, entirely, from her life. He'd embedded himself with her for so long, she didn't think absence was possible. Except, it was. He didn't reply to her texts, didn't return her calls.

As she was packing up the equipment, the bartender waved her over, offering her a shot. She shook her head: it wasn't fun getting drunk without Zach. The bartender shrugged and did it himself.

"Hey, I heard about Zach," he said. "Pity."

Adrenaline kicked her ribs. "What do you mean?"

"Didn't he quit music or some crap?"

Quit music? *Quit music?*

When Darlene visited Zach's apartment, the smiling concierge recognized her and called up. Then the smile faded.

She tried to lose herself in her EP, which all this was supposed to be in service of. In lieu of Zach's twenty-five grand, the check for which she definitely wasn't cashing, she paid for the producer's deposit with all her savings, telling herself that when she got a record deal, she could pay it all back.

But that was another avalanche of disappointment.

She submitted ten songs to the producer. They listened to them all in his Harlem studio. Her initial excitement morphed into panic as song after song received only reserved acknowledgment, no real enthusiasm. "Dark Secret" was last. It took every ounce of her strength to keep it together as the lyrics played.

> *He's my dark secret; I think he's a keeper.*
> *I like to run, but he makes me stand still.*
> *When it comes to keeping secrets*
> *I'm nothing but the best*
> *I'm a locked box, baby, I'm a treasure chest*
> *But boy you're breaking down my defenses*
> *Making me mix up all my tenses*
> *You were the only one who made me feel like coming home.*

"That," the producer said. "That has potential."

"Oh," Darlene said in pained surprise. "I sort of cowrote that. With a . . . former friend."

The producer asked if her "former friend" had signed a cowriting agreement, for the song they legally owned half of.

Of course the former friend had not. He, apparently, had "quit music."

Without it, the producer was not willing to work on "Dark Secret," and without that, Darlene was of no interest to him.

Darlene left the studio in a daze, stepping onto a street messy with car horns blaring, a woman arguing into a cell phone, music playing from a distant window, dogs barking. A rhythmless jumble of random noise.

74

Alone in his apartment, Zach stared at his ceiling in silence. His bed was covered in political books—his newfound medicine. He read, and listened to podcasts, and watched the distressing, dystopian news. He did not listen to, or play, or even think about, music. Because music was Darlene. And once you had the ear for it, *every* song was about love or women or getting your heart put through a bloody Vitamix and honestly, he couldn't handle it.

Memories of things she said or did attacked him at all hours. Strangely, there was one moment that he kept coming back to, from a wedding upstate in May, the one where Zia met Clay. Something Darlene said that he couldn't stop thinking about.

I don't want my success handed to me. I want to earn it.

He joined a local activist group aimed at registering people to vote, and this felt good; this felt productive. When a very cute fellow activist asked him out for drinks, he declined politely. He dragged his useless, broken heart around with him like a pile of trash, hoping that time would do what the expression claimed, and heal his septic wound.

It didn't. He missed her. Christ, he missed her. He made it seem like he didn't love her anymore, but that wasn't true. He couldn't turn off his feelings, even if he wanted to. He missed his bandmate. He missed his best friend. He missed his girlfriend. He just missed her. But every time she texted—*Please. Please, just call me*—he heard those words. *I'd sooner marry a donkey than date Zach Livingstone.* And his throat would get tight, and his stomach would boil, and he'd throw his stupid phone across the room. Darlene didn't care for him: she'd only said that because she felt bad she'd been caught. Kissing was easy but love was not and there was still so much he didn't understand about her, about her world and her struggles. And he'd never be able to. Because he was a stupid white guy with the brains of a witless beast.

"Can I get everyone's attention, please?" Mark Livingstone tapped his wineglass with a dessert fork. The clean, high sound rang out across the crowded room. Zach's twenty-seventh birthday party had originally been planned as a Sunday picnic, but the freezing rain lashing the East Coast moved it into the formal front room of the Livingstone estate. Relatives and family friends nibbled crustless sandwiches and petit fours, to the subdued strains of Bach's Violin Concerto No. 1 in A Minor. Zach's music buddies, scruffy-looking folk from all walks of life, looked either bewildered or snide at the chichi surroundings. Zach had been too morose to push back on his mother's planning, and so now he found himself the guest of honor at a ridiculous tea party. He didn't even feel like getting sauced.

But only a donkey would feel ungrateful surrounded by so much privilege and people who genuinely cared about him. Zach tried to feel thankful for his many blessings—and he did. But the one thing he wanted, the one girl he wanted, thought he was an idiot. So he probably was. His chest hurt. It hadn't stopped hurting since his sister's wedding. He slumped into a settee at the back of the room, only to have his shoulders tapped by his mother—*Posture, darling*—as she took a seat beside him.

"Quiet down," Mark boomed, and everyone shut up. There'd been three pretty average speeches so far: his great-aunt, one of his father's business associates, and a family friend he didn't even like. His dad, thankfully, was last. "It's been a banner year for the Livingstone family," began Mark. "Catherine has been doing wonderful work on the board of Save the Children"—his mother inclined her head at the light applause—"and many of you were present last month for the wedding of our daughter, Imogene, to her lovely wife, Mina." The applause increased. Imogene pinched Mina's bottom. Mina elbowed her, hiding a smile. "But we're here today to honor my son, Zachary Bartholomew Livingstone, on his twenty-seventh birthday." Zach managed a watery smile. Imogene caught his eye and made a sympathetic face. She and Mina were the only ones privy to the true despair felt by the man of the hour. "As many of you know," Mark continued, "Zachary enjoyed something of a . . . Bacchanalian youth."

The room tittered—they knew.

"But this year, we've started to see a real change in him. In fact, just this summer, Zachary became interested in politics. And I'm pleased to inform you he's beginning a paid internship with our local congresswoman."

The crowded clapped, surprised.

"It's only a day a week," Zach muttered, embarrassed.

His mother shushed him, whispering over the applause. "I know things didn't work out with Darlene, but we've been very impressed with you this year." She shifted closer to him across the stiff settee. "We're going to give you your trust."

The offer irritated him. If there'd never been a trust, maybe he and Darlene would've gotten together like a normal couple, and she'd be here beside him, holding his hand and exchanging secret smirks. "Thanks, Mum, but you can keep it. I'll figure all that out on my own."

His father started saying something about the value of hard work.

Catherine's forehead tried to crease. "Zach, I'm saying we'll give you the money."

"And I'm saying I don't want it," Zach said. "I'll earn it myself: I'm actually pretty capable. Donate it all to the ACLU or something."

His mother looked absolutely aghast.

"This year, we've gotten a glimpse of the man he's going to become," Mark was saying. "Responsible. Mature. Sober-minded. And I for one could not be prouder." Mark raised his glass. "To my son. Happy birthday, Zachary."

"Happy birthday, Zachary," echoed the guests.

"Thanks." Zach raised a limp hand in acknowledgment. "Thanks so much."

"All right, everyone." His mother was on her feet. "Into the kitchen for cake."

The noise level rose again. Zach willed himself to get through this last little bit. The sooner it was over, the sooner he could go back to Manhattan, pull his duvet over his head, and stay there for—

"I'd like to say something."

Zach froze. He knew that voice. That clear, musical, *beautiful* voice.

The guests shifted, parting, allowing Darlene Mitchell to step forward.

75

Time didn't make losing Clay any easier. But the one thing it did do was move the nation's obsession off the infamous naked selfie. The news cycle was moving with the pace and responsibility of a drunk driver. Clay Russo's naked body was a brief distraction from frightening new pollution statistics and arguments about health care. But Zia didn't stop thinking about it. Or him.

Was he still mad about it all?

Did he think about her?

Listen to the voice mails she'd left him?

Zia had no idea. And so, she tried to forget about Clay.

At first, taking a shift at an In Love in New York wedding at Brooklyn Winery seemed like a good idea. Close to home, good money, and working with people who were more like friends than coworkers. But as toast after toast celebrated the blissed-up couple, Zia's defenses weakened. The couple began their first dance and grief landed on her chest, full force. She found herself in the side alley, feeling stunned and breathless, talking herself out of crying. Someone said her name. Liv.

Zia startled. "I'm sorry, I was just—" Staying up late watching old movies. "Having a moment but I—" Making love in the shower. "Just, um—" Talking about everything and nothing, curled up in bed together, the city a twinkling distant dream.

It was too much. Her face fell into her hands, and she started to cry.

Liv put her arms around her, soothing. "Shhh. It's okay."

"I just—miss him—so much," Zia said between sobs.

"I know, honey. Oh, I know." And she did know. Liv was a widow. "You don't really have any family in the city, do you?"

"Not really." Zia still took her niece and nephew to the park once or twice a week. But every time she looked at her sister, all she could see was cold, cruel venality.

Liv gave her a tissue, tucking her hair out of her face. "Why don't you come over for dinner tomorrow night? Sam will cook. And we can talk about it or not talk about it. Whatever you want."

"Thank you, Liv," Zia said. "I'd really like that."

"Good. Take a minute, then get back in there. Okay?"

"Okay."

Liv ducked back inside. Zia collected herself. She would move on. She knew she had to. But at least once a day, she couldn't help picturing him. Alone in his trailer, jaw tense, gold eyes turned inward. Regretting what happened. Missing her.

76

As the intensity of the *Jungle of Us* shoot finally came to an end, Clay found himself resurfacing into a bitter, lonely reality.

It was hard for him to recognize the man who overreacted to the viral photograph. It seemed like the actions of Illusion Clay, the invented one. The very thing he was afraid of happening—Illusion Clay taking over his life—had happened.

He'd been a controlling dick. He'd blown it.

But it'd been weeks. Even though he missed Zia, the best thing he could do for her was leave her alone. When the flirty makeup artist put her hand on his thigh at the wrap party, he leaned in, feigning interest. But then he remembered Zia pretending to be a makeup artist when she returned his wallet. How easy it had been between them, how thrilling. And the spark he'd been hoping to breathe into a cleansing fire with the actual makeup artist promptly went out.

Now, back in New York, the penthouse felt huge and empty. An assistant, some eager undergrad sent to pick him up at the airport, helped Clay with his luggage, chattering about the week's schedule of meetings and phone calls and appearances and invites. Clay only half listened, inspecting the fridge. Nothing but condiments. The prospect of ordering groceries and cooking for one felt depressing. Outside the city was washed gray. It used to feel cozy when it rained, full of candles and lamp light and the smell of her essential oils . . .

"Is there anything else I can do for you, Mr. Russo?" The assistant stood by the elevator, blinking behind Coke-bottle glasses.

"No. Thanks."

"Call if you need. Oh, this came," he added. "Special delivery. From your dry cleaner."

Clay's heart paused.

From your dry cleaner, that was their joke, that was theirs!

He spun around so fast he almost lost his balance.

The assistant was holding a tux on a coat hanger, wrapped in flimsy dry-cleaning plastic.

Oh. Right, that tux, the one he wore to Dave's wedding. He'd finally gotten around to getting it cleaned. It was literally a special delivery from his actual dry cleaner.

The assistant looked at the suit. "Were you expecting something else?"

He'd met Zia wearing that tux. They'd almost kissed for the first time when she was buttoning up the wine-stained shirt. Clay hung the suit up, not sure whether to laugh or cry. There was only one person he wanted to tell that story to. One person he hadn't spoken to in six long weeks.

One person whose heart-wrenching voice mails he'd listened to no less than one hundred times.

Something stronger than lust was surging through him, building in his chest. He called.

"The number you've called has been disconnected. Please hang up and try again."

He felt his pulse all the way down to his fingertips. He scrolled through his contacts until he found Darlene's number. She picked up on the second ring, sounding surprised and slightly suspicious. "Clay."

"Hey, Darlene. Long time. I was, um, looking for Zia. Her number's disconnected."

There was a pause. "She just left."

A puff of relief. She still existed: Darlene had just seen her. "Well, when will she be back? And do you have her new number?"

"She just left for the airport."

A siren sounded in Clay's head. He stopped pacing, rooted to the spot. "Where's she going?"

Darlene hesitated. "Papua New Guinea."

The ground fell away. "What? When? Why?"

"I'm not sure I should tell you."

"*Please.*"

There was another excruciating pause. "She took one of her volunteer coordinator jobs there. There was a hurricane— Wow, you really have impeccable timing, Clay."

"Text me her flight number."

Silence. It sounded like Darlene was driving, the wet squelch of the windshield wipers moving rhythmically against glass, Jimi Hendrix playing low.

"Darlene, I messed up. I let Illusion Clay—it's hard to explain but I need to see her. Apologize. For everything."

Darlene sighed. "I'll text you. But if you hurt her like that again, I will end you."

"Sounds good." Clay hung up and whirled around. He had to put on shoes, call his driver, grab a jacket—

Wait. He came to a halt. Shook his head. Took a breath.

He wasn't really doing this. Was he really doing this? Running to the airport to get back the woman he loved?

And there it was: the woman he loved.

"Russo," he groaned, thumping his forehead with the heel of his hand. "You're such an *idiot*." He stabbed a call to his new assistant. "I need a plane ticket. To anywhere. Leaving from"—he checked Darlene's text—"uh, I don't know. Wherever Flight HA51 is leaving from."

The assistant babbled some questions.

"I don't know what airport!" Clay shoved his foot into a sneaker, hopping around on one leg. "I'll forward you a text. Wait, can I do that?"

The assistant kept blathering.

"I don't care about frequent flyer miles!" He had the shoe on the wrong foot. He almost lost his balance as he tried to switch it, the phone still jammed under one ear. The comic absurdity of it all struck him. He had a wild urge to laugh. "No, I don't need luggage! No, *don't* come back!"

In the three separate films where he'd done a run-for-your-love scene, there had never been any logistics. But this is what he wanted to remember—the messy, confusing, silly thrill of it. The parts of his life that were just for him. And just for her.

77

The sight of Darlene was water to a man dying of thirst. Her curls were natural and she was dressed simply in jeans and a blouse the color of a sunflower. She was the most beautiful woman at the party, in America, on the entire bloody planet. And she was here. In his parents' home. Staring at him with full, expressive eyes. Zach's heart, sensing the antidote to its current state, banged against his ribcage like a prisoner demanding sustenance.

"My—my name is Darlene. I'm Zach's . . ."

Zach didn't blame her. What *was* she to him? What was he to her?

"Ex-girlfriend." Is what she landed on. "But we also play—played—music together. And while I'm pleased, and honestly a little surprised, that Zach is getting into politics, I thought someone should acknowledge what a unique talent Zach Livingstone is."

Some of Zach's music buddies—really, they were Zach and Darlene's music buddies—called, "Hear, hear."

"Zach auditioned for me about two years ago," Darlene said. "He was forty-five minutes late"—the room chuckled, unsurprised—"so I was pretty annoyed when he finally showed up. Certain I'd never work with someone so unprofessional. But then, he started to play. I'd never seen anything like it. No sheet music, no warm-up. He just sat down at the piano and played like it was *pouring* out of him. I asked if he could play any other instruments. He was like, 'Yeah, a little guitar.'"

A collective titter at her impression of Zach. Mark's face was dark, but Catherine laughed too. Zach couldn't take his eyes off Darlene, a weird, warm feeling twisting up inside him. "And he picked up a guitar and started 'Voodoo Child' by Jimi Hendrix. Which, if you don't know, is a really tricky song to play, and Zach was basically doing it with his hands tied behind his back."

"I was just trying to impress you," Zach said, and everyone laughed.

"It worked," Darlene said, and her smile turned his insides into a squelchy, melted mess. "Zach has an amazing career ahead of him as a professional musician, if that's what he wants to do. And, I hope he does want that, because, well, I need him. I say this without any disrespect, Mr. Livingstone, but if Zach turns into someone who is only responsible, mature, and sober-minded, the world has lost the most charismatic, most hilarious, most fun person I've ever met."

The younger generation broke into applause. Zach felt himself smiling for the first time in a very long time.

"So let's all raise a glass to Zach." She looked right at him. "Just as you are."

The guests toasted him, then his mother insisted it was time for cake. Everyone flowed toward the kitchen.

Zach hadn't stopped staring at Darlene. She inclined her head, drawing him to an empty corner of the room. "D-Dee," he said, once they were alone. "That was lovely—"

"Zach, I'm sorry," Darlene spoke over him. "I'm so sorry for what I did. There's no good reason for you to trust me. But I hope that you do. I need you to."

The world around him stilled. "Why?"

"Because . . ." Her eyes shimmered with emotion. "Because you're the one for me."

In the kitchen someone was calling for him to blow out the candles. Zach didn't hear it.

Darlene continued. "These past few weeks apart have been the hardest of my whole life." Her voice quavered. "I've been afraid to let myself love someone. Let someone love me. But I'm not afraid anymore." She gazed at him, and it was just them, just the two of them. "I love you, Zach. So much it's kind of freaking me out."

Zach let out a breath. The painful ache in his chest was gone. In its place was pure, peaceful warmth. He smiled, and it felt like leaping over a wall. Darlene smiled back, and goddamn she was beautiful. He wrapped his arms around her, pulling her close. She let out a sound of relief and circled her arms around his neck. She felt so damn good, so damn right. He would never let her go. Ever. "I love you too, Dee. I always bloody have."

He pressed his lips to hers and she kissed him, again and again and again, until they were both laughing, suddenly self-conscious and a bit delirious.

Someone popped a bottle of champagne.

Bang. The starting gun on a new life. "Oooh, yes!" Zach grinned at his girl. "Let's get sloshed."

"That's my boy," Darlene said, and it was true. He was hers, and she was his.

Imogene put on "Voodoo Child" and people started dancing and things got deliciously hectic and celebratory and *fun.* And everything in Darlene Mitchell and Zach Livingstone's small corner of this big, unwieldy world was completely as it should be.

78

"Flight HA51 to Honolulu is now ready for general boarding. All passengers please have your boarding passes ready."

Zia grabbed her backpack and joined the queue of fellow travelers waiting to board the first of three flights to Port Moresby, Papua New Guinea. Total travel time: fifty-nine hours and forty-five minutes. She'd forgotten to pack a neck pillow. Or snacks.

Usually waiting for a flight, even a long one, filled Zia with excitement. But leaving New York had never felt so hard. Her fingers found the gold necklace that still circled her neck. The Japanese symbol for light. Every day she woke up telling herself today was the day she would take it off. And every night she went to bed with it still warm and close against her skin.

The line moved forward.

There was no line when she and Clay flew to Tokyo. After getting dropped off at a small airport in New Jersey, they were on the plane and taking off within fifteen minutes. No customs, no security, no check-in. It was less like flying, and more like relaxing in a small, comfortable room. Their friendly flight attendant (one attendant, for the three people onboard) had ordered everything off the menu at Clay's favorite Italian restaurant. They ate *cacio e pepe* and grilled swordfish, served with silver cutlery and wine pairings. But it wasn't the luxuries that caused her heart to ache. It was the company. Clay was so sweet on that trip. So attentive. So happy. So was she. Like they were at the very beginning stages of falling in love.

Forget him, she instructed herself fiercely. *You're going to help people who need it. It's going to be very* rewarding.

The line shuffled forward. Zia waved down a harried flight attendant. "What's the food like on this flight?"

The attendant looked wry. "Nothing to write home about."

Wherever that was. Zia glanced around, looking for somewhere to buy an overpriced salad.

And that's when she saw it. Some sort of . . . commotion at the far end of the airport. A man. Running toward her gate, a sizable crowd following him. A spike of panic flashed in Zia's chest—terrorism?— before she heard shouts of laughter. Whoops from the crowd.

There was something familiar about that man . . .

Everything around Zia warped, and slowed down. Her boarding pass fluttered from her fingers.

"Zia!" Clay shouted, waving. "Zia, wait!"

He was red-faced and drenched with sweat or rain, his button-down shirt soaked. There were *hundreds* of people behind him; it was like a festival or a riot. Frantic airport security were trying to disperse the crowd, but it was too big, too focused on Clay. No one was going to miss this.

Whatever this was.

He came to a stop about twenty feet away, puffing and wild-eyed. "Zia," he said between pants. "Hi."

The line for the flight had morphed into an oval encircling them. Someone nudged Zia's back. She stumbled forward a few steps. How was Clay here, out in public? How did he get to her gate—buy a ticket? For a flight he wasn't even taking? Everyone was whispering, pointing, filming them with their phones. *That's her, the girl from the photo.*

Finally Clay regained his breath. He ran a hand through his hair and good God, he looked gorgeous. Not because of the golden tan and solid muscles and the five o'clock shadow lining his jaw. Because he was smiling. A blazing, megawatt grin.

"Hey," he called to her. "You going somewhere?"

"Um, yeah," she managed, and the crowd laughed.

He squinted at her and made a face. He was *enjoying* this. "Too bad. Was gonna see if you were free for dinner."

Laughter and sighs and *oh my God*s scattered among the ever-increasing crowd. "Well, you're too late," she told him, unable to fight a smile.

"Yeah, I figured. I figured you might say that." He took a few steps toward her, the crowd moving with him like magic. His tone softened. "Zia. I've been a gigantic ass. I never should've let you go. Baby, I'm so sorry."

She could tell from the self-aware glint in his eye that Clay knew he was delivering every clichéd line spoken at every Hollywood airport set—but at the same time, he meant every word. And so it wasn't a cliché at all.

"I was an ass, too. I never should've . . ." She glanced around, self-conscious. About a million phones were aimed at her.

Clay waved a hand airily. "You can say it. You shouldn't have taken a picture of my cock."

The crowd exploded. Every inch of Zia's skin scorched. It was just so *impossible* that he was here, in *public*.

Clay shrugged, shouting over the feverish crowd. "We all make mistakes."

Someone called, "And you have an amazing cock!"

Clay laughed. He *laughed*. "See? I have an amazing cock." Then his face turned serious and the crowd quieted. He took another step forward, his focus only on her.

"Zia," he said, so softly she almost couldn't hear him. "Before you get on that plane, there's something I need to say. Something I should've said months ago."

It felt like everyone in a five-mile radius was holding their breath. Including Zia. She could barely get the word out. "What?"

His eyes didn't leave hers. Eyes the color of a sunset. Eyes she knew so well. "I love you."

Zia didn't hear the gasps and the screams. She didn't see the thousand camera flashes. She only saw Clay. She nodded, tears welling in her eyes. "I love you too, Clay."

Before her knees gave way from the sheer insanity of it all, his arms were around her, and his lips were on hers, holding her, kissing her.

Around her, total and complete mayhem. But all Zia felt was a calm, beautifully clear rightness.

She pulled back to stare at him. Her flight was still boarding. But Zia wasn't going anywhere except home with Clay. "You're crazy."

"And you're the one for me," he murmured. "Always."

And in this matter, Clay Russo was absolutely correct.

79

Henry called to Gorman, "Honey, have you seen my keys?"

"Don't think so." Gorman popped his head out from the bathroom, smoothing product into his hair. "I'll be ready in five."

It was a cold, rainy Sunday in New York. But rather than veg out on the couch in sweats, catching up on *Dancing with the Stars*, Henry and Gorman were going out for dinner at Frankies. It was Gorman's idea.

"What's the occasion?" Henry had asked, snipping the thorns off a bunch of burgundy roses. Even though the high season of summer was long past, Flower Power, Honey! was still full of customers. "The extended run?"

Tears of a Recalcitrant Snail was playing for an extra two weeks. They'd recouped their investment, and even made a little extra. Gorman downplayed it, but Henry knew he was proud.

Gorman had shrugged, twirling a fallen bloom between his fingers. "Do I need a reason to have dinner with the love of my life?"

And just like that, Henry decided.

He was going to ask Gorman to marry him.

Why wait? They were not bound by archaic gender norms. And ever since Henry had decided not to pursue Gilbert, things had changed between the couple. Become more forgiving. More loving. They bickered less. A certain selflessness set into the bones of their relationship. Henry realized he was so caught up in the timeline and to-do list that he'd lost sight of Gorman. Someone he didn't just love, but enjoyed. Admired. Now, Henry was reveling in their relationship anew, feeling his commitment returned in equal measure. He wasn't letting go of his ideal future; rather, he was letting himself enjoy how beautiful it felt to commit to the *potential* of it.

It was time. And Henry was certain—98 percent certain—that Gorman would say yes.

Still, the past few weeks of ever-present nerves had made him a bit scattered, now misplacing his keys, which he never did. Henry searched through his bags, and the entry table bowl, and in the couch cushions. He tried all his coat pockets, and then on a whim, Gorman's coat, hanging on a hook by the front door.

His fingers brushed something hard and soft. A small box, covered in velvet.

A disbelieving smile spread over Henry's face.

The gold ring glinted back at him.

Not exactly the same as the one in his own pocket at this very moment. But similar in the ways that mattered.

"Find them?" Gorman called.

Henry put the box back. He felt like laughing and crying, euphoric and silly. Then he pulled himself together and called back, "No. We'll just take yours."

Gorman came into the living room. Henry's breath hitched at the sight of him. Tall and distinguished. His man. His great love. And soon, his husband. Gorman reached for his jacket. "Ready?"

Henry pulled Gorman close and planted a long, loving kiss on his mouth. "Looks like we both are."

10

They met in neutral territory—an organic café near Prospect Park. Late on a rainy Sunday, Savannah and Honey were the only ones sitting by a window that looked out onto a waterlogged backyard. Their cute waitress—muscle tee and a crunchy thicket of dirty-blond hair—was definitely checking out Honey as she delivered two ginger teas and left them to it.

Savannah wasn't sure if this technically constituted a breakup. But it sure felt like one. As heartbreaking as it felt, she knew she wasn't ready to give Honey what she needed. "I don't want to ruin the chance of having you in my life," Savannah told her. "You've helped me realize so many things I want to be thinking about." She reached across the table to tentatively touch Honey's hand. "I wish I was in a different place; your clarity about who you are and what you need is something I aspire to. Your courage gives me courage."

Honey nodded, looking away. "I'm not going to pretend like I'm not disappointed. I really like you, Savannah. A lot. But I'm also ready for a girlfriend. Like, so ready. So, so, so ready."

They both laughed. Honey dabbed at her eyes with a paper napkin.

"You'll meet someone," Savannah said. "Someone who can see just how wonderful you are."

The waitress stopped by to refresh their cups. "Are you sure I can't get you anything else?" She ran her fingers through her mop of hair, her eyes lingering on Honey. "Anything at all?"

Savannah twirled a lock of her own hair. Maybe she should try something shorter. She'd had the same haircut for a very long time. "Oh, you'll be more than okay," Savannah said to Honey, after the waitress left. "She was totally into you!"

"Was she?" Honey craned her neck, staring after her with a bashful smile. "I should get dumped more often."

Savannah forced a chuckle, titillated, even relieved—but mostly sad. It was too soon to be talking about Honey's love life in a way that didn't involve her. But that was what happened after you let someone go.

They hugged under the café awning, and Honey told Savannah to come by the restaurant; a whiskey for old time's sake. Savannah said that she would. But she suspected this was the end of something. Honey dashed up the street, jumping puddles in a bright yellow raincoat. And then, she was gone.

Savannah pulled out her phone. It was time her parents knew two things. First, she wasn't moving back home. She was staying in New York. She had to live her life, even if that meant disappointing people. And second, Terry and Sherry needed to stop assuming that she was only looking to date a guy. Because the more she thought about it, the more it felt like that was not a possibility. She knew they'd worry about her. They just wanted her to be happy. So, she'd have to tell them that she was happy. Breakups notwithstanding, she was.

Terry answered on the first ring. "Hi, Pookie! Great timing, I'm making turkey burgers."

"Dad, can you grab Mom?"

"Sure, honey. Is something wrong?"

The rain started to relent. It was always so nice out after a deluge. The streets were washed clean and everything smelled earthy, like fresh shoots. Like new life. Savannah switched her phone to her other ear. "No. Nothing's wrong at all."

81

Liv went through the motions of her life. Fall was busy in a different way from summer. In Love in New York focused on meeting with prospective clients, doing early-stage planning for couples who were wedding next year, and finalizing the books. But Liv's mind was never far from Eliot.

Eliot had been ill.

The thing that drove him to Savannah was fear of death. The terrifying realization that all the eternal-seeming roles humans create to order our experience—becoming a spouse or a parent or a business owner—were just ways to forget about our mortality. The temporariness and seeming insignificance of anything done on earth. Confronted with that, the man she'd married couldn't inhabit his life anymore.

And he hadn't confided in her about any of it. His *wife*.

In retrospect (the place Liv was almost exclusively spending her time), there was one moment where maybe, he was considering it. Around this time last year, when the temperature had just started to drop. He'd come home late, puffing as he hung up his coat. (Out of breath from the five-minute walk from the subway. She hadn't noticed.)

"Hey." He greeted her with a paper-thin kiss.

"Where were you?" Her greeting. As cold as his lips.

He hadn't replied, chatting instead with Ben about homework until Liv sent their son upstairs for a shower. Eliot opened a bottle of red and poured himself a glass. The house was cold, and quiet. "Liv." He spoke the word in a way that was sort of . . . raw.

She was scrolling through her email, distracted. "Mm?"

"Do you ever think about your legacy?" He drew out a chair at the dining room table, sitting in Ben's spot. "What you'll be remembered for?"

Liv didn't look up from her phone. "No."

He was silent for a few minutes. "I don't quite know how to say this—"

"Oh, shit. The Robinsons want to switch their hotel block from the Marriott to the Hyatt! Je*sus*."

"Liv—"

"Yeah, I don't really have time for your legacy right now." Pushing off from the kitchen counter, she gestured at the frying pan. "There's leftovers, but can you help clean up, please? This isn't a hotel." She went into the front office and shut the door.

Was that the moment? The moment her husband of twenty-two years tried to tell her something life-or-death, and she'd unequivocally blown him off?

Over admin. Over nothing.

He was suffering, and she didn't know about it. He'd died alone in a midprice hotel room in Kentucky. The final thing he saw was probably boring beige blinds or a bathroom light, still on.

The way Eliot had decided to act didn't exonerate his deception. But it did explain it. It evolved his absence. And she missed him. She missed him in a way she hadn't in months. She missed his love of dill pickles and sour gummy worms. The way he could tell a story at a dinner party and have everyone in stitches. Even his mood swings. She just missed him.

Sam and Dottie started staying over half the week. Sam moved a bigger television into the den, and the flickering light from the screen reached further into the hallway. Pink socks and frilly girl's underwear appeared in the laundry. Some mornings, Liv would wake to the smells of stocks and marinades Sam was preparing in the kitchen. Savory but alien.

One night, as Liv chopped carrots for the kids' school lunches, she pictured Eliot, creeping up to the patio door and peering in. Would he recognize what he saw? Would he be relieved Liv had moved on? Or angry he'd been replaced?

The weather turned from fresh to cold. It was coming. One year without Eliot was coming.

It was the week before Thanksgiving. Sam, Liv, Ben, and Dottie were making homemade pizzas. Outside, it was windy. Cold air whistled under the windowsills.

"Let's add some pineapple." Liv rummaged through the pantry. "I know we have some."

"Yuck," announced Dottie. "No way."

Sam laughed, grimacing. "Yeah, I think that's a veto, love."

"We like pineapple," Liv prompted Ben. "Don't we?"

But her son just shrugged, focused on adding cherry tomatoes. "Sam, is it true these are a fruit, not a vegetable?"

The wind howled. A swell of dark emotion rose in Liv's throat. "You like it," she said, louder. "We all—Dad and I—we *like* pineapple."

"Okay, okay," Sam said, surprised. "We'll put it on half."

"No," Liv said. "*All of it.*"

A crack sounded from outside, followed by a smash. They all jumped, spinning in the direction of the backyard.

One of the limbs of the willow tree had come through the windows next to the patio door, breaking the glass. A gust of wind blew into the kitchen. Dottie screamed.

"It's okay, sweetie." Sam hugged her. "Just a fallen tree branch. Ben, why don't you guys watch some TV while your mom and I fix this. Now, please."

The kids headed off, rattled but thrilled for extra screen time.

Liv was already outside.

A sizable branch of the weeping willow had snapped off. One of its smaller branches had broken the window on the way down. Liv stood by it, dumbly, the wind whipping her hair.

"Don't worry." Sam examined where the fallen branch had come down, calling over the wind. "No real harm. I'll call my tree guy to see what we should do."

Liv sat down on the branch. It was the size of her torso and accepted her weight with a gentle give. She crossed her legs underneath her. This low to the ground, she felt childlike.

"Honey?" Sam loomed over her. "We should probably get back inside."

Liv's eyes grew hot with tears. She folded her arms. Twigs and soil blew around the dark backyard, stinging her cheek. Through the patio doors, the house was lit with warm, yellow light. Liv didn't move.

"Liv," Sam tried again.

"Leave me alone." Liv waved him away, afraid she was really going to start crying. Her skin turned to gooseflesh. She was shaking.

Sam stood perfectly still, his expression neutral; inviting explanation.

"It was *our* tree." Her gaze zigzagged from limb to limb, trying to find a place to land. The limbs heaved in the wind, a tumble of shadows far above her head. "Eliot and I planted this tree. And he—he—he was dying too."

Once Sam had gotten her inside and wrapped in a cardigan, Liv told him everything: the attorney's email, Eliot's diagnosis.

"I didn't know," Liv said, angry and heartbroken and ashamed. "He didn't tell me."

"It's okay, love," Sam kept saying, stroking her arm. "It's all okay."

"I don't know if I'm ready. I don't know if . . ."

"It's okay, Liv. Whatever you decide, it's okay." Sam kept offering reassurances, but all Liv could hear was the wind blowing against the newspaper Sam had taped up over the broken window.

After a long phone call to a local arborist, Sam deemed it safe enough for them to stay the night. "But first thing tomorrow," he warned gently, and Liv nodded.

She woke before dawn. Sam found her sitting on the back patio. The backyard looked like a war zone. Leaves and splinters of wood covered the overgrown flower beds. The earth was wounded.

Sam draped a wool blanket over her shoulders and sat down beside her. Liv turned to him. "It's not like I'm still in love with him or anything. But I can't just erase him. He's still a part of me. Of us. Of all this," she said, indicating the house, and everything inside it.

Sam nodded, his large hands clasped in front of him. "I love you, Liv. But I'm still grieving the end of my marriage, too. I don't require you to be over Eliot in order to be with me."

"God," Liv mumbled, pulling the blanket tighter. "You're so mature."

Sam's smile was wry. "Is that code for boring?"

"No." Liv let out a small laugh. "No, it's code for . . . wonderful."

Sam put his arm around her, and she snuggled closer. The cold morning air smelled like sawdust. Clean and woodsy. It smelled like Sam.

They really should spend more time out here. Reclaim the backyard. Liv pointed at the fallen tree limb. "Maybe, we could make a table out of the wood. Something long and solid that'll weather a few storms. For dinner parties . . ."

Sam's face lightened. "And birthdays."

Liv pictured Ben and Dottie in caps and gowns. Bright-eyed young adults with hopes and dreams of their own. Her throat tightened with emotion, then relaxed. "Graduations."

"And anniversaries." Sam's eyes had a question in them. If she wanted it.

She did. "Yes," Liv answered. "And anniversaries."

There was only one star left above them, brilliant as a diamond in the soft, gray sky.

EPILOGUE: IN LOVE AT HOME

TWO YEARS LATER

Liv & Sam
ARE GETTING MARRIED

Saturday, June 24
At four o'clock in the afternoon
In their backyard
Dinner around the long table
to follow

"I will love like I never forgot how."
—f. D. Soul

Not many brides spend the morning of their wedding at a cemetery. But Liv Goldenhorn was no ordinary bride.

The gravestone had weathered over the past few years, and it looked better for it. A brand-new gravestone was depressing. Now it had some character, some authority. Eliot was finally aging well.

Ben put a jar of dill pickles and a copy of the *New York Times* sports section on his dad's grave. He updated Eliot on his various interests and accomplishments: an A on a recent science quiz about the solar system, how the Yankees were doing, the worm farm Sam had built in the backyard, equally gross and cool. He'd grown eight inches in the three years since his father's death, losing the baby fat, no longer a little boy. "There was a meteor shower last week. Mom let me stay up really late to watch it." He pushed his glasses up his nose.

His newly enlarging Adam's apple bobbed as he swallowed. "I wish you'd been there."

Sam put his hand on Ben's shoulder. "Why don't we go for a walk and give your mom some time." He produced a paper bag from the tote slung over his shoulder. "Are you guys hungry?"

Dottie eyed the bag. "If it's lunch, then I'm not hungry. If it's a treat, then I am."

Liv and Sam traded an amused look. "Lucky for you, Miss Sweet Tooth," Sam said, "it's apple fritters."

As the trio disappeared over a small hill, Liv stared at the etched words and dates on the gravestone, rereading them for the thousandth time. Even after all these years, it still seemed somewhat unbelievable that he was gone. "Well, E. I'm getting married today." Saying it out loud invoked an untamed moment of laughter. She sank to her knees, settling into the grass, breathing the warm June air. "You'd like him, I think. Oh, let's face it: you'd probably be a jealous prick about the whole thing. But he's good for me. Good for Ben. He loves us. We love him."

She pulled a blade of grass from the ground, examining its soft white end. It was peaceful here. Soothing. She leaned back against the sun-warmed grave, feeling incredibly close to her ex-husband.

A few minutes passed before she spoke again. "I don't have any bad feelings, E. About us, I mean. Oh, there's things I wish we'd done differently. Ways I could've been a better wife. Probably should've worked less. Probably could've initiated sex more. But I've learned from it all. I've become a better person. I'll be a better wife this time. Don't roll your eyes at me, you bastard," she added, using the headstone to help get to her feet. "I will. I know I will."

In the near distance, Sam rounded the corner. Dottie was on his shoulders, Ben dashing ahead. Their chatter and laughter a warm, happy sound. "This isn't goodbye, E. You'll always be Ben's dad. You'll always be my first love. But this is a farewell, my darling. Because I'm giving my heart to someone else today, and I need to give him all of it, for us to have a shot. I hope that's okay." She frowned, reconsidering. "Why am I asking you if it's okay? It's my heart. I can do what I want with it."

Liv inhaled deeply through her nose. Warm fragrant earth and the sweet scent of flowers. For a place that honored the dead, there was an incredible sense of life out here. Because there always was life, always movement and momentum. If you weren't dead, you were alive. A calm sense of certainty filled her. She gave the gravestone a quick smile, turning in the direction of her family, before spinning back. "Oh, and don't get in your head about it, but Savannah Shipley has a girlfriend."

She was laughing as she walked toward her fiancé and children, imagining Eliot's stunned disbelief.

When Sam and Liv got engaged, the first thing Savannah said was, "You have to let me plan the wedding."

"Don't you mean, *Congratulations*?" Liv teased, giddy and girlishly happy.

"Oh my gosh, sorry: congratulations, and you're perfect for each other, and please, please, please let me plan the wedding." She looked equally hopeful and determined. "Just me. On my own."

Savannah had never done a wedding solo before, from start to finish. This, the vendors all joked, would be her introduction to wedding-planning society. For months, she'd been working on getting every detail perfect.

"Are you really trusting her to do *everything*?" Gorman had asked, refilling Liv's glass as they toasted (again) to sexy Sam. "Isn't that driving you crazy, Ms. Type A?"

Liv shook her head. In her leafy backyard, Ben was reading a book about space travel while Dottie was running around in a tutu. "I trust her."

Gorman twisted his wedding band absentmindedly. "Isn't life fascinating?" he murmured. "How it all turns out."

Now, as they all arrived home from the cemetery, Savannah made her go *blindfolded* upstairs into her and Sam's bedroom, where she was going to get ready. "No peeking!"

For her first wedding, at Temple Emanu-El on the Upper East Side, Liv had gone all out in a Vera Wang ball gown the size of a small planet and six bridesmaids in purple silk. This time, it was different. As soon as she'd laid eyes on the floor-length cream lace dress in a local vintage store, she knew it was the one. Simple and elegant, the dress evoked old-world glamour, and the three-quarter sleeves covered her arm fat.

Liv did her own hair and makeup. No false lashes or extensions or contouring. Her face was her face. She'd rather look like a fiftysomething than a fiftysomething trying to look thirty. She didn't want to be thirty. She wanted to be right where she was.

Downstairs, the house filled with the sound of arriving guests. Nerves bubbled up.

"Knock, knock." Gorman stuck his head around the door. On seeing her, his eyes grew wide. Then misty. He pressed his fingers to his lips.

"That bad?" Liv joked.

He swatted her. "Don't even."

Henry was behind him, both hands behind his back. "I know you wanted to keep it simple but . . ."

"Every queen needs her crown," Gorman finished. "Take it from the biggest queens of all."

The two men presented Liv with an elegant flower crown. Pink roses and purple lilacs and yellow goldenrod. "All from your garden," Gorman said proudly. "Which is looking absolutely—"

Henry elbowed him. "Don't ruin the surprise!"

Liv marveled at their creation. "It's beautiful." She hugged them both, wiping away a tear. "This day is already perfect. How can it get any better?"

Gorman offered her his arm. "Why don't you marry a deliciously hot chef?"

Savannah was in the doorway. Her face was aglow. It'd taken Liv a few days to get used to the new haircut. But the choppy platinum-blond bob suited the woman Savannah had become in New York. "We're ready for you."

Greenery wound down the staircase and lined the hallway. Liv felt like a fairy queen as she floated through the first floor of the house.

The backyard took her breath away. It was full of flowers. Hundreds of clear bottles with one or two colorful stems hung suspended along the back and side fences. More blooms wove around a wooden arbor, which was loosely wrapped with a swathe of ivory silk. The assembled crowd, brightly attired in the dress code of *summer chic*, fell silent. In her clear, pretty voice, Darlene Mitchell started "Here Comes the Sun." Her boyfriend, Zach, accompanied her on acoustic guitar. "*Little darling, it's been a long, cold, lonely winter. Little darling, it feels like years since it's been here.*" The duo had planned the East Coast tour for their debut album, *Dark Secret*, around the wedding. Their band was blowing up, but they weren't missing this for the world. Sam and Liv were part of their love story, too.

Ben and Dottie, angelic in all white, scattered wildflowers down the aisle. A wave of laughter rippled through the gathering when Dottie ran out of flowers and started throwing them from Ben's basket. Liv's heart swelled at the gracious way Ben let his almost-stepsister steal the spotlight.

Gorman walked Liv through the center of their assembled guests. All eyes were on her, but she was only looking at Sam. His kind eyes and broad shoulders and big hands. Big enough to catch her if—when—she fell. But she felt strong enough to catch him, too. She only took her eyes off him when it was time to read her vows.

"Sam Woods," she began. "I love you. Tenderly. Wildly, and with my whole heart. Because you are so easy to love."

Zach was already teary. Darlene grinned and pulled him closer.

"On the day we met, I thought you were an intruding sex pest, so I brandished a banana at you and threatened to throw you in jail."

Everyone laughed.

"And you handled that like you handle all aspects of your life. With flawless grace, generous humor, and boundless empathy."

Sam brushed away a tear.

"Gosh, you never cry," Liv murmured. "Guess I'm doing a good job."

He gave her a thumbs-up.

Standing at the side, Savannah laughed out loud. It was already going *so* well.

Liv continued. "We're not spring chickens, you and I. We're adults, with big, messy lives and big, messy hearts. I don't promise a perfect marriage: I don't believe in perfect marriages. But I believe in us. As partners. As parents. As human beings, trying to make sense of this big, messy world. Today, I choose you as my husband because you make me happy. I promise to love and trust you. I promise not to work too much or drink too much or make you eat my terrible cooking."

Zia nudged Clay, who smiled and kissed his wife's cheek. They'd gotten married last year in Hawaii, a three-day blowout with a salsa band, piles of Italian food, and two hundred of their friends and family. They honeymooned on a private beach. To remember the happy occasion, they took Polaroids.

"Sam Woods," Liv continued, "you're the one for me. Whenever I recall the first time we kissed, on the front steps of this very brownstone, one word keeps coming back to me. That word is *home*. You are my home. I cannot wait to continue our great love story, as your wife, always by your side."

The crowd broke into applause.

Gorman was weeping. Henry handed him a tissue. "You big softie."

His husband wiped his eyes. "You love it."

Henry squeezed his hand. They'd just had their final home visit from a social worker. They were ready to adopt. Gorman had painted the nursery himself. "I do," Henry said.

After the cocktail hour, dinner was served. Sam had indeed made a long table out of Liv and Eliot's willow tree, around which they'd enjoyed countless outdoor dinners and afternoon coloring sessions. Savannah rented a few more tables to fit their guests, all decorated with tall white candles, vintage crockery, and more jars of bright flowers. The feast was summer staples: watermelon and feta salad, grilled corn slathered in salted butter, roasted new potatoes. Maine lobsters and sticky ribs were served family style. Kids chased each other under the tables. Everyone was drinking Aperol spritz and rosé and champagne. A lot of it.

Darlene and Zach were seated next to Clay and Zia. After being nominated for (but not winning) an Academy Award for Best Actor in *The Jungle of Us*, Clay had solidified his place in the A-list as a dramatic actor. But at Liv and Sam's wedding, he was just Zia's husband, and Zach and Darlene's friend, watching proudly as his wife announced her latest news to her friends.

"Director of volunteer services for Southeast Asia," Zia told Darlene and Zach. She felt lit up from the inside. "I'll be overseeing all of the teams there." Zia had gone back to school to get a master's in public health. When her boss's job at Global Care came up, she went through four rounds of interviews to get it. "I'm going to be based in Bangkok for the next five months, starting in the fall. I get to expand the current programs in the region and start new ones in Laos and Myanmar. I'm psyched!"

"Bangkok." Zach addressed Clay. "Long way from LA."

"I'm going with her," Clay said, adding that Layla and her kids would be housesitting the LA condo while they were away: Zia's sister had groveled for a year for their forgiveness, donating all the money from the photograph to Global Care. "It's time Zia's career came first."

Zia and Clay exchanged a smile of understanding, their fingers evenly intertwined.

"Do you miss having a home base?" Zia asked Zach and Darlene, sampling the fresh lobster. "You guys seem to be constantly on tour these days. South by Southwest, LA, Portland."

Zach and Darlene looked at each other and shrugged, smiling. "I'm just happy people want to hear our music." Zach squeezed Darlene's thigh. Even after all this time, it sent a deliciously lazy spark up her spine. His shirt was still a little rumpled, but he wore his hair swept back off his face these days. It made him look more mature, but no less cute.

"It's like Liv said in her vows," Darlene added. "Wherever we are, as long as we're together: that's home."

Later, the tables were cleared away, and Sam and Liv cut a three-tiered vanilla cake slathered with honey-and-lavender buttercream frosting. Ben and Dottie had two pieces each and were taken up to bed before they gobbled a third. Liv was apprehensive about a DJ—her days of drunkenly thrashing to "Party in the USA" were definitely behind her. But then Darlene and Zach started a sweet, jazzy version of "It Had to Be You," and she realized it was going to be a different kind of dance floor. As the sun sank over the fence, Liv slipped off her heels and let Sam sway her around, full and tipsy and entirely happy.

"*It had to be you,*" Darlene sang, making the old words sound inevitable and romantic, classic and entirely fresh. "*It had to be you.*"

Liv and Sam were surrounded by couples in love in New York. Gorman and Henry; Darlene and Zach; Clay and Zia; Savannah and Sophie (the quirky English fashion student she'd been dating); and a couple dozen other friends and family, all twirling around the backyard, which had been strung with little white lights.

"*For nobody else, gave me a thrill,*" Darlene's eyes were on Zach, as they sang together, not bothering to hide grins. "*With all your faults, I love you still.*" And Liv thought about how love meant showing someone everything—every awkward, shameful, hidden part of yourself—and the sublime grace and freedom in having those parts accepted, and cherished. How that was, ultimately, the secret to being loved, and loving others. Seeing, and being seen.

"'*It had to be you, wonderful you, it had to be you.*'"

"How'd I do?" Savannah whispered, as Sam was saying goodbye to some friends with sleepy kids.

"I can't believe I'm saying this," Liv said. "But I'm really glad you had an affair with my husband."

Savannah blushed. "I'm glad it brought us together."

She locked eyes with Sophie, unable to stop smiling. They'd met online a few months ago. Sophie was goofy and sweet and made Savannah laugh more than anyone else in the world. Liv and Sam had dinner with the couple, and Savannah's mom and dad, when they were in town a few weeks ago. The six of them ate at a new spot in Bushwick, co-run by a good friend of Savannah's and Sam's. They were lucky to get a table: Honey's Fried Chicken was currently the hottest fried chicken spot in New York City. At the end of an indulgent dinner that even the Kentuckians deemed fantastic, Honey came by the table. The light in her eyes was explained by the fact she was in love. A food writer, Natasha, who, it turned out, fell for more than just the Southern comfort food. They'd recently gotten engaged.

"Guess it all worked out for the best," Honey said to Savannah, and Liv thought, *Ahhh*, putting the pieces together.

"You changed my life," said Savannah to her now.

Liv smiled back broadly. "You changed mine, too."

The two women hugged, holding each other close. Then Liv squeezed Savannah's arms. "All right. Go back to your lady."

Savannah's lips curved up. It took Liv a moment to realize why she looked so pretty. Savannah Shipley wasn't wearing a scrap of makeup.

Sam stepped in. "May I have this dance?"

"Hello, husband," she said, accepting his hand.

"Hello, wife," he replied. "Ooh. I like the sound of that."

"Me too." She settled into his arms. "Well, we did it. We got married."

"And it's the first day of the rest of our lives."

"I don't know about that," Liv said with a smile. "I think we're already living our lives. We just get to do it together."

"That sounds pretty good to me." He spun her around slowly, her bare feet twisting in the soft grass. "Wanna know the best part?"

"What's that?"

Sam kissed her. He tasted like whiskey and buttercream. "We're already home."

ACKNOWLEDGMENTS

If you're reading this, you've either finished this story and are feeling all the feels, or you're skimming these words in a bookstore, because the acknowledgments are a window into a writer's inner world, and you're curious. Either way, hello!

This novel was truly a team effort. It felt akin to planning my own wedding, which I was actually doing over a fair portion of the writing of this book. Both required orchestrating an ambitious, exciting event that was a meaningful celebration of true love, and a lot of drinking.

There are very few people for whom I would throw out a year's work and start again, but my agent, **Allison Hunter**, is one of those people. On her advice, I deleted the twenty-five-thousand-word sample we sold this novel off, and started from scratch. I'm so glad I did. Allison, thank you for pushing me to do what it takes and for your belief in me: it truly means the world.

Sarah Cypher of the Threepenny Editor, you're so much more than my freelance editor, you're my writing teacher. I've worked with Sarah on four novels now: her insights are transformational and, honestly, astounding. Sarah, I'm getting my MFA by working with you, and I couldn't be more grateful.

Emily Bestler, my editor at Simon & Schuster and an all-around publishing legend, thank you for your unwavering support of my work. I'm so thrilled to have had three novels published by the fabulous Emily Bestler Books. Thanks to **Lara Jones, Megan Rudloff, Isabel DaSilva, Sonja Singleton,** and everyone at Simon & Schuster.

Cheers to my enthusiastic screen agents at UTA, **Addison Duffy** and **Jason Richman**. I am positively visualizing a kickass film or show based on this book: let's make it happen!

I engaged the hearts and minds of a lot more early readers than I usually work with in an effort to create a collective vision of modern love and romance. It was nerve-racking to share the raw, first draft with so many readers (some I didn't even know, who responded to a callout in my newsletter), but their honest feedback was invaluable. Thank you to **Danielle Brennan**, **Lisa Daniels**, **Natalie Edwards**, **Melissa Epifano**, **Emily Klein**, **Melissa Kravitz Hoeffner**, **Jen McManus**, **Kari Schouveller**, and my old Showtime pal, **Adam Waring**. Extra-special thanks to the vivacious **Megan Reid**.

I love learning things from my friends and people I cold-email. This novel was brought to you by:

Amy Shack Egan, and her team at New York wedding planners, **Modern Rebel**: Amy answered all my questions about wedding planning and even let me moonlight as an assistant for one of their events, to get a behind-the-scenes peek. Wedding planners **Meredith Falk**, **Emily Love**, and **Madison Sanders** also provided crucial insight in the manuscript's early stages, all of whom I was connected to by wedding photographer **Alea Lovely**, who I met in an Uber Pool and let me take her out for lunch.

Keisha Zollar, **Clare Mao**, and **Hala Maroc** helped me illuminate the stories of young women of color. I truly could not have brought Darlene and Zia to life without you three; thank you for being such generous guides.

Jill Lamoureux, my wife's college roommate and lead singer of the band Scavenger Hunt: thank you for helping me make Darlene and Zach real musicians. You are very cool.

The fantastic **Mr. Dan Fox**, one of my best friends in the whole world: cheers for giving this book the Jew Thumbs-Up. And for always being one of my biggest fans (the feeling is mutual).

My lawyer, **Sam Mazzeo**, gave counsel on legal aspects. **Jocelyn Brewer** advised on mental health. **Richard Cooke** helped with Awful Charles. **Neil Collier**, my good friend Ally's dad, does all the medical stuff. I've sent this man some pretty weird emails, and he never flinches.

I worked on this novel at the peaceful **Spruceton Inn Artist Residency** in 2018 and the outrageously enjoyable **Rowland Writers Retreat** in 2019. Drafting happened, in part, at **The Writers Room** in

New York, where I finished in early 2020. Thanks to those who give writers places to dream.

Shout-out to my friends, near and far: my **Brooklyn gang**, **Sydney crew**, and **LA pals**.

Hello to the **New York Author Salon** fam (especially cohost **Amy Poeppel**). Thanks for the chats, cheer, and cheese plates.

The **Generation Women** and **Funny Over Fifty** communities are so special to me (join us! Generationwomen.us and funnyoverfifty.com). Thanks **Jessica Lore** for being the ultimate collaborator.

Big love to my family, the **Clarks** and the **Ratowskys**, especially my wonderful **Mum** and **Dad**, and **Will**. It means a lot to make you proud and to be a part of a loving and vibrant family.

Finally, my wife, **Lindsay Ratowsky**, to whom this novel is dedicated. I am writing these acknowledgments in May 2020, and we are (still) quarantining at home in Brooklyn. There's no one I'd rather self-isolate with than you, baby. Our wedding was part of the inspiration for this novel, and so this story is shared with you, as is everything I do. I love you endlessly.

It was a joy to create this story with everyone who read it before it got into the hands of you, dear reader (and if you are still in a bookstore reading this, that's your cue to go buy this book).